SWEETER THAN WINE

Cole's warm breath was like a caress over her skin. "Strawberry, isn't it?" he murmured huskily.

"What?" Lacey opened her eyes, overcome by the sensation that she could drown in his indigo gaze.

"Your lipstick. It's strawberry, isn't it?" Cole repeated softly, and tasted her lower lip.

"Yes," she whispered, and unconsciously swayed toward him.

"I always did have a weakness for strawberry." It was an absent comment. Lacey doubted if Cole was aware that he had said it aloud.

Then his mouth opened over hers, claiming the ripeness of her lips as his strong fingers stroked the back of her neck, tilting her head backward to make the most of the passionate kiss. He reached around her waist and Lacey let herself be arched against him.

With consummate skill, Cole demanded a response and he got it.

from "Tidewater Lover"

Also Available by Janet Dailey

Let's Be Jolly
Happy Holidays
Maybe This Christmas
Scrooge Wore Spurs
A Capital Holiday
Eve's Christmas
Searching for Santa
Mistletoe and Molly
American Dreams
American Destiny
Santa in a Stetson
Something More
Masquerade
Tangled Vines

From the Calder Series

Calder Storm
Lone Calder Star
Calder Promise
Shifting Calder Wind
Green Calder Grass

Close to You

JANET DAILEY

ZEBRA BOOKS
KENSINGTON PUBLISHING CORP.
http://www.kensingtonbooks.com

ZEBRA BOOKS are published by

Kensington Publishing Corp.
119 West 40th Street
New York, NY 10018

ISBN-13: 978-1-4201-1714-1
ISBN-10: 1-4201-1714-9

First Printing: July 2010
10 9 8 7 6 5 4 3 2 1

Printed in the United States of America

Contents

TIDEWATER LOVER

Chapter 1

The ring of the telephone checked the step Lacey Anderson had taken away from her desk, and she turned around with a sigh to see which button was blinking. It was the interoffice line. She had to answer it. Shifting the stack of file folders she was carrying to her left arm, Lacey reached across the desk. The movement swung her silky brown hair forward and she tucked it behind her right ear before lifting the receiver to the same ear. It was a balancing act, but she was used to those.

"Lacey speaking," she identified herself automatically.

"You have a call from a Margo Richards on line three," was the reply.

Her cousin. But her dark eyebrows flicked upward in surprise. "Thanks, Jane." Lacey pressed the third button on the display, wondering why on earth Margo was calling her. "Hello, Margo." She glanced at the ceiling, knowing it wasn't likely to be a short conversation.

"Hey—sorry to bother you at work, Lacey," the melodic voice rushed on with hardly a trace of sincere apology. "I don't want to get you into trouble with your boss, but I couldn't wait until tonight to reach you."

At least Margo sounded cheerful, so she probably

had good news. “It’s okay. Personal calls are allowed, so long as we don’t talk for hours.” Lacey knew her chatty cousin wouldn’t take the hint. “What’s up?”

“This is kind of last-minute, but—oh, Lacey, it’s going to be so much fun! Bob and I are leaving tomorrow to fly to Florida to visit his parents, and from there we’ll be taking a two-week Caribbean cruise!”

“Sounds fabulous.” Not for anything would Lacey permit even the tiniest suggestion of envy to creep into her voice. She adjusted a pleat on her skirt and settled down to listen to her cousin.

“It is exciting, isn’t it?” Margo gushed. “It all happened so quickly. I happened to mention to Bob how romantic a cruise like that would be—and you know how Bob is. If I wanted the moon, he’d try to buy it.”

Poor guy, Lacey thought. She hoped he would learn to say no to Margo before all their money got frittered away. Lacey was sure that Margo truly loved Bob, but she doubted her cousin would ever get tired of having her every whim indulged.

“I’ve been to the mall twice since he told me,” Margo continued. “Most of my summer wardrobe is so, um, last year. So I shopped—Lacey, I wish you could see this gorgeous gown I bought! It’s so sexy I don’t know if Bob will let me wear it. And I picked up these fantastic evening pajamas in this shimmery material that really does something for my—”

“Margo, I’d love to hear all about your new clothes,” Lacey interrupted, knowing that if she didn’t stop her now, the conversation would never end. She had a feeling Margo was only getting started. Next she would be outlining the entertainment schedule for the cruise and their ports of call.

Nothing doing. Lenient office rules aside, her strong

sense of loyalty to her job meant that Lacey wasn't going to spend an hour on a phone call like this.

"Okay," Margo said eagerly, "because I forgot to tell you about—"

Lacey hadn't been fast enough. "Ah, I am actually pretty busy at the moment, Margo. Maybe you should call me tonight."

"I can't. Bob and I are invited to a dinner party at seven—that's why I'm calling you now." There was an incredulous note in Margo's voice, as if she couldn't understand why Lacey hadn't read her mind. "I can't just whip out my cell phone and my BlackBerry at the table, you know."

You do it all the time. Lacey gritted her teeth and smiled rigidly at the receiver. "No, of course not. Anyway, I really appreciate your letting me know you're going to be leaving. Have a great time, okay?" What else could she say?

"Um, that isn't the only reason why I called. I thought I told you."

Lacey could imagine Margo's expression of wide-eyed innocence. "Told me what?" she asked, concealing an impatient sigh.

"I ran into Sally Drummond yesterday. By accident," Margo assured her as she tossed off the name of a close friend of Lacey's. "I was on my way to the car with my arms full of shopping bags and whatnot when she came out of a restaurant."

Lacey sat down on the edge of her desk, still clutching the armful of files, and surveyed the long line of boldface unopened e-mails displayed on her monitor. The first three had little red flags and required her immediate attention.

Re: Contract #4569033
Did you follow up on Carleton memo?
Fwd: call IT for defrag today!

A quick glance at the subject headings of the others told her they could wait, but the claims on her time seemed never-ending. And now—well, she had absolutely no idea what Sally had to do with this phone call and she wasn't sure she even wanted to find out. But there was simply no way to speed up Margo's explanation. Her cousin's talkativeness was irritating, and not something that could be changed.

"Anyway, I stopped to say hello," Margo went on. "Then we got to gossiping—you know how that goes. And one subject led to another until finally we were talking about you."

"How nice," Lacey murmured dryly.

"We didn't say anything bad," Margo laughed. "Honestly, Lacey, it's not like you would ever be the cause of gossip—all you do is work, work, work."

Lacey rolled her eyes for no one's benefit but her own. "That is what they pay me for. I don't have a Generous Bob in my life, Margo."

Margo blithely rolled on. "Anyway, Sally mentioned that you were going on vacation next week for two weeks, but she wasn't sure if you'd made any specific plans. Is that right?"

"Yes," Lacey admitted grudgingly. Her time off was going to consist of a no-frills jaunt close to home, definitely no big deal, because she was barely getting by financially these days. Her so-called vacation, whatever form it took, would pale in comparison to Margo's cruise.

"You aren't going away anywhere?"

"Ah," Lacey hedged. "I thought I'd spend a couple of days with my folks, but outside of that, I'm just going to relax and do nothing."

"Wow. Sounds great!" Margo declared cheerfully.

Lacey frowned. *Wow?* Though it was true enough that relaxing at home would be a refreshing change from the hectic pace of the office, she really didn't share Margo's fake enthusiasm.

Unfortunately, Lacey couldn't afford to leave the Tidewater area of Virginia to go anywhere on her vacation. Several unforeseen expenses, the biggest being some major repairs to her car, had drained Lacey's savings account, but she was too proud to volunteer that information to her cousin.

"So you called because . . . ?" She tried to hurry Margo to the point of the call. Maybe there wasn't one. Where her cousin was concerned, it wouldn't be the first time.

"I'm just so worried about our house and all the new things we bought when we decorated, Lacey," Margo said. "Situated the way we are on the beach, with no close neighbors—I mean, you never know what might happen, not that anything ever has, though. But the summer season is about to start. Someone could break into the house and steal everything. I'd be heartbroken."

"With good reason," Lacey agreed. "Have you put in a security system?"

"Bob was just talking about doing that," Margo said. "And we had new locks installed. But I think it's still best if someone is actually in the house."

"Yes," Lacey said absently. Over a month ago Margo had taken her on a tour of the place, to show off—no other term fit—her home. Lacey hated to admit to being envious but she had fallen in love with her cousin's beach house.

"I was sitting here this morning, worrying myself half sick thinking about what might happen while Bob and I are on the ship. So when Sally told me you were going on vacation, it was like, aha! You can babysit the house while we're gone!"

Lacey hesitated. "I suppose . . . I could."

As she ran over the idea in her mind, it sounded like the perfect plan. Two weeks in luxurious surroundings with the ocean and beach at her doorstep—nice. And something she wouldn't have been able to afford at twice her salary.

"I just knew you'd help us out!" Margo exclaimed.

"It really would be a pleasure," Lacey said sincerely, already picturing lazy days in the sun. Maybe she would even splurge on a new bikini.

"There is one thing." Margo paused. "I told you we were leaving tomorrow. And I just hate the thought of the house being empty for even an hour."

That was a little ridiculous. *Would the designer sofa get lonely? Tell it to hold hands with the ottoman.* Lacey kept the tart thoughts to herself, grateful for Margo's offer.

"Do you think you could stay here tomorrow night?"

Taking a deep breath, Lacey wondered if her self-absorbed cousin knew what she was asking. Commuting from Virginia Beach to Newport News during rush-hour traffic would mean practically rising with the sun. But tomorrow was Thursday. If she could arrange to have Saturday morning off, then she'd be making the round trip only once.

"Sure," Lacey agreed finally. "I'll pack and drive out after work tomorrow."

"Ooh, I will be eternally grateful for this," Margo vowed. "Now there's plenty of food, fresh and frozen, in the house and I'll leave the front door key in the flower-pot near the door."

"Great. I'll find it. If anyone asks who I am, I'll act like I own the place."

"Good idea. But if not, you could meet one of the local cops. Did I ever tell you that I always wanted to date a cop?"

"No," Lacey said.

"It wasn't meant to happen. So I married Bob," Margo continued airily. Lacey could almost see her cousin twirling a lock of hair around her finger while she talked.

"Anything else I need to know? About the house, I mean."

Margo giggled. "I don't think so. Just, um, that cell phones sometimes don't work too well out by the beach. You can use our land line—I guess I should call it a sand line. Sometimes it doesn't work either, when it gets windy."

"I'll figure something out," Lacey said. She looked again at the list of unopened and unanswered e-mails. "Actually, being out of reach sounds great."

"Really? Are you sure?"

Lacey's monitor blinked and ten more e-mails appeared in rapid succession. "Yes," she said firmly.

"I owe you for this!" Margo's bubbliness was overflowing into the receiver. "Make yourself totally at home when you get there, Lacey. Eat anything, drink anything, do anything you want. Listen, I have to go—I still have oodles of packing to do. See you when we get back from the Caribbean. Bye!"

"Bye." Her farewell was spoken to a dial tone. Margo had hung up.

Shrugging, Lacey replaced the receiver on its cradle. It was typical of Margo. Once her objective was achieved, she lost interest. But Lacey wasn't going to hold a grudge. Thanks to her cousin, she was suddenly really looking forward to her two weeks off.

Of course, she still had to talk to Mike Bowman, her boss, about Saturday morning. Straightening from the desk, Lacey walked to the banks of filing cabinets in her office and deposited the folders she'd been holding on top, tucking a few escapees back into the toppling pile.

As she opened a drawer to begin, the office door opened and in walked Mike.

"Hello, Lacey," he greeted her distractedly, frowning as he passed beside her desk to go through the stack of messages waiting for him.

Brushing aside the sleek hair that had fallen forward again, Lacey studied him for an instant. Mike was in his late thirties, a peppering of gray showing up in his dark hair; a confirmed bachelor or so he claimed. He was one of the chief engineers for the construction company, and didn't have much free time for socializing.

Even with her limited experience, Lacey knew she could search a long time and never find an easier guy to work for, or one that was more fun to be with. They had gone out occasionally in the last few months, although they'd kept quiet about it. No one else in the office knew, and truthfully, there wasn't anything to know. Sometimes a date was just a date, not a prelude to a relationship. Though Mike was good-looking in a strong, dependable kind of way.

"Judging by your expression, I won't ask how your meeting went," Lacey offered. There was a sympathetic gleam in her brown eyes.

"Please don't." The corners of his mouth were pulled grimly down. "It was an exercise in frustration. The big bosses demanded to know why the Whitfield project is so far behind schedule and I got called on the carpet. Sometimes I think if they'd get out of their offices and out on the job sites, they might have a better understanding of what I'm up against."

Lacey smiled. "Maybe you should have suggested that."

"No way." Mike sighed heavily in resignation. "They don't want to hear excuses, they want solutions. And they're right. I have to start coming up with solutions before

I create more problems. Hell, they create themselves without any help from me."

"Speaking of problems, I don't know if you remember or not, but my vacation starts next week."

Mike grimaced. "Don't remind me. I don't want to remember it until Monday morning."

She smiled again but more tentatively. "Sorry, but I was hoping you might give me Saturday off."

"Why? I thought you said you weren't going anywhere on your vacation." He frowned, his hazel eyes confused as he met her gaze.

"Um, my plans have changed," she ventured. "My cousin called to ask me if I'd stay at her house in Virginia Beach. She and her husband are going on a cruise—it was a last-minute kind of thing. That's why the short notice. They leave tomorrow, which means I want to get out there tomorrow night. I would have to commute all that way on Friday—and Saturday too—unless you let me have the day off."

"I see. Well, why not?" Mike shrugged.

"Thanks. I can work late on Friday to make up for it," Lacey promised.

"No. Get out of this madhouse at five on the dot Friday or I might change my mind and postpone your vacation," he declared in a mock threat. "By the way, who's going to take your place here?"

"Donna is." Lacey knew the reaction that announcement would produce. Donna was not one of Mike's favorite temps.

There was a skeptical glint in his eye when he heard Lacey name her replacement. "You'd better leave the address and phone number of your cousin's house with Jane, just in case Donna get things all screwed up around here or discovers she can't find something. Where did you say you'll be? Virginia Beach?"

"Yes. The house is right on the ocean. And so help me, Mike, if you call me back to work on my vacation, I'll—"

Lacey never got a chance to finish her warning words. "On the beach, huh? Nice," he chuckled, "I just might run away and join you. It sounds like paradise. You know what the travel ads say—Virginia is for lovers. Maybe we should both go and see if it's true. I need a break from here."

Both of them knew that wasn't going to happen. There wasn't a chance of Mike getting any time off.

"If you aren't doing anything on Sunday, why don't you come out?" she suggested, extending the invitation as consolation.

"It's a date," Mike replied without any hesitation, settling for a day instead of two weeks. "I'll bring a couple of steaks and we'll fire up the grill—I assume your cousin's beach house has a grill."

"A big, shiny one. About as big as a car, in fact. And almost as expensive." The new grill had been on the tour—it was Bob's pride and joy.

"Terrific." Mike smiled, a little wearily.

The interoffice line rang and Lacey walked to her desk to answer it. Jane, the receptionist, asked immediately, "Lacey, didn't I see Mr. Bowman come in? Is he with you?"

"Yes."

"Good. Mr. Whitfield is on line one for him. He's called half a dozen times." She didn't bother to add that Mr. Whitfield was already steamed about waiting. The nervousness in her voice made it clear.

"Thanks, Jane." Lacey replaced the receiver and looked at Mike. "Whitfield is on line one," she said carefully.

He blew out an exasperated sigh. "Oh, please, not that maniac. I've just gone through one frustrating series of explanations. See if you can use that soothing voice of yours and put him off for a while."

Sitting down in her chair, Lacey accepted the challenge. After all, in a sense it was part of her job to shield Mike from unwanted phone calls. Mike stood expectantly by her desk, watching her intently as she picked up the phone and pushed the button for the first line.

"Mr. Bowman's office. May I help you?" she inquired in her most pleasant tone.

"Yes," came a crisp, very male voice. "I would like to speak to Mr. Bowman."

It was a command, not a request, and Lacey could tell the difference. She didn't dare suggest he send an e-mail. Still she persisted. "I'm terribly sorry, but Mr. Bowman is on another line at the moment. May I take a message, please?"

"He's on another line, huh?" There was no mistaking the sarcastic skepticism in the response.

"Yes. May I have him call you back when he's through?" Lacey offered.

"No, you may not!" the voice snapped in her ear. "I'd bet anything Bowman is standing right there to see if you can stall me. Tell him I said hi. And that I don't like playing his waiting game."

Whether it was the accuracy of his rude comment about Mike or her temper reacting to his acid tone, Lacey didn't know, but she abandoned her attempt to be pleasant.

"He really is on another line, Mr. Whitfield. However, since your call seems to be so urgent that you feel entitled to be rude, I'll see if I can interrupt him. Please hold." Without giving him a chance to respond, she pushed the hold button, shutting him off. Its fast blinks seemed as angry as the man waiting on the line. Well, that made two of them. Fiery lights burned in her brown eyes as she glanced at Mike.

"I'm sorry that I asked you to cover for me, Lacey," Mike said immediately. "I'll take the call in my office."

"I wish you could tell him to go take a flying leap into a dry lake," she fumed.

"Believe me, it's a temptation," he sighed. "But it is his time and money that I'm spending every day that the project falls further behind schedule. He has a right to know what's going on."

"He doesn't have any right to be such a . . . a . . ."

"Careful," Mike warned with a teasing wink. "Ladies aren't supposed to use bad words."

"Get real. I don't feel very ladylike at the moment," Lacey muttered, glaring at the blinking hold light.

"Just think about the two weeks you're going to spend away from all this," Mike suggested, attempting to calm her annoyance as he started toward his private office.

As quickly as her temper had flared, it died. "I promise to feel sorry for you back at the office while I bask in the sun," Lacey laughed.

Less than a minute after Mike had entered his office, the light stopped blinking and held steady. Lacey felt sorry for him right now. Considering the hotheaded mood Whitfield was in, it wouldn't be easy for Mike to explain about the new delays on his construction project. Whitfield deserved a tongue-lashing, but she knew Mike would handle the situation in his usual calm way.

With a sigh, Lacey went back to the metal cabinets to resume filing the folders she'd placed on top. The door to her office swung completely open. Lacey glanced over her shoulder and smiled.

"Hi, Maryann," she greeted the visitor, who worked there too and was one of her best friends. "What are you doing?" It was purely a rhetorical question.

"I'm escaping," Maryann Carver declared and sank into the spare, straight-backed chair at Lacey's desk. She had the air of someone who'd been pushed to the limit. "Want some advice, Lacey? Don't ever take a job as a payroll clerk. And here's some more," she continued. "Don't ever put off going to the dentist."

"Is your tooth bothering you again?" Lacey asked.

"Yes. Do you have any aspirin for a suffering fool? I forgot to bring any with me this morning and this molar is killing me." Maryann combed her fingers through hair that couldn't make up its mind whether it was brunette or blond.

"I think there's a bottle of aspirin in the middle drawer of my desk. Help yourself." Lacey slipped a folder into its proper place. "You really should see a dentist pronto."

"I am. At four this afternoon. All I have to do is survive until then." The desk drawer was opened and pills rattled in their plastic bottle. "He's only going to fix this one tooth today. I have to go back in a couple of weeks for a regular checkup." She took a breath and rattled on. "You know, that's one good thing about mothers. They always make sure you have your regular checkups. Of course, I'll never tell my mother there are advantages to living at home. She'd have me back in my old room with the pink stuffed animals before I could say no."

"So would my mother." Lacey closed the file drawer and returned to her desk, that task finished.

"Hey, I just remembered!" With pills in her hand, Maryann paused on her way to the nearby water cooler. "You start your vacation on Monday. Are you still planning to visit your parents in Richmond?"

"Just for a weekend. My cousin Margo called a little while ago. She's going off on a cruise with her husband and asked me to stay in their beach house while they're away."

"Beach house?" Maryann wailed. "How lucky can

you get? Are you staying there by yourself? Or would you like a roommate?"

"But that roommate"—Lacey knew Maryann was suggesting herself—"would have to commute back and forth to work every day."

Maryann pouted. "You're only saying that because you want the place to yourself."

Lacey smiled away the remark. "It's going to be a better vacation than what I'd planned, that's for sure. Imagine, two weeks with the ocean at my doorstep and an uncrowded beach—bliss, huh?" Each time she thought about it, it sounded more idyllic.

"Don't rub it in," Maryann grumbled as she went out to the water cooler a few steps away in the hall.

As she set the aspirin bottle back into the middle drawer, Lacey noticed the light on the first line of the phone system had gone off. "Poor Mike. I wonder if he needs an aspirin."

"Why should he? Don't tell me he has a toothache, too." Maryann came back in with a paper cup filled with water and downed the aspirin in her hand.

"No, but I bet he has a headache." Lacey motioned toward the phone. "He just finished talking to the high-and-mighty Mr. Whitfield. That man knows how to give people hell."

"Who is Mr. Whitfield?"

"A client with a big mouth. Very rude, to the point of being obnoxious. It doesn't help that the complex we're building for him is way behind schedule. Still and all, he's a real pain. I wish Mike would punch him in the mouth someday. After the job is done and the check clears, of course."

"Tsk-tsk. The client is always right, Lacey." There was a definite twinkle of laughter in Maryann's eyes. "Look, I'd love to sit and swap horror stories all day, but we both have a lot of work to do. We'll have lunch tomorrow and you can tell me all about the beach house. You can skip your Mr. Whitfield, though."

"I plan to," Lacey murmured.

"I'm sure the place is fabulous and I'll be green with envy—you have a digital camera, right? Take pictures and e-mail them to me—"

Lacey held up a hand. "You'll have to rely on my talent for vivid description. I'm not taking a laptop and I don't know if my cousin has a computer out there. I don't want to give myself a chance to check in, if you know what I mean."

"I sure do. You're smart. Wow, going totally off-line. That sounds so—primitive."

"I'm taking my cell phone. But it might not work, my cousin said. They have a regular phone, though."

Maryann nodded. "Got it. You leave when? Sunday?"

"No, tomorrow night. I'll have to commute on Friday but Mike gave me Saturday off."

"Lucky you," Maryann sighed. "I wish I had him to work for instead of that crotchety old prune face in accounting."

Lacey only laughed. "Hope your tooth gets better," she offered in goodbye as her friend headed out.

"So do I. See you tomorrow."

On Thursday evening, her small hatchback loaded with suitcases, duffels, and odds and ends, Lacey turned into the driveway of Margo Richards's home. Her gaze moved over the simple, classic lines of the beach house, painted a pale hue that matched the foamy whitecaps of the ocean breaking beyond the dunes.

No doubt about it. She was looking forward to having

the place all to herself for the next two weeks. A faint smile curved her lips, tinted a bit with strawberry gloss.

Grabbing her cosmetic case and one of the smaller duffels from the rear seat of the car, Lacey stepped out and walked buoyantly to the front door. Looking at the flowerpot where Margo had said she would leave the key, Lacey didn't pay attention to what was beneath her feet.

The toe of her sandal hooked the roughly textured mat in front of the door, catapulting her forward. The cosmetic case flew from her hand, the lock failing to hold so that the lid snapped open and her cosmetics tumbled out onto the concrete slab. Fortunately Lacy managed to find her balance a stumbling second before she joined the case.

She told herself to pay attention to where she was going, then stopped to pick up the items scattered at her feet.

A gleam of metal winked at her near the edge of the mat. Curious, she reached for it, pushing the mat aside to reveal a shiny key that looked new—Margo had said the locks were. She studied it for a second, hoping it would work. New keys could be problematic. She tried it in the door lock. It opened with the first attempt.

Good thing she'd found it in the wrong place. It was typical of Margo to get something that important wrong. Lacey left the door open while she refastened her cosmetic case. Most likely her cousin had forgotten where she'd said the key would be and left it where everyone did. So much for Margo's concerns about security.

Inside the entrance of the two-story house, Lacey paused. From her previous visit, she remembered that the rooms on the ground floor consisted of a study, a rec room, and a utility room. The rest was taken up by a roomy two-car garage.

The main living area of the house was at the top of the

stairs to her left. Looking up the staircase, Lacey admired the tall built-in cabinet stretching from the landing of the open stairwell to the ceiling of the top floor. It was no less impressive when seen for a second time. The carved moldings of its white-painted wood were picked out with a darkly brilliant blue. Through the glass panes in its tall doors, assorted vases and figurines of complementing blues were deftly placed among a collection of books.

With cosmetic case and duffel in hand, Lacey mounted the steps. A large potted ficus tree stood near the white railing at the head of the steps. All was silent. The click of her shoes on the hardwood floor of the second story sounded loud to her own ears, but she resisted the impulse to tiptoe.

The décor of the stairwell was an introduction to the white and blue world of the living room. Matching cream-colored sofas with throw pillows of peacock blue occupied the large area rug whose pattern echoed the blue theme, positioned in front of the white brick fireplace. Again, small works of art and sculpture carried the theme of blue, accented by greenery. Hanging plants and two more potted ficus trees brought a natural look to the cool-toned room.

The dining room and kitchen were an extension of the living room with no walls to divide them. A mixture of white rattan and white wicker furniture in the dining room added an informal touch, with the emphasis subtly changing from blue to green, mostly provided by vigorous, leafy plants that obviously liked the ambient sun.

Setting her things down, Lacey walked to the large picture windows fronting the ocean. The blue drapes were pulled open to reveal an expansive view of the sea and the inviting sandy beach. She turned away. There was time enough to explore the outdoors later.

An investigation of the kitchen with its countered bar

confirmed an ample supply of canned goods on hand and three or four days' worth of fresh stuff in the refrigerator. She silently thanked her airhead cousin for not forgetting the truly important stuff, like food. Lacey decided she would fix her evening meal later. First on the agenda was unpacking and getting settled in.

The bedrooms branched off the hallway to the left of the living room. Lacey only glanced into the master bedroom. The two guest rooms were smaller, but looked really comfortable. She chose the one with a view of the ocean. Both guest rooms shared a bath that had its entrance from the hall.

Pastel yellow enlivened the predominant blues in the room's décor, giving a cheery impression of sunshine and ocean. Lacey glanced admiringly at the furnishings before catching her reflection in the mirror.

There was no question in her mind that she could get used to living here. She smiled at herself. The dark-haired girl in the mirror, her seal brown hair worn short in a boyish cut that made her look ultrafeminine, smiled back.

An hour later, she had brought in all her luggage from the car, which she'd parked in the garage. A few of Margo's winter clothes were in the closet of the room Lacey had chosen, but there was still plenty of room for Lacey's belongings. Fixing a plate of cheese, cold cuts, and fruit, she ate at the dining table, facing the ocean. Finished, she lingered there, listening to the symphony of the surf, gentle waves breaking on the endless beach. The music of the ocean was soothing and she hated to leave it, but there were other things to be done.

The picture-perfect house seemed to demand tidiness. Lacey washed and dried the few dishes and put them away, effectively removing any trace of her presence. Then, and only then, did she give in to the call of the sea and the irresistibly empty stretch of sand she could see from the windows.

The setting sun was turning the sand into molten gold when she finally retraced her steps to the house, tired yet refreshed by the salt air. After showering and setting the alarm, she crawled into bed, falling asleep almost as soon as her head rested on the pillow.

She stirred once in the night, waking long enough to identify her surroundings before slipping right back into a sound sleep. The infuriating buzz of the alarm she'd set wakened her as the morning sun was rising over the ocean's horizon. Her groping hand found the shut-off switch and quickly silenced it.

Just thinking about the long drive she had ahead of her in heavy traffic made her groan. She was glad she would only have to do it once.

Stumbling out of bed, she walked bleary-eyed into the kitchen, wearing silky pajamas that made her feel glamorous all the same. A pitcher of orange juice was in the refrigerator. Filling a glass from the cupboard, she downed the wake-up juice quickly before putting water on to boil for instant coffee.

Lacey wasted little time in the bathroom with washing and applying the minimal makeup she used. Back in her bedroom, she donned a print skirt and matching blouse in a summery mint green. She might as well get started on the season. Her return to the kitchen coincided with the first rising bubbles of the water.

With a cup of instant coffee in her hand, Lacey stifled a yawn and walked to the glass-paned door in the dining room. It led to a wood-railed upper deck overlooking the ocean. The breeze blowing from the restless sea was brisk and invigorating—exactly what she needed to chase the sleepiness out of her head.

Leaning against a rail, she watched the incoming tide,

mesmerized by the waves rushing one after another to shore. For a little while she lost track of time, sipping at the steaming coffee until the cup was drained.

The sound of a car engine broke the spell of the waves and she turned with a frown. The ocean breeze made it difficult to tell where the sound was coming from, but it seemed very near. Probably an early-morning fisherman, she decided, and went back into the house.

In the kitchen, she started to rinse her cup and spoon under the tap. Her eyes rounded in surprise at the orange juice glass sitting on the counter. Had she—

"Oh, get a grip," she told herself, a little unnerved and needing the sound of a voice even if it was hers. She picked up the used glass. "You got up too early and you only thought you'd washed it. But you didn't."

Quickly dealing with the glass, cup, and spoon, she put all three back where she'd gotten them, clean again. A glance at her watch and she knew she would be late if she didn't hustle. She collected her purse and sped down the stairs to the garage and her car.

The morning rush through Norfolk was as heavy as she'd thought it would be at that hour. And there was no getting around the congestion at the tunnel under the ship channel to Hampton Road and Newport News. She arrived at the office twenty minutes late and spent all morning trying to make up for the lost time.

Coming back from her lunch break at a crowded café that she swore ruined her digestion, Lacey stopped by the receptionist. One look at Jane's flustered and anxious expression told her that office gossip wasn't on her mind.

"That Mr. Whitfield is calling again, Lacey. And he's really upset," Jane burst out. "I told him to call back at one-thirty. I thought Mr. Bowman would be back in his office by then, but he just called to say he's tied up at another job site. Mr. Whitfield is going to be furious when he finds out Mr. Bowman isn't here."

Lacey's first impulse was to say, "Tough!" But she had noticed the steeliness in Whitfield's voice before and she knew why Jane dreaded his call. Forcing a smile, she said, "Put the call from Mr. Whitfield through to me. I'll explain."

She was barely seated behind her desk, her purse stashed in one of the lower drawers, when the interoffice line buzzed. It was Jane, relaying the message that Mr. Whitfield was holding on line two. Lacey murmured a wry thanks at the information.

She gave herself a personal pep talk, silently. *Don't lose your temper. Stay calm and pleasant no matter what he says. Don't do anything that would make matters worse for Mike.*

Excellent advice, she knew, but just before she took the call, she stuck her tongue out at the blinking light. It was an unseen expression of her true feelings at the moment, combined with relief that tomorrow she would be away from all the mean Mr. Whitfields in the construction business for two glorious weeks of solitude.

"Mr. Bowman's office." When she spoke, there was enough honey in her voice to fill a hive.

"Put me through to Bowman." Impatience crackled in the male voice.

"I'm sorry, but Mr. Bowman isn't in. I don't expect him until late this afternoon. May I help you?" Lacey kept the sweetness in her tone and waited for the explosion. It came.

"I was told—" he began with cold anger.

"Yes, I know what you were told," she interrupted him, then spoke with angelic patience, slowly and softly. That oughta get to him, she thought. "He was expected back at one-thirty, but he was unavoidably detained at one of our job sites."

"So you're claiming that he's not in the office?" came the taunt.

"I'm not claiming it. I'm stating it." It was a delight to hear the smiling confidence in her own voice.

"Hell. I know you won't tell me more than that. But you have to tell me your name."

No, I don't. Lacey fiddled with a pencil while Whitfield paused for breath.

"So who am I talking to, Miss—or is it Ms.—?"

"Miss," Lacey supplied. "You can call me Miss Andrews. I don't mind. I'm an old-fashioned girl." She smirked at the receiver.

"Isn't that nice. Well, Miss Andrews, your boss isn't at *my* job site and I'm sure you know it. And he promised me that a full crew would be." His rich voice was ominously low and vibrating with anger. "A skeleton could dance through the building and not find anyone to scare. You tell Bowman when he gets back to his office that I expect to hear from him—immediately!"

If, as Jane had indicated, there were problems on one of the other job sites, Mike wasn't going to be in any mood to contact Mr. Whitfield when he returned. Taking a deep breath, Lacy plunged into her mission of mercy. It was the least she could do after Mike had given her Saturday off.

"I'm familiar with your project, Mr. Whitfield," she volunteered, "and I do know why it hasn't been completed. Please let me explain."

"You?" The reply was not so much skeptical as mocking.

Lacey bristled, but steadfastly refused to take the bait of replying in kind. "Yes, Mr. Whitfield, me. I am aware of what's happening on all of the projects, including yours."

"Which is precisely nothing."

"That's for a very good reason," Lacey insisted, her composure cracking for an instant.

"All right." He accepted her offer to explain with a decided challenge. "For starters, tell me why there aren't any painters on the job."

"The painters aren't there because the bulk of the work left for them is in the various washrooms, rooms they can't do until the tile setters are finished. The tile setters aren't there because the plumber isn't finished. You see, Mr. Whitfield, it's a vicious circle."

"Why isn't the plumber on the job then?" he demanded. "The story you've just told me isn't new, Miss Andrews. I've heard it all from Bowman, along with a bogus promise that the plumbers would be out there today without fail."

"At the time Mr. Bowman told you that, he had every reason to believe it would happen. The problem is that the shipment of bathroom fixtures hasn't arrived. Yesterday the plumber assured us that it had come in. Later this morning, Mi—Mr. Bowman—found out differently. I know he regrets the delay as much as you do." Lacey spoke with sugar-coated politeness but she was feeling less sure of herself by the second.

Whitfield completely ignored the last comment. "Where are the fixtures?"

"I don't know, sir. I do know that they were shipped from the manufacturer several weeks ago, but they haven't arrived."

"In other words, they were lost en route and you're saying 'too bad.'"

"Of course not," Lacey protested. Why had she thought she could fake her way through a phone call from Whitfield, the client from hell? She really wasn't all that familiar with this particular job. Mike had handled it from the get-go pretty much by himself.

"Then what freight company shipped them?"

"I—I don't know."

"What about the manifest numbers, points of origin? Do you know any of that, Miss Andrews?" Whitfield continued his biting questions.

"No, I don't." She was becoming flustered, color warming her cheeks.

"Do you know if anyone is following the shipment online? Has anyone there even heard of real-time tracking or are you all old-fashioned? I'm hoping that description only applies to you. Though you do sound too young for it."

"Ah—"

"Never mind. Next question. Has Bowman or the plumbing contractor looked into alternate suppliers for the fixtures, or am I supposed to twiddle my thumbs until the happy day they show up?" he snapped.

"I'm sure they don't intend to—"

"I damn well hope not!"

"Really, Mr. Whitfield." Her lips were compressed in a tight line. Her prim façade was hard to maintain when she wanted to curse right back at him. "I—"

"Really, Miss Andrews," he interrupted in a low voice, "it seems to me that if human skill and persistence can invent satellite mapping that shows every damn house on the planet *and* the pigeons on the roofs, it should be possible to find a lost shipment of toilets!"

She was silent, caught somewhere between a grin at his absurd statement and anger at his tone.

"What do you think? I really want to know," he was asking.

"Of course it's possible," she began.

"Then may I suggest that since you're Bowman's assistant or secretary or whatever it is you call yourself, that you use your time to find out where the hell they are!"

The line went dead.

Lacey sputtered uselessly into the mouthpiece before slamming down the receiver. He really did have a point, and she felt like a bumbling idiot. The shipment should have been tracked online days ago, and follow-up phone calls made. It didn't reflect well on the company that Whitfield had been the one to point out the oversight. Picking up the phone again, pulling up a screen on her monitor, Lacey made the first steps toward correcting what promised to be a long series of careless mistakes.

Chapter 2

It was crazy, Lacey thought as she stretched lazily like a cat. Here it was a mild summer night and she had all the windows open and a fire burning in the fireplace. But it seemed to somehow fit her mood, with the breeze off the ocean carrying a tangy salt scent, the gentle sound of the breakers rushing in to the beach, and the crackling of flames dancing to the soft music on the sound system.

After the hectic last-day-before-vacation stint at the office, with the irritating phone call from that Whitfield man, and the long drive through evening traffic back to Margo's house, Lacey had virtually collapsed on Friday night, sleeping until nearly noon this morning. An afternoon swim had been her only exertion, outside of cooking a high-calorie Italian dinner all for herself.

Now, with the moonlight silvering the ocean and the yellow flames lighting up the blackened hearth, Lacey's sole desire was to curl up on the sofa and read. Kicking off her slippers, she got ready to do just that, plumping pillows and making a nest.

She caught a glimpse of herself in one of Margo's mirrors, and fluffed the ends of her silky brown hair. The new cut was short and sophisticated, and it held up, even in the damp sea air. The stylist had admired Lacey's fine cheekbones and the cut brought them out.

She sighed and turned away from her reflection. It would be nice, she thought, if she had a wonderful guy to keep her company and shower her with compliments to warm her up for . . . well, never mind.

The filmy baby-doll pajamas she'd picked to wear were going to require a robe or an afghan thrown over them before the night was over. They were decidedly brief, she realized as she tucked her legs beneath her, but what the hell. She was safely locked in—she'd double-checked that—and kept the key inside from the day she'd arrived. It was on the mantel so she couldn't misplace it. Just being careful. There weren't any neighbors close by, although a peeping Tom would have to be a giant to see in the second-story windows. Here in the flat country of Virginia's Tidewater basin along the coast, there wasn't such a thing as a hill, much less a mountain.

The blue-bottomed lamp beside the sofa cast a small pool of light on the pages of the book in Lacey's hand. Reclining against the fluffy pillows, she found her place and began reading. Soon her head began nodding lethargically until finally the book slipped from her fingers and she dozed.

An hour later something wakened her. Still tired, she glanced around and decided it had been a log cracking into embers in the fireplace. Closing the book, she set it on the chrome and white stand beside the lamp and switched off the light.

As sleepy as she was, she knew she should go to bed, but it was so pleasant and comfortable in front of the fire. Snuggling deeper into the pillows, she gazed at the yellow flames licking the nearly disintegrated wood in the fireplace.

Then it happened.

From the bottom of the entrance stairs she heard the rattle of the doorknob and the remnants of sleep fell as every nerve screamed in alertness. A burglar—someone—was breaking in! Never mind her checking the locks. There she was, all alone with no neighbor near enough to hear her cries.

Her bare feet didn't make a sound on the patterned rug as she darted to the telephone beside the other sofa. But the line was dead when she picked up the receiver. That was one thing she hadn't checked, not remembering Margo saying that the land line was iffy before she'd changed and settled in. Her cell phone was in her purse, which was in her bedroom. Great—the intruder wasn't going to wait for her to find out, she thought bitterly. Maybe she could knock him out with the useless but heavy old phone. Panic raced through her veins.

It was too late to run. The front door had already been opened and there was the quiet, even tread of footsteps on the stairs. Instinct sent Lacey racing madly to the fireplace. There was a brief clang of metal against metal as she grabbed the poker from its rack.

The footsteps on the stairs paused for an instant and she froze near the fireplace. Both of her shaking hands were clutching the poker, holding it like a baseball bat in front of her.

The steps resumed their climb. With only the flickering, dying flame of the fire to provide light in the darkened house, the stairwell was encased in shadow. Yet from these shadows a darker figure emerged and halted at the top of the steps.

Breathing became painful for Lacey. She swallowed, trying to ease the paralysis in her throat.

The figure moved nearer, into the half-light cast by the fire. Dark pants. Lighter-colored top, a knit of some sort, Lacey guessed unconsciously, judging by the way it outlined the breadth of his chest and shoulders. She was trying to memorize details for the cops.

Conservative but well-cut clothes. Thick hair that the ocean breeze had ruffled a bit. He could have stepped out of a men's wear catalogue. But that didn't mean a damn thing.

The man's face was all angles and planes, the firelight casting more shadows than it revealed. But the rough contours of his face gave her the impression that he was regarding her with curious—if not amused—surprise.

He took another step nearer and her heart jumped into her throat, blocking any bravado words of challenge. The shadows dissipated and she found herself staring into a pair of blue eyes, dark as indigo.

They began to make a slow, assessing sweep of her, traveling down the long column of her throat, over the jutting curves of her breasts, noticing the slimness of her waist and hips, and following the length of bare legs to her bare toes, then reversed the order.

Lacey wasn't aware that the fire flickering behind her made the filmy pajamas virtually transparent. Her only sensation was the way his eyes seemed to burn through her body, increasing her feelings of danger. Lacey trembled when his gaze met hers, her knuckles whitening as she gripped the poker more tightly.

"Bob told me I would find everything I want, but I didn't realize he meant it literally," the intruder mused, his tone riddled with suggestion.

Lacey brandished the poker. "Get out of here!" Her voice was a croaking whisper, making a mockery out of her attempt to threaten him.

She heard his chuckle and wanted to run, but her legs were shaking. She had never been so afraid in her life. That he had said Bob's name didn't really register in her mind. So many things could happen to her right now and she was desperately trying not to visualize any of them.

"Get out," she told him again, in a steadier voice this time, "or I'll—I'll call the police."

She glanced at the phone, inching closer to it. She knew it wasn't working, but did he? She had to take the chance that he hadn't cut the wires.

"Sorry." There was laughter in his voice, rich and low. "The telephone has been temporarily disconnected. Corrosion on the exterior jack or so I was told."

As she breathed in quickly, a tiny sob of panic made itself heard. As if hypnotized, she watched his mouth curve in a smile that was oddly gentle and a little indulgent.

"Why don't you tell me who you are and what you're doing here?"

His question struck as being so absurd that she was struck speechless. It became obvious to her, even in her state of semishock, that he wasn't going to leave on his own. The poker in her hand didn't seem to intimidate him in the slightest. She would have to think of something else.

"I'm not here alone, you know," Lacey lied. "My husband went out to the store and he'll be back any minute."

"Is that right?" The intruder merely smiled. "Okay, fine. Got a cell phone? I left mine in my car. Could you ask him to pick up a quart of milk? And when he gets here, maybe you'll put down that poker and start explaining a few things."

He took another step forward and Lacey raised the poker to strike. Her heart was hammering against her ribs, her stomach churning with fear.

"Don't come any closer," she threatened shakily. "Or I'll bash your head in!"

He stopped, the lazy smile still curving his mouth. His stance was relaxed but Lacey wasn't fooled. There wasn't any flab on his muscular frame and a man that physically fit could react in seconds, like a predatory animal.

"I bet you would," he said, but something in his tone told her that he didn't take her threat too seriously. She could see that she was no match for him even with the poker.

Behind Lacey a log in the fireplace cracked and popped loudly. The tiny sting of a few sparks flying made her stand on one foot for a second, startled more by the explosive sound.

In that second, a grip strong as steel fastened around her wrist and the poker was ripped from her hand. He tossed it away and it clanked against the fireplace bricks.

"No!" The single word tore from her throat as she struggled to regain her balance and fight him off.

Adrenaline surged through her system. Her legs had been wobbly with fright, but now she kicked and hit out at him, too, punching randomly at awfully solid muscle.

At first he was satisfied to hold her arm and only ward off the majority of her blows, but as her accuracy improved, he changed his tactics. Lacey felt herself being bodily pushed down onto the sofa. Primitive alarm raced through her frantic heartbeats when she felt the force of his weight pressing her into the cushions.

Writhing in panic, gasping, she tried her best to throw him off but remained pinned in place by his chest and his single-handed grip on her wrists. His sheer strength was setting off instinctive danger signals and she reacted with increasing wildness. But he kept her captive with humiliating ease.

As she made a superhuman effort to twist away, she felt the delicate strap of her top tear in his other hand. His touch against her now bare skin made her blood run cold.

His body heat had already made a scorching impression.

She heard him curse softly when she muffled a sob of fear by sinking her teeth into her lip. She detected a trace of liquor in the warm breath that fanned her cheek.

"Stop struggling," he demanded roughly. "I don't want to hurt you."

The words flashed through her brain—should she stop fighting? She didn't want to do anything to incite him more.

She stayed tense, though, waiting for his next move and hoping for the slightest chance of escape. Her breathing was labored and deep.

"That's better," he said with approval, and shifted to one side, easing his weight from on top of her while keeping a firm hold, as if knowing she would run at the first opportunity.

"Let me go!" Lacey cried in a hoarse voice. She knew he wouldn't, but she couldn't bear being totally submissive.

"Not yet."

In the dim light she caught the brief glimmer of white teeth and knew he was smiling—laughing at her. It stung that she was so helpless.

He seemed to move toward her and she cringed into the cushions—then he sat up. His arm reached above her head to switch on the lamp above the sofa.

Lacey blinked warily in the blinding light, calming under the inspection by the dark blue eyes. She couldn't hold his gaze for long. It got to her in the strangest way, and the sensation rattled her.

"Now for some explanations," he said, eying her steadily. "What are you doing in this house?"

"I—I'm living here." Lacey frowned in confusion.

"Really? You own it? Is that what you're saying?" he queried.

Who *was* this guy? The real estate agent from hell?

She still had to play along, much as she wanted to scratch his eyes out. He had her by the wrist, though.

"Well, no, not exactly." She wondered why his question made her feel so uneasy. She had a legitimate right to be here. For all his bizarrely casual remarks, he was an intruder.

Her left hand was free and she raised it to brush a wayward strand of hair from the corner of her eye. His narrowed gaze followed the movement, as if he was anticipating that she would try to hit him again.

"Not exactly?" He gestured toward her left hand. "You said your husband would be here any minute. Where's your wedding ring?"

Lacey had been caught in her lie and she felt as guilty as a child. "Ah—"

"Okay, maybe you left it in the pocket of those pajamas."

He grinned and she glared back. Her skimpy outfit, now torn, didn't have pockets, something he'd obviously noticed. Lacey was hotly reminded of her vulnerability, wearing practically nothing. Sitting next to her, he took up more than his share of space. She edged away.

"I don't think," he said, "you're expecting anyone."

"You can't be sure of that," she retorted. "And I don't have to explain to you. You're the one who broke into the house and accosted me. You—" She stopped short, realizing she shouldn't have reminded him that he had no reason to be there. She stared into his eyes, memorizing his features, again thinking she would have to identify him to the police. He might not hurt her, but he was crazy-calm.

The metallic glitter in his eyes spooked her. "I broke into the house?" His words held a steely coldness that sounded strangely familiar, but Lacey was too caught up in the present moment to search her memory. "No, I didn't."

"But—"

His hand moved, and in the next instant he was holding a key in front of her face. "I used a key. You're the one who broke in. Don't lie."

Lacey stared at it open-mouthed. "I'm not—that's impossible!" she declared. "Just because you say that's a key to the door doesn't mean it is."

"Believe me, it fit the lock." He smiled lazily, and happened to glance toward the mantel. "Well, look at that. Here's another one." He got up to get the key she'd set there and put the two of them together, aligning the notches until they fitted exactly and holding them up for her to see. "Where did you get this? Let me guess. You must be from a housekeeping company and you decided to copy the key and have yourself a private party in a client's house when you knew it would be empty. Sweet." He folded his fingers around both keys and placed them back in his pocket. "I hope you don't clean in that getup."

"What?"

He ignored her look of outrage. "Spare me the innocent act. Time to go. I don't know who you are or who you're really waiting for, but get dressed and get out—you have other clothes, right?"

She didn't answer, seething inside with confused fury.

"Am I wrong? Is this your night job?" he asked in a conversational tone that made her want to do serious damage to him with that poker all over again.

"Not talking—hmm. Well, if you're desperately in need of a place to sleep tonight, there's always my bed."

"You—"

His gaze traced the hollow of her collarbone, but no lower. He was courteous enough to keep his eyes up, for some strange reason. "It's been comfortable, at least for the last couple of nights. But it's really too big for one person."

"What did you just say? The last couple of nights?" Lacey burst out angrily.

"I think this house has developed an echo," he chuckled.

"And you tell me not to lie! You have some nerve," she sputtered, "trying to con me into thinking you have any right to be here. Well, you just tripped yourself up, because I've been sleeping in this house for the last two nights all by myself, and I certainly haven't seen you."

"You don't give up, do you?" he declared with an exasperated sigh, and stood up again.

"No, I don't," Lacey retorted, her brown eyes snapping. "And since you've so magnanimously offered to share your bed, I'll be leaving as soon as I can!"

"Good." His mouth thinned into a grim line. "And tell your party-hearty friend or friends who were thinking this house is up for grabs that it isn't. Got that?"

Lacey was on her feet, halfway across the living room and headed for her bedroom when he asked the question. She stopped, glaring at him over her shoulder.

"I sure do," she said quickly. As soon as she was dressed, she *was* going to get into her car and drive straight to the police. But he didn't have to know that. This guy was well dressed and authoritative—and somehow had glommed on to the right key—but you never knew who was crazy and who wasn't. Her cousin had been right to worry about leaving the place empty while she and her husband were away. Friends, hah. But it was clear Margo had made some incredibly stupid mistake, Lacey was sure of it. Without thinking, Lacey muttered words to that effect as she stormed away.

Long strides ate up the distance between them and he clasped her arm. She shrugged him off and faced him boldly.

"What did you just say?" he demanded.

"I said I would talk to my friends," she replied with irritation.

"Not that. The last part—what you said under your breath."

"About Margo . . ." Lacey trailed off, knowing she shouldn't have mentioned her cousin's name in front of this stranger.

His gaze sharpened. "Do we know the same Margo? Margo Richards?"

"Uh—"

He looked at her suspiciously. "Maybe not."

Lacey was even more nettled. "Margo Richards happens to be my cousin."

"Really?" he said with jeering skepticism. "You don't look alike. Where is she now? Would you know?"

"As a matter of fact, I do," she burst out, throwing caution to the winds. "She and her husband flew to Florida to visit his family before leaving on a Caribbean cruise. That's why she invited me to stay here, so the house wouldn't be empty while they were gone," Lacey said with all the righteous confidence she could summon up.

"How about that," he said with an odd laugh. "Her husband Bob asked me to stay."

"What?" Lacey was taken aback for a minute by his statement. Then she scowled fiercely at him. "You don't honestly expect me to believe that."

"It happens to be the truth." He reached into his pocket and took out a business card that she recognized as Bob's. "I don't know your cousin Margo very well, but Bob and I go back to freshman year at the University of Virginia."

"Prove it," she challenged him.

"You know," he said solemnly, "I usually carry my framed diploma around just in case anyone asks, but I don't happen to have it with me at the moment."

"Very funny. Bob should be with his parents now. Why don't you call him?"

He pointed to the living room phone. "It's dead, remember? Bob told me about the corrosion problem. You know how it is, waiting around for a repairman. They would've missed their flight."

She crossed her arms over her chest. "And your cell is in your car." She wasn't going to tell him she had one, safe in her purse, while she sat unsafely in the living room, thinking the land line was working.

"That's right. Want me to get it and call him?"

"Yes," she insisted. "Where I can listen." She was beginning to believe him. Then she reminded herself that he had both keys while she waited for him to get his phone. If she ran out into the night, she wouldn't be able to get back in.

He took the stairs two at a time when he returned with a cell phone in his hand, listening to a voice mail message she could hear from where she was standing.

Hello, this is Bob. I'll get back to you when we get back from paradise. Fair warning: Margo and I might be gone for good. But leave a message at the beep.

"That's helpful," the man commented, holding out the cell phone to her. "Want to say something?"

Lacey shook her head, thinking if his cell phone got service out here, hers would too. She looked at the state-of-the-art, expensive design of the phone he held and its glowing touch screen. Maybe not. Hers had been offered free with a discount plan and was cheaply made. His sleek phone obviously cost ten times as much.

"Okay. That's Bob's voice and you have Bob's number. But it's not absolute proof that you know him or that you're supposed to be here." Might as well stall. She crossed her arms over her chest, not able to think of a better plan.

He studied the glowing screen and typed in a few words to leave a text message. "Maybe he'll call back. So"—he looked up—"while we're playing this game, do you know where they went on their honeymoon?"

"Yes," Lacey admitted, but she figured it was his turn to prove himself a little more. "Do you?"

"To Hawaii. The first day there Bob stayed out in the sun too long and spent the next two days of their honeymoon in the hospital with heat stroke."

"That's right," she said with amazement. "So you really do know him."

The man rolled his eyes. "Why would I lie? If you want to know, he asked me to stay in the house a week ago. I said yes. He didn't mention you, though."

Lacey was dying to call Margo and tell her what had happened—and give her cousin hell for getting her into a pickle like this—but she wasn't going to borrow his solid gold phone to do it or dig around in front of him for her own. Little Cheepy, her nickname for it, had probably gone dead and she couldn't remember if she'd brought the charger.

Something else this guy had said came back to her. "Um—did you say you'd been staying here since Thursday night?"

"That's right."

"But so have I." She ran her fingers through the tousled thickness of her short hair, thinking hard. Pieces of the puzzle called Margo's Stupid Mistake started to fall into place. "Oh!" They began fitting together rapidly. "My gosh," she whispered, and turned the full force of her brown gaze on him. "Did Bob give you the key to the front door in person?"

"No, he left it for me."

"Exactly where did he say it would be?"

"Under the mat, but I—"

Lacey interrupted him. "You found it in the flowerpot, right?"

"Yes." He frowned. "How did you know?"

"Because that's where Margo said she would leave the key for me, only I tripped over the mat and saw the key underneath it, so I didn't bother to look in the flowerpot," she explained.

There were other things she remembered that backed up his claim that he had been in the house since Thursday. "It must have been your car I heard leaving on Friday morning," she murmured.

"I left around six-thirty, quarter to seven, something like that."

"And it was your orange juice glass I washed," she went on.

"It was late." She could see by the absent look in his eyes that he was recalling the events of that Friday morning too. "I had orange juice and didn't bother with coffee until I got to my office. But I didn't see you here."

"I was out on the deck having my morning coffee. This is so freaky," Lacey declared, moving back to one of the sofas and sinking onto its cushions. "I went to bed early both nights and slept like a baby."

"It was nearly midnight Thursday and Friday before I came in," he added.

"And when you came in tonight, I took you for a burglar." She laughed briefly, shaking her head.

"I don't blame you. And I'm really sorry that I scared you. Nice try with the poker, by the way."

She made a wry face. "What if I'd managed to hit you?"

There was a look of amusement on his face that clearly conveyed his doubt on that score. "That wasn't going to happen," he pointed out.

"Even when you put those two keys together—heck, I couldn't put two and two together if I tried." She sighed worriedly. "Wow, do I need this vacation. I've been working way too hard lately."

He chuckled. "Maybe we both have. My first thought was that you were some college girl crashing in the first empty house you found. But that outfit—um, you didn't look like someone from a cleaning service either."

No, not in see-through babydoll pajamas. She could more or less imagine what his second thought had been and reached for a crocheted afghan to drape around herself. It occurred to her that he still wasn't looking at her below the neck at all. A point in his favor.

"What a mix-up!" Lacey shook her head. "I wonder if Bob and Margo figured out yet that they each asked somebody to stay in the house."

"I doubt it." He walked to the fireplace and gazed down into the smoldering remains of the fire.

"I guess it doesn't matter," she sighed, smiling at the ridiculousness of the situation. "They're in Florida and we're here. There isn't much they can do to put it right now. It's up to us to straighten things out."

"It's too late to do anything about it tonight." Picking up the poker, he put it back in its stand. "Tomorrow is plenty of time for you to pack."

"Me?" Lacey squeaked in astonishment.

"Naturally you." He glanced over his shoulder, seemingly surprised that Lacey didn't agree.

"What? Why 'naturally' me?" she demanded.

"You don't want to stay, do you? I don't plan to be around that much and it seems to me there are safety concerns here. If I had been a burglar tonight, exactly what could you have done?" he reasoned. "There isn't a neighbor close enough to hear you scream."

"I don't care," Lacey insisted stubbornly. "I'm on vacation. This is a perfect spot and I'm not leaving. And what was that you just said about not being around much? If you—if you were a gentleman, you would go and leave me alone."

"Nothing doing. If you want a solitary vacation, go ahead and check into a hotel suite." He regarded her with infuriating calm, his rugged features set in unrelenting lines.

"I beg your pardon?"

He just looked at her for another minute without saying anything.

"No, scratch that. I'm not begging for anything. I can't get a reservation in a hotel—the season is starting. Besides, I can't afford two weeks in a suite. I'm staying here. *You* go."

"Nothing doing," he answered decisively. "Thanks to your—" He cut off that sentence abruptly and started another. "The demands of my business don't allow me the luxury of a vacation. The most I can hope for is to get away a few hours now and then where I can't be easily reached. When Bob told me the phone was out, I was happy. This place is ideal." The corner of his mouth lifted in a wry smile. "For both of us. But not necessarily at the same time. You can—hey. I don't want to keep saying 'you.' What's your name?"

"Andrews. Lacey Andrews."

A wicked glint of laughter sparkled in his eyes. "You are the redoubtable Miss Andrews?"

"I beg your pardon?" She tipped her head to one side, staring at him in total confusion. Why had he put it that way?

"Where do you live?" he asked unexpectedly.

"I have a small apartment just outside of Newport News. Why?" Except for that glittering light of amusement dancing in his blue eyes, his expression didn't tell her much.

"Where do you work?"

What does that have to do with anything? Lacey thought crossly, but answered in the hope that he would eventually satisfy *her* curiosity.

"I'm an assistant to a construction engineer in Newport News."

The wicked glint became all the more pronounced. "'I am not claiming Mr. Bowman is out. I am stating it.'" he mimicked unexpectedly.

Chapter 3

Lacey's mouth opened and closed. "You . . . you aren't Mr. Whitfield, are you?" she said incredulously.

"Cole Whitfield." He confirmed his identity with a mocking nod of his head. "At last we meet face to face. Now we can argue in person instead of on the telephone. Might be fun."

Stunned, Lacey stared at the tall, broad-shouldered man standing in front of the fireplace. His strong, carved features had the stamp of authority—he was accustomed to lording it over others, obviously. There was a warm virility about him, an aura of total maleness that Lacey hadn't picked up just from a phone conversation.

Talking to her then, he'd been abrasive—she'd thought of rough finished steel covered with a winter morning frost. Her mental image of Mr. Whitfield didn't resemble this high-energy, compelling man at all. Lacey was still gaping when he broke the silence to speak.

"Do I measure up?" he asked sarcastically.

She found her voice long enough to croak, "I'm not going to answer that."

"Suit yourself." He shrugged. "I only asked because of the way you were staring. What did you think I would be? An ogre with three heads?" Cole Whitfield's voice was husky with contained amusement. "I left the other two heads at my office."

"You—you are the rudest, most obnoxious man—" Lacey began, tripping over the words, to describe the man she had known as Cole Whitfield.

"If you had as much money—meaning my own and investors' money—tied up in that building, and you'd had to put up with all those delays, you'd be snapping at everyone too," he interrupted without a trace of apology for his behavior.

"And that's your excuse?" she demanded indignantly.

"It'll do," Cole said casually. "And maybe you can understand why I desperately need some peace and quiet. All that aggravation is getting to me. By the way"—his deeply blue eyes were laughing again—"did you ever find those toilets?"

A smile tugged at the corners of her mouth but she refused to let it show. "We're tracing them every way we can." He had a right to know, obviously, but she hadn't completely forgiven him for his rudeness. Besides, discussing the ins and outs of interstate shipping while clad only in babydoll pajamas and a crocheted afghan just felt weird. "There should be more definite information by Monday afternoon."

"Really, Lacey? That long? Even with computerized container codes?"

"Things get lost. It does happen." At the moment, she wished that he would get lost himself.

"Monday, huh? But you're on vacation, so you won't be there." He surveyed the room as if he was noticing it for the first time, momentarily releasing Lacey from his gaze. "Which brings us back to our present situation."

"Who stays and who goes." Her chin came up at a belligerent angle. Cole Whitfield seemed to get what she couldn't quite bring herself to add out loud. *Make me.*

He rested an elbow on the mantelpiece, an indolent gesture that gave her more than a hint of what he was thinking.

"Okay. Since we're both prepared to be stubborn, I think the solution is for both of us to stay," he said.

Lacey arched an eyebrow in silent surprise.

"After all, we've already spent two nights together under the same roof," he reminded her.

There was one point she wanted clarified before she considered this new suggestion. "Are you, ah, rephrasing your invitation to share your empty bed?"

"Oh, right. I did say that, didn't I?" He smiled. "Propositioning you seemed like a fast way to make you take off." He gave a brief shake of his head, then said jokingly, "I'm not interested in meaningless sex, are you?"

"No," she said tightly.

"I guess we both want peace and quiet. So we need a few ground rules. Number one: no hanky-panky. All in favor say aye."

"Aye," she murmured.

"Although"—his gaze skimmed over her mostly concealed body—"if you make a habit of wandering around in outfits like the one under that shawl thing, all bets are off," he added with a note of mockery in his voice.

His comment sent an odd tremor quaking through her. Fiddling under the afghan, she raised the drooping neckline of her pajama top and tucked the torn strap under her arm, but there was nothing she could do about the bare expanse of shapely leg and thigh that still showed.

"It wasn't ripped until you got your paws on it," she retorted defensively, referring to the torn strap.

"That really was an accident," he assured her. "I'll buy you a new set if you want."

A shopping tour of the nearest Intimates Department with him was not going to happen. Never. No way. "That won't be necessary."

He studied her face and Lacey realized that she was blushing.

"All right. But I did offer. Give me credit for that." Lacey glared at him. "So what do you think? About sharing the place, I mean."

"You just said you wanted peace and quiet. Why are you willing to have me stay here all of a sudden?" Lacey wanted to know.

"I hate arguing. And it might work. Seems to me you like to read," he said, giving a brief nod toward the paperback she'd thrown down on the sofa. "So I'm guessing you actually are relatively quiet. And you seem responsible—I seriously doubt I could get anyone else at your company from Mike on down to track that shipment."

"Whoa." She held up a hand. "I am officially on vacation and I didn't bring a laptop. Call the company on Monday." She envisioned him producing a laptop of his own and launching a wild-goose chase—no, call it a wild-toilet chase—all over the Internet, armed with the shipping codes.

Her vehemence made him smile, but he didn't reply.

She looked at him suspiciously. "That's not the reason you offered to share, is it?"

Cole shrugged. "If I tried to insist that you leave, I bet you'd fight to the last breath. And I've had all the wrangling I can handle for a while. Besides, I'm tired," he added.

Lacey noticed the lines of strain around his mouth and felt a twinge of guilt.

"I'd rather figure out something that would make both of us happy, if that's possible," he continued. "We're civilized, intelligent adults. You are an adult, aren't you?" he asked sarcastically.

"I'm twenty-four," she declared.

Again he gave her the once-over. "Close up, you look older. I don't know why I took you for a college girl at first."

"Thanks a lot!" A thread of angry astonishment ran through her voice. She was usually accused of not looking her age instead of the other way around.

"Sorry. Wishful thinking on my part." He sighed tiredly and looked away. "Must have been those pajamas. They really are pretty damn se—" He caught himself before he said *sexy.* Lacey could see the word on his lips and it disconcerted her. "Seductive," he finished. "Can I say that without risking a lawsuit?"

Lacey stiffened. "We're not in the office and I made it clear that I'm not discussing company business. But let's change the subject. Or stay on it—what were we talking about?"

"Staying here. Together."

His tone of voice confused her. An uncomfortable flush warmed her skin until she shivered under the ridiculous afghan. "Wait a minute. I want to get a robe," she muttered. He looked politely away as she scrambled off the sofa, first making sure her abbreviated pajamas weren't clinging anywhere embarrassing.

"Don't bother," he said softly. She just stood there for a frozen second until he continued, "What I mean is—if you agree with my solution, there's no reason why we can't turn in for the night right now. In separate bedrooms, of course," he joked tightly.

"I . . ." Lacey hesitated.

At close quarters, his good old-fashioned virility—there was no other word for it—suddenly held a powerful attraction. And if, as he had implied, he'd felt just as drawn to her, rooming together would be completely unworkable.

"I know what you're thinking," he said quietly—and strangely enough, Lacey believed that he did. "Things could get kinda out of control if we let them. Don't worry. I lose my temper sometimes, but other than that, I can control my animal instincts. How about you? I'm not that irresistible, right?"

"Right," she said slowly. A smile flickered over her lips. At least they both found humor in their predicament. The situation couldn't get out of control unless they permitted it.

"Does that smile mean yes, roommate?" The corners of his eyes crinkled, although the line of his mouth remained straight.

She nodded.

"Fine. Then what do you say we bring this conversation to an end so I can get some sleep?" Cole suggested lazily.

"Okay." Lacey smiled. "Good night then." She moved past him to the hallway leading to her bedroom.

Three-quarters of an hour later she was lying in her bed, dead tired but unable to fall asleep. She fought to lie still and not toss and turn with restlessness.

The previous two nights, when she hadn't known that Cole Whitfield was in the next room, she'd slept like a baby. But now, knowing he was there, she discovered she wasn't quite as nonchalant about it as she'd thought she would be. Good grief, she could even hear the squeak of his bedsprings when he moved.

Pay no attention, she told herself silently, and forced her eyes to close.

It was a long time before she was able to ignore his presence in the house and drift into sleep. In consequence it was midmorning before she awakened, vaguely irritable from having overslept.

Grabbing her robe from the foot of the bed, she pulled it on as she hurried toward the bathroom. In the hall she stopped face to face with a bleary-eyed, tousle-haired Cole, also en route to the bathroom.

His dark blue eyes made a disgruntled sweep of her and she felt a moment's relief that she'd changed into long-legged, completely opaque silky pajamas of turquoise blue. He couldn't accuse her of not being substantially covered.

The same couldn't be said for him, she realized, as she became rather uncomfortably conscious of the naked expanse of naturally tanned chest—and below that, jockey shorts. She had often seen her two older brothers in about the same state—they slept in their skivvies and generally beat her to the upstairs bathroom of the family home. Yet it wasn't at all the same when the man was Cole Whitfield.

There was a sardonic twist of his mouth as he gestured toward the bathroom door. "Ladies first." Then he retreated unselfconsciously into the second guest room.

Lacey darted into the bathroom, her cheeks burning like a schoolgirl's. Cold water from the tap was more effective than the chiding words she directed at herself. With her face washed, teeth brushed, and a touch of light makeup applied in the interests of vanity, she emerged from the bathroom.

A glance into Cole's room revealed him sitting on the edge of the unmade bed, his dark head resting tiredly in his hands.

"I'm all through," Lacey told him, with a lot more poise now that she wasn't looking at him close up. "Bathroom's yours. I'm going to start some coffee."

"Good." He sighed deeply, rubbing his hands over his face before rising.

In the kitchen, she filled the coffeemaker reservoir with water and spooned fresh grounds into the basket, quickly figuring out how to turn the gizmo on and make sure the pot was positioned correctly before the brew cycle started. She heard water running in the shower, giving her plenty of time to dress before Cole was finished in the bathroom.

Lacey poured a glass of orange juice and climbed on one of the tall stools at the counter to drink it.

As she finished the refreshing juice, the running water was turned off. Sighing, she slid off the stool and started to her room.

She was halfway across the living room when the front doorbell rang. Changing her direction to answer it, she shrugged, thinking to herself that it was probably a neighbor who didn't know that Margo and Bob were off on a cruise. She was going to have to buy Margo a nice new brain. Maybe she could get a second one at half off for Bob.

Descending the steps, she paused at the front door to look out through the peephole. A man and a woman stood outside, but Lacey couldn't see much of them. Just to be polite, in case they were neighbors, she opened the door a crack.

"Yes?" She smiled at the pair.

They were complete strangers to her. The woman had beautiful long, wheat blond hair, and makeup precisely applied to her striking features. Her green eyes registered shock at the sight of Lacey standing on the other side of the door.

Her clothes were casual, white slacks with a vividly red print top. On the blonde they looked chic—the only adjective Lacey could think of that fit.

The man, taller with sandy blond hair, seemed first surprised to see Lacey, then amused. He was very good-looking, but she suspected he was well aware of it.

She opened her mouth to explain that Bob and Margo were on vacation, but the woman spoke before she had the chance.

"We must have the wrong address, Vic," she declared in an icy tone. She would have turned to leave if the man hadn't taken hold of her elbow to keep her at the door.

Without glancing at the blonde, he directed his curious gaze at Lacey. "We're looking for Cole Whitfield. Is he here?"

Lacey became tense, suddenly aware of all the embarrassing connotations that could be read into her presence in the house alone with Cole all night. But what did it matter? She had done nothing to be ashamed of, so why act that way?

"He's here." She opened the door wide to let the couple in. "Follow me."

She started up the stairs with the unnaturally silent pair behind her. They didn't volunteer the usual *sorry to bother you* or *by the way, did we mention our names?* She wasn't going to be able to call ahead to Cole. The whole business of their arrival was awkward. Just for a minute Lacey wished she'd gotten dressed instead of having orange juice, but it was too late now.

As they passed the landing, the well-groomed blonde asked with a somewhat superior air, "Are you the housekeeper?"

That question hit a sore spot. Lacey understood that they had no idea of who she was and wouldn't have minded giving a polite explanation of how she'd come to be in the house if they'd asked differently, but—she half turned on the stairs, a hand on her hip, and gave the woman a deliberately cool look.

"Do I look like a housekeeper to you?"

Without waiting for a reply, she started up the stairs again. She could feel the blonde's freezing anger as surely as if a cold north wind were blowing.

Behind her she heard the man speak very quietly in a snotty tone. "You were really reaching with that question, Monica."

"Shut up!" was the hissing reply.

In the living room Lacey paused near the sofa. She was about to suggest that the pair take a seat while she went to tell Cole that they were here. At that same instant, she heard the bathroom door open.

"Lacey!" There was an edge in the way Cole called her name. Her head jerked at the sound, hearing his strides carrying him to the living room.

"Have you been using my razor?" he roared, rounding the hall to stop short at the sight of the three people staring at him.

A white towel was wrapped around his waist and a smaller hand towel was draped around his neck. His hair was glistening darkly from the shower and most of the shaving lather he'd had on had been hastily rinsed away. She made the obvious conclusion from his words and spotted the small spot of red where he'd nicked himself, and the tiny piece of white tissue over it.

Despite his abrupt halt on entering the living room, he made no other outward sign at first that the appearance of his visitors had upset him in any way. Then his gaze narrowed as it flicked from the woman to the man to Lacey.

Lifting a corner of the towel around his neck, he patted it against a trickle of water running down his chest. He seemed to expect a response from Lacey to his initial question.

"If you used the razor that was lying on the shelf above

the sink, it was mine," she answered smoothly. "Yours is in the cabinet."

Her reply appeared to snap the thin thread of self-control the blonde had. "Cole, I want to know who this woman is and what she's doing here!" Her voice trembled violently.

"Good morning to you too, Monica. Yes, it is a lovely day." Cole smiled but the smile didn't reach his eyes and didn't take the even sharper edge off his reply. He took the towel from around his neck and began pressing it to his soaked hair.

"I think you'd better excuse me," Lacey said quickly, praying Cole's lower towel would stay in place if he was going to dry his hair. She was certain that was only the first outburst from the obviously volatile blonde.

"Is the coffee done?" Cole asked. "I could use a cup."

"I think so," Lacey said.

He had partially cut off her retreat with his request. She was inclined to think that he'd want an opportunity to explain, once she was out of earshot, the reason she was there, but evidently he didn't.

"Haven't seen you for a while, Vic. How's it going?" Cole directed the question to the man with the blonde as Lacey walked to the kitchen.

"Not bad, Cole. Not bad," was the reply.

But Lacey could hear the underlying laughter in the man's voice. She had no idea what the relationship was between the blonde and that guy, but it was clear that Vic thought the encounter was more funny than not.

As she started to pour the coffee, a sobering thought occurred to her. Whoever the woman was, she believed she had a right to an explanation from Cole. And Lacey realized she had no idea whether Cole was married or not.

Holy cow! What if the woman was his wife? She

nearly dropped the coffeepot, the color draining from her face.

"You haven't answered my question, Cole," the blonde whom Cole had addressed as Monica reminded him. Her tone was icy, enraged.

"I didn't think you really expected an answer," he replied in a low voice. "I was sure you'd worked it all out for yourself."

The cup clattered in its saucer as Lacey carried it into the living room to Cole. Her face was pale, she saw with a sideways glance into a wall mirror, her color still stolen by the shock of her secret thoughts.

Was he married?

The three were still standing, Cole and Monica eyeing each other with almost open hostility. Lacey came up to Cole's side, offering him the çoffee she'd fixed. The clattering ceased the instant he took cup and saucer from her and set them on a nearby table.

"Aren't you going to introduce us, Cole?" Vic prodded, gazing intently at Lacey.

A muscular arm curved lightly and possessively around the back of her waist, and she stiffened in resistance to Cole's touch. Her gaze flashed to his, meeting the bland glitter in his eyes.

She thought of a cat's hiss when she heard the other woman's indrawn breath, and couldn't help noticing that Monica's green eyes were glowing with hatred. And she realized that Cole was deliberately annoying the woman rather than trying to smooth her ruffled fur.

"Hey, you haven't been formally introduced to my roommate, have you?" His steel blue gaze swung to the couple, his arm tightening around Lacey's waist when she would have pulled away.

He had referred to her last night as his roommate in a joking sense, but his use of it now was provoking and suggestive. He propelled her, stiffly resisting, a few steps forward.

"Lacey, I would like you to meet Monica Hamilton and her brother, Vic Hamilton." He identified them only by name without any other explanation.

Monica merely gave Lacey a poison green look of dislike, but her brother reached out to shake her hand. "It's definitely a pleasure to meet you, Lacey," he murmured.

He hung on to her hand a little too long. The look he gave her made Lacey feel like she was wearing a sheer black lace negligee instead of being fully covered by luxurious but modest pajamas.

"Back off, Vic," Cole ordered quietly.

Lacey's hand was released as Vic smiled in a fake way at him, then at her. "I get it. Private property, no trespassing, huh?"

"That's right," Cole agreed with a curt nod.

"Cole, don't you think," Lacey suggested with rising feeling, "that you should tell your friends how we—I—got here? In detail. Now." As far as she was concerned, this farce had continued much too long already.

He glanced at her, seeing her rigid with anger. "I don't think Monica is interested in how you came to be here, Lacey," he replied dryly. "And she doesn't want a description of what happened between us last night. She's seen all the evidence with her own eyes and used her imagination to fill in the sordid details."

"Tell her," Lacey insisted.

Giving in with a mild shrug, he swung his gaze to Monica. "No matter how it looks, this is perfectly innocent," he told her. "As a matter of fact, Lacey and I slept in separate beds."

"Before or after?" Monica snapped.

There was an I-told-you-so glint in his eyes when he glanced back at Lacey, and she acknowledged silently that Monica was beyond listening to any explanation at the moment. But Cole was to blame for that.

There was a challenge in the set of his jaw when he again turned his attention to Monica. "You didn't say why you're here."

"We came to invite you to dinner and arrange a barefoot-on-the-beach party for this afternoon," she replied caustically. "Of course, I was under the impression that you, poor baby, were here alone with nothing to do all day."

"Obviously you were wrong," Cole replied with a complacent smile.

His arm tightened unexpectedly around Lacey's waist, drawing her more fully against his toweled side before she could make a move to stop him.

"Don't!" she protested in a low, angry whisper. If she wriggled, the towel might fall. She stood stock still.

By the time his grip lessened, it was too late. Monica was already turning on her heel, her long blond hair swinging around her shoulders.

"We're going, Vic," she said huffily.

Vic shrugged as if he didn't care one way or another. "See you around, Cole." But it was Lacey he was looking at before he turned to follow his sister.

"Monica, do you remember what I told you the other day?" Cole's question halted her at the top of the stairs, her expression turned haughty with pride. "I think you understand now that I meant it when I asked you not to call."

Liquid green eyes shimmered briefly and resentfully at Lacey. Then Monica was descending the stairs with a faintly smiling Vic behind her. Neither Lacey nor Cole moved or spoke until they heard the front door shut.

"That was—" Lacey began reprovingly.

"You're a godsend, Lacey!" he laughed.

In the next second, his mouth was swooping down to claim her lips in a hard, sure kiss that took her breath away. When he lifted his head to study her, her reaction was chaotic.

The firm imprint of his mouth still tingled on her lips, the sleep-warmed scent of a man in the morning a pleasurable tickle in her nose. Her heart was tripping over itself, unable to find its normal beat. Over all that, confusion reigned at his lightning change from sarcastic coldness with Monica to this warm, hearty amusement.

He locked his hands together at the small of her back. Lacey's own fingers were spread across his chest in mute protest, aware of the solidness of his naked flesh.

His wickedly glinting eyes looked deeply into hers, crinkling at the corners while taking note of the confusion in her expression.

"I've been trying to get her off my back for several months," he explained. "I think the sight of you scared her off for good. You have my undying gratitude, Lacey."

"Who is she?" Lacey frowned.

"My former fiancée. A couple of years ago I unwisely asked her to marry me. I wanted out soon enough—not that I phrased it like that. But Monica isn't the type to take rejection lightly. In fact, she's been trying to persuade me to change my mind ever since I broke our engagement." His face was disconcertingly near Lacey's, the chiseled contours shadowed by sexy overnight stubble.

"So that's why you deliberately let her believe we'd spent the night together—like lovers, I mean," Lacey said, half in accusation and half in conclusion.

"Exactly. She wouldn't have believed me if I'd tried to convince her otherwise," Cole insisted calmly. "Knowing the way her mind works, if there'd been a video camera hidden in the house to record everything that happened—or didn't happen—last night, she still would be sure that I'd somehow erased the interesting parts."

Lacey eased free of his unrestraining hold, finding his

nearness just a bit much, especially when he was barely decent. She moved a few feet away under his watchful yet mellow gaze.

"I am sorry, though," he added. "It wasn't fair to involve you, not when you're an innocent bystander." A smile tugged at the edge of his mouth, deepening the cleft in his chin. "I hope you don't mind being thought of as a scarlet woman."

"Oh, I get that all the time," she said caustically. "Anyway, spending a night with a man is no big deal these days."

He seemed a little dismayed by that careless remark. Tough. Cole didn't have to know the reality: her love life was on hold, and no one was picking up. It had been that way for a while.

"To be honest," she continued, "I thought for a moment that she was your wife and I was more worried about being named in some divorce suit."

Cole winced. "Yikes. Please don't remind me how close I came to having Monica for my wife. I don't like to believe I was ever that much of a fool."

"She's very beautiful," Lacey said absently, picturing the green-eyed blonde in her mind.

"Hm. If the saying 'beauty is as beauty does' is true, it should be applied to Monica," Cole stated. Then he asked unexpectedly, "Can you cook?"

It took Lacey a moment to catch up with his rapid change of the subject. "I'm about average—definitely not Iron Chef material, though. Why?"

"I'm hungry and I was hoping I could talk you into making breakfast." He grinned.

"I think I'll get dressed first," she said, adding silently to herself, *before any more visitors show up.*

Cole rubbed the stubble on his chin. "Okay. I still need a second shave. You said my razor was in the cabinet?"

Lacey nodded. "I noticed it there this morning."

She was only a step behind him as he started down the hallway. When he stopped at the bathroom door, she started to walk by him to her bedroom, but he put a hand on her forearm to stop her.

"I want you to know that I didn't mean all that to happen this morning," he told her, a serious frown drawing his dark brows together. "When I made the suggestion last night that we both stay here, I had no plans whatsoever to use you to get rid of Monica."

"I believe that," she assured him. "It never occurred to me that you did, actually."

"I hope not." Cole paused for a second. "If I'd known she was coming over this morning, I would've insisted you leave rather than put you through that."

"No biggie. Give people something to talk about, I always say." Lacey didn't want to dwell on Monica's suspicions. "Would you like bacon or sausage with your eggs?" she asked, using his tactic of changing the subject.

"Bacon—crisp." He smiled, aware of what she was doing. "And two poached eggs on a slice of dark toast."

"I was asking your preferences, not taking your order," she sighed with mocking exasperation.

"Whatever's easiest for you." His smile deepened for a teasing minute before he walked into the bathroom and closed the door. Lacey stared at the white woodwork, then moved to her own bedroom.

Cole Whitfield in person was very different from the sarcastic big shot on the phone. She could really get to like this Cole.

Chapter 4

The bacon was already fried and draining on a paper towel when Cole wandered into the kitchen–dining area. Lacey lifted the poached eggs onto the dark toast.

"Looks good." He reached across the counter bar to take the plate from her hand.

Lacey hoped the food tasted good, but she didn't say so. "The silverware, salt, and pepper are on the table. Coffee to drink or would you like something else?"

"Coffee is fine." He moved to the table where a place setting and a clean cup were laid. Lacey brought him the plate of bacon, as well as the coffeepot to fill his cup. He glanced around the table, then at her. "Aren't you eating?"

"Just a slice of toast." She walked back to the kitchen area for her coffee cup and the small plate with additional slices of toast on it, one for her and the rest for him.

"Are you on a diet?" There was something disbelieving in the sweeping look he gave her as she turned to rejoin him. Lacey hoped it implied that there was nothing wrong with her shape

"No," she said. "I thought I'd go for a swim, so I didn't want anything heavy in my stomach."

She had expected him to say he would come with her,

but he only nodded at her statement. Lacey wondered what he planned to do but decided it was better not to pry. After all, nobody liked a nosy roommate.

The bamboo blinds at the dining room windows were raised, letting in the morning sunlight. Lacey nibbled at her toast and gazed at the ocean view of sparkling waves and brilliant gold beach.

"Fantastic view. Nice to get away, isn't it?"

She smiled. "It really is."

"How long have you worked for Bowman?" Cole asked with apparent casualness.

"I've worked for the company for almost three years and for Mi—Mr. Bowman for the past two." Lacey decided it was wiser if Cole wasn't aware that Mike was her friend as well as her boss.

"So you really know the business."

"Well, you might say that. I started there right out of college."

Cole smiled. "You could probably run the place by now."

"I wouldn't go that far," she said with an answering smile. "And I'm not sure I would ever want to."

"Have you decided what you want to do when you grow up?"

He was teasing but her cheeks pinked. "I got my bachelor's in business administration and I'd like to get an MBA, make a move to a national company."

"Go for it." The heartfelt statement sounded like a vote of confidence. Lacey liked hearing it.

"So where'd you grow up?" Cole was asking.

"In Richmond. My family still lives there." She dunked the last bite of toast in her coffee.

"What made you decide to come here to work? There must have been job opportunities in Richmond where you could be with your family and friends." He eyed her curiously.

"That age-old desire to leave home and be totally on my own." She shrugged and cupped a hand under the dripping piece of toast to carry it to her mouth.

It occurred to her that she had the perfect opening to ask him about his family and background. But by the time she was able to swallow the bite of toast, it was too late to take advantage of it.

"You're a very good cook," Cole stated, finishing up his food.

She shook her head in polite demurral. "I can handle the basics. That's about it."

"Basics are everything. Remind me to recommend you if you ever decide to change your profession to chef."

"Thanks." Lacey was pleased by the over-the-top compliment, though she tried not to show it.

He pushed his plate to the side and leaned back in his chair. "Since you did the cooking, I guess it's only fair that I wash the dishes."

"All right." The offer was another point in his favor. She wasn't about to morph into a maid while she was on vacation, that was for sure.

"What? No protest?" Laughter shone in his deep blue eyes.

"Are you kidding? I hate doing dishes." Lacey rose from the table, not even looking in the direction of the sink. "I'm going for my swim. Have fun."

In her room, Lacey stripped off her jeans and knit top down to the bathing suit beneath. The suit was the vacation present she'd promised herself, its few ounces of material somehow costing more than a women's business suit. But it looked fantastic. The blue-gray color had a metallic sheen and molded itself to her slender curves like a second skin.

Draping a beach towel around her shoulders, she

closed the door to her room behind her. Lacey avoided the kitchen, where she could hear water running in the sink, and slipped out through the sliding glass doors onto the deck, heading down the steps leading to the beach.

The water was cool. Lacey had second thoughts about her swim, shivering as she immersed herself in an oncoming wave. But after some vigorous crawl strokes, striking out for a while in a parallel line to the beach, she got used to the temperature of the water and decided to do a little body surfing.

Buoyant, floating, Lacey let the next wave carry her toward shore. Before her feet touched the bottom, she righted herself and started to wade back to deeper water, letting the foamy ripples of the ebbing wave run through her fingers and swirl around her thighs.

She lifted a hand to wave to Cole, farther down the beach. He'd waded out himself, wearing hip boots and casting a line from a heavy surf-fishing pole over the water to where the waves began to rise. At least she had her answer as to what he planned to do and why he hadn't mentioned joining her for a swim.

An hour later, she decided she'd had enough of splashing around in the sea and waded out onto the beach. Shaking the sand out of her towel, she dried herself off and glanced toward Cole. This time he lifted a hand in greeting and she waved back.

"Any luck?" she called.

He shook his head and shouted back, "None!"

It wasn't a response that encouraged more conversation and Lacey knew better than to distract a fisherman concentrating on the throw of his line. She walked back alone to the beach house. A quick shower washed away the ocean salt on her skin and a thorough shampooing did the same for her hair. Dressed in fresh clothes, Lacey rinsed out her swimsuit and hung it over a towel rack in the bathroom to dry.

She went out onto the deck, leaning against the rail while she idly toweled her short hair damp-dry. After several minutes, she hung the towel over the rail. The sun could finish drying her hair, she decided, and she finger-combed the strands into a semblance of order. Good enough.

She could see Cole, up the beach some distance away, still engrossed in his fishing, apparently in the same spot as before. He reeled in and cast again, throwing the line out in a long, graceful arc that soared over the waves. She thought back to their extremely brief exchange when she came out of the water.

Even dripping wet and good as naked, she hadn't distracted him much. Of course, Lacey knew she shouldn't expect things to happen just because they were staying in the same house. But she had to wonder a little about her attractiveness to the opposite sex—meaning him, now that they'd stopped arguing—if a fishing pole and a lump of slippery bait were more interesting than she was. Even if he wasn't all that interested, it would have been nice just to chat with him, keep him company while he fished away.

She reminded herself of his statement that he was there for the peace and quiet. That was why she'd kept her distance, when it came right down to it. If he wanted to be more or less alone, she respected that.

After a while, Cole bagged it, reeling in one last time and catching the hook on an invisible ring on the tall surf pole. She watched as he picked up the tackle box too and started down the long stretch of beach toward the house. She darted into the house to the bathroom, where she quickly ran a comb through her nearly dry hair and added a touch of strawberry gloss to her lips.

Inwardly she was laughing at herself all the while she was doing it, because it was kind of funny to think she might want to impress Cole. She was just stepping out onto the deck again when the doorbell rang.

Her first thought was that it was Monica returning for some nefarious reason, and she glanced at the beach to see Cole still trudging on. He wasn't close enough to hear her shout and she didn't want to make him go faster with all that fishing gear to carry. With a resigned shrug, she went down to face the green-eyed lioness alone. She walked unhurriedly into the house and down the stairs to answer the door.

But it was Mike Bowman who was standing outside when she opened it, and her brown eyes widened in surprise at the sight of him. He gave her a crooked smile.

"Took you long enough to answer the door," he teased good-naturedly. "I was beginning to think either I had the wrong house or that you'd gone somewhere."

"Hello, Mike," Lacey murmured, not fully recovered from the shock.

He waited patiently for her to invite him in. When she continued to stare at him, he rested a bent arm on the door jamb and leaned on it. "You did invite me over this afternoon. Unless you forgot."

An embarrassed flush warmed her cheeks. "I didn't forget." She lied rather than hurt his feelings. But it had completely slipped her mind that she'd asked him over this afternoon. "I just wasn't expecting you so soon." Glancing down at her shorts and crop top, she tried to pretend she'd been caught half-dressed. "I need to change."

"Not for me." He grinned.

She lifted a hand to her shining crown of silky brown hair. "And my hair isn't even all the way dry."

"You look great," Mike insisted. "Look, I'm tired of

holding up this door. Are you going to invite me in or do you want me to wait in the car until you're ready?" he teased as she continued to block the doorway.

"Come on in. You got me all flustered." Lacey forced a laugh. She swung the door wider and stepped to the side to let him pass.

Yikes. In a minute she would have to explain to him about Cole Whitfield's living in the same house with her.

The situation was on the odd side, especially because she was pretty sure she'd told Mike that she'd be on her own. She had no idea how Mike would react to that or exactly how she ought to go about telling him about Cole, considering the biting things she had said about "Mr. Whitfield" to her boss when he had been nothing more than a faceless, cantankerous client on the phone.

As she led the way up the stairs, she was still trying to decide whether she should just lay it all out fact by fact or spin it into one of life's cosmic jokes or what. One thing was for sure—she had to make up her mind pretty soon or Cole would be walking in and Mike would be totally unprepared. The whole mess was becoming more complicated by the minute.

"Yowza. This is quite a place," Mike declared as they reached the top of the stairs and entered the living room.

"It is beautiful," Lacey agreed, and began, "Mike, I—"

"It's custom-built, isn't it?" He surveyed the room with a professional eye, his gaze narrowing as he studied its construction.

"I believe so. I—"

He nodded. "It shows. This is real craftsmanship. And that fireplace is a masterpiece." He smiled at her. "No wonder you said yes to your cousin so fast. Oh—" He suddenly remembered the paper bag he was holding. "Here are the steaks I promised to bring. I had the butcher trim them just right. He swore they'd be so tender you could cut them with a fork. There's a bottle of wine too." He handed the bag to Lacey. "You can open it, let it breathe, or whatever it is you're supposed to do before you pour. Me, I just drink the stuff."

"Yes, I will." She started toward the kitchen, certain that her boss was following her. "Now, Mike, there's something I have to tell you."

Setting the bag on the counter, she waited for him to ask what. But when she glanced around, he wasn't anywhere in sight.

"Mike?" She took the bottle of wine from the paper bag and opened it. Looking around again, she saw the door to the deck standing open and hurried to it.

"This is a million-dollar view," he commented, turning as he heard her approach.

"It is spectacular." Lacey rushed on before he could interrupt, "There's something I have to explain to you."

"Look!" He pointed out to sea. "See that ship way out there?"

Lacey glimpsed the silhouette of a large, ocean-going vessel on the horizon. She saw it strictly by accident as she scanned the beach and the path to the house, looking for Cole. He was nowhere in sight. But he was bound to show up soon enough. She could almost hear the seconds ticking away.

"Really impressive." Mike surveyed the expanse of beach. "You practically have it to yourself too."

"Not exactly," Lacey qualified. "I—"

"It's fairly isolated, though," he added. "Does it bother you to be here alone?"

This was her opening. "No, not at all, because I'm not—"

"Lacey!" Cole's voice sliced off the end of her sentence. She froze as Mike jerked his gaze to the interior of the house. "I rummaged around in the garage and found Bob's portable grill." His voice was coming steadily nearer to the deck. "I decided that since you cooked breakfast this morning, it's only fair that I cook dinner."

Boom. There were no more seconds left to tick. Lacey saw the shock wave reverberate through Mike as Cole stepped onto the deck carrying the small grill.

Cole came to an abrupt halt, almost taking a step back when he saw Mike. "Bowman," he said, startled. His questioning blue gaze moved to Lacey.

"I invited him over for dinner." She didn't add that she had forgotten. It was written in the beseeching look she gave Cole that said something else. *Don't ask.*

Cole set the grill down. "Hey. It's not what you think."

"Are you staying here, Whitfield?" Mike's voice rose to a pitch of disbelief.

"I was going to tell you," Lacey inserted, trying desperately not to sound guilty.

"I see." Mike sounded grimly skeptical.

"I don't think you do," Cole joined in. "You see, there was a mix-up. Lacey's cousin asked her to stay in the house and her husband asked me. When Lacey and I discovered what had happened"—he didn't explain that part—"we couldn't decide which of us would leave. Finally we agreed that we would both stay. What the hell, right?"

"Do you mean"—Mike's frown deepened—"you two are living in this house together?"

"I really was trying to figure out a way to tell you," Lacey said, sensing his rising anger, not that her boss had a right to be angry. "I didn't want to sound, you know, like there was something going on." What she sounded like was a guilty teenager, she thought desperately.

"What she means is that we're sharing the house, not the beds," Cole stated bluntly.

He shot Lacey a bewildered look. "Really? You said last week that you wished he would take a flying leap into a dry lake."

Her darting glance at Cole saw his mouth twitch with amusement and the annoying gleam in his blue eyes. Even though she hadn't made any secret of her previous opinion of Cole, she really wished Mike hadn't blurted out her impulsive comment.

"Ah—I think it'll be better if you talk this thing out on your own, so I'll make myself scarce." Cole nodded briefly to Lacey, a smile touching the firm line of his mouth.

Lacey nodded, but offered no words of goodbye. She couldn't very well say "I'll see you later." Not without aggravating the situation.

His departure left an uneasy silence. Below her, Lacey could hear the garage door open, followed by the sound of Cole's car reversing into the driveway. She glanced at Mike's profile, determined not to apologize for a situation that was completely innocent.

"I can't believe you actually agreed to this," Mike declared, slapping his palm on the railing.

"Honestly, Mike," Lacey sighed, "you make it sound as if I suddenly deserted to the enemy camp. It isn't like that at all."

"I know," he admitted grudgingly. "It was a shock, though, seeing Whitfield here with you and then finding out that you two are living together."

Lacey bridled at his continued use of that term to describe their arrangement. "You wouldn't consider it 'living together' if we were both in the same apartment building or staying in the same hotel, right? This isn't any different."

"It doesn't matter how you put it," Mike retorted, "sharing a house isn't the same as living in the same building. Come on, you cooked breakfast for the man. You don't do that for someone who only happens to be under the same roof."

"That's not the way I see it."

He shook his head stubbornly. "Then I don't know what else to say."

"Look, we can argue about this all night, but I'm not going to change my mind." Lacey's chin thrust stubbornly forward when she finished.

Mike turned from the rail to confront her. "What do you want me to do, Lacey? Leave?" he challenged. "It's pretty damn clear that you forgot you'd invited me today, so if you'd rather forget about dinner too, I'll go."

"No, that wouldn't be right," she insisted. No way did she want to give Mike the impression that she preferred Cole's company for the evening—a conclusion he would undoubtedly jump to, no matter how she tried to deny it. "I want you to stay for dinner—as long as you agree to drop this subject. After all, you don't have any right to criticize what I do outside the office."

Breathing in deeply, he eyed her for several seconds. "All right," he agreed tautly. "No more discussion about this."

Pretending that something didn't exist didn't make it go away.

The ensuing hours added up to one of the most miserable afternoons and evenings that Lacey had ever spent. The atmosphere had crackled with Mike's disapproval, stringing Lacey's nerves to high tension.

They were both relieved when he left early. The hours they'd spent together had been uncomfortable, nothing like the companionable good times she was used to. Even after he left, Lacey remained irritated with Mike for making her feel guilty about a situation that wasn't her fault or anything to be ashamed of.

She walked the beach to try to ease her mind. It didn't work. The rush of the surf didn't soothe her nerves and there was no magic in the moonlight silvering the ocean swells. The tangy salt breeze did nothing to change the sour taste in her mouth. Finally Lacey returned to the house, but the memory of the dinner bugged her. She chose to distract herself by staring out the window at the empty beach.

Lost in reverie, she barely heard the sound of a car driving into the garage, but it was Cole's footsteps on the stairs that finally broke into her brooding. She turned around, remembering too late that she'd intended to be in bed before he returned. She glanced at her wristwatch—it was nearly eleven—just before Cole paused at the top of the stairs.

"Did Bowman leave?" he asked.

"Yes. Two or three hours ago." Lacey was unaware of the dejected note that crept into her voice.

His gaze became fixed on her, the blue of his eyes so intense that she had to turn away, afraid of what he might be seeing. There was an uneasy feeling in the pit of her stomach. A nervous reaction, she told herself.

"Let me guess—it didn't go very well," Cole said. He crossed the room to where Lacey stood.

She blinked at him in surprise, then had to look away again. He was much too observant and astute. As he stood tall beside her, she also had to admit that he was even more overpoweringly male.

"No, it didn't," she answered truthfully.

"Didn't he believe you?"

"Oh, he thought the arrangement was on the up-and-up." Lacey gave a short, humorless laugh. "He just didn't approve."

"I suppose you argued and that's why he left so early."

Lacey shook her head in denial. "We didn't argue."

Maybe it would have better if they had, but it would have created an unhappy distance between them. After tonight, she guessed they would just drift apart—be employer and employee and nothing more. Granted, office relationships tended to be tricky, if not impossible. But until now she and Mike had managed well enough. In a way she regretted that things had changed.

"I knew you worked for Bowman, but it never occurred to me that you were going out with him," Cole mused.

Her sideways glance caught him gazing out to sea, a thoughtful expression on his face. The suggestion of grimness in his bluntly carved features made her want to reach out and smooth it away with her fingers. It reminded her too much of the autocratic Mr. Whitfield who had infuriated her on the phone.

"There's nothing serious between Mike and me," she said, correcting his impression that she was Mike's girl. "We've dated a few times, that's all. It isn't likely to go any farther than that."

"Because of tonight?" Again his dark blue eyes studied her profile, alert to any nuance in her expression.

"No, not really." Which was true. "Mike tends to shy away from any relationship that could be defined as serious. I guess I'd say he's a confirmed bachelor." Lacey smiled

"And that doesn't bother you?" An eyebrow flicked upward in curiosity.

"No. I enjoy working with him and he's good company away from the office—no more than that." A breeze stirred the edge of the drawn curtain and ruffled her hair a bit.

Out of the corner of her eye, Lacey saw Cole stifling a yawn with the back of his hand. She felt a twinge of guilt. He had stayed away to give her and Mike some time alone, when he'd probably intended to turn in early after a quiet, relaxing day.

"You'd better get some sleep," she suggested. "You have to work tomorrow."

"Are you calling it a night?" He rubbed his neck, looking tired.

"No, I don't think so." A smile flitted across her lips. She wasn't sleepy. "I can sleep as late as I want in the morning. I think I'll go out on the deck for a while and enjoy the night air."

Cole didn't move as she stepped past him to the sliding glass door. She strolled to the railing, leaning both hands on it as she gazed at the moonlit ripples of the endless ocean.

It was a warm, languid night but the air had a salt tang. A firm tread sounded on the deck boards and she glanced over her shoulder, momentarily surprised to see Cole join her at the railing. She had assumed he would hit the sack.

"What's the matter, Lacey?" he asked quietly.

"Huh?" she asked blankly, then faked a laugh. "I'm fine. Nothing is wrong."

"Really?"

Cole's dark eyes were midnight blue and fathomless in the dim starlight. He kept his gaze steadfastly on her face.

"I don't know what you mean." She stared straight out to sea, fixing her attention on the moonlight on the water, a gleaming path to nowhere.

"Don't you?" His fingers caught her chin and turned her face to his searching gaze. "When I walked in tonight, I could tell something was bothering you."

"Cole—" She gently pushed his hand down.

He didn't let her reply. "At first I thought you and Bowman must have argued, but you set me straight on that score. So something else must be on your mind, and I'd like to know what it is."

"It has nothing to do with you." She decided against

turning away. Cole would get her where he wanted her again.

"Oh, I suspect it does," he said quietly. "Indirectly, maybe. I'm guessing that it's about our arrangement. Am I right?"

Lacey sighed in defeat. She had a feeling he could just about read her mind sometimes, and she didn't know whether she liked that or not.

"This is silly," she protested.

"Just tell me about it." Cole gave her a reassuring pat on the shoulder.

"Um, I don't know how to put this . . ."

"Any old way you want to, Lacey."

"Okay," she sighed. "It's just I'm beginning to realize that I'm not quite the free spirit I thought I was. Does that sound corny?"

"No. Go on."

"I never thought other people's opinions ought to bother me as long as I believed what I was doing was right. But I guess I really am a little old-fashioned. Maybe 'traditional' is a better word. I don't know."

"Okay, rewind. You weren't expecting Monica and Vic to visit," he pointed out, "let alone react the way they did. And obviously Bowman just put in his two cents on the subject. So now you're not feeling all that sure of yourself."

"More or less," Lacey conceded. She ran a hand through her hair, its dark brown sheen reflecting the moonlight. "It shouldn't matter what anyone thinks, right? This—us—it's all perfectly innocent," she insisted.

"So you're not having second thoughts about staying here," Cole finished.

"Oh, no, I'm not." Lacey laughed, a tremulous sound. "I bet you were hoping that's what I would say. Then you could have that big fat gorgeous moon all to yourself."

She gazed up at the silver globe hanging in the sky above the ocean.

A furrow made a vertical crease between his brows. "So what? The house would seem way too empty if you left."

His reply electrified her. Lacey's breath hitched and there was an odd fluttering in her pulse. He reached out, resting a hand on her shoulder this time, almost imperceptibly drawing her closer as his gaze slid to her lips. Caught in a very pleasurable spell, it didn't occur to her to resist, although Cole gave her the opportunity. His bold mouth descended to hers.

Taking his time, he explored every curve of her full, soft lips. His hand lay along the side of her neck, his thumb resting against the tiny pulse point to feel her blood racing madly. Her every nerve tingled.

He lifted his head a fraction of an inch, his warm breath a caress over her skin. "Strawberry, isn't it?" he murmured huskily.

"What?" Lacey opened her eyes, overcome by the sensation that she could drown in his indigo gaze.

"Your lipstick. It's strawberry, isn't it?" Cole repeated softly, and tasted her lower lip.

"Yes," she whispered, and unconsciously swayed toward him.

"I always did have a weakness for strawberry." It was an absent comment. Lacey doubted if Cole was aware that he had said it aloud.

Then his mouth opened over hers, claiming the ripeness of her lips as his strong fingers stroked the back of her neck, tilting her head backward to make the most of the passionate kiss. He reached around her waist and Lacey let herself be arched against his hard, muscled length.

With consummate skill, Cole demanded a response and

he got it. She kissed him back with equal ardor, letting her fingers spread naturally over his chest, then slide around his neck into the thickness of his dark hair. A melting sensuality seemed to flow through her entire body as his mouth continued its task of arousal until her desire for him became something like hunger.

The light breeze from the ocean cooled her heated skin, but it couldn't temper the molten fire spreading through her veins. His seductive skills were new to her but she gloried in it all, finding a heady exultation in his arms, and sensations she had experienced with no other man.

Then . . . the kiss that had begun so slowly ended. To her dismay, Cole pushed her gently an arm's length away. Dazed by the unexpected rejection, Lacey looked at him with inviting, luminous eyes. She could hear his ragged breathing—the soft sound made her quiver inside. Why had he stopped?

A rueful, almost wry smile curved his mouth. "You'll have to forgive me for that, Lacey." His voice was low and roughly controlled.

"Yes . . ." But the single word sounded more like a question than an answer.

"You're just about irresistible. So that means I have to control myself."

She shook her head, confused. "I don't see why you should apologize for kissing me. I may have said I was old-fashioned, but I wasn't talking about . . . a kiss like that."

"Even so." Cole seemed unable to explain himself. He let go of her arms and she had to stand without his support. Her knees trembled for an instant before she stiffened. "What happened?" she asked. "What did I do?"

"It's me, not you. Our agreement isn't even twenty-four hours old and I was on the verge of breaking one of our first ground rules," Cole stated in a mocking tone. "No sex."

Crimson flamed through her cheeks and just as quickly burned itself out, leaving her unnaturally pale as she acknowledged the truth of his observation. She had lost control too.

There was no telling just how far she might have let Cole go before she came to her senses. It was a sobering discovery. After all, they hardly knew each other. And she absolutely, positively didn't believe in instant hookups and meaningless flings. Yet . . . she wanted him. Fiercely. *Damn it.*

He watched her for a silent minute until Lacey snapped out of it. Cole smiled down at her, more gentle than ever. "Good night, Lacey." He turned without touching her again and went into the house.

"Good night," Lacey echoed faintly, doubting that her voice was strong enough to carry to him.

She pivoted back to the ocean view, shivering, in the grip of a sudden chill, which was almost welcome. The fires inside her were slowly being brought under control.

She remembered Cole saying that the situation between them wouldn't get out of hand unless they let that happen. Well, they'd both come dangerously close to that point. Cole had been the first to realize it, but it was just hitting Lacey now.

Chapter 5

The buzz of the alarm clock made her eardrums vibrate and with a groan Lacey rolled onto her side. She must have set the clock late last night out of habit.

Her fumbling hand reached for the button to shut off, only to discover the alarm wasn't turned on. Still the buzzing sound continued to drone its wakeup call.

Frowning, Lacey forced her eyes open. It was several seconds before she realized that the sound was coming from Cole's bedroom. It was his alarm clock she was hearing. She grabbed the second pillow and crushed it over her ears, trying to muffle the sound, but it continued with monotonous persistence.

"Oh, why don't you wake up and turn that darn thing off?" she moaned into the pillow. But the buzzing didn't stop. "I'll never get back to sleep!"

Angrily she tossed the pillow away and stumbled out of bed. She walked over to pound on the bedroom wall, remembering too late that the bathroom was between the two guest rooms. Grabbing her robe, she shrugged into it as she stalked into the hallway to Cole's door.

She hammered on it with her fist. "Shut that alarm off!" It kept right on buzzing. "Cole!"

There was an answering squeak of the bedsprings, then blissful silence. Sighing, Lacey hurried back into her own room and crawled under the covers, robe and all. As she closed her eyes, she heard his door open and the firm padding of his bare feet in the hall.

The bathroom door opened and closed. A few seconds later the shower was turned on full force, the hammering of its spray sounding as loud and as nerve-racking as the alarm clock.

"Make it stop. I just want to go to sleep," moaned Lacey in self-pity.

Within a few short minutes, another sound mingled with the rushing water. "Oh, no," she groaned, "he isn't!" She listened. "He *is*. He's singing in the shower. That does it!"

The bedclothes were thrown aside again. It was absolutely pointless to try to go back to sleep now. She stalked into the kitchen, opening and slamming the refrigerator door to get some orange juice and doing it harder when she put the container back.

While she sipped at her juice, she readied the coffeemaker, perversely hoping that Cole would get blasted with too-hot water when she filled the pot with cold. Switching the coffeemaker on, she hopped onto the tall stool at the kitchen's counter bar.

A quarter of an hour later, the coffeemaker had done its job when Cole walked in from the living room. He was dressed, his hands completing the knot of his tie. He saw Lacey sitting at the counter and frowned.

"I thought you were going to sleep late this morning," he said. "What are you doing up?"

"It takes gall to ask that question," Lacey declared with an exasperated look.

Cole gave her a rueful look. "Did my alarm clock wake you up?"

"Your alarm clock, followed by the shower and your stunning serenade."

He paused beside the counter to smooth his tie. There was a mischievous gleam in his eyes. "So you're not going to vote for me when I go on *American Idol*."

"Not a chance." But her tone was less sharp. Somehow he made it awfully hard to stay angry at him.

"Is there any juice?"

"In the fridge. And there's fresh coffee too," Lacey added.

"Smelled that. Want a cup?"

"Might as well," she sighed. After all, she was already awake and the just-brewed coffee had a wonderful aroma.

First Cole poured himself a small glass of orange juice from the refrigerator and downed it in one go before taking two cups from the cupboard. He filled them and set them side by side on the counter, then walked around it to join Lacey.

He caught a glimpse of himself in the mirror on the opposite wall and fingered the knot of his tie. "It isn't straight, is it?"

"No," Lacey said. When he started to try to redo it without going over to the mirror, she said, "Here, let me." Cole didn't argue.

When she was finished, he looked to the opposite wall again, inspecting his reflection with surprised approval. "Perfect. Where did you learn to do that?"

"I have a father and two brothers," she answered. "And they're all thumbs when it comes to tying ties."

"No sisters?" Cole sipped at his coffee.

"Nope."

He nodded. "I have two sisters, each married with kids."

"Neither of my brothers is married yet." Lacey tried her coffee and decided to wait until it had cooled some.

"Your parents getting anxious for grandchildren?"

"I don't know." She smiled faintly. "My mother claims she's too young to be a grandmother. She certainly looks too young."

Cole glanced at the gold watch on his wrist and gulped down the rest of his coffee. "I'm late," he declared. Hesitating beside her stool, he crooked a finger under her chin. "Sorry I woke you up this morning, sweet thing."

The devastating smile he gave her was Lacey's undoing. She couldn't even be annoyed, let alone angry, that he had deprived her of a few hours of sleep. But she wouldn't go so far as to admit that.

"I suppose I shouldn't get into the habit of sleeping late, right?" she said lightly.

"Maybe not. I like seeing you in the morning. And stealing"—before she could guess his intention, he bent down and kissed her swiftly—"a friendly smooch. You know, that could become a habit."

Lacey wished her heart would stop beating so erratically. "You're forgetting the ground rules," she pointed out primly.

"I did?" Cole gave her an innocent look. "Sorry." The gleam in his eyes said exactly what he was thinking, though. "See you tonight."

Lacey had to smile. The house seemed awfully empty when he left.

It was eight thirty-one that evening when Cole's car drove into the garage. Lacey knew exactly because she had been checking the clock nearly every five minutes since seven. But she steeled herself to react calmly and casually when he entered the living room. He looked exhausted, his briefcase bulging with take-home work.

"Rough day?" Lacey glanced up from the fashion magazine she was supposedly reading.

"More or less." He sat down on the other sofa.

"Have you eaten?"

"What?" Cole looked at her blankly before her question registered. "Yeah, I stopped for a bite on the way here."

Lacey thought of the dinner she had kept warming in the oven after having eaten her portion, too hungry to wait, but said nothing. Cole opened his briefcase and took out a sheaf of legal documents.

Lacey was about to suggest that he should relax instead of going over contracts and permits, but she told herself silently that it was none of her business if he wanted to work too hard.

For all the notice he paid to her for the rest of the evening, she could have been another throw pillow on the sofa. She tried to convince herself that she didn't care, but she knew that wasn't true. Finally, at half-past ten, she tossed the magazine onto the table and rose. Cole glanced up with a questioning frown.

"It's late. I'm going to bed. Good night."

"Good night," he returned indifferently and went back to his paperwork.

Pressing her lips together, Lacey walked away. But there were tears in her eyes and a bitter taste in her mouth.

"Oh, by the way." Cole spoke up and she glanced quickly back at him. "The toilets finally showed up today."

"They did? Isn't that wonderful."

"Turned out they've been in the city for the last two weeks, at the wrong warehouse," he replied with thinly disguised impatience. "Too bad no one bothered to check on them before."

Anger began to simmer as Lacey read implied criticism of her in the comment, but Cole's attention was now on the laptop he was booting up. She checked her biting reply, wondering if he even remembered that she worked for Mike Bowman. Holding her head high, she walked down the hallway to her bedroom.

The next two days were a repeat of Monday, with Lacey waking at the buzz of Cole's alarm and Cole returning late in the evening to bury himself in business paperwork. Except for the early mornings and late evenings, Lacey could have been staying at the house by herself, since she was either alone or left alone.

In the mornings she filled her time swimming in the ocean and strolling on the beach. The afternoons she saved for relaxing on the deck and catching up on her reading. Meals were hit-or-miss. She didn't repeat the mistake of the first night by keeping food warm for Cole. Lacey didn't want to admit it, but she was really spending her days waiting for Cole to come back.

And when he did . . . nothing happened.

On Thursday evening she went to bed as usual sometime after ten, leaving Cole in the living room with his everlasting paperwork. She fell asleep almost immediately, but it was a restless, fitful slumber that didn't last. She was awake again shortly after midnight.

Her mouth felt dry. Maybe quenching her thirst would help. She slid out of bed and padded sleepily to her door, opening it to the harsh glare of overhead light that dazzled her.

Shielding her eyes with her hand, she started to grope for the switch to turn off the hall light that Cole had left on, but the whisper of papers being halted in the living room stopped her.

She walked into the living room, her bare feet making almost no sound, her eyes still squinting at the unaccustomed light. Cole was sitting on the sofa where she had left him hours ago, going over his papers and making notes on a long yellow notepad. When had he turned from a man into a robot, anyway?

"Enough already," she said accusingly in a voice husky with sleep. "It's after midnight."

Startled, Cole looked up, his concentration broken. Automatically, he put out a hand to steady his laptop, left at a perilous angle on top of a book and about to slide off. One dark eyebrow quirked as he checked the gold watch gleaming on his wrist below his rolled-up shirt sleeve. His mouth tightened briefly before he fixated on the papers again.

"I'm almost done," he said, then asked absently, "what are you doing up?"

"I was thirsty," she retorted, and resumed her path to the kitchen, doubting that he had even heard her answer.

As she passed by the sofa, Cole rubbed the back of his neck and arched his shoulders like a big cat. "Damn, but I'm tired," he murmured to no one in particular.

"You could go to bed," she called back to him as she entered the kitchen area, went to the sink, and turned on the cold water tap. Sleep-deprived as she was, she didn't feel any sympathy for his problem. If he was tired, the solution was simple. Since he was making it worse with relentless work, she wasn't going to waste words feeling sorry for him.

"I have to get this done."

Opening the cupboard door, she took out a glass. "Didn't you ever read *Gone with the Wind?* Tomorrow is another day."

"No, I haven't read it. I need to have this in first thing in the morning," he answered curtly.

"I suppose the world will come to an end if you don't," Lacey said dryly.

After filling the glass with water, she started to raise it to her lips and, turning slightly, discovered that Cole had followed her into the kitchen. The etched lines at the corners of his mouth deepened into a smile, but he made no reply to her verbal jab.

"Is there any coffee?" he asked instead.

She glanced at the coffeemaker, noticing the cord unplugged from the socket, but not really looking at the pot. "If there's any left, it's cold."

"We have instant coffee, don't we?" Cole opened the cupboard door nearest him.

"In here." She gestured to the cupboard above her head without offering to get it for him.

Lacey did move to one side to avoid getting banged in the head when he opened it. Sipping at her water, she watched him take the jar down and spoon some dark crystals into a cup.

Her irritable mood began to dissolve as she became fascinated by his hands, strong and tanned, and the scattering of bronze hair curling on the arm exposed by the rolled-up sleeve. Her pulse fluttered and she took a quick swallow of water in an effort to forget his unsettling nearness.

He looked at her and she realized that she was standing in the way of him getting to the sink. Lacey stepped to one side, assuming he would fill the cup and microwave it.

But all he did was run not-so-hot water into the cup, stir the brew, and drink it down. Ugh. Couldn't he even take the time to boil water or program a minute into the microwave? Apparently not.

He had turned to her after rinsing the cup. "It's like medicine. Drink it fast and you don't taste it."

"That's going too far."

He shrugged, setting the washed cup in the drainboard, but he fumbled and the cup rolled onto the counter. They reached for it at the same time to keep it from falling to the floor and their hands touched.

Instinctively, they both held on, an elemental tension coursing through Lacey. She stood still, held by the velvet quality of his midnight blue eyes.

"That was clumsy of me," he said, relinquishing his grip.

Lacey set the cup upside down in the drainboard. "Maybe you don't need any more caffeine," she said. She forced an evenness into her voice. "Just come to bed. You're tired."

"Is that an invitation?" Despite the rough-edged amusement in his voice, there was a thread of seriousness that made Lacey's heart skip a beat or two.

"You know what I meant." She swirled the water in her glass and took a quick swallow.

"Mmm."

She didn't know whether that meant yes or no, and glanced at Cole to be sure. There was an unnerving sensuality in his study of her face, his gaze taking in her wondering eyes and then moving lower to the soft curve of her lips.

He didn't stop there but allowed himself to look at the slender column of her neck as if he had never seen anything so kissable or tempting. Cole didn't skip the rounded curve of her breasts either. To her embarrassment—and secret pleasure—they seemed to swell under the almost physical caress of his eyes, the rosy peaks thrusting against the silky material of her pajamas.

The sensations he was arousing inside her were dangerously delicious. She fought the urge to glide into his arms and mold her supple body against his hard, rangy length.

Things were happening too fast. No matter how much she desired him, she really didn't know him. And she didn't want to get to know him in bed.

Not yet.

"Cole, stop it," she protested shakily.

His answer was to move closer, an arm braced on the counter on either side of her, trapping her, playing a game. The next move was going to be hers.

She couldn't show weakness. But she felt altogether giddy, a feeling that increased as his muscular legs pressed against her thighs.

Bending his head, he sought the curve of her neck, teasing the sensitive skin with his mouth. And the caress held a promise of something more. He nibbled sensually on her neck, his breath warm against her skin.

"I want you, Lacey," he murmured against her throat.

When he put into words what had only been a nebulous thought in her mind, she snapped out of her pleasurable haze. *Now* he was interested . . . but how long would that last? Cole clearly had his priorities. And he had virtually ignored her for the past four days. Not a good sign.

Pliant and yielding until that thought occurred to her, she ducked under his arms and stepped quickly away. He turned in surprise as if he hadn't realized she could slip away, or that she would want to.

What an ego.

"You were forgetting the ground rules again, Cole," she reminded him breathlessly. "Besides, you have your paperwork to finish." She retreated a step from his direct gaze. "Have some more of that not-so-hot coffee. Bet it's delicious."

Cole made no move toward her and she turned to hurry to her bedroom, tossing a hasty good night over her shoulder.

As she started to close her door, Cole's quiet voice carried from the living room, even though it was soft. "You were forgetting the ground rules too, Lacey."

There wasn't any reply she could make to that.

* * *

Yellow beams of sunlight peeped through the billowing curtains. Lacey opened an eye, focusing on the dancing particles of dust caught in the early morning light.

Lifting her head from the pillow, she glanced at the clock and groaned. It was six o'clock. Obviously she'd woken up in anticipation of Cole's alarm going off. She covered her head with the pillow and waited for the customary buzz.

Ten minutes later there was still no sound of the alarm clock going off. Not that it mattered, she sighed. She couldn't drift off again even if Cole had decided to sleep in after working so late last night.

Climbing out of bed, she put on her robe and walked out the door into the hall. The door to Cole's bedroom stood open and automatically she glanced inside as she tiptoed by. The bed was made.

"That's a first," Lacey muttered. Usually he left it rumpled.

Either Cole had risen before dawn or else he hadn't bothered to go to bed at all. He had still been in the living room working when she had finally gone back to sleep. It was possible that when he finished, he had dressed and gone into the office early. Or . . .

Lacey went into the living room. There he was, half sitting and half lying on the sofa, fully dressed, with his papers and notes strewn on the cushions around him. At least he'd left the laptop in a safe place where it wouldn't slide. He looked so tired that she disliked the thought of waking him. But he also looked very uncomfortable.

As quietly as she could, she gathered up the papers scattered around him and set them in stacks on the lid of his briefcase. She managed to slip one of the throw pillows beneath his head when he moved a little in his sleep and was debating whether she could swing his legs onto the cushions without waking him.

He stirred again and she became motionless. Sleepy dark blue eyes peered at her through a screen of dark spiky lashes. Cole shifted slightly and grimaced, as if cramped muscles were making their soreness known.

"What time is it?" he mumbled.

"About fifteen minutes after six."

Groaning, he rubbed his forehead. "It can't be. I was only going to rest my eyes for a few minutes."

"From the looks of you, you could do with a few more minutes of 'rest,'" Lacey suggested dryly.

"I can't." He pushed himself into a sitting position, arching his back and stretching. "I have a meeting first thing this morning. I have to get into the office."

There was no use arguing; he wouldn't listen to her anyway. "I'll put some real coffee on," she said instead.

She did just that while Cole showered and changed. A glass of orange juice was sitting on the counter for him when he entered the kitchen. She assured herself that she had only done it because she felt sorry for him.

"That helped," he declared after downing the juice.

Maybe, Lacey conceded to herself, but the reviving effect of the juice wouldn't last long. She saw the weariness on his face plain as the breaking day.

"Really, Cole," she said impulsively. "Sleep is more important than pulling an all-nighter like that."

"The work has to be done." He shrugged and walked to the sink counter to set down the glass and pour a cup of coffee.

"So do it at your office and leave it there if you want a life. Bringing work home every night is crazy."

"I get ten times as much done here as I ever did at the

office. There aren't any distractions or interruptions." Cole paused, giving her a wink. "Or at least not as many."

Lacey pretended not to understand that comment. "Go ahead and work yourself half to death. You must be used to it." She slid off the bar stool.

"And where are you going?"

"To shower and dress." She started to go through the living room.

"Lacey—"

She paused to look at him. "Yes?"

"Thanks for waking me up," Cole said, smiling.

Returning his smile, Lacey nodded and quickened her steps to the hall. He was gone by the time she'd finished showering.

The previous days of her vacation had seemed to pass swiftly, but today the hours were dragging. It was barely the middle of the afternoon and she felt completely at loose ends. She'd baked in the sun for a while, slathered in sunblock, then moved to the shady part of the deck, stretching out on a lounge chair with a book. But it failed to hold her interest.

Sighing, she slid a piece of paper between the pages to mark her place and set it down. She stood up and walked to the railing, lifting her face to the cool breeze blowing from the ocean.

She was still wearing her shiny one-piece bathing suit, an unusual blue gray color. Maybe she should change and drive into Virginia Beach to treat herself to a dinner out.

The ring of the doorbell resounded distantly through the house. She turned in surprise, wondering who would be calling at this hour on Friday afternoon. All of her close friends were working.

Any distraction was welcome, so she went to answer the door, hurrying into the house to get down the stairs.

She peered through the peephole and frowned. It looked like Mike standing outside and she opened the door.

"I was hoping you'd be here," he announced with a smile.

"Aren't you supposed to be working?" It was almost an accusation,

"I should be," Mike agreed, stepping into the house as Lacey moved aside to admit him. "But it's been a long, hectic week and I told the big bosses I was taking off early today. And if they didn't like it, they could shove it."

"Really? Good for you." Lacey grinned, knowing that Mike would never have put it that bluntly.

She'd been uneasy about meeting him again after that disastrous dinner. But within seconds after opening the door, she was able to slip back into the easy familiarity they'd always enjoyed. It made her feel good that there was no harm done.

"How about a cold beer?"

"It sounds better than a paycheck right now," Mike laughed. "Lead the way."

"Follow me," Lacey said, going up the stairs first. "I know there's at least a couple of cans in the fridge."

A few minutes later, ensconced in a lounge chair on the deck with the promised cold beer in his hand, Mike heaved a sigh of contentment. "Now this is living. Peace and quiet and an endless view of the ocean. I kept thinking about this all week."

"And all the while, I've been thinking you'd driven all the way out here to see me," Lacey said teasingly.

"Oh, I did," he assured her, settling deeper into his chair. "I never realized what a gem you are until you went on vacation."

"How is Donna doing?"

"She's driving me up a wall, that's how she's doing," Mike grumbled.

"She really is a pretty good temp," Lacey said. "Count your blessings."

"She's okay," he said grudgingly. "Granted, she's taking on a lot of responsibility. But she chatters like a magpie all day long, asking a million questions. I can't make up my mind if she really is that clueless or if it's an act she puts on because she thinks it's cute."

"Donna isn't totally clueless," Lacey said. "Just somewhat."

"Same difference when you need something done right."

"Oh, you'll survive, Mike. Stop grousing."

"Yeah? Thank God it's only another week before you come back." Mike took a swig of his beer. "More than that and I think I'd hand in my resignation."

"Really?" A mischievous light twinkled in her eyes. "I was thinking of giving two weeks' notice and recommending Donna to take my place permanently."

She squealed with laughter as Mike came bounding out of his chair, catching her by the wrist. Gaining a better hold, he swept her into his arms and off her feet to hold her over the deck railing.

"Put me down, Mike!" She was laughing so hard she could hardly talk, her fingers clinging to his arms instinctively rather than out of fear.

"Take back what you said or so help me I'll drop you into the dunes!" he threatened. But the warmth in his smile and the strength of his hold indicated that he hadn't the slightest intention of making good on his words.

Chapter 6

"I take it back! I take it back!" Lacey promised between gasps of breathless giggling.

Mike swung her away from the railing, letting her feet slide to the floor. "Don't ever joke about a thing like that again," he warned with a broad grin.

"I won't, believe me," she declared, leaning a shoulder heavily against his chest as she struggled to catch her breath.

"You'd better—"

"Is this where you go, Bowman, when you tell your office you're on a job site?" Cole's biting question took the fun out of the moment in an instant.

Lacey turned with a jerk to see him standing in the doorway, the knot of his tie loosened and the top button of his shirt unfastened. He looked as tired and irritable as he had sounded, and coldly angry.

"The office was aware that I was through for the day when I left there an hour ago," Mike replied with commendable calm.

"That isn't what the temp said," Cole snapped, his eyes glinting like honed steel.

"Donna again!" Mike muttered beneath his breath.

And Lacey guessed that her replacement had decided it was better to tell a client that Mike was working than that he had left early. She spoke up, hoping to defuse the situation. “Hey, the temp shouldn’t have told you that instead of the truth,” she told Cole.

“Aww. Aren’t you a good little assistant. You always have his back. I guess I should be impressed.”

Her chin tilted up defiantly. “I’m merely trying to straighten out your facts,” she retorted.

“Are you?” His mouth twisted cynically.

“Yes. And while we’re on the subject of working, what are you doing here, Cole? Why aren’t you at your office?” Lacey demanded.

“In case you’ve forgotten,” he snapped, “I was up practically all night working!”

“So you decided to leave early,” she concluded and tipped her head to challenge him. “Can you be sure that’s what your assistant is telling your callers? Or will she make up some other excuse for your absence, like Mike’s temp?”

“So long as it’s plausible.” Cole’s voice was riddled with skepticism.

“The truth generally is,” Lacey flashed.

His wintry steel eyes raked her from head to toe, taking in the shiny bathing suit that clung to her curves. “But I can’t help wondering how many times this past week Bowman has been here when he was supposedly on a job site.” On the last word, Cole pivoted sharply and walked away.

The arrogant set of his wide shoulders irked her to the max, and Lacey started to charge after him. Mike laid a restraining hand on her arm.

“Let it be, Lacey,” he said, recognizing the warning signs that her temper was about to fly.

She jerked her arm away from his hand and stalked

into the house after Cole, catching up with him in the living room. In the act of stripping the tie from around his neck, Cole glanced at her coolly.

Lacey unleashed her anger in a flurry of acid words. "It's none of your business how many times Mike has been here this past week, or if he's been here at all! Furthermore, he's my guest and—"

"Listen," Cole interrupted sharply, "do you need a lesson in common courtesy? You could have simply told me you were going to entertain tonight. I would have made plans to go out so the two of you could be alone."

"So now you're accusing me of being rude?" Her hands rested on her hips, fury trembling in her voice. "What about you?"

"You mean I was rude to Bowman? Oops." There was a contemptuous twist to his mouth.

"Rudeness seems to be your default setting," Lacey snapped.

He drew his head back to study her dismissively. "How so?" he demanded.

"For one, your alarm woke me up every single day this week. You sleep right through it."

As sins went, that was a small one. But Lacey knew she was being goaded into an argument about more than just the things Cole had said against Mike. Not that she minded all that much. She'd been building up to an explosion for several days. Only a spark was needed to light the fire.

"I've apologized for that," Cole reminded her grimly.

"Apologies don't help me go back to sleep." Sarcasm iced her words.

"If you don't like our arrangement, why don't you move out?" he challenged.

"I am not moving out! You leave!" Lacey countered angrily.

"Why? So Bowman can move in? That would be cozy, wouldn't it?"

He was being ridiculous, but the comment still stung. Lacey sputtered for a second. "I'd prefer his company to yours any day."

"Of course you would. No ground rules. No separate bedrooms. No sleeping solo." Cole snapped out the words almost savagely.

"You have a dirty mind," Lacey said spitefully. "Too bad you didn't marry Monica. You're two of a kind."

"Hey, you two," Mike declared from the door to the deck. "I didn't come here to start a free-for-all. Mind if I leave?"

Lacey turned with a start. For a few minutes she'd forgotten Mike was even there. "Don't go, Mike. Cole was just leaving," she insisted tightly.

"Like hell I am!" Cole growled. "You can either do your entertaining while I'm in the house or you can go somewhere else. But I'm staying."

"Fine." Lacey clipped out the word and glanced at her boss. "Mike, give me a couple of minutes to get dressed and I'll go with you."

He gave her a brief nod of agreement and Lacey walked purposefully to her room. Peeling off her bathing suit, she put on underwear and bra, and a flowered sundress. A taut silence stretched from the living room, its oppressive stillness spreading all through the house.

Mike was waiting at the head of the stairs when she reappeared. Keeping her distance from the grim-faced Cole, she walked to the staircase to join Mike. He shifted uncomfortably as Lacey paused to cast a fiery look at Cole.

"The house is yours for the evening," she told him with a cloying smile. "You get to have all the peace and quiet you want." The sweetness turned sour as she muttered, "Enjoy it."

With a toss of her head, she swept past Mike down the steps to the front door. Outside, the staccato click of her sandal heels on the pavement gave away her simmering anger. Mike moved forward to walk beside her, lengthening his strides to keep up with her rapid pace.

"Considering the present circumstances, Lacey," he began hesitantly, "don't you think it would be better if you moved back to your apartment for the rest of the vacation?"

"And let that man win?" she flashed. "Not on your life! I wouldn't give him that satisfaction. I can make his life as miserable as he makes mine."

Stepping beside his car, she waited without thinking for him to open the door for her. Mike liked to observe traditional courtesies and she generally let him. When he didn't make a move, she glanced at him and noticed the rather pained expression on his face.

"What's wrong, Mike?" she demanded, the crispness of leftover anger still in her voice.

"I don't know how to tell you this," he murmured uncomfortably.

"Tell me what?" Her patience was in short supply.

His gaze ricocheted away from hers. "I have a date tonight," he announced flatly.

"You have a *what?*" Lacey felt worse than ever. So good old dependable Mike had plans and they didn't involve her. But there was nothing she could do about it.

"I'm sorry," he offered. "I thought I'd stop by for a couple of hours to relax and talk, then get out before Whitfield came."

She was still kicking herself for assuming that he had arrived for the evening to see her and only her. Surprise, surprise, she scolded herself. Mike had a life outside of work. Maybe it was time she got one too. But current circumstances were definitely conspiring against her.

She glanced back at the house. She simply couldn't go back there, not until much later. Cole would never let her hear the end of it if he learned the truth.

"It's all right, Mike," she said finally. "Serves me right, I guess."

"Huh? What do you mean?"

"Nothing. Just indulging in a little self-pity." She straightened up. "Don't worry. I'm not going to burst into tears."

"What are you going to do?"

"I'm not going to go back there and have Cole start gloating, that's for sure," she declared emphatically. "I'll go somewhere, that's all. Would you mind waiting a couple of minutes while I get my car out of the garage?"

"No problem." Mike smiled tentatively, like waiting was the least he could do after letting her down.

Lacey hoped it would look to Cole as if she and Mike were going somewhere but in separate vehicles. As she backed her car out, she glanced up to the second-story window of the living room and saw Cole looking out.

A surge of anger washed through her and she reversed recklessly out of the driveway without looking for oncoming cars. Immediately she shifted gears, and pressed the accelerator to the floor, the tires squealing faintly as the car shot forward, leaving Mike far behind.

At the major highway intersection, Mike finally caught up with her. His honking horn made Lacey glance in her rearview mirror to see him motioning her onto the shoulder. Still steamed, she pulled over anyway. He parked behind her and climbed out of his car to walk to hers.

Mike bent down to peer into her open window. "What the hell are you doing, burning rubber like that? You trying out for NASCAR?"

"Is that why you stopped me? Just to criticize my driving?" Lacey was in no mood for a lecture.

"Beats a moving violation, doesn't it?" He frowned as a highway patrol car went by with flashers on. "Would you rather talk to that guy?"

"I don't want to talk to anybody."

Clearly Mike wasn't going to back down just because she was in a foul mood. Lacey slumped down in her seat and started to count the smashed bugs on her windshield as he kept on talking.

"Look, Lacey—I do feel responsible for what happened back there. That spat with Whitfield started because you were defending me, whether I asked you to or not."

"No big deal. An argument was inevitable." Her fingers drummed the steering wheel. Lacey was impatient to be on her way, even if she didn't know where she was going to go.

"I put you in an awkward position. I should have told you when I first arrived that I had a date with someone else tonight." Mike gallantly took the blame for her present dilemma.

"It isn't your fault," Lacey sighed. "I was the one who put my foot in my mouth. I didn't need help from anyone to do that."

"What are you going to do tonight?" His look was sympathetic, even compassionate. She cringed inwardly.

"I don't know." Her gaze skittered away from his face.

"I don't like the idea of you being alone. I could round up one of the guys for a double date," he suggested.

"No. I couldn't fake a good mood if I tried. But thanks. Besides, I wouldn't want to cramp your style." She attempted a smile but it wasn't very successful.

"What are you going to do, Lacey? You can't just drive around all night."

She hesitated before answering. "Maybe I'll stop by to see Maryann."

Her statement seemed to satisfy Mike. "You do that. And drive carefully, will you, Lacey?"

"I promise." As Mike straightened, Lacey shifted her car into gear.

She checked for oncoming vehicles before pulling into the traffic lane, waving to Mike. Obeying the speed limit, she drove thoughtfully to the apartment complex where Maryann lived. She parked her car in the visitors' lot and walked up the stairs to her friend's unit. Lacey rang the doorbell and waited.

The door, still secured by a chain latch, opened a crack. Looking over the latch, Lacey glimpsed washed-out brown hair, that dark blond shade that was so distinctively Maryann's.

"Hi. It's me, Lacey," she identified herself to her cautious friend.

"Lacey, what are you doing here?" The door closed a moment, then swung wide to admit her. "I thought you'd be having a clambake or something on the beach tonight."

"No such luck." Lacey's smile was wry. "Actually, I came to see if you had a hot dog to share." As she walked in, she noticed that her girlfriend was wearing a robe. Only then did it occur to her that it was Friday night and it was very likely her friend had a date too. "I bet you're going out, aren't you?"

"No, it's just another Friday night for me and my cat. We have big plans for sitting on the sofa. C'mon in. I was changing out of my work clothes when you rang the doorbell. Both of us are happy to see you," Maryann insisted as a pumpkin-colored cat sauntered from the kitchen to rub against his mistress's leg. "I don't have any hot dogs, but I do have some hamburger."

"That's fine." Lacey really didn't have any appetite.

Maryann closed the door, locked it, and refastened the chain. "You never did say what you're doing here. Did it get too lonely out there in the fabulous beach house?"

"No, it wasn't lonely. Far from it," Lacey declared.

"What do you mean?" Maryann frowned. "I thought you didn't have any close neighbors."

"It's a long story," was the sighing answer.

Her friend waved away that excuse. "I have all night if you do."

"It isn't lonely because I'm not staying in the house by myself," announced Lacey.

"You're not staying in the house alone." Maryann repeated the statement to be sure she'd understood it. "That means someone is staying with you. Am I an ace detective or what?"

Lacey nodded in answer to the rhetorical question. "Absolutely."

"So who is it?" Maryann wanted to know.

"Cole Whitfield."

"Who is—" Almost immediately a light dawned in Maryann's eyes. "Whitfield? You don't mean the sarcastic Mr. Whitfield who was giving us all hell?"

"That's him."

Maryann's mouth opened in astonishment. For several seconds, she was incapable of getting any words out. Finally she managed to ask, "How? What is he doing there?"

"It seems that Cole is an old family friend of Margo's husband. There was a mix-up. Margo, the airhead, asked me to stay at the house and her husband asked Cole."

"But when you found out . . ."

"I know it's hard to believe, Maryann. I thought he was a burglar when he got into the house. He scared me half to death." Lacey went on to explain how she and Cole had come to the agreement to share the house.

"And you actually agreed to that, after the things you said about him?" Maryann was incredulous.

"Look, in person, he really isn't so bad. What am I saying?" Lacey caught herself angrily. "He's worse. His alarm wakes me up in the morning. He sings in the shower. He works late into the night, then he's grouchy as a bear in the morning."

"Lacey—" Maryann gave her a long, considering look. "Fill me in on a few things. How old is Cole and, um, what does he look like?"

"He's in his thirties."

"Unmarried?" Maryann asked.

"Yes. As far as I know."

"Good-looking?"

"In a rough kind of way," Lacey admitted. "He has nice blue eyes, though."

"And all you are doing is sharing the same house." Her friend eyed her skeptically. "Very practical. Nothing romantic about that."

"I don't know what you mean by romantic. I sleep in my room and he sleeps in his."

"And he hasn't made a single move?" Maryann took one look at Lacey's face and had her answer.

Lacey couldn't conceal what she really felt a second longer. "It's all so crazy. I'm half in love with him already. Lord knows he doesn't give me much encouragement."

"What happened tonight? Does he have a date with someone else? Is that why you came here? To show him that he isn't the only pebble on the beach?"

"He doesn't have a date. He came home sooner than usual, that was all." Lacey was unaware that she had referred to the beach house as home, but that was what it had become to her since she'd started sharing it with Cole.

"I see."

"Mike was there. He'd stopped by for a beer. Cole got all hostile because he'd called the office, and dopey Donna told him Mike was working at another job site instead of simply saying he'd left early. We started arguing and the whole thing got personal."

"So you lost your temper and stormed out of the house," Maryann finished for her.

"Cole thinks I'm going out with Mike tonight. Which I'm not, because Mike already has a date," Lacey explained.

"When did you find that out?"

"After I had stormed out of the house," Lacey said with chagrin. Instantly her chin lifted to a defiant angle. "I wasn't going back in."

"So you came here."

"I didn't know where else to go." Lacey shrugged and glanced apologetically at her friend.

"Hey, we're pals and I do have plenty of food. Don't worry." Maryann grinned. "Salad, hamburgers, wine—how does that sound?"

Lacey hesitated only for a second. "If you trust me with a knife, I'll fix the salad."

After their meal, they sat around Maryann's small living room, talking and listening to a forgettable playlist of love songs while they sipped at a couple of strawberry daiquiris, no rum, in lieu of dessert. The wine had given Lacey a slight headache, and besides, she had to drive home. Or drive somewhere. A little after eleven, Lacey saw Maryann stifling a yawn.

"I'm sorry. I forgot you have to work tomorrow even if I don't," Lacey said. "I'd better leave so you can get some sleep."

"You don't have to go," Maryann protested, rising to her feet when Lacey got up.

"It's late. I think it's safe for me to go back now," she joked weakly.

"Call me and let me know what happens," her friend urged, then clicked her tongue. "Do you have a land line out there?"

"It doesn't work. My cell should, but I haven't tried it yet," Lacey said.

"So tonight you will. Call."

"Okay, okay. Let's have lunch next week and I'll fill you in on the exciting details. If there are any," she laughed. "More than likely Cole is in bed and snoring."

"Sounds like you two are married," Maryann said, then clapped a hand to her cheek theatrically. "Oops. Shouldn't have said that."

"Don't worry. Not a chance in a million of that happening. Anyway, he won't care what time I come in."

"Make a lot of noise and wake him up, just for the hell of it," Maryann said with a conspiratorial giggle.

"Cole sleeps through his alarm. I think he'd sleep through an atom bomb explosion." Lacey started for the door. "Thanks for the dinner . . . and the company."

"It was fun." Maryann reached down to pick up her cat. "Wasn't it, Oscar?" The cat purred and rubbed its head against her chin. "He likes songs of unrequited love, you know. I don't usually put on that playlist."

"Lucky me." Lacey grinned. "Good night, you two."

Once outside in the pleasant coolness of the night air, her expression sobered. She really wasn't ready to return to the beach house yet, and she sure as hell wasn't up to teasing Cole. Content to be in her car, Lacey drove aimlessly through the empty streets, the radio off. Finally she ended up on the Virginia Beach side of the bay along the oceanfront.

Not thinking about the lateness of the hour, she parked and strolled along the silent beach. The time she'd spent with her friend had provided a breather, but Lacey still felt depressed. Finally the strengthening breeze drove her back to the car and she headed homeward.

All in all, it hadn't been the best evening, but thanks to Maryann, not the worst, Lacey thought as she drove the car into the garage. She had left her watch on the bedroom dresser and the digital clock on the car's dash showed three faint zeros. She had no idea what time it was, though she knew it had been dark for hours.

Shivering at the now too-cool-to-be-comfortable night air, she hurried through the connecting door from the garage to the house entrance. Wearily she began the tedious climb up the stairs.

Three steps from the top, the back of her neck prickled in warning and she glanced up to see Cole towering above her.

His white shirt was unbuttoned and loose. The T-shirt underneath was still tucked into his jeans, but even so. There was a dominant quality to his stance that made her nervous, and his gaze was shadowed, his features rugged and tense.

"Where have you been?" he asked.

"That's none of your business." Lacey attempted to brush past him, but he clasped her wrist to stop her.

"Do you know what time it is?" Cole demanded.

"No, I don't. Check your laptop. Or your gorgeous gold watch. Don't tell me you haven't been slaving away as usual. You never seem to stop."

"It happens to be almost four o'clock in the morning," he informed her. "I want to know where you've been."

Lacey strained against the grip on her wrist. "I don't have to account to you for my whereabouts. Let me go," she ordered. "I'm exhausted."

"I'll let you go," Cole promised, "as soon as you tell me where you've been."

"I told you it's none of your business." She was tired and had no desire to engage in a battle of words with Cole Whitfield.

"I know you weren't with Bowman," he snapped.

Lacey paled visibly but challenged him, "Wasn't I?"

"No." There was no trace of uncertainty in the single word. "Because I went to his place to find you. Bowman told me you'd said you were in no mood for company and that you'd left."

Silently Lacey thanked Mike for inventing a face-saving answer—face-saving for her, not him—instead of admitting that he had a date with some other girl that night. But it still didn't get her out of her present situation.

"Guess what. I'm still not in the mood for anyone's company—least of all yours! Now let me go!" She tried twisting her arm to free it from his grip.

But Cole used the movement to curve her arm behind her back and haul her against his chest. "I don't care what you're in the mood for. You're going to answer my questions."

"I am not!" Lacey protested vehemently.

His other hand lifted to her hair, stroking it soothingly as he let her go at last. She wanted to scratch his face, but settled for a glare.

"You've been drinking, haven't you?" he asked.

"I stopped by a friend's place and had a glass of wine," she said truthfully. "Is that a crime?"

"Considering the way you drove when you left here, it borders on attempted suicide," Cole said, the underlying tension in his voice breaking through. "I called the police half a dozen times. I was sure you'd had an accident, especially after I found out you weren't with Bowman."

"I didn't have an accident. I arrived safely." Tears were

misting her eyes. "I seem to be more in danger of being hurt by you than anything."

"I let you go. Did you notice?"

Lacey rubbed her wrist. "I'm beginning to get feeling back, so the answer is yes."

"Don't exaggerate. After what you put me through—"

Pent-up anger flared in Lacey and she went for him, only to have her wrist grabbed again. This time he used his superior strength to pull her against his rigid length.

"What the hell do you mean?" Lacey's laugh was bitter. "Listen to me, you arrogant, bullheaded—"

Cole gave her no time to finish the insult. His mouth pressed hers into silence as his powerful arms molded her to his body with a sensual economy of movement. The unexpectedly tender kiss ignited a bewildering response in Lacey. She had meant to struggle, to fight his embrace, but her hands were sliding inside his shirt, seeking the fiery warmth of his naked skin. Her head was whirling, thoroughly confused by her reaction.

When Cole lifted his head, she could not open her eyes to look at him, quivering all over with the feeling of his kiss. She felt his mouth and chin rubbing against the hair near her forehead.

"For God's sake, Lacey, tell me where you were all this time." There was a funny throb in his voice, almost like pain, as his mouth moved against her hair while he spoke, roughly caressing. "I was half out of my mind thinking that something had happened to you."

"Really?" she breathed, almost afraid to believe him.

"Yes, really." He smiled against her cheek and she felt the uneven thud of his heart beneath her hands. "Your friend, the one you had a drink with . . ." His arms tightened around her, demand creeping back into his voice. "Male or female? Okay, you don't have to answer that," he added quickly, looking a little ashamed of himself.

"But you just thought you'd ask, right? That wasn't a casual question, Cole."

"Even so."

"I was with a girlfriend. Maryann, from work." Lacey tipped her head as he began nuzzling her ear. "And I promised I'd call her." She fumbled for her cell phone and sent a brief text instead to get out of the inevitable conversation, then put it away.

"I'm not sure that's better," he grumbled with mock annoyance. "Bet you two were gossiping up a storm while I was pacing the floor all night."

"You poor thing," she murmured without a trace of sympathy. His hands were roaming over her bare shoulders and Lacey was shamelessly enjoying the sensations they were creating. "We weren't talking about you the whole time, if that's any comfort. And I left around eleven."

He lifted his head, frowning, his gaze narrowing. "Where have you been since then?"

"Oh, I hit the bars and did some tequila shots. I can't remember how many—five? No, six. I got loud so they eighty-sixed me. My rear end still hurts. But I treated myself to a couple of tattoos at a drive-through tattoo parlor. You know how it is when your mind's messed up."

For a fraction of a second, he looked ready to believe her. Lacey grinned. "I went for a walk on the beach."

"For three hours?"

She did the math in her head. "That sounds about right."

"Alone?"

Lacey nodded, knowing full well she'd been taking a chance, but here she was, safe and sound. "Do me a favor and skip the Safety 101 talk."

"You were actually walking on the beach for three

solid hours?" He repeated her statement as if he still couldn't believe she had said it.

"I have the sand in my shoes to prove it." She couldn't bring herself to worry about the risk.

"Oh, Lacey . . ." He sighed with exasperation and held her tightly in his arms. "I knew I shouldn't have let you walk out that door with Bowman."

"You couldn't have stopped me," she laughed softly. "I was so mad when I left that a brick wall couldn't have stopped me. And that's all your fault."

"Oh yeah?" Cole tucked a finger under her chin, tilting her face up and gazing at her quizzically.

"You started the whole thing," she reminded him. "If you hadn't been so rude to Mike, I would never have lost my temper."

One of his dark eyebrows quirked at her answer. "What was I supposed to think? I call his office and someone tells me he's out on a project. But when I get here, I find him carrying you around in his arms like he's Prince Charming."

"You could have given him the benefit of the doubt," she pointed out, feeling resentment build again, "instead of jumping to conclusions that are completely wrong and unfair."

"I'm not so sure I was *completely* wrong," Cole argued.

"You were. Mike isn't like that." Stiffening her arms against his chest, Lacey arched away from. "He's honest and intelligent and he works as hard as you do. Your project isn't the only one he's in charge of, in case that hasn't occurred to you."

"But—"

"The delays on yours were unavoidable."

"There you go again, defending him." Cole's mouth thinned. "Mike never makes a mistake, according to you."

"What am I supposed to do when he isn't around

to defend himself?" She twisted completely out of his embrace.

When she would have walked away, he caught her wrist, holding it firmly. "Lacey, I don't want to argue with you." His voice was husky, its demand low and urgent.

"No?" Looking into his dark blue eyes, Lacey knew that wasn't what he really wanted and answered her own question. "No. You want to make love, don't you?"

His gaze searched her face with unnerving thoroughness. "Don't you?"

Lacey's pulse hammered in instant reaction, a heady intoxication filling her senses. But her mind refused to be overwhelmed by physical attraction.

"Actually," she began, her tone faintly breathless as she tried to figure out what to say, "no. I don't."

"Liar," he said, one corner of his mouth curving into an oddly irresistible smile.

Its charm was potent and Lacey had to breathe in deeply to keep it from weaving a spell around her. It took all of her willpower to not give in to his subtle and powerful appeal.

"You've accused me of that more than once, Cole," she said tightly. "And you're wrong this time too."

With a quick tug, she pulled her wrist free of his hold and turned away. She could feel his gaze on her, compelling her to come back. She had to force herself to walk calmly and unhurriedly from him and not give in to the impulse to bolt like a scared bunny to the safety of her room.

As she closed the bedroom door behind her, a delayed reaction set in, with a strength that had her trembling. She was dangerously attracted to him. She recognized the symptoms, the combustible chemistry. But that was all it was.

Cole was aware of it too. He'd made no secret of his attraction to her and he had no reason to think she was unavailable. His desire wasn't going to go away when they were sharing the same house. But Lacey's instinct for self-preservation, which she hoped would prove to be stronger than her physical reaction, told her she would never be satisfied with him as a temporary lover. Yes, she wanted him with the same intensity that he wanted her, but not for a fling.

And yet . . . if that was all she could have, shouldn't she allow herself that pleasure?

A tear slipped from her lashes, its warm wetness surprising her as it trailed down her cheek. She flicked it away with her finger and began undressing for bed with awkward, hurried movements.

One tear followed another. By the time she had her pajamas on and was crawling into bed, her cheeks were damp all over from the confusing sadness that made her heart ache.

As she was about to switch off the bedside light, her door was pushed open. Her fingers stayed on the switch, unable to move. Cole stood in the doorway, his masculine bulk filling the frame. The roughly planed features of his face were set, one half in shadow from the uneven light streaming over him. The rich umber of his hair gleamed nearly black. His eyes shone with a smoldering desire that just might be her undoing.

A wave of intense longing washed through Lacey and she fought silently to deny it.

"Cole, I'm going to bed," she declared shakily.

"Change of plans," he said with a snap. His long strides carried him into the room, all the way to her side. "You're going to my bed—where you belong."

As he reached for her, Lacey made an attempt to protest before realizing that she didn't really want to tell him no. All the same, she grabbed the spare pillow on the double bed and threw it at him, hoping for a few seconds to escape his hands. But he knocked it aside with a swing of his arm and succeeded in getting her around the waist before she could slide out the other side of the bed.

Effortlessly he slung her bodily over his shoulder. A caveman move, but she secretly loved it. Still, token resistance was called for. Her bare feet flailed in the air but her doubled fists found their target and she pummeled at his broad shoulders and back.

"Want me to put you down?" he asked in a friendly voice.

Lacey tried to twist so she could slide down but his incredibly strong hands kept her exactly where she was. She thought about screaming. She didn't.

The door to his bedroom was ajar and he kicked it open the rest of the way to dump her unceremoniously on his bed. Her startled cry was muffled by the pillow she fell into. Out of breath, half loving what he was doing, half hating it, it took her a second to react.

Rolling onto her side, she saw Cole shrugging out of his unbuttoned shirt. The T-shirt beneath was next, and along with it he seemed to be shedding the veneer of civilization that separated man from beast.

However, he was a gorgeous beast, totally gorgeous. Her eyes widened at the expanse of bare chest, powerfully muscled yet sinuously lean.

As he reached to unbuckle his belt, she recovered from that momentary pang of pure desire and started to finish her roll off the bed. His hand reached out to capture hers.

"Going somewhere?"

Lacey thought . . . then shook her head. Slowly. The masterful sensuality he conveyed, the warmth of the hand that clasped hers, the look in his eyes . . .

everything compelled her to stay. But she didn't want to tell him that.

He lowered himself over her, the superior strength and pressure of his body secretly thrilling her. The last shred of her resistance burned away against his physical heat, her thin, silky pajamas the only barrier left between them.

She trembled, not quite ready to go this far. Her hands strained against the rippling muscles of his biceps, trying unsuccessfully to push him away. By turning her head far to the side, she managed to elude his searching mouth, but that didn't stop him from exploring the area of her cheek and neck she had exposed. Despite her attempts to get free, a sensual response to his rough caresses raced through her.

"Cole, what about the ground rules?" she gasped, her heart pounding frantically.

"To hell with 'em," was the terse reply.

The warmth of his breath seemed to set fire to her skin, the sensation quickly spreading. She didn't know how to cool it down—or even if she wanted to.

"You're tired, Cole. You don't know what you're doing," she protested weakly, not sure any longer if she knew what she was doing herself, or why.

"Maybe," he agreed in a throaty murmur that tantalized her with its gruff, soft sound. "But I'm enjoying it, whatever it is."

His fingers caressed her cheek, sliding into the short hair near her ear. He moved her face to his, his mouth at last finding the softness of her lips. Hungrily he explored their sweetness, kissing her deeply, with a very male intensity.

"Mmm. You taste like strawberries," he whispered, rubbing the pad of his thumb over her full lower lip when the kiss ended.

Lacey's hands curled into his shoulders to cling to

him. Cole shifted his attention, nuzzling her earlobe and chuckling softly in triumph. "You're enjoying this, aren't you? Don't deny it." Lightly he nipped her skin, the tiny pain becoming exquisite pleasure.

Her surrender wasn't complete and she began a protest. "Cole . . ."

"Strawberry girl," he repeated, his moist mouth investigating the trembling curve of her lips. And the protest died in her throat. "Not ready in the morning, ripe red and sweet at night."

Then his mouth was closing over hers again, his burning kiss drawing her into the vortex of his desire. Everything went spinning. Lacey had no idea where or when the sensations would stop. Or which of them would win or lose. It was a wild, dizzying merry-go-round.

His hands seemed to know exactly where to touch her and arouse her to the full pitch of sensuality. Limp with pleasure, she let her feminine curves be molded to fit his hard length.

Her hands slid over the steel-smooth skin of his back. The pressure of his body was deeply satisfying and she answered his rising need with instinctive movements of her own, all too aware of a yearning ache within her lower body.

At that instant she realized she was losing control. She was letting herself give in to pure desire, without a thought for any of the consequences.

"Don't do this, Cole, please," she whispered in desperate protest.

"Lacey, for God's sake," he muttered thickly, seeking her lips, caressing her wildly. "You know you want me to love you . . . I'll make you admit it."

Yes, she did want him to love her, but not just in the physical sense. His words troubled her and she stiffened without meaning to.

"I'm not going to submit. I don't like this game."

"It isn't a game, Lacey." Cole breathed in tightly, levering himself up on one elbow, the brilliant blue of his gaze moving darkly over her face. Lacey knew the advantage was suddenly hers. She couldn't weaken.

"Damn it," he groaned finally, and rolled on his back, dragging her with him.

His strong, open hand pressed her head against his bare chest, rising and falling with his uneven breathing. Lacey could hear the hammering of his heart. Its beat was as erratic and aroused as her own.

She closed her eyes, letting the circling band of his arms hold her to the comforting warmth of his chest.

That was all he did from then on: hold her. He made no attempt to caress her or carry out his threat to make her admit their mutual desire. All of a sudden, she wasn't going to be seduced.

She wasn't too happy with that either.

It was a long time before his jackhammer pulse settled into a calmer tempo and his breathing became relaxed and level. The contentment of lying in his arms was nearly as satisfying as his experienced lovemaking.

The warm glow and the late hour combined to make sleep inevitable—her eyelids were heavy. Unwillingly she realized that she had to leave the comfort of his arms, but as she started to disentangle herself from his hold, his muscles tightened. He wasn't letting her go that easily.

"Stay here, Strawberry." His voice was husky with sleep, a drowsily warm sound that she couldn't bring herself to fight.

Cole himself was minutes away from conking out. Lacey snuggled against his body heat, assuring herself that she would stay just until he fell asleep, then she would leave. At her lack of protest, he sighed, his breath stirring the feathery locks of her tousled hair.

It wasn't easy staying awake. The one thing that helped was the bedroom window that was propped open. The cool breeze blowing in from the ocean through the curtains danced over her skin, its brisk chill just enough to keep her awake and aware of her surroundings.

At one particularly strong puff of sea air, Lacey shivered. Cole immediately shifted her from his chest, reaching down to pull the covers over both of them before nestling her against his side again. The bed became a warm cocoon, relaxing and safe.

"Go to sleep, Strawberry," he whispered, and brushed his mouth briefly across her hair. Despite the casualness of the good-night caress, there was something intimate and loving about it.

"Yes," Lacey replied.

But she wouldn't really go to sleep and she was only pretending to agree. When Cole was really out, she would leave, she reminded herself.

Her lashes fluttered tiredly down and she decided to rest her eyes just for a few minutes. His arm was a heavy, warm band around her waist, possessive and gentle.

Chapter 7

The alarm buzzed loudly, almost right in Lacey's ear. She struggled to open her eyes, not understanding why it should be so loud.

A heavy weight was around her waist, pressing her to the mattress. She started to push it aside, hugely irritated by the buzz and wishing Cole would shut his alarm clock off just once in the mornings.

As her fingers touched the weight, she felt the roughness of wiry hair and discovered that the weight was an arm—Cole's arm, to be precise.

Instantly she was wide awake, remembering the events of last night—or more correctly, early morning. And the hard, long shape in the bed beside her was most definitely Cole.

Careful not to disturb him, she reached out, her fingertips just able to reach the button that turned off the noisy buzz. For once she was glad that Cole slept through his alarms. It would give her a chance to slip out of bed before he awakened.

But as she tried to slide away from him, he reached for her. "Don't move, Strawberry." His voice was thick with sleep.

Lacey guessed that it was a momentary alertness and within seconds he would again be sound asleep. "Your belt buckle is poking me," she lied, to explain the reason she'd moved away from him.

Cole mumbled something unintelligible and rolled onto his side. Lacey remained completely still for several minutes until she was satisfied that he had fallen back asleep. Then she slid silently out of bed and tiptoed to her own room.

Dressed, with coffee made and a glass of orange juice in her hand, she walked back to Cole's room. She paused in the doorway, gazing at him, still out cold. Sighing, she remembered how late it had been last night before Cole had slept, and the previous night when he had drifted off on the sofa. She simply couldn't bring herself to wake him and deprive him of the sleep he needed.

Turning around, she went back to the kitchen and put the glass of juice in the refrigerator. The morning sun sparkled on the ocean, reflecting shifting dots of light onto the walls of the living room.

With a cup of coffee in hand, Lacey moved onto the deck. She hesitated, then descended the steps to the inviting stretch of empty beach. The peace of the morning was broken only by the waves licking the shore and the occasional cry of a seagull on the wing.

Only it wasn't quite empty, she discovered as she strolled along the sand. An older woman in a sunhat, ancient jeans rolled up to her knees, was wandering along, intent upon the treasures washed up by the tide.

Sitting down on the sand, Lacey watched the woman for a while before the soaring acrobatics of a gull got her attention. The ocean was in one of its serene moods, its surface calm.

Contentment filled Lacey's heart, and she sat quietly

on the sand, not conscious of thinking about anything, her mind seemingly blank.

Time seemed to slip away. Only the growing brightness of the rising sun and the increasing warmth of its rays offered any change. The ocean and sky remained the same, and the woman was still scouring the beach for shells and driftwood.

"Lacey!" Cole impatiently shouted her name, breaking off the lonely cry of a gull.

Turning to look over her shoulder, she saw him standing on the deck, naked to the waist. Even from this distance, she could see how wrinkled his pants were after being slept in for a night. His dark hair was tangled and he was attempting to comb it into order with his fingers.

She waved to him, her heart somersaulting in reaction to all that glorious virility radiating from him, male and powerful.

"Why didn't you wake me?" he called. "I was supposed to be at the office an hour ago."

Lacey was piqued by the accusation in his tone. "I thought you needed your sleep!" Lacey cupped her hands to her mouth to shout the answer.

"The next time, don't think! Wake me up!" His shouted reply sounded more like a roar.

As he turned from the railing to enter the house, she stuck out her tongue at him, more amused than angered by his grouchy behavior.

Getting up and dusting the sand off her bottom, she wandered toward the water. The woman beachcomber glanced up, and a smile wreathed her face, which was lined from years of sun, despite the hat she wore.

"It's a beautiful morning, isn't it?" she commented.

"It certainly is," Lacey agreed, and stopped where she was. "Found anything interesting yet?"

"Nothing spectacular." The older woman straightened

from her bent position and pressed a hand to the small of her back.

"Do you collect shells?" Lacey looked curiously at the pail slung over the woman's arm.

"Well, yes, I do," she admitted after a second's hesitation. "But my main hobby is making things with shells and other objects that I find on the beach."

"Oh, like jewelry." Lacey had noticed the string of shell beads around the woman's neck.

The woman touched the necklace with her finger. "Yes—I do earrings and necklaces. At the moment I'm making a picture with shells. That's why I'm collecting all of these little mauve shells," she explained, reaching into the bucket to lift out a handful of the tiny shells. "There are any number of things you can make with shells—mobiles, wind chimes, lots of things."

"Sounds fascinating," murmured Lacey with a trace of envy in her voice. She wished she had the time to do projects like that, although her creative talents seldom stretched to more than attempting a floral arrangement from time to time.

"It's very enjoyable," the woman said. "And now that I've retired, it keeps me busy."

"Lacey!" Cole was calling to her again and she turned to the house to answer. He stood on the deck, this time dressed in a lightweight summer suit. "I'm leaving now. See you tonight."

Lacey waved to let him know she'd heard. He gave her a brief salute and went back into the house. She smiled to herself, tickled by the difference a morning cup of coffee and a shower made in him.

"Your husband's very thoughtful," the woman commented. "My John always lets me know when he's leaving the house too."

"Cole isn't my husband." Lacey made the correction automatically and without thinking.

"Oh." The older woman was momentarily startled by the answer. "Oh!" The second time the word was drawn out a little. She gave Lacey a look that seemed vaguely disapproving but she left it at that, not adding anything like *you young people these days*.

Lacey blushed. She didn't want to launch into a long, detailed explanation of the circumstances surrounding their decision to share the house. But Lacey didn't attempt to justify their arrangement. She wasn't sure the woman would believe her anyway.

"Um, I have to go. I enjoyed meeting you and—and I hope the picture turns out. Have a nice day," Lacey offered and self-consciously walked down the beach.

When she was several yards away, the breeze passed along the older woman's soft comment, not meant to be heard. "Lovely girl. That fella shouldn't take her for granted . . ."

The rest of it was lost as Lacey walked faster, her lips compressed in a thin line.

Sometimes being polite meant putting up with more than you'd bargained for. But what could she do? Tell a nice old lady that she'd gotten it wrong?

There wasn't much to do back at the house, but she puttered around, tackling minor chores like watering the plants and handwashing some delicate items of clothing. It was just after twelve noon when she fixed a sandwich and some fruit, donned a light hoodie, then settled into one of the lounge chairs with a book.

She put it aside for a few moments, realizing she hadn't applied sunblock. That necessary task done, she opened the book again.

The sun overhead was warm and relaxing. Combined with her lack of sleep for the last two nights, its heat made her drowsy and soon she was setting her book aside to take a short nap.

The next time she opened her eyes, they focused on a familiar brown leather briefcase. Immediately she looked for its owner and found Cole sitting in one of the deck chairs, his long legs stretched out in front of him and a can of beer in his hand. Dark spiky lashes screened the expression in his eyes, but he was watching her.

His mouth twitched briefly in a smile. "So you're finally going to wake up, sleepyhead. Good thing you put sunblock on or you'd be brick red by now."

Lacey scrabbled for the capped tube and threw it at him. It landed at his feet.

"Don't get mad."

"I'm not," she yawned. "But you shouldn't watch me while I'm sleeping." Then she remembered she'd done the same to him. She wasn't going to admit it, though. "What time is it?"

"Four-thirty or thereabouts." He shrugged, uninterested in the exact time although his gold watch was around his wrist, making it easy enough to verify.

"I didn't realize I was so tired." She rubbed her eyes and covered another yawn with her hand. "How long have you been here?"

"Since just after two."

Which was only a little while after she'd fallen asleep. "Don't tell me you sat there from then until now." She blinked in disbelief.

Cole nodded. "I did. The fresh air was great. Very stimulating. So was the view."

She suddenly felt a lot more alert. "I bet." Lacey really wanted to ask what he'd been looking at and a hand strayed to the zipper of her hoodie. It was pulled up to her collarbone. Then her vanity kicked in. Had her mouth been open as she dozed? Not even Sleeping Beauty would look good like that. But it was another question that wasn't going to get asked.

She noticed the hint of weariness in his posture. "You should have napped too," she said, sitting upright.

"Maybe," he conceded, "but I wanted to be here when you woke up."

That didn't make sense. "Why?"

"Because I wanted to apologize for last night."

"Oh." His statement suddenly made her uneasy, especially with his dark blue gaze watching her so intently.

She walked to the deck railing, wishing Cole had pretended last night had never happened rather than alluding to it on their first real meeting. At the same instant, she realized she'd escaped to the beach in the morning before he had awakened to avoid this confrontation after the events of last night.

Footsteps indicated his approach and she tensed, her heart beating rapidly as a hummingbird's wings. Cole stopped directly behind her and she could sense his gaze on her.

"Aren't you going to accept my apology?" he asked.

"For what?" She shrugged nervously. "Nothing happened."

"We came close," he said in a gently mocking voice.

Lacey was flustered. Forget about poise—she felt like skittering away like a sand crab. What had happened to all her self-confidence and her ability to handle any kind of a situation? What power did Cole have to reduce her to a quivering mass of nerves?

His hands rested lightly on her shoulders to turn her around. She refused to look up, just stayed focused on his shirt collar, the top two buttons of the shirt itself unfastened, giving her a glimpse of his bare chest. The sight held her still. She might be better off gazing into his magnetic blue eyes.

He crooked a finger under her chin to lift her head.

"I knew you'd be a temptation from the first night, but I thought I could handle it." He paused, frowning at the agitated look in her eyes. "I was tired and irritable last night. And we'd argued over Bowman—"

"Cole, please," Lacey interrupted tightly. "I don't want to dissect all the events and emotions from last night. It won't change anything. Don't do this to me."

"Don't do this to you?" He laughed without humor. "What about what you do to me?"

Troubled, distracted by thoughts he couldn't bring himself to share, he began to rub her shoulders and upper arms in what amounted to a circular caress, unaware of the bone-melting sensations he was causing in her. Lacey didn't protest, powerless to stop what he was doing.

"Do you know how I felt when you drove away from here yesterday?" His voice lowered to a husky pitch, demanding an answer. "Or when I found out that you weren't with Bowman? Do you know what it was like waiting for you to come home last night?" His fingers dug briefly into her flesh. "You don't have to answer. But think about what it's like for me, going to bed each night and imagining you in the next room in your cute little pajamas?"

She knew she was a breath away from trying to fix that problem for him. Nothing doing. She was not going to have sex with a man she'd known less than a week. "Then leave. Move out," she challenged in desperation.

"And worry about you being here by yourself?" Cole argued. "I'd be trading cold showers for ulcers."

"Deal with it," she snapped. "Next I suppose you'll ask me to move out. In writing, with a copy to your lawyer."

"Come on, Lacey, don't be like that. Although it would solve things if you went somewhere else."

"Would it?" she countered with a funny ache in her throat.

"I don't know." Cole sighed heavily, releasing her to turn away. Raking his fingers roughly through his hair, he let his hand rest on the back of his head.

"Hold that thought, because I'm not moving out," she declared, even though every logical cell in her brain told her to do just that. "And you're in my way." She started for the door to the house, brushing past him. "I want to see what there is for dinner."

"No!" Cole spun around, the edge in his voice stopping her. "We'll eat out tonight."

She hesitated only for a split second. "You can eat out if you want. I'll fix something here for myself."

Refusing his invitation wasn't that hard. The prospect of going out with him on what would seem like a date was as unsettling as staying in the house with him for the evening.

"Damn, Lacey," he muttered, "I thought I'd made myself clear. I'm not letting you stay in this house alone at night. I'm a little uneasy that you're by yourself in the daytime, but you're a big girl, so what can I do?"

"Back it up. You're not *letting* me!" Lacey's temper flared at his arrogant statement.

"That's right, I'm not letting you," he repeated forcefully. "And you can argue about that for as long as you like, but either we both go or we both stay. That's the way it's going to be."

She crossed her arms over her chest and glared at him like a balky mule.

"Look, just go out to dinner with me this once. We need to get out of this house and rejoin the human race."

"Speak for yourself!"

"I'm trying to, Lacey."

Their eyes locked in a clashing, silent duel that lasted

for several seconds before Cole asked, "So what's it going to be?"

He actually was right about one thing: they needed to get out. Staying here and squabbling was pointless. "Give me a few minutes to change clothes," Lacey agreed grudgingly.

"Fine." The roughness hadn't completely left his voice. "We'll go somewhere for a drink first."

He sipped half a beer, she downed a mojito. It was only after they left the swanky cocktail lounge for the restaurant that the tension between them began to ease. The hostess seated them at a table with a view of the ocean and outside spotlights that highlighted the white, rolling surf.

"What looks good to you?" Cole asked, glancing up from his menu to Lacey.

"I'm trying to decide whether to have the deviled crab or the steamed blue crab," she answered, nibbling thoughtfully at her lower lip.

"Have both," he offered as an alternative.

"Are you kidding? I'd be so full I couldn't move. You'd have to carry me out of here," she joked, dismissing his suggestion.

"It wouldn't be the first time I've carried you somewhere," he reminded her quietly.

The way he was looking at her made her glow all over. Feeling instantly warm, she focused on her menu, aware of his soft, almost silent chuckle. She closed the menu and set it on the table in front of her.

"I'll have the steamed crab," she said quickly in an effort to change the subject.

The waiter appeared at Cole's left. "The steamed blue crab for each of us," he ordered. "And a wine list, please."

When the waiter left, a silence ensued. Lacey nervously fingered the prongs of her fork, unable to think of any small talk to get her through this awkwardness. Cole spoke first.

"I was only teasing you," he offered in apology, "when I reminded you about last night."

"I know, but it's nothing to joke about." She glanced up and found she was unable to look away from his compelling gaze. Her heart turned over, not helped by the tingling warmth that had returned to drive her crazy.

"Well, well, well," a male voice said from behind Lacey. "You two have finally ventured out of your little love nest."

Lacey cringed. Crawling under the tablecloth and out the door suddenly seemed like a great move. She didn't turn around. Cole's gaze flicked in back of her.

"Hello, Vic," he said blandly.

She'd surprised herself by recognizing the voice of Monica Hamilton's somewhat sleazy brother. At that moment, Vic came around the table.

"Hey, Cole." He nodded first to him, then turned his wide smile to Lacey. "We meet again. How's it going?"

"Hello." She returned his greeting coolly, not liking his attitude any more now than she had at their first meeting.

"Good to see you." His smile got wider but that didn't make it any warmer or more charming. "My sister has been gnashing her teeth over you all week. Really, Cole"—he turned his attention away from Lacey—"I think you could have let her down a little more gently."

"There is such a thing as being too gentle," he replied. "She doesn't seem to realize that it's over and has been for some time."

"Yeah? Not by her. She's always yapping about you," Vic commented absently. "Monica prefers to forgive you for your"—he nodded in Lacey's direction—"you know.

Your indiscretions." His pointed words made Lacey bristle with indignation and embarrassment.

Cole's mouth twisted. "Is that what Monica said?"

"Yeah. She said to tell you that if I happened to run into you. And here we all are." He put his hands in his pockets and jingled his change.

"You've delivered the message," Cole said indifferently.

"Now you want me to run along and leave you alone, is that it?" Vic shrugged. "Okay with me. Enjoy your evening."

When he'd wandered off, distracted for a few seconds by a waitress's cleavage, Lacey sputtered indignantly, "Why didn't you set him straight? He isn't Monica."

Cole rolled his eyes. "You mean set him straight about my indiscretions? Want me to deny that we've slept together?"

"You know nothing really happened," she retorted.

He leaned back in his chair, studying her thoughtfully. There was a coolness in his eyes that dismayed her. "You seem so eager to deny any relationship between us. And just because Vic happened to slither by our table—are you attracted to him?"

"Of course not." Lacey scowled. "He's a reptile. 'Slither' is the right verb for that guy."

"Thanks. But he has some things going for him, at least according to some other women I know."

He had to say that, she thought crossly. She wasn't even going to ask who they were, but he continued, "The Hamiltons are rich. Really rich. And by some standards, Vic could be classified as a very handsome man. Quite a catch, in fact."

"I'm sure the same could be said about Monica, couldn't it?" she argued.

"It could," he said almost affably. "But we aren't talking about Monica."

"Listen, I'm not on Vic's side, but maybe you should take his advice and beg her forgiveness. Then the two of you can get back together."

His mouth thinned. "You enjoy starting arguments, don't you, Lacey?"

"I don't start them. You do."

"Let's end this one by dropping the subject," he suggested briskly.

"Gladly," Lacey agreed.

The waiter arrived with their dinner, negating the need for immediate conversation to fill the awkward silence. With good food and a glass of wine, the silence was eventually broken.

"How's the project coming?" Lacey asked, using her knife to pry off the bottom flap of shell on the underside of the crab.

"Moving right along. Didn't Bowman mention that the crew was making up for lost time?" Cole asked idly.

"No." With more shell discarded, Lacey broke off the claws and set them aside to pick the meat out of them later.

"You've done that before," Cole said.

"What? Oh, you mean the crab." She smiled at him. "Yes, I have. They're a lot of work but it's fun."

"Glad to hear it." He returned to the previous subject. "Considering the various snafus along the way, I'd think Bowman would be bragging about getting caught up."

"Mike's not like that," Lacey said. "He considers it his duty to do the best he can. He never lets a problem become an excuse. He tries to solve it, which is why it was so unfair when you blamed him at first."

Cole ignored the last red-flag remark. "Bowman mentioned the two of you had been discussing business, so I presumed he was referring to the progress on the project. What were you talking about, or am I cruising for a bruising with that question?" Amusement glittered faintly in the look he gave her.

Lacey hesitated, her knife poised to slice through the crab. "When did you ask Mike what we had been discussing?"

"When you were in your room, changing clothes to leave with him."

"And he told you we were talking about business?"

"Yup. At the time I found it kind of hard to believe. I don't know any guys who can hold a gorgeous woman in their arms and talk shop," Cole admitted.

"And you still don't believe it, do you?" she challenged.

"With you, I'm learning that anything is possible. But I have to say I'm beginning to sympathize with that crab on your plate." The laugh lines around his eyes deepened but his mouth didn't smile. "So . . . were you talking business?"

"We were talking about the temp who replaced me while I'm on this fabulous vacation," she explained. "Donna knows the fundamentals, but her personality can be very irritating."

"I've talked to her a couple of times." Cole didn't elaborate.

"Then you understand what Mike's been going through this week." A smile teased the corners of her mouth.

"Yes. And I sympathize," he said dryly. "But that doesn't explain why he was dangling you over the railing."

"Oh, that." Lacey didn't attempt to hide her smile this time. "I was teasing him. I told him I was thinking about quitting and I suggested Donna as a permanent replacement. He was threatening murder if I did."

Cole made a frown. "Like he needed a reason to sweep you off your feet." She chose not to respond and he cleared his throat and continued, "Are you thinking of quitting?"

She dug out tender shreds of crabmeat, shaking her head. "No. I like working there for now. The company's relatively small. I can learn a lot and move to a bigger firm when I'm ready and the economy is on the uptick."

"Spoken like a true businesswoman."

It was difficult to make a casual response to that. If anyone else had been that interested in her future career, she wouldn't have thought much about it one way or the other. But because it was Cole who was asking the questions, she was answering carefully. She was more than half in love with him right now, and the future was a loaded subject.

"How about marriage, kids, all that? Part of the plan?"

"Wha-at?" She didn't believe he'd asked that, even though it was as legitimate a topic of conversation as any other. But there was only so much one could say about a crab on a plate waiting to be eaten. He'd asked an awfully personal question, though, and his interest didn't seem casual.

"Sorry. Maybe I shouldn't have asked."

"No, it's all right," she assured him. "I just haven't given the subject a lot of thought."

"I was just wondering," Cole said.

She poked and picked at the crab. "I'll get back to you on that," she said. "Dinner's getting cold. Let's finish eating."

"Do you mean we've found something else we can agree on besides sharing the house?" Cole declared with mock astonishment, a wicked glint in his indigo blue eyes. "Amazing," he drawled, and Lacey laughed.

Their earlier disagreement over Vic and Monica Hamilton was forgotten. By the time the plates were taken away and a light, lemony dessert to share was put on the table, they'd found a lot of things to talk about that weren't potential bear traps. Then they'd lingered over coffee until it was nearly ten.

All too soon, it seemed, the bill was paid and they were on their way, and Cole was driving the car into the garage.

Concealing a sigh of regret that the evening was coming to a close, Lacey stepped out of the car, instinctively taking the door key out of her purse. Both stepped forward at the same time to unlock the connecting door, bumping into each other.

"Allow me," Cole offered with a gentlemanly flourish that made her giggle.

"By all means," she agreed, putting the key back in her purse.

In the lower entranceway, he paused to lock the door behind him while she slowly began to climb the steps. She was reluctant to have the evening end so soon.

"How about if I—"

"Let's make a pact," Cole interrupted, right behind her on the staircase. "You don't offer to make coffee or a drink and I won't show you my etchings. I don't have any etchings anyway."

"I figured," Lacey said.

She knew exactly why he'd made the tame joke. They were back in the house again, and its privacy and isolation suggested an intimacy they were both trying to avoid.

His hand took hold of her elbow, his touch impersonal and light as he guided her across the living room to the hall leading to the bedrooms. As they started down the hall, Lacey wanted to protest that she wasn't sleepy, but she knew it wasn't wise and kept silent.

At the closed door of her bedroom they stopped, and Lacey turned hesitantly to him. An elemental tension crackled between them.

"Do you know this is the first time I've escorted a date directly to her bedroom door to say good night?" Cole's tone was wry.

"It's a first for me too." Lacey tried to respond in the same blasé way, but her voice sounded a little shaky.

His large palm cupped the side of her face in a caress that was gentle rather than arousing. "You'd better go straight to bed," he said. "After these last couple of days, you need a good night's sleep."

Something in the way he said it made her ask, "What about you? Aren't you going to bed right away?"

"No. I thought I'd take a walk on the beach before I turn in."

"But—" Lacey was going to suggest that she go along, but his thumb pressed her lips into silence.

"Not a good idea." His gaze dropped to her mouth for a fraction of a second. "I know what I'm talking about, Lacey."

Her heart was skipping beats all over the place and her brown eyes were round and luminous. She only nodded in reply, and was surprised to see a flash of anger in his eyes.

"Hell. Why did I say that? I'm not cut out for sainthood. And neither are you. Don't be so damned meek," Cole growled. "It doesn't suit you."

"I—" Lacey started to defend herself, annoyed by his moodiness.

"Just shut up," he interrupted her, and she detected the faint groan in his throat before he let his mouth replace the thumb that had been pressed against her lips.

The hard, searing kiss flamed through her as his arms crushed her against his male length. The lean warmth of his body added to the fire already raging inside her. The fierce, sensual masculinity he embodied was irresistible to her.

Lacey's lips parted under the bruising urgency of his mouth, permitting him to deepen the kiss with delicious expertise. She felt his tenseness, his muscles like coiled springs in an effort to keep control, while she herself had none. But she had long ago realized that in Cole's arms she lost her inhibitions, and that made his touch doubly dangerous.

He broke off the kiss, lifting his head. A muscle twitched in his jaw as he stared into her dazed, love-softened face. He breathed in deeply—and then he turned away.

"Good night, Lacey," he said softly.

For an instant she was incapable of speech. "Good night," she answered finally, but he was already striding into the living room, not glancing back when she spoke.

Not until she heard the sliding glass door to the deck open and close did she enter her bedroom. She was emotionally shaken by the feelings and sensations he had aroused. She knew she couldn't possibly sleep so she walked to the window, gazing out at the moon casting a pale, silvery light on the sand.

In seconds Cole came into view, his long strides taking him to the edge of the waves. His hands were thrust deep in his pockets and his attention fixed on the ground. Lacey watched him until he walked out of her sight, striding along the beach into the night.

Changing into her pajamas, she crawled into bed. She didn't attempt to close her eyes as she listened to the clock on the bedside table tick the seconds away. The hands of the clock were nearly together just before the midnight hour when she finally heard Cole enter the house.

His pace had slowed considerably as he wandered into the hallway. He stopped outside her door. When she saw the knob turn, she closed her eyes, faking sleep.

Opening the door, Cole made no attempt to enter the room, but stared at her for several silent moments before he closed the door. She heard him go to his own room. The pounding of her heart became almost an aching pain as she turned onto her side and tried to sleep.

Chapter 8

The next morning Lacey awoke early from habit. She lay in bed for several minutes listening to the sounds of Cole stirring about.

Finally she threw aside the covers and got up, realizing that she couldn't get back to sleep, not with all that sunshine, which was growing brighter by the minute. Pulling on her robe, she stepped out into the hall.

At that moment Cole came out of his room softly whistling a tuneless melody. He was wearing swimming trunks, chocolate brown with tan stripes. He smiled when he saw her. "Good morning," he said cheerfully.

"You must have been up for a while," Lacey observed, her own voice still husky from sleep.

"I have. How did you know? Did I wake you?" he asked, waiting for her and falling into step beside her.

"No, you didn't. I just guessed you'd been up because you're usually grouchy when you first wake up," she replied.

He reached out and ruffled her short hair. "You aren't exactly Miss Sunshine first thing in the morning yourself," he commented.

"Don't do that!" she protested, and tried to brush her hair down with the flat of her hand.

"See what I mean?" He winked, a light dancing in his dark blue eyes.

"Okay, I admit I'm not Miss Sunshine. The cure is caffeine. Did you make coffee?"

"Not yet. I was on my way out for a morning swim, hoping you'd be up and have it ready when I came back," he replied honestly, the mocking amusement still gleaming in his look.

"Hmf. You could have fixed it and had it ready for me when I got up," she countered, unable to take offense this early in the day.

"I could have," he agreed. "Anyway, want to come for a swim with me? I'll wait."

"No, thanks." Lacey didn't even glance at his lean, browned physique, which was altogether too virile for her senses to cope with when she wasn't fully awake.

"Okay." He moved away from her toward the deck door. "See you later."

He seemed to take a lot of the morning sunshine with him when he left. Lacey halfheartedly got the coffeemaker ready and switched it on. She took her orange juice onto the deck, her gaze searching the waves until she found Cole. He was a strong swimmer, as she'd guessed he would be. She watched him for a long time before finally reminding herself to get dressed.

Showering first, she put on cute shorts with a white top. The coffee was brewed when she returned to the kitchen. She poured a cup and wandered again to the deck, her gaze once more drawn magnetically to the beach.

Two figures caught her attention. One was Cole wading out of the ocean, lifting a hand in greeting to someone else. It was the woman in the sun hat Lacey had talked to the previous morning.

She paled slightly as Cole stopped to talk to the woman, who was searching the beach for shells. His tanned body gleamed like bronze from the water still beading on his skin.

Lacey had no idea what the two were chatting about, but Cole was listening attentively. Once he glanced to the house, spying Lacey on the deck.

Apprehension shivered over her skin. The woman surely wouldn't mention her impression that she and Cole were living together or say anything disapproving. They were from very different generations, but old people seemed to be beyond finding most things shocking nowadays.

Soon Cole was nodding a goodbye to the woman, his long legs striding across the sand to the stairs to the deck. Lacey was tempted to retreat into the house, but she forced herself to stand her ground and react calmly to his return.

"Did you have a good swim?" she asked.

"Great." His hair glistened darkly in the sunlight as he effortlessly took the stairs two at a time to reach the top. "Ah, the coffee's done," he said, seeing the cup in Lacey's hand.

"I'll get you a cup," she offered quickly, finding an excuse to leave.

"It can wait." He walked to the railing near her, leaning both hands on it and gazing silently at the ocean beyond.

Then, unexpectedly, he looked at her, his gaze piercing. He was so alive, so male, a bronzed statue come to life, that her breath caught in her throat.

"I just had an interesting conversation with that woman on the beach," he said. "A Mrs. Carlyle—she lives a few houses down. Do you know her?"

Something in the inflection of his voice told Lacey

that he already knew the answer, possibly recognizing the woman from yesterday.

"I talked to her for a few minutes the other day," she admitted, "but I didn't know her name." Slightly flustered, she knew there was a tinge of pink in her cheeks. She sipped at her coffee, pretending the tepid brew was hot. "She collects shells and does crafts with them—jewelry making, stuff like that."

"So she told me, among other things." There was a hint of laughter in his reply, but his intent gaze didn't soften. "I'm curious about what you told her."

"Me?" Lacey swallowed nervously.

"Mrs. Carlyle is under the impression that we're living together. And I got the impression that in her day, that was no way to treat a woman you loved."

"I was afraid she was thinking along those lines," Lacey admitted after a second's hesitation.

"So what did you tell her?" he prodded, a smile playing around the corners of his mouth.

"She assumed we were married and I automatically said you weren't my husband. I had to let her draw her own conclusions from that," Lacey said self-consciously.

"You left out a detail or two. Maybe she thought you had some other husband—not me."

That honestly hadn't occurred to Lacey at the time. Okay, a few things could still be considered shocking. "I don't really know, and you're right, I didn't tell her everything. It would have been such a long, drawn-out story, Cole. And she is a stranger." She curled her hands around her coffee cup. "What did she say to you?"

"I got a very stern lecture." Creases deepened on either side of his mouth, triggered by amusement at Lacey's obvious discomfort.

"Oh," was all she could think of to say, and she stared at her half-empty cup of coffee.

Cole reached out and removed the cup from her hands, setting it on a deck table. Before she could protest that action, he was curving both arms around her. She pressed her hands against his chest, her fingers coming in contact with the cloud of moist dark hairs.

"She was trying to convince me that if I had any respect for you at all, I'd make an honest woman out of you." He smiled down at her, the dampness of his legs against her thighs oddly sensual. "What do you think?"

"Cole, I—" Her throat constricted.

He bent his head to brush his mouth over the soft curve of her jaw. The tangy ocean scent clinging to his skin assailed her senses, overstimulated in an instant by his touch. He teased the sensitive skin of her neck, his breath dancing warmly over her flesh.

"How about if I make an honest woman of you, Lacey?" he asked playfully, not a trace of seriousness in his voice.

She swallowed hard to ease the tightness in her throat and pushed away from his disturbing nearness. "Don't be ridiculous, Cole." Truth be told, she didn't feel like joking about a touchy subject like marriage. Deep down, it meant something to her, even though it seemed trivial to him.

He made no attempt to recapture her as he watched her widen the distance between them with quick, retreating steps. Yet behind his obvious amusement, his expression seemed guarded and alert.

"Maybe I should make a dishonest woman of you first," he said, again in that same laughing tone that indicated he was teasing. "But it really is up to you."

Lacey felt light-headed and unable to match his bantering words. "Oh, go get some coffee and sober up," she said. "You've had too much ocean or too much sun."

"Nope. Neither. It's you, babe." His sudden look of longing conveyed a lot more than those few words.

The undercurrents vibrating in the air intensified. Lacey paled, unsure of how long she could resist before succumbing to the sheer force of the growing attraction between them. She nearly jumped out of her skin when Cole moved unexpectedly.

But he swept past her, speaking abruptly. "I'll shower and dress first, then have coffee."

"I'll start breakfast," she offered, in need of something ordinary to do. She had to pay attention to something besides him, she thought, watching him walk away. She might as well cook.

Bacon was sizzling in the skillet when he entered the kitchen, wearing khakis and a polo shirt that emphasized the width of his shoulders and molded the muscled leanness of his torso. The clean fragrance of soap mingled with something else: pure him.

Lacey couldn't help being aware of the heady combination as he helped himself to coffee and moved to the counter near the stove. He was brimming with vitality, making her weak in the knees with the force of his presence.

She began turning the bacon strips with utmost care to keep them from burning, aware that he was watching her intently with his disconcerting gaze.

"Do you have to stare at me like that?" she asked impatiently, not letting herself look up from the skillet.

"Sorry." Cole made the offhanded apology and took a sip of his coffee. "Do you have any plans for today?"

"Let me think," she said, stalling for time. "Um, so far, no. Just working on my spatula skills at the moment."

"You're doing an awesome job. In fact, I could watch you do that all morning," he teased. "But I was thinking maybe you should get out of the kitchen."

She shot him a peeved look. "I'm doing for this you, you know."

"Thanks. Glad it's me and not Bowman."

"Would you stop? He didn't mention coming by." She added a pat of butter to the other skillet she'd set aside to do the eggs, turning on the gas beneath it.

The bacon grease popped, splattering the back of her hand, and she jumped back from the stove with a muffled exclamation of pain. Cole immediately got hold of her arm and practically dragged her to the sink. Turning on the cold tap, he thrust her hand beneath the running water.

"Keep it there," he ordered.

"Watch the bacon," Lacey said, beginning to flinch. She could feel it now.

"I will. You just let that cold water run on that burn for a while," he ordered, moving back to the stove to rescue breakfast. Lacey did as she was told and the stinging pain was gradually reduced to numbness.

"How does it feel?" he asked when she turned off the water to pat her hand dry.

"It's fine." There was a barely discernible red mark where the hot grease had splattered on her hand.

"Aren't you going to ask me why I wanted to know if you had plans?" He broke an egg into the melted butter in the second skillet.

She hesitated. "Why?"

"Want to drive over to the Eastern Shore for the day?" He added another egg to the skillet. "How do you like your eggs cooked?"

"Over easy." Lacey answered his last question first—it was the easiest.

"So . . . what about going to the Eastern Shore?"

"It sounds like fun," she said.

"Good." He grinned at her. "Made the toast yet?"

"Oh—um—no." Lacey reached for the bread.

* * *

An hour later breakfast was over and the dishes washed, and they were on their way to the Eastern Shore of Virginia. As they traversed the seventeen-mile Chesapeake Bay bridge-tunnel, Lacey watched a navy ship some distance away in the Atlantic Ocean to her right. It moved steadily closer to the ship channel leading to Chesapeake Bay on her left.

But Lacey didn't look that way at the warships and merchant vessels more easily viewed in the waters of the bay. The confines of the car had heightened her awareness of Cole, if that was possible.

Without glancing at him, she was conscious of everything about him, from the way his dark brown hair curled near his shirt collar to the strength of his sun-browned hands on the wheel. She seemed to have an inner radar system tuned strictly to his presence.

"Anyplace special you want to see when we get over there?" he asked, his gaze sliding from the road to her for a brief instant.

"No." Lacey shook her head, unable to think of a single place she particularly wanted to visit. She really had been sitting in the office for far too many months, with never a thought of going places.

"Let's drive to Chincoteague," he suggested.

They were approaching the concrete island in the bay where the bridge dipped beneath the water to become the tunnel under the ship channel.

"That's nearly a hundred miles, isn't it?" She frowned, turning to study his strongly defined profile.

"About that far, yeah." The cavernous tunnel swallowed them, a ribbon of lights overhead.

She glanced at her watch. "Do you realize how late it will be when we get back? You have to work tomorrow. You should make it an early night."

There was a wry look on his face, but his gaze never

left the tunnel stretching ahead of them. "Let's stay off the subject of sleep and beds, okay? I suggest we just enjoy the day."

Turning her head to the front, she stared straight ahead at the sunlight beckoning at the tunnel exit, fighting back a flash of anger at his unnecessary comment.

His hand reached out to stroke the back of her neck. His fingers felt the taut muscles and began to massage them gently.

"Relax, Lacey," he said in a coaxing tone. "And stop hugging the car door. I'm not going to bite."

"I'm not so sure," she retorted, already stung by the point of Cupid's arrow.

"You don't have anything to worry about." He smiled. "I promise—no bites. Not even a nibble."

With that, his gaze slid to the exposed curve of her throat, its brushing touch as effective as a caress. Immediately he withdrew his hand and returned it to the steering wheel.

"This afternoon we're just going to be a couple taking a Sunday drive," he stated.

And Lacey felt a twinge of regret that their time together would be nothing more than that, regardless of how sensible it was. Ignoring her longings would be easier if he weren't so attractive. She managed a stiff smile of agreement.

The Cape Charles lighthouse poked into the sky, signaling that the ocean was near. Shortly after, the bridge curved to an end on the jutting finger of land that was Virginia's Eastern Shore.

The modern highway made its way up the length of the unspoiled peninsula. Lacey caught glimpses of the windswept Atlantic coast and the islands scattered out from its beaches.

It was impossible to ignore the charm of the landscape

for long. Its natural beauty cast a spell, the minutes slipping by as fast as the miles.

As they neared the Maryland border, Cole turned off the main highway, crossing the bridge to the island of Chincoteague. They traveled through the small town of the same name and on, across a second bridge to Assateague Island.

Declared a national seashore, the island was the refuge for the wild Chincoteague ponies, believed to be descendants of horses from the wreck of a Spanish galleon more than four hundred years ago. On the island they ran free as their ancestors did, drinking from the freshwater pools and grazing in the nutritious salt marshes. Inbreeding over the years had stunted the horses to pony size, yet the clean-limbed, delicate conformation remained in the descendants.

To keep the herds' numbers at a level the island's food supply could support, there was a roundup every year by the residents of neighboring Chincoteague Island. The sick and injured among the ponies were treated and a certain number of the new foals were sold at auction.

Although there was a bridge to connect the Assateague Island refuge with Chincoteague Island, tradition demanded that the ponies swim the short distance between the two islands. The annual July event drew thousands of visitors to witness it and attend the auction.

There was no one around, though, when Cole and Lacey spied a herd of the small ponies and stopped to watch them. The pinto stallion kept a wary eye on them and they took care not to alarm him. He tolerated their presence at a distance, leaving Lacey and Cole free to enjoy the antics of a cavorting pair of young foals.

All the ruckus was more than the stallion would permit in his domain. With his head low to the ground, he began moving his mares away, nipping at the recalcitrant ones slow to obey his commands.

"They're beautiful!" Lacey breathed when the last of the ponies trotted out of sight ahead of the stallion.

"Are you glad you came?" Cole asked, smiling.

"Of course," she responded naturally, a happy light in her brown eyes.

"So am I," he agreed, and glanced at his watch. "We aren't likely to see any more this late in the afternoon. I don't know about your stomach, but mine says it's been a long time since breakfast. Let's go to Chincoteague and find a place to have dinner before the drive back."

The summer sun was setting as they finally began the trek back to Virginia Beach. Its golden glow made a serene ending to a relaxing afternoon and evening. Sometime during the long ride, Lacey closed her eyes and forgot to open them. The next thing she was aware of was a hand gently nudging her awake.

"We're home, Strawberry," Cole's voice came to her through the mists of sleep.

Lazily raising her lashes, she focused on him, bent a bit to hold her car door open. She smiled at him, unaware of the curious dreamlike quality of her expression.

"Already?" she murmured.

"Yup." His helping hand got her out of the car.

Not fully awake, she took advantage of the support he offered, leaning on him as they walked slowly to the garage entrance to the house. His arm remained around the back of her waist until they reached the top of the stairs and the living room.

"I think I'd better put some coffee on." Lacey yawned, trying to blink away her drowsiness.

"Not for me." Cole moved away from her to the sofa, bending down to pick up his briefcase.

With a feeling of annoyance, she watched him slide

out his laptop and open it, booting it up and waiting. The faint bluish glow radiating from the screen made his thoughtful face seem cold.

"What are you doing?" she asked, frowning.

"Work, what else," he answered without looking her way.

"After all that driving?" She couldn't believe he was serious.

"I have to stay on top of this project. I'm in charge." He reached into the briefcase and took out a folder and note pad, frowning at the spreadsheet on the glowing screen.

Within seconds, Lacey was completely shut out. She stood uncertainly in the center of the room before finally wandering out onto the upper deck.

Leaning against the railing, she experienced a curiously letdown feeling. The night sky was alight with stars that seemed to stretch on as endlessly as the emptiness inside her.

Shivering, she reentered the house. "It's getting chilly out," she commented, but the temperature inside seemed several degrees cooler after Cole's indifferent nod. "Do you have to work?" she demanded with a flash of irritation.

There was a remoteness in the blue gaze that sliced to her. "I don't happen to be on vacation, Lacey," he reminded her.

"I wish I weren't," she declared, suddenly regretting the moment she had met him.

He turned back to his all-absorbing work, muttering, "So do I. Then you wouldn't be here. You'd be in your own apartment where you belong."

The last trace of the enchanted mood of their afternoon together vanished at that instant.

"Oh. I see. That's what you want? For me to move

out?" she asked tightly, a pain squeezing her chest like a constricting band.

Again his cool, glittering blue eyes leveled on her. "I thought I made it clear that was what I wanted all along."

Lacey paled slightly. "I had the impression you'd changed your mind," she retorted.

There was an unfriendly gleam in his gaze. "Because I wanted to make love to you?" he asked. "For God's sake, Lacey, you're a really gorgeous woman. Intelligent. Easy to be with. And passionate. Any man in my situation would want to make love to you, given half a chance."

"I see," Lacey murmured stiffly.

If she'd asked him outright whether or not he had any serious feelings for her, she couldn't have received a more explicit answer. The moves he'd made had been strictly that—moves.

She was available and had been available. She should have been glad that he let things happen instead of rushing her or taking advantage of her vulnerability in some other way. But the ache she held inside was too painful for her to feel grateful for small favors like that.

"Now, if you'll excuse me, I'll get back to work." Cole shuffled his papers noisily, bending over his laptop again.

Aha. She was being dismissed. That rankled. "Go ahead," Lacey urged him. "Don't let me disturb you, whatever you do."

Her sarcasm seemed mostly lost on him. "You disturb me just by being here," he muttered almost beneath his breath, but he stared fixedly into the laptop screen, not glancing her way.

She had the impression that he hadn't meant her to hear the remark, but there was no consolation in that. She wanted to disturb him—emotionally, not just physically.

Turning on her heel, she walked rigidly to her bedroom

and closed the door. Her eyes were hot with tears, but she didn't cry. Instead she walked to the closet and took out her nightclothes.

Lying in her bed, she stared at the ceiling. Her door was shut, but the light in the hallway streamed through the narrow slit at the bottom of the door. From the living room came the whisper of papers moving against each other, and the soft clicking of the laptop keyboard.

Chapter 9

Outwardly the pattern of their days didn't change during the next three, but subtly it had altered.

Cole's alarm still awakened Lacey in the mornings while he slept through its buzz.

They shared orange juice and coffee together, talking with superficial friendliness. But it was a forced effort to maintain the previous week's atmosphere for both of them.

As before, Cole returned late in the evening, eating elsewhere, and spent the remainder of the time engrossed in paperwork or reviewing spreadsheets on his laptop. There were no more physical encounters, though, and no chance contact, because neither of them was leaving anything to chance.

For Lacey, it was like a rocket countdown. Five nights to live through before her cousin Margo returned, then four, then three. Now it was Thursday and the number was down to two.

The agony of being near him was almost over, but she was afraid of what was to come. She found it almost impossible to believe that in the space of one short week a man could mess up her mind and her life the way Cole had done.

"You're a fool and a half," she muttered angrily as she climbed out of her car. He had never asked her to fall in love with him. It was her own dumb fault. Mostly.

"You're talking to yourself, Lacey. That's a bad sign," Mike teased, walking up behind her. "What's on your mind?"

Recovering from her surprise, Lacey shook her head. "Nothing in particular—just life in general."

"And here you are. Hmm. Did I lose a few days somewhere? Is this Monday? I don't think so. But the office awaits, as always. Abandon all hope." He glanced ahead of them at the office building housing the construction company where they both worked.

"You haven't lost any days, Mike," she assured him, attempting a smile.

"You just couldn't stay away, huh?" Mike laughed.

"Something like that," Lacey agreed.

"Kidding aside, what are you doing here? You should still be out soaking up the sun while you have the chance." His hazel eyes began inspecting her closely, noting the way she avoided looking directly at him and the tension behind her carefree expression.

"I drove over to my apartment this morning to pick up the mail and make sure everything was all right there," Lacey explained, striving to seem offhand so he wouldn't guess it was her own company she particularly wanted to avoid. "Since I was in the neighborhood and it was lunchtime, I decided to stop by and have lunch with Maryann."

"I'm afraid you're out of luck." He winked at her. "Maryann took off to visit the dentist again. I'd buy you lunch, but I'm just coming back from the deli myself." He glanced at his wristwatch. "And I have an architect coming in for a conference in about twenty minutes."

"That's okay." Lacey shrugged, turning back to her car. "I should have called Maryann first instead of driving by." She didn't want to prolong the conversation with Mike. "See you Monday if not before, then."

"Don't be late," Mike warned jokingly, waving a goodbye.

In no hurry to return to the beach house, Lacey took her time on the way back. As she passed one of the more lavish resort hotels, she studied it absently. Giving in to an impulse, she left the highway and retraced the route to the hotel.

She was going to treat herself, thinking that this so-called vacation ought to amount to more than a broken heart and useless what-if memories.

Parking her car in the lot, she strolled into the hotel lobby, not giving herself a second chance to consider whether she should spend too much money on a mere lunch. Well, it was her vacation and she wouldn't have another one for a year.

She hesitated near the lounge, trying to decide if the big spree should extend to a cocktail before lunch. Maybe something really frivolous with a tiny umbrella—no. Sweet, silly drinks really snuck up on her. Maybe a glass of chardonnay. No again. The thought of sitting alone at a table for two sipping a glass of white wine was too depressing. She started toward the restaurant entrance.

"Lacey!" a male voice declared, its tone somewhere between surprise and curiosity. "I thought that might be you—nice to see you!"

Him again. Stopping, Lacey turned to stare at the good-looking blond guy coming out of the lounge. Her own surprise was mingled with dismay as she waved, not with joy, at Monica's brother, Vic Hamilton.

"Oh, hi." Her greeting was cool. She hoped he would get the message and not hang around to chat.

"Forgot my name? It's Vic," he said smoothly, and clasped both of her unwilling hands in his. "You look fantastic in that turquoise sundress—and don't you have pajamas in that color?"

A passing couple gawked at them, and Lacey flinched. There was no need for him to remind her of the circumstances of their first meeting, especially in a public place like this. Lacey managed to pull one hand free but he held the other. He'd had a manicure, she noticed. It was definitely possible for a man to be too well-groomed, she thought.

"Do I?" She smiled with artificial politeness.

"Hey, sorry. Me and my big mouth. Anyway, what are you doing here?" His smirk didn't hide the shrewdness in his eyes. "Don't tell me you're meeting Cole."

"No, I'm not." Lacey had to check herself to keep from snapping out the answer. "I just stopped by for lunch."

"Alone?"

"Yes," Lacey answered decisively.

She'd said the wrong thing. Her answer seemed to please him. "I can't let you do that. Eat with me. Come on, we'll have a drink first."

"No, thanks," she refused, trying to discreetly pull her hand free.

"If you're worried about Cole being upset if he finds out we had lunch together, I wouldn't." There was secret amusement in his look, and something knowing. "Let's give the wait staff a break. Two people shouldn't occupy two tables when they can sit together at one."

As if he cared. Lacey pressed her lips together while she tried to think of a way to discourage him.

"If you like, we'll go dutch and you can pay for your own meal," he said.

Getting stuck with him and the bill was not the deal of the century. What was it going to take to convince this blond god of her total lack of interest, Lacey wondered impatiently. Probably no one had ever told him no before and actually meant it.

"I . . ." she began, but the sound of Cole's laughter coming from somewhere to her left cut off her retort.

The rich, throaty chuckle was instantly recognizable. Turning at an angle, she saw him looking rugged in an expensive gray suit. As always at the sight of him, her breath hitched a little. Cole's good looks and blatant masculinity overwhelmed Lacey.

She stood up straight. Someone—not her—was with him, on the receiving end of his flashing smile and virile charm. Lacey forced herself to look at the green-eyed blonde clinging to his arm.

Monica Hamilton laughed up at Cole. Everything about the woman's manner said that he was her exclusive property. And Cole didn't exactly seem to be fighting her off.

"You didn't know Cole was going to be here, did you?" Vic murmured.

Lacey began to tremble. She unconsciously reached out to Vic for support and he obligingly offered the same hand as before.

"No." Her voice was low. "I didn't know."

"I guess you didn't know that he'd be with my sister either," Vic continued.

Not wanting to hear the ring of satisfaction in his voice, Lacey was more aware of the ache in her heart. So much for treating herself to a good time. The universe just was not on her side today, that was all.

"No," she said again, her voice almost inaudible.

Vic wrapped an arm around her shoulder and turned toward the entrance to the lounge. She had the fleeting sensation of deep blue eyes narrowing on her in recognition before she was faced in another direction.

Numbed by the fierce pain, she didn't remember taking the steps that brought her to the dark corner of the lounge. The next thing she was aware of was Vic helping her into a cushioned booth.

He snapped his fingers for the cocktail waitress's attention and called an order, but Lacey didn't hear—or care—what it was. He slid onto the seat beside her. She wasn't thinking of him at all, until he covered her suddenly cold hands with his own. Someone stopped at the booth, then Vic was pressing the rim of a glass against her lips.

"Drink this," he ordered, and tipped the glass a fraction of an inch.

Automatically Lacey parted her lips, coughing and choking as vodka laced with slivered ice burned a path down her throat. Once again she could feel, but she wasn't certain she was grateful for that. Seeing Cole with Monica hanging all over him left her with the feeling that she had been betrayed and used. And worst of all, he'd looked happy.

"Cole didn't mention to you that he's been seeing Monica, did he?"

Panic raced through her at his implication: it wasn't the first time. She gave him a stricken look, then lowered her head. "No."

"Didn't you ever wonder where he was having supper?" Vic chided her.

"No, I . . ." She faltered and stopped. It had never occurred to her to set the record straight that she and Cole were not living together in the intimate sense of the phrase. "I thought he was going to a restaurant somewhere, I guess. Actually, I didn't give it much thought."

"He's spent the last three evenings at our house, having dinner with Monica," he informed her.

"I see," Lacey murmured.

She saw that she'd been deluded to hold on to hope where Cole was concerned. The hand covering hers tightened protectively, squeezing a warning an instant before a tall figure blocked the light—what there was of it. Lacey guessed it was Cole before he spoke, her nerves on edge.

"What are you doing here, Lacey?" His voice was low and tautly controlled.

She looked up at him, her eyes bright with foolish tears. The hard angles of his face were set in expressionless lines, yet she sensed his anger simmering just beneath the surface.

He could think what he liked. And she didn't have to come up with an explanation just to soothe his manly ego.

"What am I doing? What most people do at a place like this," she retorted, her tone brittle. "I'm having a drink before lunch."

"Lacey took pity on me being alone and was kind enough to join me," Vic said, and Lacey didn't deny the lie.

The muscles along Cole's jawline tightened noticeably as he flashed an accusing look at Lacey. Monica appeared at his elbow, eyeing Lacey for a brief second before smiling possessively at Cole.

"They're holding our table," she reminded him huskily.

Distracted, Cole glanced down at her. He hesitated for a fraction of a second, then his gaze pinned Lacey again, sharp and metallic blue.

"Want to join us?" he requested stiffly.

"No," she refused, lowering her gaze to the liquor glass on the table.

Beside her, Vic spoke up. "The lady says no, Cole. And I don't have any reason to change her mind."

"Our table," Monica prodded.

Out of her side vision, Lacey saw Cole abruptly pivot away from the booth and walk away with Monica cooing in his ear.

Lacey wanted to gag. But she felt a certain sense of relief in knowing the truth at last.

"You're in love with him, aren't you?" Vic's sardonic question got to her in the worst way.

Pale and shaken, Lacey knew she couldn't escape the truth, so she nodded a silent admission. There was a strange unreality to the situation, as if none of it was really happening.

"You poor kid." But he sounded more amused than sorry for her. "You thought you had a chance against Monica. If you'd asked me, I could have told you it was inevitable that Cole would end up with her."

"Really?" Tears made her lashes wet. She flicked them away with her finger, refusing to give in to a crying jag. She breathed in deeply, sniffling a little, regaining her self-control.

"Monica's got it all," Vic told her smugly. "Besides, Cole is just the man she needs. He would have been hers two years ago if she hadn't started ordering him around and throwing tantrums when he wouldn't do what she wanted. After that, they were kinda on-again, off-again. You just happened to meet Cole when the off switch got stuck."

"Maybe so," Lacey said tightly, not about to explain now how they'd met.

"I'll be honest with you. I'm totally in favor of the marriage," he went on. "With Cole for a brother-in-law, I know my dad will get off my back. I don't have a head for business and I don't want anything to do with the family holdings."

He slid an arm around her shoulders again. Unthinkingly, Lacey accepted its comfort. "Cole's all business. He never thinks about anything else. Not me. I have a gift for making beautiful women happy. Like you, Lacey."

She stiffened at his words. "If you're the consolation prize for losing Cole, I'm not interested," she declared and removed his arm from around her shoulders. "Okay. Let me out of this booth. This is ridiculous," she snapped. "And I don't want this drink." She shoved it away from her. Vic frowned and picked it up, slurping it down to half in about a second.

Cheapskate. Just looking at him made her shudder.

Vic was more or less oblivious to what she had really said, and went off on another tangent about being irresistible to women. Being with him was only going to remind her that Cole was with Monica. At long last she understood what a fool she'd made of herself by falling in love with Cole. There was no reason to make matters worse.

"What's up? Where are you going?" He appeared incredulous that she was actually rejecting him.

"I'm leaving. Where is my business," she retorted.

"You don't mean that."

"Yes, I do. So if you don't want me to create a scene, you need to move."

He gave her an ugly smile. "You'll be sorry. Once a girl says no to me, she doesn't get a second chance."

"No, Vic. No, no, I don't want you ever," Lacey repeated, enunciating each word.

White with anger, he slid out of the booth but not before completely finishing the glass of iced vodka. "Okay, have it your way. You're nothing special, if you really want to know the truth," he jeered. "I don't know why I bothered coming on to you."

His spiteful words bounced off her, not leaving any marks, as she swept past him into the lobby. When she stepped outside into the sun, the tears on her lashes streamed down her cheeks.

Once she was in her car, instinct took over, making all the right turns to take her to the beach house. She drove the beginning of the last two miles in a sea of tears that made the road blurry. Lacey stopped, pulled over, and scrubbed fiercely at her eyes. She wasn't going to end up in a ditch because she couldn't figure men out and couldn't stop crying. On a scale of one to ten, a jerk like Vic rated a minus-two and Cole, a nine point five, but they were both trouble as far as she was concerned. When she was calmer, she drove on, singing loudly to keep herself from sobbing.

Bolting into the house, she stumbled up the stairs to sink into the nearest chair, thinking that the décor matched her mood: blue, more blue, endlessly blue. She was sick of it. And she hated being sandbagged by despair and its best friend, self-pity.

Outside a car roared into the driveway, brakes squealing, coming to a halt, by her guess, right in front of the garage door. Obviously it was Cole. She'd gotten so used to him she recognized the sound of his engine. How pathetic. The reverberation of a car door being slammed echoed into the house.

Something told Lacey she'd better bolster her courage. She quickly wiped away fresh tears and was blowing her nose as he slammed more doors on his way in, climbing the stairs two at a time.

He was angry. Big deal. Lacey was beyond being intimidated by his anger; he'd hurt her too much for that. She met his stormy gaze without flinching.

"It's a little early for you to get here, isn't it?" she asked.

"You know damn well why I did," he growled. His hands clenched. "I want to know what you were doing at that hotel with Hamilton."

Lacey tilted her chin defiantly, pain hammering at her throat. "None of your business."

If she had any doubts about saying something like that to him, they faded into nothing when the memory of seeing him with Monica, billing and cooing, hit her again. She started to pivot away from him, but he caught her wrist.

"You can do better than that. Lie to me. Have some fun." His voice was low and hurt.

She whirled around and he was forced to let her go. "I certainly didn't go because I thought you were going to be there!" Lacey choked out the answer, fighting the tears that were once again stinging her eyes.

"But you arranged to meet Vic, am I right?"

"Yes, I met him there. Is that what you wanted to hear?" she cried in challenge.

With fire still raging in his eyes, he looked away in angry exasperation. He let his gaze slice back to her, analyzing her silently. She hated it.

"I knew it was only a matter of time before Vic tried something, but I thought you were smart enough to deal with him," he said with contempt. "I guess the combination of money and looks works for you. How many other times have you met him before today?" He didn't wait for a reply and she hardly felt he was entitled to one for asking something that stupid.

"What do you care?" Lacey said anyway, massaging her wrist where he'd gripped it. "I've never asked you how many times you've seen Monica!"

"Monica has nothing to do with this, so just leave her out of it!" he snapped.

"Gladly!"

Lacey stalked out of the living room onto the deck. Her fingers clutched the railing, her nails digging into the smooth painted surface. Waves of emotional pain racked her, leaving her shaken.

She was angry with herself because she was letting Cole get to her even more than before. The damage he'd already done was beyond repair. She used her simmering anger as a shield against him when he followed her outside.

"Lacey, I want you to stay away from Vic Hamilton." His own anger seemed held in check—for the moment. She'd bet anything the slightest provocation would set him off.

"Don't give me orders," Lacey retorted in a low, fierce voice. His overbearing attitude really grated on her. "You don't have the right to tell me who I can see!"

Sure enough, he snapped. He grabbed her shoulders like he was going to shake her—and then let her go, not gently. "Someone ought to shake some sense into you!"

"Try. Just try." Her laugh was brittle, her heightened senses in worse shape than before.

"No. But I wish you'd listen." He gritted his teeth. "Just stay away from him."

Lacey was infuriated all over again. "I don't have to listen to you!" she cried, her voice ringing with the pulsing hurt inside, her nerves raw. "You don't have any right to tell me what to do or not to do! I don't tell you who you can have for friends and you're not going to tell me!"

His smoldering gaze flashed past her for an instant. "You don't have to shout, Lacey," he said in a low, sharp tone.

Automatically she glanced over her shoulder to see what or who had distracted him. An older woman wearing a sun hat was on the beach near the tideline. Lacey recognized her instantly. Mrs. Carlyle, of course. She was searching the beach for seashells, and she was staring toward the house. Their raised voices had carried to her.

"I'll shout if I want to." But Lacey did lower the volume a few bars. "And if you don't like it, you can leave!"

"We've been through that before," Cole retorted.

"Yes, we have." Her chin quivered traitorously. "And you'll be happy to hear that you finally won that argument. I'm leaving!"

Cole frowned, his gaze narrowing at her announcement. Lacey didn't wait to hear his response, but darted past him into the house, not slowing until she reached her bedroom. The decision had been made on impulse but she knew it was the only sane thing to do.

Gulping back sobs, she dragged her suitcases and duffel from the closet and tossed them on the bed with such force that the suitcases popped open. She gathered up armfuls of clothes and threw them in with careless fury, jamming it all together with no thought to organizing any of the damned stuff. She hesitated for a split second when Cole appeared in the doorway before continuing her frenzied attempt to pack.

His mouth was a controlled line, but there was regret flickering in the hard blue steel of his gaze. "Lacey, I—"

"There's nothing left to say," she interrupted him, wishing she wasn't so aware of the way his tall, muscular body filled the door frame. "I have three full days of vacation left and I'm not going to let you ruin those too."

Impatiently he burst out, "I don't want to! Lacey, I'm not trying to ruin anything for you. I—"

"You're doing a first-rate job for someone who isn't trying!" She slammed a handful of underwear into one of the bags, her voice ragged with emotion.

"You don't understand," Cole muttered.

"Isn't it time you were going back to your office?"

challenged Lacey, scooping cosmetics from the dresser and dumping them into their small case.

"Yes, it is, but first—"

She turned on him roundly. "I'm leaving, got that? The house is yours! Isn't that what you want?"

His expression hardened. "Yes," he snapped after a second's hesitation. "That's exactly what I want!"

In the next instant the doorway was empty. Heavy, angry strides took him away down the hall. Lacey resumed her packing, moving even faster, faltering only when she heard the door slam below.

An hour and a half later, she was lugging the last of her belongings into her own apartment. Setting the duffel and suitcases on the floor, she collapsed into one of the chairs, burying her face in her hands.

She didn't cry. There didn't seem to be any tears left inside her. She was just a big empty ache. Something vital had been torn out of her and she had a feeling she wasn't ever going to get it back.

The phone rang. It seemed like an eternity since she'd heard the sound. She stared at it blankly for several rings before pushing herself out of the chair to answer it.

"Hello," she said in a tired and dispirited voice.

"Lacey?"

It was Cole. The sound of his voice seemed to slash at her heart like a knife.

"How did you get this number?"

"That doesn't matter—"

Lacey hung up on him to stop the piercing hurt but within a minute it was ringing again. She'd made up her mind not to answer it when her hand picked up the receiver of its own volition and carried it to her ear.

"Don't hang up, Lacey." The remnants of his temper

were evident in his irritated tone. "I'm at my office, so I don't have time to argue. We're going to get together tonight so we can talk this thing out. I'll be free around eight thirty."

That would be . . . after he'd had dinner with Monica, Lacey realized. "Leave me alone!" she cried angrily. "Get out of my life and stay out of it! I don't want to see or hear from you again—ever!"

She slammed the receiver down, breaking the connection, but Cole was as stubborn as she was. He would call back. Lacey picked up the phone again, hesitated, then dialed in a number.

When the call was answered, she said, "Jane? This is Lacey. May I speak to Maryann?"

"Sure," was the reply. "How's your vacation?"

"Fine," Lacey fibbed. "I'm having a great time. I'll bring you back some sand in a bottle for a minibeach."

"Thanks," Jane sighed. "Put a sexy man in the bottle too. I could use some fun. Hold, please."

Lacey heard the clicks while the call went through. "Hello, Maryann."

"Hi, Lacey," was the cheerful response. "Mike told me you stopped by for lunch. I wish I'd known you were coming—it would have given me a perfect excuse to cancel my dentist's appointment."

"Nothing doing. You take care of those teeth," Lacey said firmly.

"Yes, Mom," Maryann teased. "What's up? How are you enjoying the sun and the sand and the surf?"

"Ah, that's what I'm calling about," she began hesitantly. "I'm not at the beach house. I moved out."

"Huh? What happened?" Maryann asked with instant concern.

"It's a long story." Her friend already knew part of it

from Lacey's Friday night visit. "I was wondering if I could sleep on your couch for a few nights."

"Of course," was the puzzled reply, "but I thought you were going to Richmond to visit your parents this weekend, after Margo came back."

"I was, but I've changed my mind."

The mere thought of her parents patiently listening to her explanation of everything that had happened to her was heartbreaking, and Lacey knew she would never be able to keep it from them. They were too close. And she couldn't stay in her apartment. Cole would keep calling her land line and her cell, and he was very likely to come over. Had Mike given out her contact info? He was going to get chewed out for it, big time, if he had. No doubt he thought Cole was a good guy because he'd been so concerned for her the night she took off in a fury.

"What happened, Lacey? Did—"

"I'll tell you all about it tonight," she promised. "What time do you get off work?"

"I can leave by five, I'm caught up. But I have to stop at the bank and the store." Maryann paused. "Why don't you come by the office and I'll give you the key to my apartment? That way you won't have to wait for me."

"Thanks." Lacey swallowed, her throat suddenly constricting.

"Oh, I have a motive," her friend laughed. "If I have to wait until tonight to find out what happened, I'll go crazy. When you stop by, you can give me an outline, okay? Details later."

"All right."

Chapter 10

Returning to work on Monday morning, Lacey hoped her job would take her mind off the dead ache in her heart. So far that hope hadn't shown much promise. She had difficulty concentrating. Composing a standard business letter was proving to be an impossible task, even with the spell-check function pointing out a constant stream of mistakes. Her fingers kept on hitting the wrong keys, and spell-check didn't catch everything.

"You look as if you could use some coffee. Want me to pour you a cup?" Mike offered, pausing beside her desk to reach for her coffee mug.

"Please," Lacey sighed, then peered into her computer screen at an error underlined in wiggly red.

Mike went out to the coffee station and returned with the whole pot. He filled her cup as well as his own and set it back on her desk. "It's only ten o'clock in the morning and you look wiped out. I think that's a symptom of just-back-from-vacation-itis," he teased as his assessing gaze swept over her.

"Could be catching," she said. "Are you going to put that pot back?"

He looked at the coffeepot as if he hadn't realized he was still holding it and smiled sheepishly. "Yes."

She heard him come back in as she clicked Print on the pull-down menu and reached for a sheaf of paper the printer had produced. "Here are the letters you wanted to go out this morning."

"One of these days I'll write my own," he said not quite seriously. "It's not like I don't have a computer, right?"

"Right," Lacey replied absently. She really didn't care at the moment. He gathered up the sheaf of letters and went to the connecting door to his private office, pausing in the doorway. "It's good to have you back, Lacey."

"Thanks." A weary smile accompanied her reply, etched with strain.

As he closed the door behind him, she rested her elbows on the desk top. Her shoulders slumped as if the weight of pretending she was her normal self had become too much to maintain when no one was around to see.

With the tips of her fingers, she rubbed the throbbing pressure point between her eyebrows. She blinked at the tears that unexpectedly sprang into her eyes.

The door to the main office area opened and she straightened, suddenly conscious of her poor posture. The smile of polite greeting she forced her lips to form vanished when Cole walked into the office.

He looked haggard and worn, but there was a resolutely unyielding set to his jaw. It seemed to match the determined glitter in his indigo blue eyes.

Recovering from her initial shock, Lacey reached for the phone, ringing the interoffice line to Mike. "Cole Whitfield is here to see you, Mike," she said the second he answered her buzz.

"What?" His stunned reaction made it clear that he hadn't expected Cole.

Lacey's pulse skyrocketed in alarm but she lowered her voice. "Do you want me to—"

Cole reached over her desk and pushed the button to end the connection. "I'm not here to see Bowman," he stated. "It's you I want to talk to, Lacey."

Hastily she replaced the receiver and gathered the miscellaneous papers and folders from the filing basket. She rose from her chair and went over to the filing cabinets, wanting distance between herself and Cole.

"Did Margo and Bob get back safely Sunday night?" She tried to make the question sound nonchalant, faking indifference to his presence as she pulled open a file drawer.

Cole was right behind her to push the drawer shut. Her heart began leaping like a jumping bean. A raw, aching nervousness assailed her.

"As a matter of fact, they did," he said tersely. "But that's not why I'm here and you know it."

The connecting door opened and Mike came out, shooting a bewildered frown Cole's way. "Sorry, Cole. There seems to be some confusion. I guess Lacey's replacement forgot to leave a message that you were coming this morning. What was it you wanted to talk to me about?"

Cole flashed an impatient look at him, annoyed by the interruption. "It isn't you I'm here to see," he repeated. "I want a few words with Lacey, if you don't mind."

The latter phrase was barely polite. Lacey was sure Cole would stay whether or not Mike gave permission.

"We have nothing to discuss," she told him stiffly, and brushed past him to return to her desk.

"That's where you're wrong," Cole said. "We have a great deal to discuss."

"Lacey, that's up to you." Mike gave Cole a warning look, then glanced her way.

"I'm fine, Mike," she reassured him. "This won't take long."

"I'm right here if you need me," Mike muttered and retreated behind his office door.

Lacey turned to call him back and came face to face with Cole. All her senses were heightened by his closeness; she was quivering in reaction to his forceful presence.

"Why don't you go away and leave me alone?" she demanded hoarsely. "Can't you see I'm working?"

"Yes. And I apologize for not waiting."

"How about for ambushing me at the office, where I have to be polite to you? Do I get an apology for that?"

"That too. I really am sorry. I couldn't," Cole informed her. "You know I wanted to speak to you. I've been trying all weekend to reach you, but you've been hiding somewhere."

"I wasn't hiding!" she lied, and angrily shoved the rest of the papers back into the filing basket.

"Oh?" He raised one dark brow in skepticism. "What do you call it?"

"Enjoying what remained of my vacation," Lacey retorted, and started to walk away from him again.

His hand gripped the soft flesh of her upper arm to stop her. "Will you stand still?" he demanded in an exasperated breath.

His touch seemed to burn through her and Lacey reacted with surprising violence, trying to wrench her arm free. Cole merely tightened his hold.

"Let me go," she hissed, pathetically vulnerable to the sensation of his touch.

Desperate, she grabbed for the first item on her desk that could be used as a weapon. It turned out to be a stapler. She raised it to strike him, but Cole captured her wrist before she could even begin the swing.

"This is where I came in, isn't it?" The grim line of his

mouth twisted wryly as she was pulled close by her struggles. "Only the other time you were trying to bash my head in with a poker."

"I hate you, Cole Whitfield!" Her voice was breaking. "You are the rudest, most arrogant—"

"You said something like that before, too." He pried the stapler out of her fingers and put it back on the desk. "Now, do you think we can sit down and talk this out like two civilized human beings?"

Averting her head from the tantalizing nearness of his sensual mouth, she nodded reluctantly. "Yes."

"Sit down." Cole more or less pushed her into her chair and drew up a second for himself opposite her.

"I still don't see that we have anything to talk about," she insisted stubbornly, her pulse behaving quite as erratically as it had seconds ago in his arms.

"For starters"—his direct blue eyes studied her closely—"why didn't you tell me that you didn't go to the hotel to meet Vic Hamilton?"

"You weren't in any mood to listen to me and I didn't see why I should explain." After that defensive answer, she hesitated and asked, "How did you find out?"

"From Vic, after a little prompting," Cole said with a half smile. "Luckily for him, he was too concerned about having his handsome face messed up, so it took only a few threats. As angry as I was, I would have gotten the truth out of him."

"It still wasn't any of your business," Lacey muttered, looking away. She refused to read anything into his overly personal involvement in her life.

"Wasn't it?" he asked quietly, his low voice rolling over her skin.

The interoffice line buzzed and she reached for the phone, grateful for the interruption. But Cole took the receiver out of her hand. "Hold all calls," he ordered. "And don't put any more through." He hung up.

"Hey, you can't do that," Lacey protested in astonishment.

"I just did," he countered with a laughing gleam in his eye.

"You know what I mean," she retorted impatiently.

"But do you know what I mean?" His voice was wistfully soft and enigmatic.

Its tug on her heartstrings was more than she could bear. Agitatedly she rose from her chair, her hands clasped in front of her.

"There isn't any point to this conversation," she insisted. "Everything has been said. Our little interlude, affair, whatever you want to call it, is over. You're free to go your own way and I'll go mine."

"Is that the way you want it?" Cole sounded skeptical.

Lacey knew she had to convince him somehow that it was what she wanted, even though she knew with all her heart that it wasn't.

"Yes, it is," she said. "So I don't see what there is for us to discuss."

In a fluid move, Cole was behind her, his hands settling lightly on her shoulders to get her to face him. Lacey could not find the strength to resist such a gentle touch.

"The point to this conversation is that I miss you," he said quietly. He ran his gaze over her face and her breath caught at the fires smoldering in his eyes. "It's been pure and simple misery since you left. You're not there in the mornings anymore to wake me up when I sleep through the alarm. No coffee, no orange juice made. I never minded coming home to an empty house before, but I do now after having you there to greet me. And in the evenings I can't get any work done, because you aren't there."

"You make me sound as if I've become a habit." The painful lump in her throat made it difficult to speak.

"A very enjoyable habit I don't want to give up," Cole responded, stroking a hand over her cheek into the silken brown of her hair.

"What are you suggesting, Cole?" Tears misted her eyes when she met his gaze, her doubt stealing pleasure from his words. "That we go back to living together, throwing out the ground rules?"

"And if I said yes, what would you say?" That glowing look in his eyes was tugging at her heart.

Lacey struggled with her pride. "I would say thanks, but no thanks. I'm not interesting in taking on a lover at the moment." Just for a second, she weakened to ask, "That is what you're suggesting, isn't it?"

"Not quite." His slow smile was disarming. "But love has everything to do with it. I want to marry you, Lacey. I want you to be my wife."

"Oh!" The tiny word escaped in an indrawn breath of surprise as she melted slightly against him. "Are you serious? What about Monica?"

"Monica?" A curious frown creased his forehead. "That's over."

"I don't think so." She was confused and uncertain about the conclusion she'd previously drawn. "You had dinner with her all last week, didn't you?"

"At her parents' home, yes, and she was at the table, but it was her father I was meeting, not Monica," Cole explained with amusement. "Who told you I was there? Vic, right?"

"Yes." Lacey sighed when his arm tightened around her waist. "He said that ever since you broke your engagement with Monica, you went on seeing her."

"And you believed him."

"Well, yes. You were there at the hotel with her, having

lunch. He said your relationship with her had been an on-again, off-again kind of thing, and that I met you during one of the off-again times. It seemed logical," Lacey said, trying to defend her mistake.

"I should have known he would make trouble," Cole concluded, bending his head to brush his mouth over the warmth of her skin, teasingly near her lips. Her lashes fluttered in tempo with her heart. "I'm doing business with Carter Hamilton, her father. That's the only reason I was there."

Her hands slipped nearer to the collar of his shirt. "I didn't know," she whispered. "I thought—at the hotel, you looked so happy with her. Not like the other time when you were—"

"Really rude."

Cole was honest, she'd give him that. "Well, yes. Strutting around in that little towel and acting like we'd just rolled out of bed."

"That Sunday? Monica arrived uninvited and I never could stand her brother."

Lacey silently echoed that sentiment.

"I saw no reason to be courteous to people who weren't welcome in my own house. And if you got the impression that I was happy to be with her at the hotel, I'm a better actor than I realized. No matter what it looked like, I was being polite to the daughter of a business associate. She could have been a dog, and I would have been polite."

"Monica's beautiful," Lacey protested.

"That, my love, is in the eye of the beholder. Now when are you going to stop talking so I can kiss you?"

"Now."

Her hands slid around his neck as she raised herself on tiptoes to meet his descending mouth. Joy spilled over, lighting every corner of her world.

The taste of his mouth possessively covering hers was like a sweet wine that went to her head, and Lacey felt drunk with the bliss of love returned. When the kiss ended on a reluctant note, she rested her head on his shoulder, deliriously happy in a quiet kind of way.

"You haven't said you'll marry me yet." His voice was a husky tremor.

"I'm not going to," she replied with surprise. Tipping her head back, she smiled at his soberly rapt expression. "I hardly know you."

"Want a crash course?"

She had to laugh. "I think I just had one. That was an amazing two weeks."

He did the math in his head. "Two weeks less three days is eleven days. Let's try for a lifetime. I know what I want, Lacey."

"So do I. Let's try acting like normal people and take our time."

He gave her a warm hug, satisfied for the moment with an approximation of yes. "When we're done with that, do you have any objections to a midnight elopement?"

"You could probably talk me into a midnight anything." She lifted a hand to let her fingertips trace the forceful line of his jaw. "Why did you let me leave last Thursday? You acted as if you were glad to see me go."

"I was." He caught her hand, lightly kissing the tips of her fingers. "It was sheer torture lying in bed at night with you in the next room. If you'd stayed those last two nights, I knew I would throw those stupid ground rules out the window. When you decided to leave, I never expected you to disappear. It turned out to be worse not knowing where you were or who you were with."

"I stayed at a girlfriend's," Lacey answered his unspoken question.

"While I went quietly out of my mind," Cole said wryly.

"I'm sorry," she whispered.

"You should be," he declared with mock gruffness.

"I wasn't having an easy time of it, either, this weekend," Lacey reminded him. "I kept imagining you with Monica and wondering when I would read about your engagement online or in the newspapers."

"There's never been any reason for you to be jealous of Monica," Cole assured her.

"I know that . . . now." But she hoped she would never have to live through another weekend like that again.

The remembered pain must have shown in her eyes, because Cole's dark gaze suddenly became very intense. "Never forget that I love you, Lacey." He kissed her hard and fiercely, as if to drive out the wrong memory so there would only be room for his love.

The interoffice door opened and Mike walked through, stopping at the sight of the embracing pair. "Sorry. It was so quiet out here I thought you'd gone, Whitfield." He seemed to be on the verge of retreat.

"There's no need to leave, Mike," said Cole. "Lacey and I were just going."

"Where?" Mike frowned and Lacey stared at Cole, baffled.

"I'll send someone over to replace her in half an hour," Cole continued. "She's going to have a lot to do for the next few months. She has to get to know me. It could take up to a year. And after we're married—I'm not so sure I want her to be anyone's assistant but mine. But that's up to her."

"But—" Lacey didn't know what protest she could make since she didn't really object to Cole's plan.

"In the meantime," Cole interrupted, "there's something I want to show her."

She forgot all about Mike and how he would get along without her.

"What?" Her curiosity was aroused.

"Get your purse and let's go." He smiled mysteriously.

"Congratulations," Mike offered as Cole hurried Lacey out the door.

As Cole was helping her into his car, Lacey repeated her question. "What are you going to show me?"

"You'll see," was all he would say.

"Give me a hint at least," she persisted.

But his only response was an enigmatic smile as he pulled out of the parking lot into the street.

In a few minutes, she realized they were driving toward Virginia Beach, crossing the Chesapeake Bay bridge-tunnel into Norfolk. When they turned down on a side road she recognized, she became thoroughly confused. It led to her cousin Margo's place.

"Why are we going to the beach house?" She frowned.

Cole reached for her hand and held it warmly in his. "Patience."

At the house, he parked the car in the driveway and turned to face her, smiling. "Would the future Mrs. Whitfield like to see her new home?"

"What?" She gave him an incredulous look and he chuckled softly.

"When Margo and Bob came back from their cruise, he told me they were moving to Florida near his parents as soon as they could make all the arrangements here." He reached in his pocket and handed her a key. "So I bought the house for us. After all the frustrating nights I'd spent here with you, it was time to turn things around."

"You've bought it?" Lacey stared at the key in the palm of her hand, not sure she had really understood him.

"You did like the house, didn't you?" Cole was watching her carefully, a trace of uncertainty in his voice.

"I love the house!" she declared. "I just can't believe you did that so soon—"

"I'm for sooner. I don't believe in later, honey."

A sound, somewhere between a laugh and a cry, came from her throat as she threw her arms around his neck, happiness and love bubbling from her heart. Cole took away the need to express what she was feeling with words. Deeds were much more enjoyable.

Her arms were locked around Cole's neck when he finally lifted his mouth from her lips. "Would it be against the rules to carry my bride-to-be over the threshold right now?"

"Go right ahead," Lacey said, laughing. "You've already carried me into your bedroom."

"So I have." He grinned and swept her up into the cradle of his arms.

The key to the front door was still clutched in her fingers. Lacey was positive Cole was going to drop her before she could twist around and get it into the lock to open the door. Laughing himself, he carried her into the house and up the stairs, kissing her sensually as he set her on her feet. Lacey glanced around, catching back the sob in her throat.

"What's the matter?" Cole frowned curiously.

"I'm afraid this is all a dream and I'm going to wake up," she murmured. He pinched her arm. "Ouch!"

"It isn't a dream. I'm still here and you still have the key to our house in your hand," he told her, his eyes crinkling at the corners.

"I can't believe it," Lacey insisted with a shake of her head, adding a quick, "but don't pinch me again. That hurt."

"Done deal. Sorry." He laughed. "Now, when we leave here, we'll drive to Richmond. Your parents might like to meet me before I marry their daughter."

"Holy cow!" The truth of his words hit her all at once. "My parents have never even heard of you. I haven't called or written since I met you. What will they think?"

"They'll think I swept you off your feet. It's allowed. We're in love."

She laughed. "Just wait until I tell Maryann."

"Who is Maryann?"

"My friend. My very best friend." Lacey made the definition a little more emphatic.

"The same one you stayed with on the weekend?" Cole asked.

"That's right."

"I suppose she's the one you'll run to whenever we have an argument."

"More than likely," Lacey retorted.

"Please provide her address and phone number so I know where to send roses before I come crawling on my hands and knees to beg your forgiveness the next time I work late," he teased.

"Do you think there will be a next time?" She tipped her head to the side, finding it difficult to imagine that she could ever get that angry with him again.

"Probably," Cole sighed. "I'm ambitious and so are you and we're both pretty stubborn."

"But you're more stubborn than I am," Lacey reminded him.

"You see?" He tweaked the tip of her nose. "You're already trying to start an argument."

"Seems to me that a smart guy like you might be able to figure out how to shut me up." Her brown eyes were bright with silent invitation.

"I'll give it my best shot," he declared before seeking her lips.

Cole waded out of the water, a bronzed sea god emerging from the ocean, and love tingled over Lacey's skin at the sight of him striding toward her, the flashing white of his smile lighting her life.

An interlocking diamond solitaire ring and gold wedding band sparkled on the fourth finger of her left hand, beautiful proof that she really was his wife. Yet she still fought the sensation of being in a dream. Every time she looked at Cole, touched him, she fell in love all over again.

Reaching her side, he dropped to his knees on the sand, droplets of salt water clinging to him. For a minute he simply studied her, stretched on the sand in her metallic blue-gray swimsuit.

Instantly every nerve was alert, her senses quivering at the obvious passion in his look. He reached for her hand, pulling her into a sitting position, then kissing her with familiar ease.

"Happy?" he murmured, raking his fingers through her hair and cupping the back of her head in his hand.

"Heavenly happy, if there is such a thing," Lacey answered softly, a delicious warmth spreading through her.

"Even though we have to set the alarm to get up in the morning?"

"Yes. Are you dreading breaking in your new assistant?" she teased.

"I don't know." The creases along the side of his mouth deepened in a very sexy way. "I've certainly enjoyed breaking in my new wife these past few days."

"Have you?" Her lips parted, inviting his kiss.

His dark blue gaze flicked to them for a tantalizing second, a fire smoldering to life in his eyes. Then he was straightening, pulling her to her feet along with him. The kiss he gave her held a promise of more to come behind the closed doors of their beach house.

When he turned toward the house, his arm curved around Lacey's waist to tuck her close to his side. A woman was walking to their right, intent upon the sand at her feet. The old-fashioned sun hat on her head instantly identified her to Cole and Lacey. He stopped.

"Hello, Mrs. Carlyle," he greeted her.

The woman glanced up, a little startled. "Well, hello." Her gaze took in their affectionate closeness. "I see you two made up after your spat." Despite the friendliness in her remark and her smile, there was a very faint shadow of lingering disapproval in her expression.

"We did," Cole admitted, adding with a dancing light in his eye, "and I took your advice too." He held up Lacey's left hand, showing off the gold band encircling her ring finger. "I made an honest woman out of her."

Immediately Mrs. Carlyle's smile turned into a radiant beam. "I'm delighted for both of you, really I am. Congratulations—I wish you a lifetime of happiness."

"Oh, we're just getting started." Cole smiled down at Lacey's upturned face. "And it's going great. Because I honestly love her."

"And I love you," Lacey murmured.

"That's how it should be," said Mrs. Carlyle kindly.

They waved goodbye to her and walked down the beach hand in hand, together at last.

THE WIDOW AND THE WASTREL

Chapter 1

Elizabeth Carrel stepped through the door of her home, a tennis racket tucked under her arm. It was a scorching August day—even the doorknob felt hot in her hand. The muggy warmth and her exertion combined to leave her feeling drained and exhausted as she leaned against the hardwood door for just a moment.

"Elizabeth, is that you?" The mature, feminine voice held an authoritative ring.

Pushing thick, raven black hair away from her face, Elizabeth straightened away from the door, her sneakers carrying her into the brick-tiled foyer where it was blessedly cooler.

"Yes, Rebecca," she answered, not bothering to glance into the priceless antique mirror hanging on one wall.

At the archway into the living room, she paused, her green eyes gazing at the sophisticated woman who was perched on a sofa. Rebecca barely dented the cushions. Her perfectly styled silver-gray hair gleamed from beneath a blue summer hat, chosen to complement an opaque flowered dress of paler blue, impeccably tailored to show off her slenderness.

The outfit was chic but subtle, expensive yet restrained.

Elizabeth noted the finishing touches—a sapphire and amethyst brooch, bone handbag and shoes—and sighed inwardly. Her mother-in-law was perfect as usual. Elizabeth, a single mom who kept busy and tended to look frazzled a lot of the time, wasn't.

And she had come back from the courts five minutes late.

"I thought you would have left for lunch by now," Elizabeth said.

"I would have," Rebecca Carrel replied. The melodic smoothness of her tone held a note of censure. "But I sent your daughter to her room an hour ago to get ready for her piano lesson. She hasn't come down yet. I have no idea what's keeping her."

Elizabeth smiled wanly at her mother-in-law. "I'll go see."

The stairway leading to the upper floor of the old house was in a hallway off the foyer. Her sneakers were nearly silent on the hardwood steps, the patina of many years adding to their high polish. At the door to her daughter's room, Elizabeth paused and knocked once.

The Carrel mansion seemed to demand good manners, as if the formal atmosphere of the house was emanating from the walls. And if those walls could talk, they would say *this is how we do things here.* In a voice like her mother-in-law's, of course. The thought brought a smile to her lips as she waited.

Rebecca was a staunch believer in tradition and chose to keep on living in a house where the major innovation had been embroidered bell pulls—and those had been installed more than a century ago. Her mother-in-law regarded newer inventions, like cell phones and computers, as a menace to personal sanity and human civilization, and wrote all her correspondence by hand on engraved stationery and didn't approve of e-mails. Elizabeth kept her laptop out of sight and didn't use it all that often, and the same went for Amy's hot-pink, stickered-up model, which she was allowed to use for homework and not much more.

After a grumbling acknowledgment from inside the room, Elizabeth entered.

There was an understanding light in her eyes as she looked at the child staring out of the window. She prepared herself to do battle with her rebellious daughter.

"Hello, Amy."

A head of curling brunette hair turned to her, brown eyes wide with indignation. "Mom, do I have to have my lesson today? Can't I miss it just once? If I was sick, you wouldn't make me go."

The impulse to agree was there, but Elizabeth squelched it. She walked farther into the room. Her daughter was contrary enough without encouragement.

"No. I think you'd better have your lesson. There will be other days when you'll have to cancel because you're sick or there's something special going on."

"When?" Amy wanted to know.

"Sooner or later. Things happen. In the meantime, your grandmother's waiting for you downstairs."

"I know." The admission was made through gritted teeth. "I just hate these lessons! Mrs. Banks keeps making me play the same thing over and over."

"And what is that again?" Elizabeth asked absently.

"'Swans on the Lake.'" Amy faked the fingering in midair. "Dum-dum-de-*dum*-dum, de-*dum*-dum—it's so boring! And that fan she has keeps making clinkety noises and the room is so hot."

"I thought you told me that you liked playing the piano," Elizabeth said gently, a smile held in check at the vehemence in her daughter's voice.

"I do, but I don't like lessons and practicing those stupid scales!"

"If you want to get better at it, you have to have both."

"Oh, Mom!" Amy sighed.

A sigh usually meant Amy had given in. This time Elizabeth didn't hold back her smile, but let the warmth of her love show through as she tilted up the girl's downcast chin.

"You'd better find your music books and hurry downstairs, or your grandmother will be late for that fancy lunch she got all dressed up for," she said lightly. "You know how impatient she can be."

"Ohh-kay. The sooner I go, the sooner I can leave." Amy sighed again, pretending adult resignation.

"Gee, you're enthusiastic!" Elizabeth laughed softly and pressed a quick kiss on her daughter's forehead, then watched her gather up everything she needed.

She didn't follow Amy down the stairs, but remained at the top of the landing near the door to her own room, staring after the girl running down to her grandmother. She was a beautiful child who would be an even more beautiful young woman someday. Elizabeth could only marvel that this exquisite little human being was her flesh and blood.

When she sighed and went into her room, the photograph on the dressing table reminded her that she hadn't created Amy all on her own. But the man in the picture was like a stranger to her. They'd been married only a short time when he was killed in a car crash. At the time, she hadn't even known she was pregnant with Amy. It was difficult to remember that she'd ever worn a wedding ring. That had been discreetly taken off and tucked away years ago,

Of course, she had been Jeremy Carrel's wife or she wouldn't be living in his family's house today. And Amy resembled her father with her dark brown hair and eyes, but her personality was nothing like his. Ditto her attitude.

Jeremy, though he wasn't a mama's boy, had accepted the role his family played in the community, society, business, and leadership. When Elizabeth had married him, he'd been marking time, preparing for the day when he would take control of the Carrel law firm and its holdings from his father. Never once did he chafe at the invisible bonds of social propriety the way Amy seemed born to do. He never did anything extreme.

Turning away from the photograph, Elizabeth saw her full-length reflection in the antique cheval mirror in the corner of her room. Her tennis whites showed off slender, athletic legs and slim but rounded hips that curved into a trim waist. The line curved back out higher up around her breasts. She didn't need the mirror to tell her that she was a beautiful woman and hardly looked old enough to have a nine-year-old child.

Vanity satisfied, Elizabeth got busy stripping off her tennis clothes, putting them in the hamper, something her stubborn daughter never did unless specifically asked. Maybe, she thought, putting a positive spin on it, Amy's stubbornness did come from her father's unshakable determination. And her own as well. She simply hadn't been able to guide Amy to find more constructive outlets, and the minor blowups seemed to have increased in the last year. Elizabeth wondered if the lack of male relatives in her daughter's life was the cause.

Amy's grandfather, Jeremy's father, had been taken from them quite suddenly by a heart attack almost two years ago. But he wasn't the demonstrative type and had never spent much time with Amy even though they lived in the same house. As a result, Amy showed him more respect than affection. It was better than nothing and she couldn't tell Amy what to feel. Sometimes Elizabeth found it hard to know what her daughter was thinking.

Hesitating in front of the open door of her closet, she

shrugged away the thought of dressing and reached instead for a cotton gauze caftan. Its loose-fitting folds would be much more comfortable on this hot, stickily humid day.

Downstairs again, Elizabeth paused in the roomy, old-fashioned kitchen long enough to fix herself a cold glass of lemonade. She'd already had a light lunch with her tennis partner and friend, Barbara Hopkins. Besides, with the house this quiet, it was the perfect time to read through the plays the local theater group was considering for their late fall season.

Although there was no longer a Carrel in the business community, Rebecca Carrel hadn't relinquished her leadership in other areas. Elizabeth had the impression that, with her father-in-law now gone, his wife actually enjoyed being the sole center of attention, no longer needing to share the spotlight with her husband.

It was an unkind thought since Elizabeth knew very well how devoted Rebecca had been, always the perfect wife and partner while maintaining her social position and never allowing the two to conflict.

Rebecca Carrel was a marvel of organization and Elizabeth had learned a lot from her. Now she herself played an active role in the right circles. She was a Carrel, and younger, socially ambitious women and some men cultivated her acquaintance and the influence she could bring to bear through her mother-in-law. Her life was full to the point where she rarely had a moment with nothing particular to do. Maybe that was why she never missed Jeremy as much as she thought she would.

In the beginning, Rebecca hadn't allowed her to grieve too much, knowing that she might be pregnant and fearing somewhat irrationally that some harm would come to her unborn grandchild. Elizabeth remembered being mostly numb. Then Amy had come along, a beautiful, happy baby who didn't much like to sleep. Those early years were a bit of a blur. Soon enough her tiny, energetic girl had turned into a toddler, then a first grader, and now her daughter was nine.

How had ten years gone by so fast? She couldn't begin to figure that one out.

As she entered the living room, Elizabeth stopped, and with a smile, walked to the piano in the small alcove. She ran her fingers lightly over the ivory keys, remembering her own rebelliousness over practicing scales. Amy did seem to have talent, though, and when left to her own devices, her enjoyment was obvious. She had never pushed Amy into learning, but there was no getting around the necessity of learning scales.

Setting her lemonade glass down on a small table where it couldn't be knocked over, she began picking out the melody of a song. More memories came flooding back as her fingers warmed up.

It was at a piano recital that she'd first met Jeremy. He had come with his parents and they'd been introduced at the reception following the performance, a benefit for her high school's music program.

Elizabeth had known who he was before anyone said so—everyone in the county did. Gossip had it that he didn't want anything to with local girls, which probably had to do with his mother's formidable reputation, but when she saw the admiring light in his dark eyes, she'd felt hopeful. Young as she was, Elizabeth had wanted the security of marriage. In truth, she'd set out to catch him. It had been very easy to let herself fall in love with Jeremy.

Mary Ellen Simmons, the aunt who'd raised Elizabeth after her parents died when she was eleven, hadn't entirely approved of the marriage. She had insisted that at eighteen Elizabeth couldn't possibly know that she wanted to spend the rest of her life with Jeremy Carrel, fearing that her niece was more impressed with his background than in love with him. Her suspicions were never proved one way or another. In fact, Elizabeth hadn't given them a thought until this minute.

It was strange. Her fingers slipped into a slower, more pensive tune. Why was she suddenly dwelling on what happened so many years ago? She had never asked herself before whether she'd truly loved Jeremy or not. The answer seemed to elude her.

A surge of restlessness burst through her for no apparent reason. Her fingers came down on the keys, hitting notes that were discordant and harsh. Anger turned inward—she'd wasted time daydreaming when she could have been studying the theater's proposed plays.

Sliding to the edge of the piano bench, Elizabeth reached for the glass of lemonade and got up with it in her hand . . . then froze. A man was leaning against the archway of the living room.

A cold chill ran down her spine: he was grubby and showing a lot of bare skin. A sweat-stained light blue shirt was half-unbuttoned and revealed a powerful chest tanned teak brown. His lean legs were covered, more or less, by old jeans that had once been dark blue but were too covered with dust now to tell their true color. The stubble of unshaven beard darkened the chiseled angles of his face. A well-worn aviator jacket was slung over one shoulder and a battered duffel bag was sitting on the floor beside him.

His hair wasn't too messy—thick, tobacco brown locks had been combed away from his face by the fingers of one hand. He returned Elizabeth's frightened scrutiny with lazy calm.

"What are you doing in here?" she breathed, suddenly

conscious of how isolated the house was in its country setting.

"Is the concert over?" he asked in a deep, husky voice.

She forced an icy imperiousness into her reply. "Get out. Right now, before I call the police." She would call them no matter what he did—but she would have to reach a phone. He was positioned to stop her.

There was a flash of white teeth in the beard growth as the man smiled and stayed where he was.

"If you're looking for a handout or something, forget it. The highway is a half mile down the road. Get going. And I mean it about calling the police!"

With the threat voiced, she braved the possibility of him stopping her and dashed to the phone, picking up the receiver. Any second she expected him to pull a gun or a knife. Her hand fumbled over the buttons and she misdialed.

"Slow down. Press nine-one-one," he offered and she stared at him, not expecting him to say that. "And say hi to the deputy for me."

"What?"

"You heard me. What's for lunch?"

Even more rattled, Elizabeth pressed the buttons in the wrong order and heard nothing, then a long, jarring buzz.

The man laughed. "You're going to feel like a fool, little sister. But it might be interesting to see a Carrel with a red face, even if you're only one by marriage."

For the second time, Elizabeth froze, her green eyes swinging back to the stranger in the archway, looking confident. But then crazy people often did. He wasn't the least bit intimidated by her threats or her calling the police. And . . . he seemed to know her. Or at least he was aware of her connection with the Carrels.

"Who are you?" she demanded. Her fingers were still tightly clutching the receiver.

"Have I changed that much?" A brow lifted as he asked the question. "Well, it's been years. But I would have recognized you anywhere."

The receiver nearly dropped out of her hand. "Jed?" she whispered in disbelief.

"The one and only," he confirmed, straightening from his slouching position against the doorframe. "Did all of you give me up for lost?"

"We haven't heard from you—" Elizabeth began, then stopped. "Jed, your father—he had a heart attack almost two years ago. He's—he's dead." There seemed no way to put it less bluntly and trite phrases of comfort would be somehow wrong. She hoped her sympathy showed in her eyes.

He didn't comment on that right away, just looked around the house. "I see things haven't changed much." His tawny gold gaze swept the room, then it returned to her. "I heard about Dad," he said finally, with little emotion visible on his unshaved face. "My mother's letter caught up with me about a year ago. I didn't see the point of returning then."

"Why . . . why have you come back?" she asked.

He shook his head in mock reproof. "It's bad manners to ask questions like that, Liza."

"Elizabeth," she corrected automatically, and he laughed.

"Still huffy about that, are you? Why?"

"I don't like the name 'Liza.' It's too—"

"Ordinary. At least that was the word you used way back when."

She nodded, remembering. So did he.

"It was just after you got engaged to my brother and you were trying to seem poised and sophisticated for my parents. You were totally ticked off when I called you Liza in front of them."

"Don't remind me." A tenseness crept into her expression as she avoided his intent gaze. He seemed to enjoy getting a rise out of her.

"Where is my mother?"

"Having lunch in town," Elizabeth replied.

"Of course. It's Thursday, isn't it? I had forgotten that she holds court every Thursday." A hard smile tightened his mouth.

He didn't seem to be expecting a reply to that snide comment and she didn't make one.

Elizabeth covered the awkwardness of the moment by pointing down the hall. "Ah—if you would like to clean up, the room at the end of the stairs doesn't belong to anyone. You can put your things there. There are fresh towels in the bathroom."

His expression didn't change. "Is that a subtle hint that I look less than presentable?" Jed asked. "It was a hot, dusty walk out here."

"Do you mean you walked from town?" She frowned at him in surprise.

He glanced down at his dust-covered boots and jeans. "The outskirts, yeah. My feet were the only transportation available. The local taxi was probably taking my mother's friends to their luncheon, as she calls it, with her."

"You could have waited or called," Elizabeth murmured.

"I wanted to see if the old saying was right. That you can't go home again," he clarified at her confused look. "So far I would say it's true—and by the way, who's in my old room at the head of the stairs?"

"It's Amy's now." She bristled faintly at his attitude. They had met only once. They were virtually strangers, so why should he expect her to welcome him back with open arms?

"Amy?" Jed lifted a dark brow in inquiry.

"My daughter." Her chin lifted fractionally to a defiant angle.

His mouth moved into something resembling a smile. "Oh, right," he said. "You and Jeremy had a child. Sorry, I didn't get updated too often. And the whole world isn't wired. Where I was, the mail generally came in on a cargo plane and not that often."

"You don't have to apologize." Still, she felt herself softening ever so slightly.

"Amy was my grandmother's name."

"We named our Amy after her," Elizabeth admitted.

"My mother must have liked that. Or was it her suggestion?"

He had that right, but Elizabeth wasn't going to say so. "There were several names on the list before Amy was born." She turned away abruptly. "Have you eaten? I can fix you a light lunch."

"Breakfast, please," he requested instead. "I haven't adjusted to the time zone change. For me, it's tomorrow morning. Omelet and toast would be great. Thanks."

He was picking up his duffel bag and striding to the hallway door. Elizabeth stared after him, noticing the catlike smoothness of his walk.

Great build. Lean. Masculine. The words came to mind without her consciously thinking them. He unsettled her.

After almost a decade she couldn't be blamed for not expecting to see her husband's brother again, or for practically forgetting his existence. In the last few years, his name had been mentioned only once that she could recall, and that had been when Rebecca, his mother, had wanted to notify him of his father's death.

They'd only received three cards from him that Elizabeth could remember, short notes with postmarks of different foreign ports in the Pacific and Southeast Asia.

Just saying his name had almost been forbidden in the house, as far as she'd been able to tell.

Of course, when Elizabeth had first met Jeremy, she'd known that he had a brother, younger by about a year. Jed was wild, so the rumors said, expelled from prep schools and colleges, ignoring every edict and precept of social behavior that the Carrels stood for.

Her only interest had been in Jeremy. The escapades of his brother were of no importance to her. If she'd considered him at all, it had been only fleetingly: black sheep or no, he had to have some input on her becoming a member of the family. She'd always known that if Jeremy's family didn't approve of her, there would be no marriage, no matter how much he professed to love her.

Caught up in memories of days gone by, Elizabeth turned to the kitchen, thinking that she'd been spending too much time there lately, distracting herself with cooking and baking while she pondered the type of questions that hit women nearing thirty. Not finding a husband and not whether to have a baby—she'd done both. No, they were more like what-do-you-really-want-out-of-life questions. Finding the answers just might mean going back to the past. Jed's sudden arrival brought her back to a time when she had been standing on a threshold, unable to see the future ahead of her.

What had she wanted then?

Her thoughts focused on her single previous encounter with him.

It had happened only a day or two after Jeremy had proposed. She'd met his parents once, briefly, at a country club dance. After his proposal, she had been invited to dinner. Elizabeth had fretted over not having an engagement ring to flaunt—he hadn't bought one yet, was all. But to his parents, its lack might signify a lack of seriousness on his part.

When they had arrived here at his childhood home, which seemed very grand to her, she'd been a bundle of nerves, terrified that she would do or say the wrong thing. Jeremy hadn't known how to be supportive, growing quieter with each step they took toward the door. His parents and Jed had been in the living room awaiting their arrival. The hostile atmosphere had almost smothered Elizabeth, sure that the strange feeling in the air was because of her. It was quite a while before she realized that it had to do with Jed.

At first he'd been silent, although he managed to convey his cynical amusement. Elizabeth picked up on that—and that Jed wouldn't care in the least about his parents' approval or disapproval of whatever girl he wanted to marry, but that he thought it was funny Jeremy wanted it so much. At the time, Elizabeth had been angry that Jed couldn't understand the necessity for it.

Except for the initial exchange of hellos and an occasional comment at the dinner table, Jed really hadn't spoken to her. Not that she'd cared. In fact, she was glad then that he hadn't singled her out for attention. She didn't want his parents' anger at him to rub off on her. Somehow she sensed that he knew she'd silently taken the side against him and understood why.

After coffee in the living room, she assumed it would be best for her to make a discreet withdrawal and give Jeremy a chance to speak to his parents in private. She was quickly assured of that by the smile that flashed across Jeremy's face when she excused herself on some trivial pretext.

Fussing with her hair and makeup didn't last very long, however, and she ventured into the hallway, crossing her fingers that she wasn't returning too soon. Jed was there. Something in his manner prevented Elizabeth from walking past him.

"So you're the angel of virtue that my brother adores," he murmured. "Not what I expected. Anyway, welcome to our little heaven," he added mockingly.

Her nervousness increased. She could think of no way to reply to that strange comment, so she smiled weakly. "Jeremy will be wondering where I am. Excuse me."

The light touch of his hand on her arm stopped her. "Doesn't it bother you that they're in there deciding whether to allow you the dubious privilege of becoming a member of the Carrel family?"

"I wouldn't marry Jeremy without his parents' permission," she answered. He had to know that doing otherwise wasn't a good idea.

"How old are you?" His unusual, hazel-gold eyes moved over her face and figure, looking her over in swift appraisal. He seemed to like what he saw.

"Eighteen. Old enough to know my own mind," Elizabeth asserted defiantly.

"And you're in love with the idea of becoming Mrs. Jeremy Carrel," Jed mocked.

"I want to be his wife more than anything else in the world. I love him."

"But you wouldn't marry him if my parents disapproved."

"Of course not."

Jed seemed skeptical. "I don't believe you really love him or you'd fight tooth and nail to have him. But you're okay with passively waiting for someone else to decide whether you'll marry him or not."

"It's my life and my decision and none of your business!" His cutting jibe prompted a furious retort.

"Don't marry him, Elizabeth." There was a hard, warning note in his tone. "Don't get caught up in what the Carrel name supposedly means. You're about to make a mistake you'll regret."

"Aren't you going a little fast, Jed?" she asked haughtily. "It's possible that your parents will disapprove of me."

"Not likely." A corner of his mouth curled cynically. "My moralistic father sees you as pure and untouched. And by the way, he's investigated your background to be sure there's no scandal attached to your name. But my mother is glorying in the worshipful attention you've been paying her. She's already deciding that she can mold you into exactly the daughter-in-law she has in mind. Someone who bows down to her like Jeremy does."

"That's not a very nice way to talk about your parents." The elation she'd felt at his saying they would give their permission for the marriage was soured by his sarcastic analysis of their reasons.

"The truth is often unkind, Liza."

"My name is Elizabeth." Her dislike of him increased. "I don't like nicknames. Especially that one. Liza just sounds—ordinary."

"Sorry, oh queen," he said mockingly. "Forgive me if I don't bow."

"Forgive me if I find it hard to believe that you and Jeremy are brothers," Elizabeth retorted acidly.

"Don't apologize for that. That's been a puzzle almost since the day I was born. All I ever heard was 'why can't you be more like your brother' until I was sick of it." Jed laughed with unconcealed bitterness. "I make too many waves but I don't intend to change. I'm just not like him."

"How so?" she challenged.

"For one thing, I'm not content to walk in my father's shadow. I'll blaze my own trail in life."

"So you condemn Jeremy because he's joining your father's firm?" she asked coldly.

"Not if that's what he wants."

"It is his decision, Jed."

"Speaking of that, are you sure about your decision?"

"I know exactly what I want," Elizabeth stated without qualification. "To marry Jeremy."

"Do you?"

His fingers closed over her chin and tilted it up. Her green eyes rounded in surprise as she stared into the lean face bending closer to hers. The astonishment at his action was so complete that she spoke not one word of protest or attempted to draw away. Nor was she prepared for the hard, passionate possession of his kiss, the raging fire scorching through her veins. Inexperience made her frightened of what was happening. When the sensual pressure eased, Elizabeth had only been able to stare into the satisfied gleam of his gold-flecked eyes, reminiscent of a cat playing with its prey.

"I bet Jeremy never kissed you like that, Liza." Jed smiled mirthlessly. "He doesn't have what it takes."

"Oh?" Elizabeth whispered breathlessly, her pulse throbbing in her throat.

She and Jeremy had kissed many times—warm, satisfying kisses. But she really hadn't been left with the knee-buckling sensation that she was about to be seduced.

"Jeremy r-respects me too much to treat me like that," she'd added in a more forceful voice that was still quivering slightly.

"Oh, is that what you want from him? Respect? Not just the Carrel name?" He was making fun of her but she didn't know what to say to stop him. "He will be making love to you, you know."

"But with gentleness and consideration." A flush began creeping into her cheeks at his open discussion of such an intimate subject.

"I hope someday, Liza, you'll be honest enough to tell me if that's what you really want." He sounded almost sorry for her.

"What? How dare you talk to me like that?" she'd demanded, angry that he seemed to think she should be pitied.

"Wake up, little girl. Jeremy isn't the man for you," Jed pointed out smoothly, looking amused at her display of temper.

"What's going on here?" Jeremy was visibly bristling at the end of the hallway, looking accusingly at Jed and Elizabeth.

With a guilty start, she had pulled away from the hand along the right side of her neck in an obvious caress. There was a strong possibility that Jeremy would misunderstand and think she'd asked for this accidental meeting with his brother.

"I was just coming in—" she began to explain, but Jed broke in calmly.

"Yes, she was," he agreed, "but I waylaid her before she could hurry back to the safety of your side. I wanted to be the first to officially kiss your bride-to-be. I didn't want her to have any doubts that I would welcome her into the house with open arms."

The suggestiveness of Jed's last remark rubbed Jeremy the wrong way. Elizabeth sensed that Jed was deliberately goading him into losing his temper.

"You keep away from Elizabeth," Jeremy had growled. "She's mine now. And forever."

"Okay. I guess congratulations are in order." Jed turned to Elizabeth, who was still too paralyzed to move, and smiled. "The verdict is in and the sentence is likely to be life. I wouldn't expect much in the way of mercy if I were you, Liza. The Carrel family doesn't forgive or forget—I know from firsthand experience."

"Elizabeth, come here," Jeremy ordered crisply.

As she started to walk by Jed, she read the silent message in his hazel-gold eyes, repeating again that she was making a mistake. Her response was to practically run to Jeremy's side, letting his arm circle her shoulders and draw her to him. She smiled into his face, seeing that her action had taken the edge off his anger.

Then Jeremy's dark gaze had turned to his brother, standing alone several feet away. Jed's eyes were half-closed, the expression in them veiled by thick lashes.

"Mother suggested you should be the best man. For the sake of appearances, I guess," Jeremy said.

"I guess I'm supposed to be honored to be included in the festivities at all. Are all of you hoping I'll be on my best behavior if I have a major role?" Jed had mocked.

"Jed, you heard me," Jeremy had stated stiffly. "I would like you to be my best man. You can say yes or no."

Without answering, Jed had turned and walked away.

Chapter 2

A flash of total recall brought that long-forgotten incident vividly back to life. Elizabeth's fingertips were unconsciously pressed against her lips. In retrospect, Jed's long-ago kiss didn't seem frightening or unpleasant. The discovery was unsettling now.

Jed had not been best man at their wedding. In fact, a few days after she'd been introduced to him, Jeremy told her that his brother had left, destination unknown. Although he hadn't added it, Elizabeth had sensed that Jeremy wished Jed well on what was likely to be a long journey. Secretly she'd been surprised that his parents had been all for it, but mostly she'd felt relief that Jed would not be around.

The brothers really didn't resemble each other, except for the brown hair. Jeremy had been an inch or two taller than Jed's six feet, broader and more muscular than his brother, who was lean. In Elizabeth's opinion, Jeremy had been the handsomer of the two, with a fine-featured, strong face.

At twenty-three there had been a chiseled hardness to Jed's features that the intervening years had intensified. Yet it had been his overpowering air of maleness that had left Elizabeth feeling insecure and inexperienced. She'd known she could become the kind of socially acceptable wife that Jeremy wanted, but the thought of Jed as her brother-in-law had made her very nervous. Then, suddenly, he was gone, and her fear and uncertainty vanished too.

Now Jed had returned. Why? It was a question without an answer, one that he had dodged successfully when she'd asked him. If he'd come back after Jeremy's death or his father's, Elizabeth would have understood. But there seemed to be no particular reason for this unexpected homecoming. She couldn't believe it was prompted by reawakened loyalty to his family or a driving desire to return to where he'd been born.

If either were true, he wouldn't have shown up unshaven and disheveled. No, if he were hoping to get back in his mother's good graces or somehow become the man of the family—he was the last male Carrel—he would have arrived in style. Rebecca certainly would expect him to look and act like a Carrel, and not come walking across fields with a backpack slung over his shoulder, looking like he'd slogged through ditches to get there.

"A penny for your thoughts—or does it cost more than that to find out what a Carrel is thinking?"

Elizabeth blinked, startled by the question. She was uncomfortable under his steady gaze, gold-brown and arrogantly—feline, she thought, searching for the right word. Though he was far from tame. The way Jed walked, turned, even how he was waiting now, reminded her very much of the restrained but graceful power of a big cat, with more than a hint of the ability to strike fast.

She took a deep breath to control the sudden acceleration of her pulse. "They aren't worth a penny."

Jed switched the subject, but she continued to stare at him. "My omelet?"

"Oh—coming up."

She turned quickly to the refrigerator, tearing her gaze from his face. He'd transformed himself in the space of a few minutes. The beard growth was gone, revealing a lean jaw and high cheekbones. The heady but subtle scent of good aftershave drifted to her. His tobacco brown hair gleamed a darker brown, thanks to the shower spray, its natural waywardness giving him a rakish look even when it was combed.

Again she was struck by his masculinity, her awareness triggered by the way his clean khakis fit his muscular legs and the plain but crisp white shirt he hadn't buttoned all the way. The rolled-up sleeves showed off bare arms rippled with more sinewy muscle, and the dark curling hair she could just glimpse on his chest heightened his natural tan. His leanness only emphasized his obvious strength. An inner sense told her that he would look just as good in formal clothes.

It was difficult to work with her usual efficiency in the kitchen when he seemed to be watching her every move. Elizabeth forced herself to concentrate on what she was doing.

She glanced to where he sat, straddling a kitchen chair. "Do you want your omelet plain or with cheese or ham?"

"Plain is fine," Jed answered.

He waited until she'd cooked and served it up with toast before saying anything else. "Where's your daughter?" he asked.

"In town with Rebecca. She has a piano lesson today."

"Does she play as well as her mother?"

The question flustered Elizabeth. For an instant she didn't quite get that Jed was referring to her.

"Amy is just a beginner." She reached for the coffeepot

to pour herself a cup, not caring about the hot day. She needed the caffeine. "She's only been taking lessons for a little over a year. But she's quite good."

"Does she look like you?"

Elizabeth didn't turn to the table immediately but took her time adding a spoonful of sugar to the black coffee. "No, she takes after her father."

"That's a shame," Jed responded dryly.

Elizabeth shrugged off that comment. "Jed, there's something I would like to ask you."

"Go ahead. Or should I say here we go again?"

Had he read her mind? But she had to know. Her wary gaze met his. "Please tell why you've come back."

"Do I have to have a reason?"

"I just want to know." She let him look at her for what felt like an interminably long time before he returned his attention to the plate on the table.

"Maybe because I've been gone too long," he sighed. "Knocking around the world, doing this and that. It gets old. My roots are here, no matter where I go."

"But is that the whole reason?" she asked, not ready to accept the ambiguous answer he'd given her.

"It's as good as any," he said. "You know how it is—you can't stay away from civilization forever."

She only nodded, hardly able to imagine being away from her routine, let alone out of the United States for that long.

"When will you be leaving?"

"Maybe tomorrow. Maybe never." He shrugged, white teeth flashing as he bit into the slice of toast and finished the rest of his breakfast.

"I still don't understand why you've come back now." She brushed the raven hair away from her face, a slight frown creasing her forehead.

"You probably don't even know why I left, do you?" The hard mouth curved into a wry smile.

"I know you argued with your parents," Elizabeth hedged.

Jed pushed the empty plate toward the center of the table. "That was nothing new. The whole time I was growing up it was one argument after another. For some dumb reason, I thought I could make my parents understand that all I wanted to do was live my own life."

She nodded without comment, hoping he'd continue.

"When you and Jeremy got engaged, I'd been kicked out of three law schools. My father gave me the news that night that he'd used his influence and money to get me into another. He refused to accept that I didn't want to be a lawyer, wanted no part of the family business. A couple of days later I left."

"I see," she murmured.

"I don't think you do." His voice had an edge of mockery that brought her head up sharply. "Actually, I didn't expect to find you here in Rebecca's house when I came back."

"Where did you suppose I'd be?" Elizabeth didn't understand what he was getting at.

"In your own house. Remarried. You're a beautiful woman." It was a statement more than a compliment. "Hard to believe no one even tried to sweep you off your feet in all these years."

"I haven't dated all that much since Jeremy died. Never on a regular basis." Elizabeth turned her back on him, looking to change the subject. "Would you like some coffee?"

"Please." When she set the cup before him, Jed spoke again. "My turn to ask why."

"Ah—it's not that I don't want to date. I just don't have a lot of free time. I have my daughter and—"

"You could find the time."

Momentarily at a loss for words, she couldn't decide whether his words or his condescending tone irked her more. "I was very happy with Jeremy," she said coldly. "Which is probably why I haven't been interested in anyone else."

"My brother was the man, huh?"

"Yes!" she flashed angrily.

"You sure?" Jed asked softly.

"Yes. You heard me," Elizabeth declared. Her throat tightened. "You haven't changed, Jed. I thought you were insulting and arrogant the first time I met you."

"That was years ago."

She was incensed by his attempt to dismiss what she'd said. "You tried to turn me against Jeremy then and you're still doing it now when he isn't here to defend himself. That's just wrong. And you know it."

He looked at her with serious thoughtfulness. "You grew up, didn't you? God, were you innocent back then. I like you better like this."

Elizabeth looked into his eyes, seeing a reawakened desire in their depths that made her want to bolt.

"You're a woman now. All the way down to your toes and all the way up again." His voice was husky and caressing.

"Stop it!" She wanted to put her hands over her ears—or use them to slap him. She kept them at her sides, clenched into fists.

"Sorry." His raw sigh stopped her. "Looking back, part of the reason I left was you. That night I couldn't stop myself from kissing you, even though I knew I'd frightened you. I frighten you now too, don't I?" His hands suddenly closed over the soft flesh of her upper arms. "I really am sorry."

She closed her eyes to keep from quivering at his

touch. It was strangely comforting all the same. "No, you're not."

"At least give me credit for leaving then." There was a plea in his voice. "If I'd stayed—hell. I couldn't. You were pure temptation, even if you were about to become my brother's wife."

"I don't want to talk about the past!"

"Then let's deal with the here and now." Jed slid his hands down her arms, letting his fingers close around her slender wrists. Crossing her arms in front of her, he drew her against his chest. "There. You're protected."

"No," she gasped.

"Not that I don't want to hold you. Or bury my face in your silken black hair."

Elizabeth gasped again as he did just that. "Let me go!" She tried to twist away from the sensuous nuzzling near her ear. His warm breath caressed her cheek and throat. She lacked the will to fight back, because it simply felt so good . . . and it had been so long . . .

"Elizabeth!" The appalled voice came from the hallway door.

Flames of red burned her cheeks as Jed slowly released her, his tawny eyes moving over her face with something like tenderness until she turned to her mother-in-law. Jed didn't follow suit, keeping his back to Rebecca.

"Ah—I—" Elizabeth began, fighting to find the right words and realizing how guilty she must look. Not that she had anything to feel guilty about, she thought with a rebelliousness that surprised her.

But she didn't get a chance to identify Jed as Mrs. Carrel broke in with haughty indignation. "Elizabeth, what on earth do you think you're doing? Suppose Amy comes running in here and sees you in the arms of a stranger? Who is this—"

"Hello, Mother." Jed turned and spoke before she finished her slashing barrage of questions.

Rebecca's mouth snapped shut, arching her finely plucked, penciled eyebrows in something considerably less than overwhelming joy at her son's return. "You." The single word was flat and condemning.

"That's right," he said casually. "I'm back."

Rebecca scarcely paused to take a breath. "Your brother and father have been in their graves for quite a while, Jed. Why have you bothered to come back now?"

"I keep getting asked that." The tense line of his mouth thinned even more into a cold smile. "Let's just say I can't do without motherly love forever," he responded cynically.

"How long do you intend to stay? Or are you just passing through?" His mother's expression was still rigidly controlled.

Jed shrugged, squarely meeting her dark gaze. "I haven't made any plans."

"I can believe that," Rebecca said in cutting reproof. She took a deep breath and didn't hold back. "Your father and I did everything we could to give you a decent start in life and you threw all of it away, even the opportunity for a law degree. You refused to plan, always insisting that you knew it all and didn't have to listen to us. What has it gained you, Jed? You've hopped all over the Pacific and God knows where else, and what do you have to show for it?"

Jed seemed determined to control his temper. The only indication Elizabeth saw of it was the slight clenching of his jaw. Other than that, he withstood his mother's tirade without any show of emotion.

"I didn't come back to argue whether what happened in the past was right or wrong," he told his mother. "I guess I wanted to come back when I'd made my fortune."

He smiled in self-reproach. "When I got your letter about a year after it was written and realized that Dad was gone, I knew it was time to set aside my Carrel pride and come home and make peace. If that's possible."

Again there was a long, measured look between them. Elizabeth unthinkingly held her breath, believing the sincerity in Jed's voice but not sure that his mother did.

"Hm. We shall see," Rebecca said.

Jed took a moment to reply and his tone was noncommittal when he did. "All right then."

"You can have the room at the end of the stairs as long as you're here," Rebecca finally said. "Amy, Jeremy's daughter, has your old room."

He nodded. "Liza already offered me the other room a little while after I arrived. I"—he glanced down at his clean clothes—"I needed to get cleaned up after walking here from town."

"You *walked* from town?" his mother exclaimed in distressed anger. "Did anyone see you? For heaven's sake, why didn't you take a taxi? What would people think if they saw you walking along the highway?"

"Probably that I was on my way home."

"I wish you would be more conscious of our position in the community." His mother sighed bitterly. "But then you never were."

At that moment Amy appeared in the kitchen doorway, changed into an everyday outfit of shorts and top. She looked curiously at the stranger in their midst, and Elizabeth realized it was probably the first time her daughter had seen a man in the house during the daytime since before her grandfather had passed away.

As she made her way to Elizabeth, Amy kept right on looking at Jed. There was no shyness in her silent appraisal, and she didn't flinch when he looked back at her.

"Hello, Amy." Jed's greeting was casual, not forcing any undue warmth or gladness into his voice.

Amy tilted her dark head back to look at Elizabeth. "Who is he?" she demanded in a clear voice that nonetheless bordered on rudeness.

"Mind your manners, Amy," Rebecca reprimanded her.

Except for a stubborn tightening of her mouth, Amy pretended not to have heard her grandmother's words. Elizabeth had the fleeting thought that her daughter's somewhat rebellious nature might run in the family. Jed certainly had it.

"This is your Uncle Jed. He was your father's brother, Amy," Elizabeth explained patiently.

Curiosity sparked again, Amy turned her attention back to Jed. "Oh. Did you know my dad?"

"Yes. We grew up together," Jed answered, calmly returning her scrutiny.

"Did you know me when I was a baby?"

"No, I was on the other side of the world when you were born."

His explanation didn't impress Amy. "I didn't know my dad. He died before I was born, you know," she informed him matter-of-factly.

He nodded. "So I understood."

"Did you like him?"

"Oh, Amy, what a question!" There was a brittle quality to Elizabeth's laughter, as she gave Jed a pleading look. "Your dad and Jed were brothers. Of course they liked each other."

"That's not exactly true."

So he saw fit to ignore her silent request to keep Jeremy's memory untarnished. "Jed!" Elizabeth's tone held an angry warning.

"He was my brother," Jed continued with a faint smile. "And because he was, I loved him. But I didn't necessarily like him. Brothers tend to fight and argue a lot, Amy. Your dad and I didn't agree about a lot of things."

"What did you fight about?" Amy looked a little too interested.

"Enough questions, Amy," Rebecca broke in coldly. "Your uncle is probably very tired after his long journey and you're supposed to be practicing the piano. Mrs. Banks told me you didn't do very well today, so from now on you'll practice an extra fifteen minutes every day."

"Mom, no!" Amy protested to Elizabeth, frowning her appeal for the edict to be lifted.

"Your grandmother isn't wrong," Elizabeth answered calmly. "But if you do better at your next lesson, we'll consider eliminating the extra fifteen minutes."

"Mrs. Banks is stupid," Amy grumbled.

"Hey, I was thinking about taking a swim in the pool sometime today," Jed said quietly—too quietly, Elizabeth thought. "Maybe you can join me when you finish that fifteen minutes of practicing."

The frown was replaced by an immediate smile as Amy rushed to accept his invitation.

"Have you forgotten, Jed?" his mother asked crisply. "In this house there are no rewards or bribes for doing what you're supposed to do."

With that parting shot, Rebecca Carrel turned around and left the kitchen. Seconds of heavy silence ticked by as Jed stared after her, emotion smoldering in his eyes.

"I'm sorry, Amy," he said simply, turning back to the crestfallen child. "Maybe another day."

"I s'pose so." She sighed as if she didn't hold out much hope for that nebulous day to come, dragging her feet as she left the room.

"Nothing's changed," Jed muttered.

Elizabeth knew the comment wasn't directed at her, but at his mother's insistence on strict, consistent discipline.

Several times she herself had gone to bat for Amy, but Rebecca's argument that it had to be that way for Amy's own good seemed unassailable. The rules were never bent, but Elizabeth was convinced that was the only way to keep her daughter's sometimes overly assertive personality under control. On her own she wouldn't have been as unwavering as her mother-in-law, though.

"Why are you living here, Liza?" Jed asked as she began clearing the dishes from the table. "Jeremy must have left you enough for you to be independent. And my father probably set aside money for you and Amy too. Am I right?"

"They did," she acknowledged, not pausing in her task. "But this has been my home for a long time and it's always been Amy's. That counts for a lot with me."

He gave her a long look that got under her skin. She decided to set him straight on one other thing while he wasn't talking.

"By the way, Jed, and I hope I'm saying this for the last time—my name is Elizabeth. Not Liza."

Shrugging, he ignored that. "What about the house you and Jeremy had? Wasn't that your home?" he countered.

"We lived here after we married."

He laughed in disbelief. "Really? Poor you. My mother running your lives, no privacy, no chance to get to know each other—"

"It was only a temporary arrangement!" His mocking tone stung her. "We had bought a house, but the whole place needed to be redecorated and furnished and the kitchen remodeled. We couldn't live in that kind of chaos."

"I guess it never occurred to either of you to move into it and redo the house in stages," Jed offered dryly.

"That was Jeremy's decision," Elizabeth said, "and besides, he was working long hours with your father. It was only natural for him to want to come home to an orderly house at night."

"What did you do all day?"

"If it's any of your business," she snapped, "I was planning the remodeling."

"Under my mother's supervision, right? I bet she had final say on every swatch and paint chip."

Elizabeth's eyes narrowed. He happened to be right, but she wasn't going to tell him that.

"I didn't have much experience and I was glad to have her help."

"So the house was never completed?"

"No, it wasn't." She turned away to the sink as she made the clipped response. "We were going to move into it anyway, but Jeremy was killed in that car crash and I . . . I couldn't bring myself to live in the house without him."

"So you stayed on here," he muttered.

"After I found out I was pregnant with Amy, there was nowhere else for me to go. My aunt had severe diabetes and she ended up in the hospital with complications—"

"And my mother came to the rescue, right?" Jed asked in a harsh voice. "I can fill in the blanks. When Amy was born, you were too young to know much about babies, so you accepted her guidance again."

"Jed—" Elizabeth began with exasperation.

"You could have found a better teacher. In fact, you probably could have fumbled through on your own with better results. A lot of women do, and without the financial cushion you were lucky enough to have."

"You weren't there. Just what makes you so damn sure that you're right?" Elizabeth retaliated.

He didn't respond to that. She was silent for a few moments, trying to figure out how they'd gotten this far, this fast. She was almost sure he was deliberately trying to provoke but she had no idea why.

"You have no idea what it's like to be lost and alone and frightened. Yes, I needed emotional support and I'm not ashamed to say so. I doubt if you know what it's like to need anyone!"

"Believe me, I do." His voice vibrated huskily. "If I didn't, I wouldn't have come back. So far, it's one hell of a homecoming."

"Don't blame me for that. You were the one who left! And three letters in nine years hardly sounds like you were homesick!"

That pointed remark hit a sore spot. "Hey, would you like to know how many letters I got from my parents?" Jed flashed. "Exactly two! One telling me of Jeremy's death and the other was about my father's. My efforts to keep the lines of communication open weren't exactly encouraged. I felt as if I was bashing my head against a brick wall ten feet thick!"

"Then why did you come back?" she lashed out, angry that he was taking his years of frustration out on her. "You still haven't said!"

"You know, I've been asking myself that question ever since I got here. I should have realized the age of miracles is over. And I thought," the smile curving his mouth mocked himself this time, "if I came back willing to make peace, my mother would meet me halfway, maybe even accept me for who I am. Nothing doing. She doesn't think much of me and she never will," he muttered. "The only thing that impresses her is success. On her terms."

"She is who she is. You can't change her. Why would you even try to?" Elizabeth asked heatedly. "You can't just walk in here and expect everything to be perfect."

His eyes were as hard and unyielding as topaz, full of dark fire. "I didn't. And I love my mother, but that doesn't make me blind to her faults."

Elizabeth's righteous anger got the better of her. "She's

right about some things now and then. What's wrong with being ambitious? Or wanting to better yourself?"

"God, you sound so much like her. So, you followed the rules and now you're at the top of a small-town social ladder. What do you think of the view? Is it what you expected?" Jed countered. "Is being a Carrel the best thing that ever happened to you?"

"I can't change it, can I?" she retorted. "My daughter's a Carrel too. Are we supposed to be ashamed of it? And just so you know, I happen to like my life. I don't just sit around and arrange flowers or whatever. I do a lot of charity work, for one thing. It's very rewarding helping deserving people."

"Deserving by whose standards? My mother's?" He punctuated the words with a short, derisive laugh. "But no one's ever good enough for her."

"You know something? I'm beginning to think you could be described that way."

He drew in a breath and let it out slowly. "Anything else negative you want to say about me?"

She was on a roll now. "I almost don't know where to start. You're judgmental. You hold grudges. You're hot-tempered. You think you're God's gift to your mother and women in general—hey!"

He took her by the arm and she shrugged him off.

"That'll do for now," he said. "Fair's fair. Let's talk about you again. I find you a lot more interesting than myself if you really want to know," he added.

"Hah. I don't believe you."

Jed forged ahead. "Here's my list. You're shy. Stubborn, too. You'll never admit you've been lonely too long." He studied her for several seconds. "Right so far?"

"I'm not going to dignify that question with a reply." Inside she was shaking but outwardly she was perfectly calm.

"Don't get me wrong. I think you're a great mom to Amy and it's obvious that she loves you. So, just one more question. Do you ever miss having a man's arms around you?"

"That is really, really none of your business, Jed Carrel." Her chin rose to a defiant angle. "Shut up. Now." Her seething temper was proving difficult to control.

"Okay. You talk."

How to put him in his place, she wasn't sure. She would have to say something, though—they were going to be living under the same roof for an indefinite period of time to come. And he was Amy's uncle and Rebecca's son, even if it was hard for Elizabeth to think of him as her brother-in-law. To her, he was just . . . Jed.

"You don't know much about me," she began.

"I'd like to."

She didn't trust his conciliatory tone. "Then listen. Long story short, I was raised by my aunt, who was single all her life. And Jeremy was killed so soon after we were married that I never really became accustomed to a man's attention. So I know how to get along without one. It's no big deal and I don't think of myself as lonely."

"Glad to hear it," he muttered.

"As far as dating, I'm in no rush. For one thing, I'm not going to go online and deal with all those liars and married men. And around here—well, as you say, it's a small town. There's not much of a selection. But it doesn't matter to me. Like I said, I don't need a man to be happy."

"Really?" Jed asked, a note of challenge in his voice.

The instant he started walking toward her, Elizabeth backed away. Her bravado didn't stand a chance if he decided to test her assertion.

He stopped and chuckled softly. "I was just going to

get a cup of coffee. Did you think I was going to demand physical proof?"

"You did before," she reminded him, with distrust flashing in her eyes. "Long ago and just now."

"Sorry about that." His expression hardened briefly. "I know I said that I wanted you, but that was out of line. As of now we have to live under the same roof and—and not drive each other crazy."

"Funny, I was just thinking along those lines myself," she said wryly.

"You don't have to be afraid. I don't intend to touch you again."

Jed spoke so emphatically that Elizabeth had to believe him. But his necessary rejection of her as a woman was more of a blow to her self-esteem than she expected. She ought to be happy about it, but instead a strange depression settled over her.

"Aren't you relieved?" His soft voice seemed to enfold her.

"Of course." She turned away, running a nervous hand through her ebony curls, pushing them behind her ear. Fiddling with her hair had to look silly and schoolgirlish, she thought. So much for her poise. "Very relieved," she added for emphasis.

"That's what I thought you'd say."

"I guess we understand each other," Elizabeth murmured. "Help yourself to the coffee. I have some reading to do." She avoided looking directly at him as she exited the kitchen, grateful that she had a good reason to be alone for a while.

Chapter 3

"Put the roast at the head of the table, Elizabeth," Rebecca instructed. "Since Jed is here, he can carve it."

As she started to transfer the platter of meat to the opposite end of the table, Jed appeared in the dining room archway. He was wearing the same white shirt and khaki pants as before.

"I'm honored that you put me at the head of the table," he said to his mother. The edge in his voice let them know that he'd heard their conversation from the hallway.

"The eldest male Carrel always sits at the head of the table," Rebecca responded curtly. "In this case, you happen to be the only male Carrel." Her disapproving gaze took in his casual attire. "We can delay serving for a few minutes while you change. I'm sure you must have forgotten that we always dress for dinner."

"Actually, I hadn't." Jed continued into the room, drawing the end chair where Elizabeth stood from the table. "Unfortunately I couldn't fit my black tie getup and cummerbund into my duffel bag."

"Don't exaggerate," his mother snapped. "A simple suit will do."

"I didn't have room for one of those either. You'll have

to take me the way I am," Jed stated, reaching for the carving knife and fork that Elizabeth had placed near the platter.

Rebecca's lips pursed with annoyance, but she said nothing in response. Waving an imperious hand at Elizabeth and Amy to be seated, she took the chair at the opposite end from Jed.

"By the way"—he set a perfectly sliced piece of meat on Amy's plate—"where's Maggie? Is this her day off?"

Maggie Connor had been the cook-housekeeper for the Carrels for years, an almost permanent fixture in the house when Elizabeth had married Jeremy.

"She retired after your father died," his mother explained. "We no longer entertained much, so there was no point in retaining her for just the three of us. Your father provided a generous annuity for her in his will and I let her go."

"Sounds reasonable." Jed looked at the various platters set out on the table. "Who does the cooking now?"

"Elizabeth does for the most part, although I occasionally lend a helping hand."

Only Elizabeth knew how rare that helping hand was. Not that she objected. She preferred having the kitchen to herself.

"A Carrel who cooks?" He shot her a disbelieving look. "Where did you pick up that skill, Liza?"

Elizabeth felt put on the spot and made him wait a bit for an answer. His use of the nickname she disliked was a further irritant. "Oh, I learned to cook as a child," she responded after a moment. "My aunt thought it was essential, so I fixed a lot of our meals. After Jeremy and I were married, I hung out with Maggie in the kitchen so I could learn how to prepare his favorite foods. Later I simply helped out."

"Maggie was beginning to show her age by then," Rebecca said. "Her retirement was long overdue."

"Wasn't Maggie a year or two younger than you, Mother?" questioned Jed, a sharp glitter in his eyes.

Rebecca bridled visibly. "I really don't have any idea."

"Do you do the housework too, Elizabeth?"

The faint emphasis he put on her full name was somehow more annoying than the nickname. "My share of it, yes. Amy picks up after herself and does some household chores. That's how I was raised."

"We have a woman come in two or three times a week to take care of the general cleaning and the laundry," Rebecca said quickly, as if such things were far beneath her.

"I like Mary," Amy spoke up. "She's really a nice lady. We fold all the towels together."

Rebecca winced but Jed smiled at his niece. "That's great." His next question was addressed to his mother. "So, do the Reisners still own the farm down the road?"

"Yes, they do. You went to school with Kurt, didn't you?" His mother looked up to receive his answering nod. "He's taken over the farm from his father and his parents have moved into town. Why?"

"I thought I'd stop by and see them tonight." He paused for a beat. "If I can use the car."

"There's a set of spare keys in the china cabinet," Rebecca said.

Elizabeth had to restrain herself from audibly sighing in relief. She hadn't been looking forward to an evening of stilted conversation. Despite the veneer of politeness, the atmosphere between mother and son was more than a little hostile. Her own inclination was to avoid Jed as much as she could. He was much too curious about her personal life, asking questions that were none of his business and laughing at her answers. Arm's length wasn't far enough away.

The instant supper was over, Jed excused himself and went out to visit the Reisners. He hadn't returned by the time Elizabeth went to bed after ten o'clock. Although she lay awake in the double bed for nearly an hour, she didn't hear him come back.

The next morning Elizabeth discovered that coffee was already made when she went into the kitchen. Breakfast dishes for one were washed and sitting in the drainboard by the sink. Rebecca didn't get up that early in the morning, so the dishes could only be Jed's. But there was no sign of him anywhere around the house.

Not until she'd returned to the kitchen to fix toast and juice for herself did Elizabeth find the note he'd left under the bowl of fruit on the dinette table. Her fingers crossed as she wished fervently that Jed had left for good. Nope. The bold handwriting on the note informed her that he wouldn't be back for lunch, but said nothing about where he was going.

If he was touching base with old friends, the only logical place he would be at this hour of the morning was the Reisner farm again. The few times she'd met Kurt Reisner, he hadn't mentioned anything about being friends with Jed, but then, why would he?

Even though they were neighbors, Elizabeth didn't know Kurt that well. She knew he'd been married at one time and was now divorced. That information had come from his sister, Freda, who was a year or so younger than she was. She liked Freda and would have seen her more often if she hadn't sensed that Rebecca would disapprove of the friendship, though she felt a little ashamed that that had been enough to stop her. She could just imagine Jed's contempt if he ever found out.

He could think what he liked, she told herself. His opinion didn't have to matter to her any more than Rebecca's did—and her mother-in-law was someone she had to live with, unlike Jed, who wasn't likely to stay long. He'd leave or get himself kicked out by his mother.

She wished that he hadn't returned. Life had been very smooth. Now she was seeing all sorts of chuck-holes in the path. For her own peace of mind, she would have to learn to rise above his ill-considered remarks—and ignore his undeniable good looks—for the duration of his stay.

"Good morning, Elizabeth." Rebecca entered the kitchen looking youthfully fresh in a pink satin robe, her silvery hair carefully styled and light makeup applied to her face. "Is there any fresh grapefruit?"

"Yes, I'll fix it for you." Elizabeth slid back her half-eaten toast and went to the refrigerator.

"I see Jed isn't up yet. I suppose he'll sleep until noon." Rebecca sniffed her disapproval.

"Actually he's up and gone." She sliced the grape-fruit in half and began cutting around each little section.

"How do you know that?"

"He left a note saying he wouldn't be back for lunch," Elizabeth answered. "He was considerate enough to wash up his breakfast dishes before he left, so he must have been up really early."

"Good," Rebecca declared with a wide smile of satis-faction.

It took Elizabeth a second to realize that her mother-in-law was commenting on his planned absence rather than the fact that he'd cleaned up after himself, and she was glad that Jed wasn't around to hear it.

"You're going into town this morning, aren't you, Elizabeth?"

"Yes, I have a committee meeting. I'm keeping track of ticket sales for the charity dinner at the country club." She set the grapefruit half in a bowl, then put it in front of her mother-in-law, adding a spoon and napkin.

Rebecca slipped a manicured hand into the pocket of her robe. There was a faint rustle, then she was handing a slip of paper to Elizabeth.

"While you're in town, I want you to stop by Shaw's Men's Store. I've made a list of things that Jed needs. The sizes are listed on the right," Rebecca stated. "I'm sure Fred will reopen our account."

Elizabeth stared blankly at the paper. "But how can you be sure these are the right sizes? I mean . . . wouldn't it be better to send Jed himself when he comes back this afternoon?" She wasn't about to go shopping for him, no matter what Rebecca said.

Her mother-in-law gave her a severe look. "Don't be obstinate. As for the sizes," Rebecca paused, "I've already checked to be sure they were correct."

Glancing from the list to the woman delicately spooning out a grapefruit section, Elizabeth knew without a doubt Rebecca hadn't asked Jed. He would have laughed off her bossiness or told her to buzz off.

"Do you mean"—the question she was about to ask was a little strange, to say the least—"that you went through his things?"

"He doesn't even have a sports jacket, can you imagine?" Rebecca shook her head in prim disbelief. "After the way he was raised, I was sure he had some decent clothes tucked away in that disreputable bag, so I went through it last night while he was at the Reisners. I hope he doesn't intend to get too friendly with them."

For the first time that she could remember, Elizabeth was offended enough by the snobbish ring in Rebecca's voice to talk back. "They happen to be very nice people," she said firmly.

Her mother-in-law's mouth opened to comment, then she met the flashing defiance in Elizabeth's green eyes with a look of silent surprise. She took the time to spoon up another section of the sour grapefruit, slipping it between pursed lips and chewing it slowly before she swallowed. “I suppose they are,” she agreed with a marked lack of interest.

“Excuse me while I go see what’s keeping Amy,” Elizabeth murmured, moving away from the kitchen table.

“Be sure to put that list in your purse so you won’t forget it,” Rebecca reminded her.

Her fingers crumpled it slightly. The impulse burned to hand it back to her mother-in-law with the retort to do her own busywork, but Elizabeth held it back. The animosity in the air since Jed’s return was beginning to weigh on her.

“I won’t forget,” she promised, and walked from the room.

It was nearly noon when Elizabeth paused beside the storefront of Shaw’s under the old-fashioned awning. She wished she hadn’t left a cold lunch for Rebecca and Amy before heading out this morning. Cooking would have provided an excuse to delay this mother-knows-best errand. It was ridiculous, totally ridiculous. Outside of a few Christmas gifts for her late father-in-law, she had never bought any clothing for men. During their short marriage, Jeremy had always preferred to choose his own.

Nervously she ran her fingers along the scalloped neckline of her white sundress. Squaring her shoulders in determination, she walked to the door. A bell jingled above it as she entered.

The balding head of Fred Shaw, the owner, turned away from the customer he was helping to glance toward the door. He waved to a male clerk to take his place as he excused himself to see what Elizabeth wanted.

It flashed through her mind that this was usually the case. The owners or managers of the various stores in Carrelville were invariably the ones who assisted her, sometimes even letting other customers wait while they did. That struck her suddenly as being very unfair.

"Good morning, Mrs. Carrel." A wide, professional smile spread across his face while his eyes crinkled at the corners behind steel-rimmed glasses. "It's going to be another hot one today, isn't it?"

"Yes, it is," Elizabeth agreed, wondering if her vague embarrassment showed. "If you're busy, Mr. Shaw, I don't mind waiting a few minutes."

"Not at all, not at all," he assured her quickly. "I'll bet I can guess why you came in. I was just saying to my wife last night that we forgot to buy tickets for the charity dinner. She suggested I get a couple extra so we can take our daughter and her husband along."

"That's very generous of you, Mr. Shaw, but actually"—her smile faltered slightly—"I stopped in to buy a few things. Of course, I'd be happy to sell you the tickets."

Elizabeth knew he would be curious about whom she was buying clothes for, but he didn't comment until the money and tickets had been exchanged.

"Now, what can I show you?" he asked.

Elizabeth took the list from her purse and handed it to him without saying anything.

"This is almost a complete wardrobe." He peered at her over the top of his glasses. "Is—er—the rumor true? Jed came home?"

"Yes, Jed is back," she said, feeling very awkward.

"For good?" Then, as if he thought the question was too personal, Fred Shaw shrugged it aside. "You know, with Jed it's impossible to be sure." He led her toward a rack of expensive dress suits. "Craig Landers said that he thought he'd recognized Jed at the airport yesterday. Craig owns a small plane and the engine was being overhauled, that's why he was out there. Jed flew in, didn't he?"

Since Elizabeth hadn't asked, she could only assume that was so. "I believe he did."

"This is a nice one." He removed a suit from the rack for her to examine. "Craig mentioned that Jed looked a little the worse for wear. Has he been ill?"

"He didn't say." Elizabeth guessed it was a reference to the grubby clothes he'd arrived in. "Of course, he'd had a long trip. He was really tired when he got to the house."

"Where has he been? I heard once that he was living on some South Pacific island."

"More than one, I think. I don't remember what they were called—too many vowels." She fingered the material of a charcoal gray suit. "He travels a lot," she replied, remembering that the three letters had been postmarked at different places.

"What's he been doing all this time?"

That was another question that Elizabeth hadn't thought to ask him. "Oh, this and that," she hedged.

"Jed never did seem to be the type to settle down to one thing. Never seemed the type to settle down at all." Fred Shaw laughed as though he had made a joke. "You probably never got to meet him before now. I think he'd already left by the time you were engaged to Jeremy."

"No. He left just after we announced it," Elizabeth clarified. She tried to distract him from the subject by questioning him about the material in another one of the suits.

Once he'd answered, Fred Shaw got right back to Jed. Elizabeth sighed inwardly.

"Yes, I remember now. You and Jeremy got engaged just before Jed took off to wherever it was he was going. We all expected him back for the wedding, but that didn't happen. He wasn't dependable like his brother. Now Jeremy was a son that would make any parent proud.

He was a fine young man, trustworthy and a hard worker. But I guess I'm not telling you anything you didn't already know."

"Jeremy was a wonderful husband," she murmured. The garrulous shopkeeper was setting her nerves on edge.

"His death was a real tragedy." He shook his head and sighed. "It's always hard to accept that someone like Jeremy would be taken. He could have done so much good for the community. Jed was always the reckless one with that bad attitude of his."

She nodded, forced to listen.

"Why, I remember in his teens he'd disappear for a day or two, then show up and claim he'd hitchhiked to Dayton to see the Air Force Museum. Heaven only knows where he really went."

"Yes, well—"

"That was one boy who brought more than his share of heartache to his parents. And they tried so hard to see that he had all the advantages Jeremy had. Mr. Carrel insisted that he get a law degree, but every time Jed was expelled, his father would look for another place that would take him, paying whatever money was necessary. It was a shame, truly a shame."

"That was all very long ago, Mr. Shaw," Elizabeth said coldly.

Lost in thought as he was, it took several seconds for her remark to penetrate. By then it had lost some of its strength.

To her annoyance, he agreed with her—and kept right on talking. "Yes, it was. But after losing both Jeremy and Franklin, your mother-in-law is probably happy to have Jed back. Who knows?"

Elizabeth only nodded in reply and began selecting clothes from various racks and shelves. She was fully aware that the instant she left the shop, the news would spread all over town that Jed was back. The not-so-subtle barrage of questions she'd endured led her to believe that Rebecca had sent her so that *she* wouldn't have to answer them.

Choosing quickly, Elizabeth picked clothes that she thought Jed would look good in, knowing that Rebecca wouldn't necessarily agree with her choices. Tough luck. Rebecca wasn't here. It was a relief when most of the items on the list were checked off and the clothes carefully folded into boxes. She signed the charge ticket with a flourish, anxious to be on her way before old Fred started talking again.

Her car was parked at the end of the block. Elizabeth walked swiftly ahead of the clerk who'd been assigned to help her with the cumbersome boxes. Opening the rear door on the driver's side, she stepped back to let him pass.

"Elizabeth!" A male voice spoke her name in warm surprise.

Turning, she saw Allan Marsden standing on the sidewalk in front of her car. He was the administrator at the local city-county hospital and had been for the last year and a half. There was some question as to how long he would stay in Carrelville when the town had to compete with larger cities that could offer him more prestigious jobs and better salaries. He was in his late thirties, which was young by the standards of local officials, and talked about as if he was destined to go places.

"Hello, Allan." Her greeting wasn't as friendly as usual. Elizabeth really wanted to get home.

"I had no idea you'd be in town around lunch hour or I would've invited you to join me." His sandy brown hair looked bronze in the sun when he inclined his head toward her.

"I had a committee meeting and a few errands to run.

I'm kind of pressed for time," she said, hoping he would take the hint.

"There. You're all set," said the young clerk as he closed the rear door of her car. "Mr. Shaw wanted me to be sure and remind you that everything can be returned if it doesn't fit."

Elizabeth nodded. "Tell him thanks."

There was a puzzled light in Allan's eyes as he watched the clerk go back to Shaw's Men's Shop. When his gaze swung curiously to Elizabeth, she didn't much want to explain. But she liked Allan. She had gone out on three dates with him, the last nearly two weeks ago.

He was a pleasant guy and undemanding. Although what she'd told Jed was true: she really didn't feel the need for a man's constant attention or companionship. But with Allan standing right there, it didn't seem polite to let him wonder why on earth she was buying men's clothes. Especially considering that the news would be all over town within an hour that Jed was back, and even a relative newcomer like Allan Marsden would hear it.

"As you can see, I was on a mission." Elizabeth smiled, gesturing toward the boxes piled up in the rear seat of her car. "My brother-in-law just came back to Carrelville after being away for ages. His clothes haven't caught up with him yet, so I was appointed to buy him a few things."

"Your brother-in-law?" Allan lifted a sandy eyebrow in surprise. "Sorry. For some reason I thought your late husband was an only child."

"Jed's younger. He's been out of the country for several years."

"Then you and Mrs. Carrel must be enjoying the reunion." He smiled.

"Yes," she agreed. Never in a million years would she discuss what was actually going on at home. It wasn't necessarily going to last much longer and people didn't have to know.

"Oh, by the way, I intended to call you tonight." Allan stepped down from the curb, coming closer to her. "I bought two tickets to that charity dinner and I was hoping you'd go with me. I'd be honored."

There was no reason for her not to accept, but Elizabeth found herself refusing. "I'm sorry, Allan, I can't. For one thing, I have to be there early to supervise the arrangements. And I'm the committee's organizing chair, so I'll have other duties, to be announced. You know how it is. Maybe it would be best if we just planned to see each other there," she suggested.

She sensed he wasn't thrilled by her suggestion, but he didn't say that in so many words or allow any disappointment to show. If he was interested in her, and she was pretty sure of that, he seemed not to want to rush her. Maybe he didn't want to risk offending a Carrel, especially her mother-in-law. The thought was distasteful.

"The weatherman said Sunday is going to be beautiful. How about you and me and Amy going for a picnic? Say, around two?" Allan countered.

Hesitating for an awkward second, Elizabeth was unwilling to refuse a second invitation from him even though she was just as reluctant to accept it.

"Ah—can you call me early this evening, Allan?" she stalled. "I just don't know if Rebecca made plans, what with Jed back and all."

"Sure." He gave her a big smile. "I'll keep my fingers crossed."

"Okay, thanks. I should know more by then," Elizabeth promised, reaching for the handle of the car door. "I really have to get back."

He looked at his watch. "I'm due at the office myself. I'll talk to you tonight, Elizabeth."

He was still standing on the sidewalk as she backed out of the parking space. She waved to him self-consciously, wishing she had refused the second invitation outright and wondering why she didn't want to go.

The Carrel house was two miles outside town, built decades ago by an ancestor who had combined his career as a distinguished judge with that of a gentleman farmer. More recently, their semi-isolation from the rest of the community seemed to reinforce the image of the Carrels as high and mighty.

Elizabeth didn't drive into the garage but parked in the driveway to make it easier to carry in the boxes and whatnot. Amy was on the far side of the lawn under a large shade tree playing with her dolls. She waved, but didn't come running to her mother.

Balancing a precarious stack in her arms, Elizabeth opened the front door of the house and walked in. She spied her mother-in-law in the living room talking on the phone first, then saw the pad on the table beside her and the pencil in her hand. Rebecca glanced up, quickly removing the reading glasses from her nose. Eternally vain, Elizabeth thought.

Placing her hand over the receiver, she asked, "Did you get everything on the list?"

"Almost," Elizabeth replied. She'd skipped the underwear. No way was she choosing between briefs and boxers for a man she didn't know, and Rebecca hadn't specified either type.

"You'd better take it all upstairs and hang things up before they get creased and need pressing," Rebecca instructed. Orders given, she resumed her phone conversation.

It was tricky negotiating the stairs when the boxes kept her from seeing her feet, but Elizabeth made it to the top. Walking to the end of the hallway, she found the door to Jed's bedroom ajar and pushed it open. She paused on the threshold, reluctant to step inside.

There had always been an impersonal air to it before, making it just another bedroom. Now, there was something strangely different about it. For one thing, it smelled good. Glancing around, the only thing she saw in the room that belonged to Jed was the duffel bag sitting in one corner. The bed was expertly made without a wrinkle. Considering the way the washed dishes in the sink had been precisely placed in the drainboard, Elizabeth was certain that Jed had made the bed and not her mother-in-law.

Entering the room, she set the boxes on the bed. Curiosity got the better of her and directed her footsteps to the adjoining bathroom. There she found neat evidence of Jed's being there, what with razor, toothbrush, comb, and aftershave with an unmistakably male fragrance sitting on the counter next to the sink.

Elizabeth decided that had to be the distinctive scent she'd noticed when she entered the bedroom. With a guilty start, she realized she was snooping and backtracked swiftly.

Needing something legitimate to do, she began opening the boxes and removing the clothes from the folds of the protective tissue. There was a funny sensation in the pit of her stomach and a faintly embarrassed warmth in her face.

She told herself not to be so silly. She'd handled men's clothes before, for goodness' sake. Why should she be self-conscious about it all of a sudden?

Elizabeth straightened a suit on its hanger and turned to walk to the closet, finding herself staring straight at Jed. He was leaning against the door jamb in much the same lazy, slouching pose as yesterday, his hands stuffed in his pockets. The unreadable expression on his face was enlivened by the faint amusement in the topaz brown eyes that studied her intently.

Her fingers closed nervously over the sleeve of the suit jacket as his gaze swept from her to the open boxes on the bed, and back again. Faking a poise she didn't feel, Elizabeth walked to the closet, trying to make what she was doing seem natural.

"Your mother thought you needed some new clothes," she said. "So she sent me out to get them."

"Thanks a lot." His reply had a definite edge.

Chapter 4

"Did she decide that when she went through my things last night?" His footsteps made no sound on the carpet, but Elizabeth, her back still to him, could tell by the direction of his voice that he'd moved to the bed. "You have great taste, Liza. I should have you pick out my clothes all the time."

"How did you know—" She spun around in surprise.

"That it was you?" Jed finished the question for her, amusement showing in his expression now. "Because it's hard to imagine my mother running the gauntlet in town when she could send you."

It had occurred to Elizabeth that she'd been enlisted for just that reason, but she wasn't about to agree with Jed. She hung the suit in the closet and carried another hanger back to the bed.

"I opened our old account with Shaw's," she told him. "If there's anything else you need, you can get it there."

"Oh, I'm sure the list was as thorough as the search," Jed said dryly.

"What makes you so sure that I wasn't the one who went through your stuff?" Elizabeth asked, driven by a surprising impulse to defend Rebecca.

"You don't seem like the snooping type," he said bluntly.

Bending over the jacket lying on the bed, she made a pretense of straightening the lapel to conceal the color that had swept into her cheeks. Good thing he hadn't come in while she was in his bathroom.

"You did have your lunch, didn't you?" she asked in an effort to direct the conversation away from herself.

"Yes, at the Reisners'."

"You went out so early this morning that I thought you might have gone there." Elizabeth kept moving, occupying her hands with the clothes and going back and forth to the closet to avoid looking much at Jed.

"Freda, Kurt's sister, seems to like you," he commented idly. "As she puts it, you're not a snob like my mother."

"I like Freda too. She's very nice."

"It's strange that with you two living so close, you don't see each other that much. Freda said that mostly you just bump into each other in town."

"Well, you know how it is." She gave a stiff little shrug. "I'm usually busy with a meeting of one kind or another. The free time that I do have, I like to spend with Amy."

"I'm sure Freda wouldn't mind if you brought Amy along. She likes kids. As a matter of fact," he continued with a smile, "I'm invited to dinner there on Sunday and Freda wanted to know if you and Amy could come too."

"That's impossible," Elizabeth refused immediately.

"Why?" For all the softness in his voice, there was an edge to his question.

"Because I've already made other plans." She was suddenly glad that she hadn't refused Allan's invitation. It provided a perfect excuse.

"Really?" he mocked.

"Yes, really." Irritation flashed in her green eyes that

he doubted her. "Amy and I were invited to a picnic on Sunday."

"Well, since you have a prior commitment, I'll convey your apologies to Freda." His tone was still skeptical.

"Jed, I'm not making it up," Elizabeth said angrily. "Allan Marsden did ask us out this Sunday. As a matter of fact, he's calling tonight to confirm it. I thought your mother might plan something for your first Sunday back at home, or I would've said yes to him right away." It was a small white lie, but one that she thought was justified under the circumstances. "Anyway, you're not going to be home, and there isn't any reason not to make it definite with Allan."

"Allan Marsden?" Jed repeated. "Not a name I know. He must be new around here."

"He's the hospital administrator."

"Oh. Did the hospital ever raise the funds for that new clinic?"

"No." Suspicion loomed suddenly and she frowned. "Why?"

"Just curious. It's been in the planning stages since forever. When you mentioned the hospital, the clinic came to my mind."

Elizabeth didn't believe his question had been prompted by casual curiosity. "If you're implying that Allan is seeing me in the hopes that your mother could be persuaded to make a great big donation and get the ball rolling, you're wrong."

"I'm sure I am," he agreed smoothly.

"Allan leaves all that to the hospital's fund-raising committee."

"Of course."

Her lips tightened, and Elizabeth knew she was on the verge of losing her temper. His complacent gaze studied the flashing fire in her eyes.

"I very much doubt that he'd even mention the hospital while we're together," Elizabeth added defensively, tugging impatiently at the suit jacket on the hanger.

"He wouldn't be much of a man if he did," Jed said with a suggestive smile. "A warm summer afternoon, a shady glade, a blanket on the ground, and you next to him—hell, I wouldn't be thinking about work."

"Which is just one reason why I'm going out with Allan, not you, Jed Carrel." Stalking to the closet, she jammed the hanger hook on to the horizontal pole. "Don't get it twisted."

"Did I?" He looked at her with laughing inquiry.

"Shut up, okay? Just shut up."

"But I was going to apologize."

"Don't bother to pretend that you're sorry," she said sharply. The last outfit was in the closet and she began busily gathering up the boxes and tissue, loading her arms with them. "Excuse me. Recycling. Coming through."

He didn't get out of her way. "Then please accept my heartfelt thanks for choosing my new clothes."

"It's only sheep's clothing, Jed," Elizabeth tossed over her shoulder as she left the room. His laughter followed her down the hall.

Supper was usually on the table by seven o'clock, a time that had been chosen not because Rebecca liked to eat relatively late, but because her husband had always stayed in his office past five. The habit of eating at seven had been too deeply ingrained to change after his death. Elizabeth had never minded it. It seemed to make long evenings go by faster.

Allan Marsden called as promised, but the phone rang just as she was setting plates on the table. She was on the living room extension when Jed walked into the room. Staring at the charcoal gray suit he was wearing, one that she'd chosen, she was stunned by the way it enhanced his dark virility. The suit fitted his muscular leanness so perfectly it could have been tailored just for him.

For a full second Elizabeth was aware only of his disturbing presence. Then she realized that Allan's voice was repeating the time of their planned outing and waiting for her to say something. Forcing herself to ignore Jed, she tried to think.

"Ah—Sunday at two is fine, Allan," she said brightly. "Amy and I will be ready a little before that. Is there anything I can bring?"

"Nope. It's all taken care of already. I didn't allow myself to consider the possibility that you might say no. I'm glad you didn't, Elizabeth."

"Yes, well—" She glanced apprehensively at Jed, knowing that he was aware she was talking to Allan. Aware, hah. He was deliberately eavesdropping. Anger at him flashed in her green eyes but it only seemed to prompt a flicker of amusement in his tawny gaze. "I really have to go, Allan. We were just sitting down to dinner."

"Of course." Allan didn't seem bothered by her sudden desire to end the conversation. "I'll see you Sunday."

"Looking forward to it," she said quickly. "Goodbye, Allan."

She was already replacing the receiver as Allan's goodbye echoed into the room. There was an instant's hesitation as she considered asking Jed why he'd stuck around while she talked. She was tempted to tell him off for his bad manners. Jed gave her a wink. His hands were thrust into his pockets as if he was bored and just happened to be standing in the same room, killing time instead of listening in.

No, she wasn't going to say anything about his behavior. She didn't need the aggravation he would give her in return.

"The food will be on the table in a few minutes," Elizabeth stated, turning away from him as she spoke.

"No need to hurry on my account," Jed responded calmly.

Even that bland remark annoyed her. But she wasn't going to be baited. Elizabeth walked out of the room. Maybe he didn't feel the need for haste, but she did. She wanted to get supper over with as quickly as possible. A little voice told her that she was becoming much too conscious of him and, furthermore, that she'd be a fool to let him get under her skin.

In the middle of the meal, Elizabeth remembered that she hadn't told Rebecca about Allan Marsden's invitation. She disliked going into the specifics in front of Jed, but she knew her mother-in-law had a church group meeting that evening and would be leaving before dessert was served.

"Amy and I will be out this Sunday afternoon, Rebecca," she said with false casualness. "We've been invited—"

"Oh, are we going to the farm with Uncle Jed?" Amy burst in excitedly.

"What farm?" Rebecca demanded, her dark eyes centering immediately on Elizabeth, her interest not nearly as vague as it was a moment ago.

Darting a poisonous look at Jed, who appeared immune to its sting, Elizabeth replied firmly, "Amy and I were invited on a Sunday picnic by Allan Marsden—"

"Phooey." Amy frowned across the table, disappointment starting to cloud her face. "Aren't we going to the farm?"

If it hadn't been for the distinct impression that Jed was deriving some sort of amused satisfaction from all this, Elizabeth's response would have been gentler.

"We will be outdoors, Amy. Picnics usually are. You know that."

"What farm is she talking about?" Rebecca inserted, looking pointedly at her son.

"I was invited to Sunday dinner at the Reisners'." Nonchalantly, he buttered a hot crescent roll. "Kurt suggested that Elizabeth join us and bring Amy, but she made plans with Marsden and had to say no."

"I see," was his mother's clipped response.

"But I wanted to go to the farm," Amy declared with a pleading look at her mother.

"Well, we're going on the picnic and that's that." Even as she spoke, Elizabeth knew she should have quietly explained that they could go to the farm another time, instead of issuing a coldly worded order. Too late now.

"I don't want to go on your stupid old picnic!" Amy let the silver fork in her hand clatter loudly onto her plate, and put on a sulky face. "I want to go to the farm and see the animals. I don't want to go with you!"

"That's enough, Amy," Elizabeth warned with firm softness.

"Maybe you can go another time," Jed said, a warm smile turning up the corners of his mouth.

Elizabeth scowled at him. This was pretty much all his fault.

"I never get to do what I want." Amy's lower lip jutted out in a self-pitying pout, as she flashed a resentful look at her mother. "It's not fair!"

Elizabeth was incensed at Jed's attempt to smooth things over. If he hadn't mentioned his going out to the farm in the first place, there wouldn't be hard feelings between her and her daughter. But she directed her angry feelings at Amy instead of the man at her right.

"Don't be such a brat. And don't talk to me in that tone of voice."

"I just don't want to go on that picnic!" Tears began filling her daughter's brown eyes.

"I think you'd better go to your room, Amy." Elizabeth tried to speak calmly and control her own growing temper. "When you can behave at this table, you can come back."

"No! I won't go to my room!" The held-back tears made Amy's voice tremble.

Aren't we just one big happy family, Elizabeth thought bitterly. Jed was the instigator—and Rebecca seemed to be choosing to mind her own business for once. That right there was something to think about, but Elizabeth wasn't going to argue with mother or son. Although she hadn't handled the situation too well, she had to follow through. Amy's behavior was way out of line, regardless.

Flashing Jed a look of barely controlled fury, Elizabeth rose from her chair and walked round to the opposite side of the table where Amy sat.

With downcast eyes, Amy pushed her chair away from the table. A tear slid down a round cheek as Amy refused to look at her mother, letting her sense of injustice be known.

"Come on, Amy," Elizabeth said quietly. She touched the girl's shoulder and immediately Amy pulled away to walk toward the hall, playing a tragic, misunderstood young heroine to the hilt.

As Elizabeth turned to follow, she caught Jed's annoyingly bland expression. "It's not her fault, Liza," he said.

"Oh, I know," she snapped. "You had no right to even mention the invitation to the farm to her without consulting me first. If anyone's to blame, it's you!"

Her long legs moved to follow her daughter's dragging steps. Once she was out of Jed's presence, she would explain to Amy why they were going on the picnic instead of to the farm. And yes, she would summon up the patience she should have shown in the first place. Yet there was the nagging thought that she had seized on Allan's invitation in order to have a plausible reason for refusing Jed's.

The area rug cushioned the sound of another chair being pushed back from the table. Not until a hand took hold of Elizabeth's wrist to stop her forward movement did she realize that Jed had followed her. Her hair swirled around her face in a cascade of ebony curls as he turned her around to face him. His eyes narrowed on her expression of astonished outrage before they flickered briefly to Amy, who had paused to listen near the stairwell.

"Go on up to your room, Amy," Jed said firmly, but without anger. "I want to talk to your mother for just a bit."

Amy hesitated and then Elizabeth heard the sound of her footsteps slowly going up the stairs.

"I don't see that we have anything to discuss," Elizabeth said tautly, tossing her head back to glare at him.

"Yes, we do."

"Well, maybe so," she agreed suddenly with a haughty lift of her chin. She didn't attempt to pull free of his grip. "Go ahead and explain. After I'd already turned down the invitation, I think it was really manipulative of you to mention it to Amy and try to use her to persuade me to change my mind." She drew in a long breath.

"Are you finished?"

"Yes."

"First of all, I didn't tell Amy about the invitation," Jed answered curtly.

"Do you expect me to believe that?" Elizabeth demanded. "I hadn't even mentioned to her that we were going on the picnic Sunday, let alone tell her that we'd turned down your invitation. There's no one else who could have told her except you!"

His gaze narrowed. "The only conversation I had with your daughter was about where I was this morning. I did tell her I'd been at the Reisners' farm."

"And that you were invited on Sunday and so were we," she pointed out. "And now she's starring in her own little drama and I get to play the supporting role of Mean Mom."

"Okay, I also said I was going there on Sunday," he admitted, "but I never mentioned that you'd been invited or that you'd made other plans for the day."

"Then where did she get the idea that we might be visiting the farm?" Elizabeth asked with cold disbelief.

"As I recall"—there was a warning look in his eyes—"Amy asked if she might go over sometime to see the puppies I'd told her about. I said she would have to ask you."

"That's a likely story," she scoffed. "Why can't you just admit you were trying to get her to influence me?"

"Hey, I don't care whether you ever go to the Reisners' or not," Jed snapped. "I only passed along Kurt's invitation. If I wanted you to change your mind, I wouldn't go through Amy, not in a million years. I just wouldn't do something like that."

"Then why did you bring up the subject of the farm with her at all?" Elizabeth continued to protest angrily. "Were you, oh, jealous of the fact that I have a really good, warm, loving relationship with my daughter?" Her temper really got the better of her when he didn't answer. "Did you want to make it as miserable and bitter as the one between you and your mother?"

"I don't give a damn what you think!" He released her wrist, fury in his eyes. "But if you want to think of me that way, go ahead! The only opinion that matters to me is my own."

In the next second he was striding away and Elizabeth was staring after him in angry amazement. He disappeared into the front hallway. Then the front door slammed with resounding violence.

"Elizabeth!" Rebecca Carrel's voice called imperiously from the dining room. "Was that Jed who just stormed out?"

"Yes," she said, her voice low with indignation.

"You might as well come back in here and finish your meal," her mother-in-law ordered.

As if she wanted to. Elizabeth glanced to the dining room archway, then toward the stairway and the room at the top where Amy was waiting. She forced herself to swallow back the tight knot of anger.

"In a moment, Rebecca," she said in a more controlled tone. "I want to have a talk with Amy first."

"I think it would be best if you left her alone for a while. It will give her an opportunity to consider how unforgivably rude she was. She must apologize." There was a light pause before Rebecca added in a sour tone, "Clearly, she doesn't take after her father."

She acts just like Jed, her uncle. Elizabeth mentally finished the sentence for her mother-in-law, who for some reason had waited a long time—for her—to speak up about Amy's behavior. But there was truth in what the older woman said. Amy's independent nature and penchant for talking back were a lot more like Jed than Jeremy, even though she barely knew her uncle. Like him, Amy tended to ignore rules that didn't make sense to her.

Taking a deep breath again, she walked toward the steps. In the back of her mind, she knew that when she'd explained to Amy why they were going on the picnic, she was going to find out exactly what Jed had told her daughter about the farm. She still didn't believe Jed's version.

But after talking with Amy, Elizabeth had to. Amy's imagination had been enough to make her jump to the conclusion that the three of them were going to the farm. It was a fairly logical line of reasoning from a child's point of view, Elizabeth decided silently, since it was the farm, and the puppies, of course, that were uppermost in Amy's mind.

As far as the picnic was concerned, Amy remained completely unenthusiastic. She grudgingly agreed to go to it by the time their talk ended, but refused to return to the dinner table. The sulky look on her daughter's face stayed right where it was. Elizabeth's lighthearted coaxing didn't cheer her up in the least.

Amy's boredom couldn't have been more plain if she'd spent the entire afternoon sitting on the picnic blanket and yawning. Elizabeth had been too self-conscious and irritated by her rudeness to react naturally. The responses she made to Allan's attempts at small talk were stilted and fake, not helping the uneasy mood of the outing. Her embarrassment had increased when Allan suggested they call it a day at four o'clock, barely two hours after they'd unpacked the basket.

To make matters worse, Amy mumbled an ungracious thank-you and bolted from the car the minute Allan stopped it in front of their house. Elizabeth stared after her for a full minute before turning to Allan, and noticing his wry smile.

"Sorry. She wasn't on her best behavior, was she? She really isn't a brat, but—"

"You don't need to explain." Allan smiled understandingly. He took one of the hands that were twisted together in her lap and held it in his own. "Maybe she just didn't feel like sharing you. Kids can be selfish about getting attention, especially when they have only one parent."

"It wasn't jealousy." Elizabeth shifted uncomfortably.

"The other day I was angry at someone else and—and I kind of took it out on her. She hasn't forgiven me for it."

"I can't imagine you being angry. You're much too beautiful." The smooth compliment sprang easily from his lips.

She smiled nervously. "Oh—thanks. But I do get angry. I'm human."

"That's encouraging." His gaze swept over her wind-tousled hair and she glanced in the corner of the rearview mirror for a second. She ran her fingers through the jet black curls and cast a critical look at her rosy cheeks. With all that fresh air and sunshine today, she shouldn't feel unhappy.

Suddenly, leaning forward, Allan surprised her by pressing a warm, lingering kiss against her lips before he spoke again. "I'll see you at the dinner next week, okay?"

When he straightened away from her, Elizabeth's green eyes had a flustered look. It wasn't for romantic reasons, that was for sure. But there was nothing wrong with the way he kissed.

Elizabeth reached for the door handle, then paused with the door a little bit open. "Thank you, Allan, for everything," she offered in gratitude for his understanding.

"Maybe another time the three of us can do this again."

"Sure. Why not?" She hoped he didn't pick up on the uncertainty in her voice.

Waving once as he reversed out of the drive, Elizabeth walked toward the house. Amy's behavior shouldn't be allowed to go without comment, but she was reluctant to lecture her about it. Sighing heavily, she opened the front door.

The sound of Amy's laughter stopped her on the threshold. The entire afternoon, her daughter had barely smiled at all and now she was laughing.

Elizabeth's chin lifted at the sight of her daughter with

Jed. His tawny gaze took her in, a watchfulness in his expression despite the grin on his face. Then Amy glanced over her shoulder and the smile faded from her mouth. Apology flickered in her dark eyes before she dashed toward the stairs.

Jed just stood there as Elizabeth shut the door behind her. A flash fire of irritation raced through her, angry that he'd been able to make Amy laugh when Allan had tried so hard and failed.

"I didn't expect you back so soon," Jed said.

"That makes two of us, because neither did I," she retorted coldly.

"What happened?"

There was an ironic arch of her brow. "Didn't Amy tell you? Her sulking made the picnic totally miserable for everyone."

"No, she didn't mention it," he replied evenly.

"Really? I was sure that's what the two of you were laughing about," she said in a faintly accusing tone. It completely slipped her mind that she hadn't apologized for doubting his word the other night. She hadn't had an opportunity to speak to him alone and she had no intention of apologizing to him in front of Rebecca or Amy.

"I wouldn't worry." Jed studied her for a long moment. "Your boyfriend won't care if one afternoon wasn't perfect."

"He's not—" Elizabeth checked herself, not willing to deny that Allan was her boyfriend. It would only trigger another snide comment. "As a matter of fact," she said coldly, "I'll be seeing Allan at the charity dinner next Saturday night."

"I hope you didn't agree to let him escort you," he observed dryly.

"That's none of your business, Jed."

"Hmm. You could be right. I guess it would be

Mother's business, not mine." The curl of his mouth hinted at something he knew that she didn't.

"Rebecca doesn't dictate my social life," Elizabeth said emphatically.

"You can argue that point with her." His expression showed little interest as he turned away.

"What are you getting at?" she demanded, drawing an over-the-shoulder glance from Jed.

In that fleeting instance, she caught a flash of a bad boy, all grown up, but still very much a rogue. His eyes glittered with mischievous satisfaction, totally erasing the cynicism that was generally there. He had, so often, the hard look of a man who'd been dealt a difficult hand in life, and now it was gone. Strange.

"My mother has decided that I'm going to make an entrance, possibly to the sound of trumpets, at your dinner next week," Jed replied. "She intends the Carrel family to attend this social function together."

"And you're going?" she murmured doubtfully.

"You've forgotten, Liza." His gaze narrowed slightly. "I came back to make peace. That requires compromise. So yes, I am attending your black tie banquet. Are you excited?"

Chapter 5

"Jed has arrived with the sitter, Elizabeth. Are you ready yet?" Rebecca called.

Halting the tube of lipstick an inch from her lips, Elizabeth answered, "In a minute!"

"Well, please hurry," her mother-in-law said impatiently. "I don't want to be the last to arrive."

Sighing ruefully, Elizabeth looked into the mirror, wishing for the millionth time that she hadn't let Rebecca persuade her to make that grand entrance as part of a trio. No trumpets, apparently. Just her, her daughter-in-law, and Jed, dressed to kill and smiling like a toothpaste ad.

She'd thought she would have the perfect excuse: the supervision of the predinner arrangements. But Rebecca had adamantly insisted that as organizing chair, Elizabeth should appoint someone else to the task. Now she realized that she had given in because of the subconscious echo of Jed's words on compromise and making peace.

Bah. She'd compromised her better judgment by going along with Rebecca's self-centered plan. She had no idea what Jed really thought of it; he hadn't exactly said.

The silk underlining of her white lace dress rustled as

she went to the hallway door. Turning the doorknob, she remembered her matching shawl and evening bag were lying on the bed. She retrieved them quickly from the blue satin coverlet. Her pulse was behaving erratically and her nerves were so jumpy that she was sure she hadn't been this skittish on her first date in junior high. But her outward composure revealed none of her inner agitation.

Amy was waiting for her at the bottom of the stairs. Her brown eyes widened and her mouth rounded into a sighing "Oh!"

A smile of genuine pleasure eased the tense muscles around Elizabeth's mouth. "Do I look all right?" She turned slowly for her daughter's benefit.

"Mom, you look beautiful!" Amy assured her in a breathy voice.

"Hello, Cindy," Elizabeth greeted the teenager standing in the hall.

"Hello, Mrs. Carrel. That's a gorgeous dress." The young girl gazed almost enviously at the perfectly fitted gown and its sweeping skirt. There was a telltale glimmer of braces when she spoke. Elizabeth remembered her own schoolgirl dreams of enchantment whenever she'd seen adults in formal clothes, and she smiled.

"Thank you." She wished she could forget her misgivings about the evening and catch some of the stardust in Cindy's eyes. "Did my mother-in-law give you all our cell numbers? You can also reach us through the country club desk."

"I have that number too," Cindy said. She smiled down at Amy. "I'm sure everything will be fine, right, Amy?"

The younger girl nodded eagerly and slipped her hand into Cindy's.

Rebecca stepped into the arch of the front hallway. "Elizabeth, Jed is waiting in the car."

Bending to kiss her daughter's cheek, Elizabeth teased, "Be good for a change, Amy."

"I'll try," she said as she wrinkled her nose impishly.

Following her mother-in-law to the car, Elizabeth took her place in the backseat, murmuring polite thanks when Jed held the door open for her. The country club and adjoining golf course were only a mile or so from the house, which made the journey short. But she was conscious of Jed's faint air of preoccupation. She was almost sure his silence couldn't be blamed on the event ahead of them.

The entrance lights fully illuminated the expertly tailored suit he wore, a last-minute buy and not from here. He opened the car door for her, offering her his hand to help her out. Elizabeth looked at him in bewilderment. The material of his suit and the white silk shirt were much more expensive than anything at Shaw's.

"What's the matter?" One corner of his mouth lifted as he tossed the car keys to the parking attendant. He touched the dark lapel with his finger. "Don't you like the suit?"

"Yes," she answered quickly, avoiding the gleam in his eyes. She made a pretense of adjusting her evening shawl. "It's just that you didn't mention you'd bought anything when you went to Cleveland last week."

"I wasn't aware that I needed to," he replied, lightly touching her elbow to guide her around the car to where Rebecca waited.

Pressing her lips tightly together, Elizabeth didn't comment. Jed had been absent most of the week, something that had bothered her since she'd never been entirely sure when he might turn up. His explanations, even to his mother, as to where he'd been were vague and uninformative. Elizabeth couldn't make up her mind whether his mysteriousness was deliberate or just how he was.

When they reached Rebecca's side, she preceded them into the club, her head tilted regally as though she were leading a royal procession. As if on cue, heads turned at their approach. Curiosity was the main reaction, covered up by friendly greetings and handshakes. The farther they walked into the small reception area where cocktails were being served, the more conscious Elizabeth became of another reaction.

Her gaze slid to the man at her side. Six foot, lean, with thick, carelessly waving brown hair and rakishly carved features, Jed Carrel was a compellingly attractive man and quite sexy. He was not the handsomest or tallest man in the room, though. And Elizabeth realized that he wasn't holding everyone's attention simply because he was a Carrel or because he was the black sheep of his rich family, come back to the fold for reasons unknown.

He had a worldly air, for one thing, that hinted at a life where he walked on the wild side now and then, a life no one from around here knew about. But more likely, Elizabeth thought, it was Jed's obvious virility that women in particular reacted to—and that men saw as potent competition.

She was still studying him on the sly when Jed turned his head and held her gaze. In that charged second she knew he'd been aware of her scrutiny all along.

"What do you suppose they're thinking?" he murmured to her in an aside, in between greeting the various dinner guests who came up to them.

Elizabeth said a quick hello to Mr. Shaw and his wife before answering Jed's question in a voice as soft as his. "I'm not sure. But you seem to have surprised them. You look really handsome in that suit. Almost civilized."

"Civilized, huh?" Jed gave her a wink. "That's an illusion. Nice to know anyone believes it."

The smile she gave him as she looked into his face was cool and controlled. "I'm sure the mothers are wondering if they should let their daughters near you and"—she paused for emphasis—"whether they're too old to catch you themselves."

His quiet chuckle was meant only for her to hear. "I didn't expect cynicism from you, Liza."

His captivating smile caught her by surprise. She hadn't realized he could be so charming. She quickly averted her gaze, feeling the warmth rising in her neck and making her cheeks pink.

"I didn't mean to sound cynical," she replied.

At that moment Barbara Hopkins detached herself from a younger group of adults and glided forward to meet Elizabeth. Her friend's eyes kept straying to Jed. That was to be expected, Elizabeth thought. After all, Jed could be classified as an eligible bachelor and there was a shortage of unattached men in Carrelville.

"Elizabeth!" Barbara called, then reached out with a ringed hand in greeting. "That's a beautiful gown."

Elizabeth returned the compliment—Barbara did look great, but then she always did—before introducing Jed. Barbara's coy gaze vaguely irritated Elizabeth when it was directed at Jed, but it didn't seem to bother him.

"So you play tennis with Elizabeth?" He smiled, holding Barbara's extended hand longer than Elizabeth thought was necessary.

"Yes, I do. About once a week. Do you play, Jed?"

Oh, please. Elizabeth didn't say it out loud, just looked at him as he nodded. Then at her friend, brightening. Barbara, Jed, Barbara, Jed. The small talk started and the flirtation was on. Elizabeth felt like her head was turning at a tennis match, watching them talk.

"We should play doubles." Barbara looked pointedly at Elizabeth, letting her know it wasn't an idle suggestion. "Can you ask Allan to be your partner?"

The reference to Allan Marsden made Elizabeth conscious of the man standing to her left. At the mention of his name he stepped forward, handing Elizabeth one of the drinks he held in his hand.

"Hello, Elizabeth. I've been waiting for you to arrive. Good to see you." He smiled pleasantly as he spoke, a questioning light in his eyes.

Not meeting his gaze squarely, she replied, "Ah—there was a last-minute change to the schedule," remembering only too well that she'd discouraged his offer to escort her tonight because she was supposed to be here early.

Jed's hand shifted from her elbow to the back of her waist as he leaned around her, a subtle intimacy in his touch that she found unnerving. "You must be Allan Marsden. Elizabeth's mentioned you." He extended a hand. "I'm Jed Carrel."

"Welcome home," Allan said, shaking hands firmly. "You've probably heard that often enough, right?"

Jed glanced at Elizabeth for a fraction of a second, then he replied, "Not so often that I'm tired of hearing it, put it that way."

Her fingers tightened around the glass Allan had given her as she wondered if anyone from the immediate family had said anything like that. Certainly she hadn't and neither had his mother. It would be ironic if his first words of welcome came from a stranger. Ironic and cruel.

"I see you've been here long enough to find the bar," Jed observed, nodding at the iced drink in Allan's hand.

"Let me show you where it is," Barbara offered quickly.

Her friend was wasting no time in staking a claim on

Jed, Elizabeth thought with a flash of bitterness that startled her. Jed's gaze seemed to laugh openly at the darkening green of her eyes.

"Please excuse me." The grooves around his mouth deepened with a suppressed smile.

"Of course." Her skin felt suddenly cool where his hand had warmed the back of her waist. Some of the chill crept into her voice, tight and dull.

"He isn't what I expected," Allan said as he watched Jed following Barbara through the crowd.

"Oh? Why not?" Elizabeth's attempt at nonchalance came out frosty and defensive.

Allan glanced at her, taking his time to answer. "Well, I heard the rumors, and I imagined someone arrogant, who had a big chip on his shoulder. He seems pretty self-assured. And he knows how to turn on the charm."

"Hmm. I think he works at both." But Elizabeth didn't want to discuss Jed and didn't let herself look his way. He was on the other side of the room by now anyway.

"Was your husband like him?"

"No. Not at all. They were total opposites," she answered curtly. Then she abruptly changed the subject. "Allan, I want to apologize for the mix-up this evening. I hope you didn't arrive too early thinking you'd find me here."

"No, I didn't." The reply had an easygoing lightness for which she was grateful.

But it was impossible to completely avoid the subject of Jed. Nearly everyone she and Allan talked to had some comment or question about him. And her sensitive radar never lost track of where he was in the vast room. No matter how casually she glanced around, her gaze invariably landed on him. She couldn't help noticing his ability to hold himself somehow apart from others while appearing to join in with their laughter and conversation.

At the long dinner table, Elizabeth and Allan were seated on the opposite side from Jed and Barbara. Fortunately the other couple was several chairs down. Yet Elizabeth couldn't avoid seeing him whenever she glanced in that direction.

As the meal progressed, she found herself becoming increasingly irritated by her girlfriend's behavior. The way Barbara kept leaning confidentially toward him and accidentally brushing against him was just too obvious. The boldness of the flirtation left little to the imagination and there were plenty of onlookers.

Jed didn't bother to dodge Barbara's moves. In fact, Elizabeth was sure that the amused interest in his eyes was meant as encouragement.

By the time the last course was served, anger was smoldering inside her, igniting into hot flames whenever she looked at Jed, which was increasingly often. The merry sound of Barbara's laughter distracted her again, but this time her gaze was met and held by Jed's. His mouth quirked. Did he get her distaste and disgust at the show they were putting on? Hard to tell.

Then Barbara's hand was touching the sleeve of his jacket in light possession, drawing his attention back to her. Elizabeth stared at her untouched dessert plate, her nerves so taut that she felt at any moment they might snap. Smiling stiffly at Allan, she excused herself from the table, desperate to get away so she could think for a few minutes.

Once in the powder room, she stayed in the section with the mirrors and small scented candles decorating the marble sinks, taking deep, calming breaths and willing herself to relax, glad that there was no one there but herself and an attendant who seemed to understand that she needed to be left alone. Turning on the cold tap, she let the water flow over the insides of her wrists to cool the feverish heat in her veins.

But when she left the powder room, Elizabeth still didn't feel like returning to the table. Luckily, being the organizing chair of the dinner committee meant she could go into the kitchen without anyone asking why. She deliberately took her time, waiting until the moment the guests were leaving the dining area to return to the reception room where a dance band was warming up.

Oh, no. Allan was standing with Jed and Barbara.

Elizabeth hesitated for an instant, about to change direction, when Jed saw her. Fixing a smile on her face, she tried to pretend that she had just that moment seen them, but she didn't think Jed was fooled.

"There you are. Everything going okay?" Allan asked with a concerned smile.

"Swimmingly." She added what she hoped sounded like a satisfied sigh.

"I'm glad all I had to do was sell tickets," said Barbara, her hand resting on the inside of Jed's arm. "Now I can just enjoy the party."

"That was smart of Elizabeth," Jed murmured, glancing at the blonde. "I doubt that there's a man in this town who wouldn't buy from you, unless his wife was around."

"Jed Carrel!" Barbara sounded properly shocked, but it was only a pose.

Elizabeth moistened her lips and turned to Allan. "I hear the band is very good."

As if on cue, the band played the opening chord of the first song. A male hand touched her arm. Elizabeth glared at its owner, unable to keep her disdain from showing.

"Come on," he said quietly, "it seems only fitting that we should lead the first dance."

If she hadn't been so sure that it was what Jed expected,

she would've refused. Instead she inclined her head in agreement and allowed him to take her hand. She sensed that neither Allan nor Barbara approved, but there wasn't any way they could protest.

Two couples had walked out onto the empty dance floor when they heard the band launch into the first notes of "Beautiful Ohio." They moved back when they saw Jed leading Elizabeth there. In the center of the floor, he turned her into his arms and stopped. He chuckled faintly as he looked down at her almost grim expression.

"I feel like I'm holding a cold fish. Relax, Liza," Jed chided softly. "And smile. This is supposed to be fun."

"Is it?" But she smiled sweetly, forcing her body to become pliant and glide with him into the first few steps.

The firm pressure of the hand at her back made it easy for her to follow his lead. With each step she moved more easily, her rigidity lessening as if answering the challenge of his natural grace. Looking up into his eyes, shadowed by his lashes, Elizabeth found herself momentarily fascinated by the darkening amber hue, feeling a little giddy. They went twice around the dance floor before the first couple joined them. Jed slowed their steps and confined their dancing to a smaller area.

"Best to get these duty dances over with fast, don't you think?"

The spell of the dreamy, sentimental music was broken by his faintly sarcastic tone.

Trying to break free, Elizabeth kept herself from looking into his eyes and concentrated on the stark contrast between his white shirt collar and tan throat. Her own throat felt dry and parched from an inner heat. Having his hand spread on her back and the rock-hard muscles of his thighs against her body was causing that.

"You're right about that," Elizabeth agreed huskily,

straining slightly against his arm so she wouldn't be held too closely against his hips.

"I bet everyone is saying how well we dance together."

She glanced around. They did seem to be the object of interested scrutiny and admiring murmurs. "Maybe so."

"If I hadn't danced with you, they would've been wondering why not for the rest of the night," he said.

It was an explanation she hadn't asked for. "Would you have cared?" she challenged.

Jed grinned. "I wonder what they would say if they knew you're nowhere near as sweet as you look."

She was taken aback. "What—"

"Let me explain. They regard you as brave, rising above the tragedy that befell you so young. Always behaving with the utmost decorum, faithful to the memory of your husband. Ever think about applying for sainthood?"

A betraying crimson flush raged across her face. "I believe you have to be nominated for that honor. And I'm not on the list."

He raised one eyebrow. "You should be. Look at that innocent blush. Very pretty."

"What are you getting at, Jed?"

There was the sensation of an invisible shrug. "Some people are just too good to be true."

"So? What does that have to do with me?"

He gave her a hooded look that deflected her outrage. "Maybe nothing. Jeremy would qualify for the definition, though." A strange sigh escaped him. "I used to get so tired of being reminded of what a good boy he was when I knew all the time that he wasn't any different from me. I took the blame for some of his pranks too many times."

"Oh, grow up. That was ages ago." She held up a hand to stop him from saying anything more. "Hey, I don't even know how we got on the subject but I'm not going to discuss Jeremy with you."

Her spirited defense silenced Jed for a few moments. But it occurred to her that since he'd returned, something odd had happened. She hadn't been able to visualize her late husband's face without looking at a photograph of him. It was as if Jed's compelling presence had knocked Jeremy out of her mind.

"Sorry. Didn't mean to bring up all those memories," Jed said. His gaze narrowed on her averted profile.

Ebony dark curls touched the bareness of her back as she tilted her head, glaring at him with resentment. She longed to startle him and say that her recollection of being Jeremy's wife was hazy, that their time together had been so brief that she was beginning to forget he'd existed—until Jed returned. The memory of her first meeting with Jed was clearer and more vivid than her wedding night with her husband, his brother.

But a sense of caution stopped her from admitting one word of that.

"Think what you like," she replied bitterly. "You will anyway, regardless of what I say."

"Do you know what I'm thinking?" he murmured with piercing softness. "I'm curious why you get so defensive every time I mention his name."

"Maybe it's because you're so obnoxious."

The music ended and she moved as swiftly as possible out of his arms. Her legs were treacherously unsteady. She realized that they had been all along, but Jed's supporting hold had made her unaware of it. His rangy stride had him at her side almost instantly, an arm at her waist as he guided her off the dance floor.

"You're shaky."

"Not really. Just relieved that I don't have to dance with you again," Elizabeth said under her breath.

"Ah, there's your adoring Allan." Jed smiled wickedly. "He's waiting patiently for me to return you to him. You know, he reminds me of Jeremy."

"He's nothing like him," she answered sharply.

"I didn't mean looks," Jed chuckled, "I meant personality. Allan will never make waves. He'd be scared to death of rocking the boat."

"What's the matter, Jed?" Her temper flared. "Isn't there anything you're afraid of? It's not his fault you're a failure. Are you jealous because Allan is a decent guy? And a success?"

"Hell, no. Liza—" There was anger in the way he said her name despite the tight control in his voice.

Elizabeth almost ran the last few steps to Allan, intimidated more than she cared to admit by the dark emotions she'd triggered in Jed. She should never have sunk to his level—but damn it, he'd provoked her. She reached for Allan's hand and clung to it.

Barbara had been waiting with Allan for the dance to end, and she stepped forward quickly to meet Jed. He smiled at her as if in answer to the silent promise in her eyes. The same feeling of distaste began to tie Elizabeth's stomach into knots again.

"I think I need a drink, Barbara," Jed stated, sliding an angry look at Elizabeth. "Let's head back to the bar."

"Would you like a cocktail?" Allan asked Elizabeth.

She was very much in need of a jolt of alcohol, but there was no way she was going to tag after Jed and Barbara to get it. "No, thanks."

The evening had been hopelessly ruined, but she fought against it, determined to have as much fun as Jed. Allan was attentive and her smiles and laughter encouraged him even more. It was unkind and unfair to look away from him to Jed so much. No matter how she tried, Elizabeth was unable to ignore him.

Despite Barbara's attempt to monopolize Jed, Elizabeth noticed when he danced with others. More duty dances, she thought resentfully. But she thought worse things every time she saw Jed and Barbara on the dance floor.

By midnight her head was pounding from the tension of constantly suppressing her emotions. She was sure she couldn't endure another minute without screaming. Her nerves were beyond raw. She nearly cried with relief when she saw Rebecca coming over.

"I think it's time we left, Elizabeth," her mother-in-law said after smiling politely at Allan. "We promised Cindy we wouldn't be late."

Elizabeth knew perfectly well that Rebecca wasn't motivated by consideration for the babysitter. Just as her mother-in-law didn't like to be the first to arrive, she didn't like to be the last to leave. Besides, it wouldn't be right for a Carrel to enjoy a party too much.

Allan began to hem and haw about something unimportant and Elizabeth suspected he was about to offer to take her home. She knew that once outside the country club, she would not be pleasant company. Considering the way she'd behaved toward him all evening, he would find her changed attitude puzzling and totally unlike her. Before he could speak, she did.

"I'm ready whenever you are, Rebecca," she said quickly, then turned to Allan. "Let's have lunch. Maybe this week. Or the next."

"Yes—" He hesitated slightly before resigning himself to her half promise. "Yes, we'll do that."

Brief farewells were exchanged all around, and Elizabeth and Rebecca were heading for the exit. "Did you get the car keys from Jed?" Elizabeth asked, clicking open her evening bag on the chance she'd brought a spare set.

"What? Jed is having the car brought around now." Rebecca frowned. "Where did you think he was?"

Elizabeth glanced back toward the group, nonplussed to see Barbara smiling and dancing with someone else. "I—I just thought he was going to stay for a while."

"No, he's leaving with us," was the firmly maternal response, as if any other action was unthinkable.

The car was at the door when they walked out and the parking attendant had already opened both side doors. Jed was behind the wheel with the motor running. He didn't seem at all surprised that Elizabeth was going back with them and not Allan. The instant the attendant closed the doors, he put the car in gear and turned it down the lane.

"It's such a relief to be away from that noise," Rebecca sighed. "It's overwhelming after a while."

Rebecca's throbbing temples echoed in agreement, but she couldn't blame the party for her headache. In the concealing darkness, she looked daggers at the strong profile of the driver.

"I was talking to Clive Bennet tonight," her mother-in-law continued. "He's one of the directors of the country club. The position of club manager will be vacant on the first of September. I sounded him out on the possibility of you taking it on, Jed. The club pretty well runs itself. The golf pro manages the greens, and the restaurant manager sees to food and liquor orders and staff hiring. Yours would be a strictly supervisory role."

"Thanks, but no thanks," Jed said evenly.

"What exactly is it that you intend to do?" Impatience sharpened Rebecca's voice to a cutting edge.

"What I've been doing."

"Which is nothing," she retorted.

He smiled thinly. "I know you were motivated by the best of intentions to ask about it on my behalf, Mother, but I believe I can decide for myself what I want."

"I swear you'll be a wastrel for the rest of your life," Rebecca muttered.

"But then, it is my life, isn't it?" His gaze slid to Rebecca before returning to the highway.

He was so arrogantly sure that he knew what was right. Elizabeth seethed but said nothing. She saw him glance at her reflection in the mirror and directed her gaze out the side window. If only he would leave, she wished silently. The quiet rhythms of her life seemed to have been permanently disrupted.

Chapter 6

"Did Amy behave herself?" Elizabeth removed the required amount of money from her purse and handed it to the babysitter.

"She's a great kid. No trouble at all," Cindy assured her, stifling a yawn as she stuffed the bills into her shoulder bag.

"I hope we didn't keep you too late." Elizabeth brushed back a strand of black hair, aware of Jed watching them near the front door, where he was waiting to take Cindy home. "I wouldn't want your parents to worry."

"Oh, no, Mrs. Carrel, I'm sure they're not worried. I explained that you were going out to a dance tonight and they weren't expecting me back until late."

Nodding, Elizabeth turned to Jed, who straightened up and jingled the car keys in his hand. "I'm the chauffeur service. Ready when you are, Miss Cindy."

It was an innocently teasing remark, but Cindy blushed. Elizabeth suddenly remembered her own teenage years and pressed her lips together—she knew the symptoms of a schoolgirl crush. Jed just naturally had that effect, even on women in their sixties. It seemed every female was potentially vulnerable to his masculine magic. The knowledge irritated her, perhaps because she was so vulnerable herself.

Cindy walked by Jed and out the door, looking over her shoulder to say good night to Elizabeth. A tiny smile that bordered on flirtatious turned up the corners of the girl's mouth, not quite wide enough to reveal the corrective braces on her teeth. Jed, oblivious to it, was asking her questions, his voice fading away as Elizabeth whirled away before the door closed behind them.

Beset by strong emotions she didn't quite understand, she went swiftly up the stairs to her room, but found no comfort in solitude. The sudden tautness of her nerves didn't abate just because she was alone—if anything, the pain in her head throbbed more than before. She paced the room restlessly for several minutes, wishing she could drink something that would ease her tension, but she was reluctant to go back downstairs to get it. Rebecca would be sure to hear her and come to find out why she was still up—and undoubtedly say something nosy or critical. A conversation with her mother-in-law was the last thing Elizabeth wanted.

With impatient movements, she stripped off the lace evening dress. Tears of frustration filled her eyes when she snagged a fingernail on the lace and tore the nail down to the quick. She clipped the rest of it off, annoyed with herself for being angry over something so trivial.

After slipping her pale green nightgown over her head, she donned the matching silk robe, tying the sash around her waist, and went into the adjoining bathroom. After searching the medicine cabinet for a moment, she found and swallowed two aspirins, washing them down with a glassful of water and praying they would work fast.

She slapped on facial cleansing cream and got rid of her glamorous makeup in a hurry. Without it, she lost her air of sophistication.

There was a vaguely yearning light in her green eyes when she studied herself in the mirror, a light that reminded Elizabeth of something. Then the answer flashed through her mind. She had the same wishful look as Cindy. She slammed the jar of cream onto the shelf in disgust.

Swiftly she returned to the bedroom. It took only a glance at the small clock near her bed to work out that Jed would have already dropped Cindy off at her parents' house. Now he was en route to—where?

She scowled. He would undoubtedly be returning to the country club and Barbara. Make that Barbara's waiting arms, she thought grimly. He'd willingly left to bring her and Rebecca home so they wouldn't get in his way later. He and Barbara would have the night free to . . . she left the thought uncompleted as a nauseating shudder trembled through her. She didn't want to think.

Her imagination was working overtime as it was. She needed a reality check. Elizabeth went into the hallway, quietly turned the doorknob to her daughter's room, and walked in. The covers were half thrown off and Elizabeth pulled them back over her daughter. A serene joy filled her heart during moments like this, a contentment in knowing that, God willing, she would always be there to look after her daughter.

Sighing wistfully, she turned away from the bed. If only she had someone of her own to look after her and protect her from—she halted in midthought.

Protect her from what? What was it that suddenly made her feel frightened? She shook her head firmly and scolded herself for being nonsensical. There was nothing threatening her.

As she turned to close Amy's door, the sound of footsteps on the stairs penetrated her consciousness. The door clicked shut behind her and she was left in plain view. Elizabeth froze; the footsteps halted as well. Jed was midway up the stairs, a hand on the partially unknotted black bow tie at his collar, his well-cut black evening jacket swinging open. His tawny gaze held her captive and she sensed his animal virility. He seemed about to pounce.

Elizabeth still didn't move, watching the unconscious grace of his movements. Not until she was again looking into his eyes, tilting her chin slightly upward now that he had reached the hallway, was she aware that she had waited for him and not retreated as she should have done.

His gaze swung from her to the door she was standing in front of. "Is Amy all right?"

"Yes." Her answer was short and frayed. "She's sleeping."

Her fingers closed around the neckline of her robe, a defensive action although there had been no outward move from Jed to warrant it. A watchfulness came over his face as he remained standing in front of her, not taking a step to continue down the hall to his room.

"What is it, Liza?" There was a drawling laziness to his voice that was highly sensual.

"I don't know what you mean," she answered, turning away.

"Something's on your mind," he said deliberately.

"If anything, I'm surprised." She kept her voice low so as not to disturb her sleeping daughter and worked to put chilling indifference in it. "I didn't expect you back until the morning."

"Where did you think I'd be?" He drew in a deep, impatient breath and exhaled it slowly in challenge as he waited for her to reply.

There were icicles in her voice. "Oh, who knows? Some out-of-the-way little place, I suppose. Just right for you and Barbara. But that's none of my business."

He gave her a wary look. "You know, I thought Barbara was your friend."

"She is," Elizabeth snapped.

"Then why are you so indignant because I was friendly to her?"

"Friendly?" she said with a note of outrage. "You two were practically making love on the dance floor. I'm not the only one who noticed."

"Whatever." He made no attempt to deny her accusation, a fact that further incensed Elizabeth.

"Acting like that in public is just plain disgusting." Too late, she heard the prim hysteria in her reply. Lowering her head, she took a deep, calming breath.

"Well, I had help. Barbara felt like having fun. She was more of an instigator than a victim, believe me."

"Am I supposed to feel sorry for you?" Elizabeth still wasn't going to admit that much of the blame could be assigned to Barbara.

He gave a snort of contempt. "You don't have the right to judge me."

Elizabeth started toward her door.

Jed stood in her way, his hands on his hips. "I can't make up my mind if you're an ice princess or just not interested."

"Either way, the answer is not going to flatter you," she retorted. "Now move."

He stepped aside and she brushed past him, cursing the static electricity that made her silky robe wrap itself around one of his legs. Even her nightclothes were against her. She jerked the material free, turning her back on him as he laughed.

She whirled around. "Listen, you—" But he was several steps closer now and her move put them body to body. The imprint of his hips made itself felt through the silkiness of her robe as Elizabeth arched herself away, pushing her hands against the solid wall of his chest.

He captured her wrists—gently.

"You said you didn't want to touch me," she reminded him frantically.

"I changed my mind." His voice was low and persuasive. "How about you? Let's start something."

"No. Let go!"

He did. But his gaze held her spellbound—she would rather be held by his hands. Physically, she could fight him and win. Or at least leave some spectacular and very visible scratch marks he'd have a tough time explaining.

"What's the matter?" he said huskily. "Did you forget who I am? I'm Jed, the worthless son, the black sheep. Don't you know that I'm not to be trusted?"

"I'm getting the idea."

He smiled, as if her raw-voiced answer pleased him. Then, very slowly, he lived up to his reputation and stole a kiss, giving her a fraction of a second to push him away again before his mouth closed over hers.

She could have refused him. She didn't. His sensual skill was her undoing. She wanted that, wanted everything that he so obviously knew how to do. Molded to him, her body betrayed her by silently begging for more. Long-suppressed desire carried her to dizzying heights of passion that she had forgotten existed—if she had ever even reached them before.

Her arms slipped beneath his jacket, circling the lean waist, the thin material of his white shirt like a second skin. The caress of his hands began as an intimate exploration that went deliciously too far, and left her weak from the completeness of her response.

"Damn," Jed muttered softly in self-reproach and she understood the reason. She hadn't wanted to feel this way about him either.

As he cupped her face in his hands and held her away, her lashes fluttered open. She was frightened by the depth of her desire for him and at the same time asking him to make his possession complete. Gold fires blazed in his eyes as he read the message in hers.

"Liza—"

She hated the calm control that had entered his voice. "Please . . ." She closed her eyes again, melting against him and nuzzling her cheek against the palm of his hand as a cat would nudge the hand that had stopped stroking it. "I don't want to talk."

He allowed her to cuddle into his chest, his hands unconsciously caressing her shoulders and back. She craved his touch, leaned into him—and felt him stiffen slightly.

"I have to say I'm a little confused," he said cynically. "Am I supposed to feel honored now that you want me to make love to you?" But he kept on holding her.

She gasped. "Please!"

"Please what?" His mouth moved along her temples. "Please understand? Please forget all the insults? Please make love to me? What?" Jed prodded unmercifully.

"Don't," Elizabeth murmured, shame creeping in to steal her pleasure.

He gave a heated sigh as his hands took her arms and pushed her away.

It wasn't a genuine rejection because she knew he wanted her. She wasn't an inexperienced girl. She was a woman and she knew when she had aroused a man's desire. Still it hurt.

A tear quivered on the edge of her eyelashes. Jed touched it, his forefinger catching it as it fell. Pride kept her gaze fixed on his impassive face, an aching need still pulsing through her body.

"I'm sorry, Liza," he said again in a gentler yet just as

firm tone. "There really is such a thing as the right place and the right time. I thought I'd stopped wanting you but I haven't."

"Then why—" she started to ask, brokenly, but his finger touched her lips to silence them.

"Not now. That has to be enough." He smiled wryly. As crimson heat colored her cheeks, he shook his head and took her in his arms again. There was too much restraint in his comforting embrace for it to be sexual. His voice vibrated with charged emotion near her ear. "This could get crazy. I don't want that to happen," he said in a low, grim voice.

"I don't understand." Elizabeth had buried her face against his neck and now she raised it to gaze at him bewilderedly.

"I know you don't." The sensual smile he bestowed on her didn't change the ruthless glint in his eyes. "Maybe someday . . ." Jed hesitated.

She felt him withdrawing from her emotionally as well as physically, detaching himself from her arms with impatience. "Good night, Elizabeth."

Turning, he walked down the hall, not looking back once, not even when he walked through the door of his own room and closed it behind him. Empty and cold, Elizabeth stood where he had left her, wanting to follow him and frightened by the vague warning he'd given her. Finally she went back to her own room and crawled into bed, her ears straining for some sound from his, but the walls of the old house were too thick.

She hadn't known what he might act like the following morning. He was such an enigma to her that she hadn't been able to guess whether he would make fun of the way she'd thrown herself at him or pretend that it had never happened.

Her own emotional upheaval was difficult to understand.

She couldn't make up her mind whether she'd been carried away by a wave of love or just feeling sexually starved. In the end, she decided on a wait-and-see approach, and let Jed make the first move.

The first day there had been the crushing sensation that he was completely indifferent to her, even aloof. The way he had of holding himself apart from others was more pronounced than ever. Then, that evening, she'd sensed him looking at her with thoughtful, almost brooding intensity. He rarely addressed any comment to her, sticking to small talk with his mother.

At least he didn't subject Elizabeth to verbal jabs or mocking looks.

The waiting game was a difficult one for Elizabeth to play. Hope would alternately rise and fall until she felt like she needed a barometer to record the erratic fluctuations. The physical attraction she felt to Jed was undeniable. The slightest accidental contact had her senses leaping in immediate response. And she guessed that he had only to take her in his arms and she would be his for the asking.

Five days had never passed so slowly.

Jed's previous routine didn't vary very much. He spent most of the day away from the house and some evenings too. Yet there was never any pretense on his part that nothing had happened. The very second she thought there was, Jed would send her a look that was meant to remind her.

How much longer was this going to go on?

Elizabeth sighed to herself. With painstaking care she trimmed off the crusts from bread, preparing canapés and finger sandwiches, varying the design of each slice from circles to squares to triangles. Two flaky cherry pies were cooling on the counter. The food was for the meeting of the Literary Club, one of Rebecca's monthly obligations. Of course, she'd asked Elizabeth to take on the task of fixing light refreshments.

"Can I help, Mom?" Elbows propped on the table, chin cradled in her hands, Amy glanced up at Elizabeth.

"May I help," she corrected automatically. She pushed the small bowls of egg salad, ham salad, and tuna salad to her daughter along with a wide-bladed filling spreader. "Yes, you can help me with the sandwiches."

"*May* help." Amy corrected her mother with impish humor.

Elizabeth smiled ruefully, acknowledging her own grammatical error. Not that it mattered much. She was glad Amy wanted to help. Cooking and baking were Elizabeth's hobby, interests that Amy appeared to share.

"How long are those ladies going to be here?" Amy asked in a less than enthusiastic tone.

"Probably until after four," Elizabeth answered. Her daughter made an unhappy face. "It would be best if you stayed in your room until it's time for the refreshments."

"I suppose Mrs. Cargmore is going to be here," Amy grumbled, then adopted a mimicking voice, "'Children should be seen and not heard.'"

"At least not too often," Jed added in conclusion.

The bread knife clattered to the floor, narrowly missing Elizabeth's foot as she spun around to face him. She tried to cover her confusion by bending to the floor to retrieve the knife, but in the next second, Jed was kneeling beside her and handing it to her. His smile was devastatingly warm.

"Someone should teach you to be careful with knives," he scolded gently.

Her pulse was revving up. She straightened quickly, trying to quell the excitement that brought an emerald brilliance to her eyes. "You startled me."

"Sorry. I didn't mean to." Looking away from him,

Elizabeth realized that he knew he got under her skin all too easily. He made a leisurely appraisal of her from head to toe, his eyes twinkling merrily when they returned to her face. She caught her breath at the change in his manner. The aloofness was gone, but what did it signify?

"This is a lot of food. Are we having a party?" Jed shifted his attention to the finger sandwiches Amy was stacking neatly on a platter.

"Not exactly," Amy explained. "Mom and I are doing the refreshments for Grandma's club meeting."

"Looks like I'll have to change my plans for the afternoon. I thought we'd spend it around here, but not if we're about to be invaded." He shook his head.

"It isn't that bad," Elizabeth murmured, her heart sinking slightly. She wished she knew if there was a particular reason why Jed had intended to spend the afternoon here—possibly with her? Was that it?

"Well, I sure wish I had somewhere else to go." Amy licked the salad dressing off her fingers and picked up another slice of bread.

"Amy, you shouldn't do that. Now wash your hands." Elizabeth shot her daughter a disapproving look.

There was a disgruntled sigh as Amy replaced the knife and bread and walked to the sink. Jed was leaning against the counter, smiling faintly at Amy.

"So you have to spend the afternoon here? Is that like being grounded?" he teased.

"Sorta. I have to stay in my room," Amy answered with an expressive widening of her brown eyes. "Not very exciting."

"Well, you can always sit and count how many times Mrs. Garth sneezes," he suggested dryly. "That's what we used to do. Her record was twenty-four times as I recall."

Amy giggled. "Did you really count?"

"Don't encourage her, Jed," Elizabeth sighed, but with humor. "Your mother already thinks Amy doesn't respect her elders."

"On second thought"—Jed's faint smile grew wider—"why don't you come with me this afternoon. I thought I'd visit Maggie."

"Could we stop by the farm and see the puppies too?"

"Amy, you—" The quick words were interrupted.

"Ask your mother if you can go," Jed suggested.

Amy rebounded to Elizabeth, not allowing her time to bask in the unexpected grin he gave her. "Please, Mom?"

"If Jed is sure he wants to take you, I don't mind," Elizabeth said. Her gaze stayed on his lean, carved face, less cynical now with its expression of patient indulgence, but not less compelling.

"Oh, he's sure, aren't you, Uncle Jed?" Amy hastened to say.

Jed straightened from the counter, the muscular length of him standing at full height. Elizabeth felt the force of his masculinity even with the width of the table separating them.

"You bet." The grooves around his mouth deepened as he ruffled the top of Amy's head. "I think we'd better go, though, before your grandmother discovers what we're up to and changes us into a couple of bookworms!"

Amy was already giggling again and racing for the back door. Silently Elizabeth observed that her daughter seemed as eager for Jed's company as she was. If only she could react that naturally and with such obvious pleasure. But her uncertainty dogged her.

"I'll look after her," he said quietly, misinterpreting her slight frown.

"Thanks." Elizabeth smiled wanly. "Go on out, you two."

Jed studied her for a long moment, and Elizabeth was sure he could read her mind. There wasn't much left of her poise and she wasn't sure how much longer she could pretend to be unaffected by him.

"We'll be back later this afternoon, with luck, after the dragons have left." He followed the path Amy had blazed out the door.

Despite her agitation or perhaps because of it, she stared after him, admiring his build from the back—wide shoulders tapering into a lean waist and hips always did it for her. Elizabeth wished they'd asked her to come along. She couldn't have, of course, turning her attention to the bread slices on the cutting board.

Fortunately she didn't have to take part in the afternoon meeting. As a silent participant, she wasn't required to comment on the book reviews being given. Once the meeting was over and the refreshments served, the women seemed to intend to linger indefinitely, gossiping in high voices. Mrs. Garth sneezed again and Elizabeth hid a smile.

This won't do, she told herself sternly. One more time and she would laugh aloud when she saw Mrs. Garth raising the embroidered handkerchief to her nose. As unobtrusively as possible, Elizabeth excused herself from the two ladies she'd been sitting beside, guessing they wouldn't miss her since she'd said nothing of consequence.

The sound of a fit of sneezing, almost too many to count, followed her as she left.

On the third trip, she found Jed and Amy seated at the kitchen table. Amy raised a conspiratorial finger to her lips.

"Ssh!" she whispered. "We don't want Grandma to know we're back yet. Did she say anything?"

"Only that she hoped you'd behave yourself," Elizabeth answered. She didn't want to mention Rebecca's initial surprise or her doubts about letting Amy go with Jed. "Did you have a nice time?"

"Oh, yes. Maggie was so glad to see me and Uncle Jed,"

Amy said proudly. "And you have to see the puppies! Freda said I could have one when they're old enough to leave their mother."

"We'll see about that." It was difficult to keep her gaze from straying too often to Jed. An odd breathlessness had claimed her lungs from the moment she'd entered the room and encountered his tawny gaze. She carefully stacked the dishes in the sink, trying to control her schoolgirl reaction to his presence. "There's some cherry pie left. Would you two like some?"

"Yes, please." Amy accepted eagerly, while Jed only nodded.

Just as Elizabeth set the platter of sliced pie in front of them, a sneeze echoed into the room.

Jed darted Amy a knowing look and smiled at her. "There goes Mrs. Garth again," he said dryly.

Amy suppressed a giggle with her hand. "How many times do you suppose that is?" she whispered gleefully.

"Sevent—" Elizabeth bit her lip, suddenly and guiltily aware that she had been counting. A red glow of embarrassment colored her cheeks at the mocking light in Jed's eyes.

"You've been counting!" Amy's eyes rounded in astonishment.

"No way. I—" Her defensive protest was automatic, but she stopped when she saw their expressions of disbelief.

"How many times, Liza?" Jed prompted softly.

Flustered for a second, Elizabeth turned back to the counter, fighting a smile.

"Make her tell, Uncle Jed." Checked laughter rippled through Amy's voice. "I knew she was counting!"

At the scrape of the chair legs, Elizabeth glanced over her shoulder. The sight of Jed's deliberate approach made her heart patter wildly against her ribs.

"We shouldn't be making fun of Mrs. Garth this way," she protested again. For too many years, her life had been ruled by strict courtesy, and Elizabeth couldn't quite shake it now. "She can't help it."

"How many, Liza?" Jed's wide smile was daring her not to laugh out loud.

Elizabeth pivoted to face him, her fingers closing over the hard counter top pushing into her back. "It isn't polite." Her good judgment and discretion were ignored.

"How many?" Jed was persistent.

He was in front of her now; his nearness weakened her resistance. A smile started to break through and Elizabeth pressed her lips tightly together, glancing wildly at her daughter. But it was too late, he had seen the laughter in her green eyes. The touch of his hands on her shoulders brought it bubbling to the surface in soft giggles.

"Jed—please!" It was a halfhearted protest through laughter—she had to give in. Her palms spread across his chest in an effort to keep him at an otherwise safe distance.

Victorious, he chuckled quietly and drew her closer, locking his arms around her waist. "You can't escape, Liza, until you tell us."

"Seventeen!" Her answer was immediate and breathless.

Another sneeze was heard and they all broke into open laughter. Tears filled Elizabeth's eyes and she couldn't remember the last time she had laughed this hard. It was a wonderful, joyous sensation, especially since she was sharing it. Gradually it lessened into deep breaths to regain her self-control. She found herself nestled in the crook of his arm, her head resting against his shoulder.

Curving his hand under her chin, Jed raised it to inspect her face, and Elizabeth was much too contented and happy to do any more than gaze at him as he grinned at her.

"I've never seen you look more beautiful," he murmured huskily, the gold light in his eyes burning. "You should laugh like that more often."

"Really?" she whispered, basking in the fiery warmth, unable to decide whether the heat racing over her skin came from the contact with him or from inside herself.

"Yes, really." Although there was amusement in his voice, that wasn't the message she saw in his gaze as he slowly turned her into his arms, his hands moving in an arousing but discreet caress down her shoulders and spine.

A tiny sound from the table reminded Elizabeth that they were not alone. Amy was watching them with obvious interest. The moment of unthinking closeness was broken.

"Jed," she whispered with a self-conscious glance at Amy, "not in front of your niece."

He lifted his head a few inches from hers, a crooked smile on his mouth.

"Amy, do I have your permission to kiss your mother?" he asked quietly. He ran his fingers over the sudden rush of pink in Elizabeth's cheeks.

"Not if it's a mushy kiss," Amy said pertly.

"I promise it won't be. I'm talking about the kind of kiss the handsome prince gives the beautiful princess when the cartoon ends and the bluebirds of happiness flutter around in the sky."

"I guess that's okay, then," Amy replied. She settled into her chair to watch.

"You see?" he said to Elizabeth.

She was doomed.

He took her chin and held it firmly as his lips touched hers—and just like a silly cartoon princess, she surrendered to the romantic whirl of it.

A horrified gasp broke through the dreamy haze that Elizabeth was lost in. As she moved, startled, slightly away from Jed, she saw the shocked faces of three of the older members of the Literary Club. At her twisting turn, Jed partially released her from their clinch, but he kept one hand around her waist, in plain view of the onlookers. Before he glanced their way, his eyes mocked Elizabeth's crimsoning complexion.

"Hello, ladies. Was there something you wanted from the kitchen?"

One of them sniffed. "We were just leaving."

"But we did want to see Elizabeth and say goodbye," a second responded, arching a disapproving eyebrow at her.

The third woman merely looked from Elizabeth to mischievous Amy and back to Elizabeth. Her indignant silence was more condemning than words could ever be.

Embarrassed beyond belief but not about to apologize—they had walked in unannounced, after all—Elizabeth stiffly thanked them for coming.

The three women were barely out of the kitchen before a rapid exchange of twittery voices could be heard, making assumptions and jumping to conclusions. Only then did Jed let her go completely, grinning at Amy before he turned to notice the uncomfortable warmth still reddening her face.

"They're off and running. Does it bother you that you're going to get talked about?" The question held a challenge despite the softness of his tone.

"Yes." Elizabeth swallowed. "It does a little."

"Jeremy was always the big man around town and I was the one with the bad reputation. Are you ashamed to be seen with me?"

Her gaze could not withstand the coldness in his eyes. "No, that's not the right word," she hedged. "I would have been self-conscious, though, with anyone."

Jed studied her face for a long moment. The expression on his own was unrelenting. Then he turned to walk away.

"Jed." Her whispered plea begged for his understanding.

Without glancing back, he paused beside her daughter's chair, and Elizabeth noticed that he seemed to soften when he spoke to her daughter.

"Your mother has her own way of looking at things, Amy."

"Is that bad?" Amy breathed.

There was a resigned shrug of his shoulders that was hardly encouraging when it accompanied a negative shake of his head. "No, it isn't bad." Finally looking at Elizabeth, he added, "I'll be back for dinner," and left from the rear door of the kitchen.

Chapter 7

"Is that everything, Mrs. Carrel?" The woman clerk paused before pressing the key for the total.

"Yes, thanks." Elizabeth responded, absently glancing to make sure Amy was still by her side.

"It's quite a production getting children ready for school these days. The list of things they need keeps getting longer and longer." The woman sighed. "With five of my own, I ought to be an expert on it."

"I think this completes Amy's list." Elizabeth smiled as she took the lightest bag and handed it to her daughter, juggling the heavy one into a comfortable position on her wrist, so she could still carry her other purchases.

"Are you ready for school to start?" The clerk smiled down at Amy.

"I think so," she said shyly.

"And I thought you were looking forward to it." Elizabeth looked at her daughter in surprise.

"Not since Uncle Jed came back. It's much more fun at home now that he's there," Amy said.

"Uncles usually are more fun than school," the clerk agreed, darting an amused look at Elizabeth.

"Jed is the best. He even makes Mom laugh," asserted Amy.

Another customer approached the checkout counter and Elizabeth was relieved to direct her talkative daughter to the exit. The clerk's look had been tinged by speculation after Amy's last comment. Elizabeth didn't doubt that the story of the kiss witnessed by the three members of the Literary Club had been transmitted all over town.

She exhaled a faint sigh of frustration as she went outside with Amy. In truth, she'd expected Jed to seek her out again, but over the weekend he hadn't once indicated that he wanted to be alone with her. Yes, there had been moments of fun, but that was about it.

"Good morning, Elizabeth. We seem destined to meet on the sidewalks of Carrelville. Hello, Amy."

Focusing on the man who had stopped in front of them, Elizabeth realized that she hadn't even noticed Allan coming their way.

"Hello, Allan. How are you?" She amped up the warmth to cover the blank look she'd given him at first.

"Fine, thanks. Looks like you two have been doing a little shopping."

"It's back-to-school time," Elizabeth explained.

"Oh, right." Allen looked down at Amy with a smile, but she didn't even seem to be aware that her mother was talking to him. The smile disappeared when he turned to Elizabeth and she knew he was irritated by Amy's attitude. However, she felt the same way as her daughter did about Allan, but was basically too polite to let it show.

Allan cleared his throat. "I was just on my way to the restaurant for morning coffee. Would you two care to join me?"

"I'm not old enough to drink coffee." Amy scuffed the toe of her shoe on the sidewalk before giving him a bored look.

"How about milk and doughnuts, then?" Allan suggested with thinning patience.

Elizabeth was no more enthusiastic about having coffee with Allan than Amy was, but her daughter had been awfully rude. Allan had always been kind and considerate. He didn't deserve to be treated that way, and she wasn't raising a brat.

"That sounds like a great idea," she said quickly, sending a warning look to Amy, whose mouth was opening in protest. She shut up and glowered at the sidewalk. "Our car's just across the street. We'll drop off the bags and join you."

"Let me help you carry some of that," Allan offered.

"Oh, no thanks. The bags aren't at all heavy," Elizabeth assured him as he fell into step beside them as if he was making sure she wouldn't change her mind and bolt with her daughter once they reached the car. "Besides, I have them balanced just right. If you took one, they'd all fall."

At the intersection, they waited for the light to change. Elizabeth asked about the hospital just to make small talk and only half-listened to his reply. Across the street a set of broad shoulders looked achingly familiar. A second later the man they belonged to turned away from the shop window and she saw his rugged profile.

Jed. Her heart skipped a beat.

Another second later Elizabeth saw the woman with him. Barbara eased her arm through Jed's and stayed close to him as they started down the street toward the same intersection she was waiting to cross. Just her luck.

Jealousy had always been an alien emotion to her. Now she felt its strong grip for the first time and she hated it. She tried to swallow back the hot lump in her throat without success.

Do you see? a malicious inner voice whispered. *Do*

you see the way he accepts all that attention as if he had a right to it? That's what he wants from you. He'd be happy to add you to his string of conquests. Once he gets you to fall in love with him, do you really think he'll marry you? No way. He's not the marrying kind.

"Look, Mom!" Amy cried excitedly. "There's Uncle Jed!" She waved the bag in her hand to get his attention.

Glancing away from the blonde molded to his side, Jed saw them. A frown of displeasure crossed his face, although it didn't make him less good-looking.

When she saw it, a wave of proud irritation washed over Elizabeth. She reminded herself somewhat bitterly that she had just as much right as he did to be in town.

The light changed. With a toss of her head she started across, but she was still distracted by the sight of the two of them, and misjudged the distance from the curb to the pavement.

She stumbled and the bags in her arms and everything in them tumbled into the street as she let go to try to check her fall. She wasn't even aware that she had cried out or that Allan reached out to catch her.

He didn't succeed. A little stunned, she lay on the pavement for a few seconds to try and collect herself. She smiled weakly at Allan as he bent anxiously beside her, then pushed herself into a sitting position.

"Are you all right?" He frowned, making a quick examination of the scrape on her elbow.

Elizabeth nodded, unable to speak, partly from having the breath knocked out of her and partly from humiliation. Her fall brought a lot of people over and they gathered in a tight circle around her.

"Stand back. Give her some room," a familiar male voice was ordering crisply, and the onlookers obeyed as Jed pushed through them. Elizabeth studiously brushed the dust from her skirt, avoiding the sharpness of his gaze. Her heart beat erratically when he kneeled beside her and made his own examination of her minor injury. "Are you hurt anywhere else, Liza?"

"No, I don't think so. I—I'll be all right, I guess," Elizabeth murmured, trying to withdraw her scraped elbow from Jed's hold.

"She fell down," Amy said anxiously.

"So I noticed," Jed said. He was completely ignoring Allan, who hovered to one side, his position usurped by Jed's authoritative manner. He chucked Elizabeth under the chin. "Is your middle name Grace?"

The pink intensified in her cheeks. "Ha ha. No, I simply misjudged the step."

"Did you twist your ankle?" His fingers scorched an inquisitive trail along her shinbone to her ankle, which he turned, very gently, from side to side. She didn't flinch.

"I may not be a practicing physician but I am a doctor," Allan put his two cents in, trying to reassert his position as Elizabeth's rescuer.

"Really. What with one thing and another, I could qualify as a battlefield medic," Jed snapped. "I've probably treated more injuries than you have." Seeming satisfied that there was no indication of a sprain, he slipped a supporting arm around her waist. "Let's get you on your feet."

"I'm all right," Elizabeth repeated.

"Oh, Jed, there isn't anything really wrong with her," Barbara said. "Let Allan take over."

The blonde's comment wasn't even acknowledged as Jed lifted Elizabeth up. She didn't know whether to blame her light-headedness on the fall or on the steel-strong muscles of the arms that held her close and safe. The dislike in Barbara's cold blue eyes did make her reel instinctively toward Jed, though. His arms tightened a little more.

"I'll carry you to the car," he said, sliding his other arm around the back of her legs and easily swinging her off her feet.

Unfortunately for all concerned, some smart-aleck had to mutter, "Looks like he's done that before."

Jed's eyes narrowed on the man and Elizabeth shivered uncontrollably as he lowered her to her feet. Allan was left to pick up the scattered school items. Oh, well, she thought irrationally. Someone had to.

Jed's voice was dangerously level when he spoke. "I believe you owe the lady an apology, Mick. Someone could take what you just said the wrong way."

"I didn't mean anything by it, Jed." The man named Mick shifted uncomfortably, as the crowd began to scatter some. But new people took the open places. The air crackled, invisible electricity snapping at hidden nerves. The arm Jed kept around her waist was now tight as an iron band. Elizabeth knew he wasn't aware of the force he was applying. She also knew Jed wouldn't calm down until he got an apology.

"Please." Jed paid no attention to her whispered request to stop it, so Elizabeth turned to Mick. "You don't have to apologize and you're not the only one who thinks like that. Everyone in town has heard about me and Jed."

"But I am sorry, Mrs. Carrel." His gaze skittered across her face to Jed's and fell away.

"Here's your stuff, Mrs. Carrel." Allan had enlisted a couple of helpers and one stepped forward with the refilled bags.

"You're big enough to help your mother," Jed said to Amy, handing her one of the bags, and keeping the others while keeping an arm firmly circling Elizabeth's waist. She couldn't very well protest without causing more comment, not that it would be public this time. Anyway, she welcomed his support.

"Elizabeth, that scrape should be cleaned and disinfected," Allan said quietly.

"Yes, but I'm not going to the hospital," she said, feeling more than a little rattled. "This really isn't a big deal, people."

The crowd began to thin again, this time for good. The sting of her injury was beginning to turn into a heavy-duty aching, but all she wanted to do was leave, as fast as possible.

"I'll take care of it," Jed said firmly. He was scowling at the last of the stragglers, as if the force of his glare could dispel them. Not surprisingly, it did.

Amy clung to her mother's hand and looked up at him. "Thank you, Uncle Jed," she said in a soft little voice.

"Well, then," Allan said to Elizabeth, "I suppose I should go." With a nod to all parties, he left after she thanked him.

"What about me?" Barbara demanded.

"I'll see you later," Jed replied. The light had changed again and Jed was nudging Amy to start across the street to the car, not at all concerned or interested in Barbara's indignant question.

"I might just be too busy to see you," she retorted haughtily.

Except for a cynical twist of his mouth, there was no reaction from Jed as he got Elizabeth across the street with her daughter. Obviously he didn't have to care about Barbara one way or the other. It was disturbing to think that there were very few women who wouldn't take him back. And Elizabeth had the dreadful feeling that she was one. It was a severe blow to her pride.

"Well, thanks for shooting off your mouth, Miss Diplomat," Jed snapped as they reached the car. "Where are the keys?"

Elizabeth fumbled nervously through her bag and handed them to him. They all got in and Amy buckled herself in the backseat, going through the bags with a typical child's eagerness, now that her mother was okay.

Huddling next to the passenger-side door, still feeling rather banged up, Elizabeth tensed when she heard the car spring to life, growling with all the suppressed power of its new driver. Even inanimate objects reacted to Jed.

She finally responded to his comment. "I didn't do anything wrong. Unless avoiding a fight is wrong," she said defensively.

"Whether you like it or not, you labeled yourself as my property." As they left the city limits, he accelerated until the car was whizzing by the telephone poles at an alarming rate.

"What does that mean?" Amy looked up enough so that Elizabeth could see her in the rearview mirror.

Elizabeth hushed her. "That's not so," she said to Jed. "You were spoiling for a fight. And could we keep present company"—she tipped her head toward Amy, who had gone back to investigating the stuff in the bags—"in the dark about this discussion?"

"She was there and she heard what that guy Mick said."

"That doesn't mean she has to hear anything more, Jed."

"Okay," he huffed, "I'll speak in general terms. When a man defends a woman's reputation, even if she's a relative by marriage and not his one and only or anything like that—hell. Never mind." Glancing at the rearview mirror, he, too, caught Amy's expression of wide-eyed interest in the bizarre problems of grown-ups.

"What does it mean, Mom? How can you be Uncle Jed's property? I thought people couldn't own people."

"You're right," Elizabeth replied with brittle patience. "They can't."

"Then—"

Jed answered the little girl this time. "Your mother and

I are more than friends, Amy. We don't date anyone else but each other."

Elizabeth looked at him wide-eyed.

"Oh. Mom can't go out with anyone but you? Not even Mr. Marsden?"

"That's right," Jed said in a clipped tone.

"Good!" Amy declared with one vigorous nod of satisfaction. "Because I don't like him very much."

"Amy!" Elizabeth's chiding was automatic.

But Jed had thrown his head back and was suddenly laughing. The deep, hearty sound was contagious. It dissolved Elizabeth's tension until she, too, was laughing.

"Oh, Amy!" Jed shook his head and gave an amused sigh as he turned the car into the house lane. "You're a treasure. Let's get your mother's arm bandaged up and see if we can persuade your grandma to let us have lunch outside."

"Like a picnic! That would be awesome!" Amy agreed. "But Grandma hates to eat outside. There's too many bugs."

"Don't worry." Elizabeth was still smiling. "Your grandmother won't be here for lunch today. It's—" An expression of dismay swept across her face. "Heck. Amy, it's Thursday! Your piano lesson."

"Oh, Mom, no!" Amy wailed.

"Come on, Liza." Jed switched off the motor and turned to her. "What's one piano lesson in a lifetime of piano lessons?" he said gently. "Call her teacher and say the car won't start."

"Please," Amy echoed. "Please-please-please."

"What if we eat later, after your lesson?" Elizabeth suggested. "You can skip practicing this time and we'll still have our lunch outdoors if you like."

"Instead of that," Jed countered, "why don't you let

Amy practice for half an hour while you're fixing lunch and skip the lesson?"

"Wouldn't that be just as good, Mom? Please?"

"Well, all right," Elizabeth conceded, glowing a bit at Jed's approving wink. Amy's shriek of joy forced her to add, "But only if you practice for half an hour."

"I will!" her daughter promised fervently, pushing the door open and hopping out of the car. "I'll start right now!"

She was ready to race into the house when Jed whistled for her to a stop. "Don't go in empty-handed," he said. "Take one of the bags."

Grabbing one and sticking in a few extra items for good measure, Amy was careening toward the front door again, not waiting for Jed and Elizabeth. He got the remaining bags and walked away from the car when Elizabeth did.

"That's one happy kid. You would think I just gave her the moon on a string." She smiled tenderly after her daughter.

"Playing hooky is always fun, even when you have official permission." His lazy smile was captivating as he fell into step beside her.

"Hmm, I heard you were an expert at it once upon a time," she teased.

"I probably was absent at least as often as I was present," he admitted with a twinkle. "I seem to remember that the truant officer described me as 'absolutely incorrigible.'"

"I can imagine."

"Well, I'm not exactly proud of it, but I probably understood earlier than most how to apply what I learned in school to real life."

"I remember," Elizabeth said thoughtfully, "your father once said that you had a very analytical and logical mind, and that you could have been a brilliant lawyer if you weren't so . . ." She hesitated.

"Incorrigible," Jed supplied. "He used that word for me too. When did he concede that I might possibly have some brains?"

"Shortly after Jeremy was killed." He held the front door open for her. "I think he was really hoping you would come back then."

"To his way of life." There was a bitter, downward twist to his mouth. "Come on, let's clean up your elbow."

"I'm sure he only wanted what he thought was best for you," she murmured.

"Maybe he meant well." Jed motioned to a kitchen chair. "Sit there." Then he walked to the cabinet where the first-aid kit was kept. "I forgave him for his good intentions a long time ago. The trouble is, he never forgave me for going my own way."

In the next instant, antiseptic gel was stinging the skin around her elbow. Her quick gasp of pain brought an apology from him, but Jed continued until the scrape was clean. By then the conversation was forgotten and Amy was at the piano faithfully practicing "Swans on the Lake."

While Jed disappeared to wash, Elizabeth called Mrs. Banks, Amy's piano teacher, thankful that the woman accepted her explanation. Elizabeth didn't fib about having car trouble, and only said that Amy wouldn't be having a lesson today, adding that the time would be paid for.

Working in the kitchen had always been satisfying to her, but she discovered there was a special contentment within her today as she set about fixing the noon meal for just the three of them. When she saw Jed standing on the patio, she realized this was how she wanted her life to be for always. The depth of her love for the man out there frightened her. She knew she was in over her head but not what would happen next. For the present Jed was hanging on to her. But what would she do if he ever let go? With Jeremy, her feelings had been nowhere near this strong. Elizabeth turned from the window, fighting back the panic that nearly sent her racing to Jed's arms seeking reassurance that he truly cared. It couldn't be only physical, not if he was that protective.

But even so . . . the agonizing pain of the morning was vividly recalled, that twisting, sickening jealousy when she had seen him with Barbara. And Barbara expected to see him again today.

It was difficult to regain the sensation of contentment. Elizabeth was on edge all through lunch, waiting for the moment Jed would say he was going. While she cleared the table, Amy proposed a game of croquet. Elizabeth fretted silently, sure that behind his laughter and teasing conversation with her little girl, his mind was thinking of something or someone else. It was hard to know if she should blame her overactive imagination, but she couldn't shut off the troubling thoughts.

The game was over with Jed the winner when Elizabeth finished washing up the lunch dishes. She brought a pitcher of fresh lemonade with her as she returned to the patio.

"You read my mind," he said lazily. "We'll drink that whole pitcherful before this afternoon is over. It's going to get hot."

She poured him a glass, concentrating on not spilling it. "What about Barbara?" Elizabeth tried to sound nonchalant.

"What about her?" He took the frosty glass, sipping it appreciatively.

"Isn't she expecting you this afternoon?"

He gave her an amused look, as if sensing the underlying emotion in her question. "That wasn't anything definite." He leaned his head back against the cushion, running the ice-cold glass along his temple. "Besides, it's too hot to play tennis this afternoon."

"Is that what you were going to do?"

"What did you think?" He studied her downcast gaze over the rim of the glass as he drank more.

"I didn't actually think anything," she answered. She didn't really believe Barbara planned to play tennis all afternoon if she could relax and have Jed all to herself.

"Liar," he taunted. "I think I detected a hint of jealous green in your eyes just then."

"You're imagining things."

"No, I don't think so." Jed closed his eyes against the sun, smiling a little. "But since I made it unbelievably clear that I preferred the company of you and your daughter to her, I was hoping that you would unbend and let me know how you feel about me."

The gaze she'd kept averted swung to him sharply. She was afraid that he might be making fun of her again but she prayed that he was speaking the truth. Jed reached out and found the fingers that were clutching the arm of her chair. Her heart quickened at his touch.

She still quailed, though, under the enigmatic warmth of his golden eyes. "No reply? It's true, Liza. I do prefer you," he said evenly and naturally.

"Why?" she asked breathlessly, still wondering whether he was playing with her emotions.

"Why do you think?" There was a husky, seductive note in his countering question that sent fire through her veins.

"Let's play another game of croquet!" Amy came bounding between the two chairs, breaking the magic spell that Jed had cast over Elizabeth.

"No, honey. It's too hot now." He smiled at her.

"Come on," Amy pleaded, taking their hands and tugging hard to get them to rise to their feet.

Jed surrendered. "One game."

Amy was delighted to have both her uncle and her mother to play with for the entire afternoon. Her constant presence meant that the conversation was prevented from turning personal again. Elizabeth didn't know whether to be grateful for that or not. An inner perception told her that she would never find out more than Jed wanted her to know. While she—oh, what was the point? She had a bad habit of overthinking nearly everything.

It was ironic now, so many years later, to remember how innocently confident she'd been when she'd decided on Jeremy. From the first time she met him, she'd been determined to marry him. Had it ever been love—true love? When the accident had claimed his life, it had been shock rather than grief that she'd felt. Looking back, she understood how very young and immature she had been at the time. Now she was a woman with a life that wasn't simple anymore. Love had become complicated.

But how she longed to plunge into it—and to have Jed for her own. The feeling was almost painful.

She told herself to quit obsessing over things she couldn't change or necessarily control. It was a beautiful day. She should be enjoying it and stop looking around every corner for some impending disaster.

"What's the frown for?" Jed tilted his head inquiringly, his thick brown hair gleaming in the afternoon sun. Before Elizabeth had a chance to answer him, he glanced toward the house. "Aha. My mother's home," he sighed. "She knows how to spoil a party. Even a little one like this."

Elizabeth turned as Rebecca came through the French doors from the living room. "There you are. It's disgustingly hot out here, isn't it?" Her dark gaze swept over the three of them and she nodded in response to their hellos.

"It is a bit warm," Elizabeth agreed.

Rebecca Carrel focused intently on her. "I heard you had a slight accident today, Elizabeth."

For an instant Elizabeth held her breath. She hadn't dreamed her tumble at the intersection would have been relayed to her mother-in-law that quickly.

"Yes. We were in town. I fell and scraped my elbow. Nothing serious," she shrugged.

"How convenient that Jed was there to take care of you." Rebecca's sharp gaze swung to her son.

The cat gold glitter in his eyes challenged her in return. "If I hadn't, plenty of other people would have helped her."

"Well, at least you look none the worse, Elizabeth." Rebecca's saccharine smile didn't soften her haughty features. "Was there anything you would like me to help you cook for dinner this evening?"

"No," Elizabeth refused the offer stiffly. "I was going to put a roast in the oven. I think I'll do that now."

She rose, leaving Amy to chatter to her grandmother and getting nearly to the French doors when she heard footsteps behind her, strong quiet strides that belonged to Jed. She turned, trying to fight away the awkwardness triggered by Rebecca's arrival.

"I meant to tell you earlier." Jed stopped beside her, drawing her away from the French doors and inside where his mother couldn't hear. "I won't be home for dinner tonight."

"Oh—of course." Her reply sounded half-frozen in the warm air of the late-summer day. Obviously, Jed hadn't gone to see Barbara this afternoon because he planned to see her tonight.

"Of course?" A curious frown creased his forehead. "Why do you say 'of course'?"

"No special reason," she lied. "It was only an—acknowledgment."

"Have it your way, Liza." He smiled mockingly and walked toward the stairway.

At that moment, she totally despised Barbara. She could have cheerfully clawed her eyes out if the other woman had been there. Jealousy was an ugly thing.

Chapter 8

It was the second cup of coffee she'd stared at until it got cold, Elizabeth thought resentfully as she poured it down the sink. If she wasn't so angry at herself for being dumb enough to believe that Jed might care about her, she would be crying.

Yesterday afternoon he'd said that he wouldn't be home for supper. She had stayed awake until well after midnight, lying in bed feeling miserably sorry for herself before drifting into a restless sleep without having heard Jed return. With good reason. He hadn't.

After the first wave of angry jealousy receded, fear had set in. There could have been an accident. She'd frantically called the police to see if anything had been reported, terror filling her heart that she might have lost Jed as she had Jeremy. But nothing had happened and he hadn't been admitted to the local hospital with acute appendicitis or anything. The emergency room intake clerk on duty confirmed that for her in yet another embarrassing phone call. That left only one place for him to be—with Barbara.

Tears scalded her cheeks and she scrubbed them away with her hand. She was not going to cry because of her own stupidity. She should have had more sense than to fall in love with someone like Jed. The bitter taste of her own foolishness nearly gagged her.

The front doorbell rang. Who could that possibly be at this hour of the morning, she thought wearily. She was in no mood to entertain any visitor for Rebecca. The coffee cup clattered against the side of the porcelain sink as the doorbell sounded impatiently again.

Smoothing her hair away from her face and breathing deeply, Elizabeth walked through the kitchen into the hall, her nerves stretched to the point where she wanted to scream. She was sorely tempted to do just that when the doorbell rang again. The smile on her face was less than welcoming as she opened the door.

"Freda?" she said in surprise. "What are you doing here?"

Freda Reisner's hands twisted nervously in front of her. "Jed . . ." she began hesitantly.

Elizabeth immediately stiffened. "I'm sorry, he isn't here this morning."

"I . . . I know he isn't." Freda faltered at the chilling coldness that underlined Elizabeth's reply. "He's at our farm."

"At your farm?" Elizabeth asked worriedly. "I thought he was—is he hurt? Has there been an accident?"

"No, nothing like that." Freda shook her dark blond head quickly to banish that thought. "But he's sick—quite sick."

"Oh, no," Elizabeth whispered.

"He had supper with us last night and fell asleep on the couch. Then later . . . he had a fever. We think it might be a bad flu. He made Kurt promise not to tell you."

"Have you called a doctor?"

"Yes, before I came over, but Jed refused to go to the hospital. Maybe he'll listen to you," Freda sighed.

"May I drive over with you?" Elizabeth asked.

"Of course." Freda Reisner turned away from the door, hurrying down the sidewalk to her waiting pickup truck.

"Amy! Amy!" Elizabeth called to her daughter playing in the back of the house. She had barely explained what was going on before she was hurrying into the truck with her daughter and Freda was reversing down the driveway.

The doctor's car was already at the Reisner farm when they arrived. Elizabeth recognized it as belonging to their family doctor, which probably accounted for the fact that Freda was able to persuade him to come out.

"Where is he?" Elizabeth glanced anxiously at Freda.

"In the downstairs bedroom, second door on the right in the hall." Freda pointed.

"Stay here with Freda, Amy," Elizabeth asked, and went in the direction Freda had indicated.

Pausing in the open doorway, she stared at the man lying in the double bed. Jed was pale beneath his tan, and sweat gleamed on his forehead and upper lip. His eyes were closed but she guessed from weakness rather than sleep. Her gaze swung to the tall, stoop-shouldered man who had just taken Jed's pulse.

"How is he?" Apprehension made her voice one degree above a whisper.

"Ah, hello, Elizabeth." The doctor smiled. "Kurt said you and Rebecca were probably on your way over."

At the sound of her voice, Jed moved slightly, his eyes opening to focus vaguely on Elizabeth. Resentment filtered through the glaze of fever in his eyes when he glanced at the second man standing near his bedside.

"Rebecca didn't come," Elizabeth murmured, trying to return the smile of encouragement Kurt Reisner was giving her. "She's in town at a meeting or something." Her mother-in-law's whereabouts were of no concern to her at the moment. Not with Jed lying there so listlessly. "What's wrong? Do you know? Is it that flu that's going around?"

The doctor cast an appraising look at Jed before moving toward Elizabeth. "This is one case where I'm accepting the patient's diagnosis." His reassuring smile told her that there was no need for alarm. "He picked up a type of low-grade relapsing fever in the tropics, and he tells me that he's had bouts of it before."

"Is it contagious?" Freda wanted to know.

"No. It's only transmitted by a biting insect from that part of the world. A rare one. Not mosquitoes, if that's what you're thinking. Of course, all of you should observe the usual hygienic precautions, wash your hands frequently, and so forth."

"Not a problem," Kurt said.

"A physician in Hawaii treated him for it. I'm going to call and see if I can get Jed's medical files e-mailed to me. And I drew a blood sample to test for it. Best to confirm things like this, I think. But it will be a few days before I get the results."

"Jed says it'll be over with in a couple of days," Kurt inserted.

"So you're sure it isn't that really bad flu," Elizabeth said.

The doctor shook his head. "I really don't think so but the test will let us know if it is. In the meantime, he'll be a sick man, but there will be no lasting effects."

"Shouldn't he go to the hospital?" Elizabeth wasn't as convinced as the doctor that there was nothing to worry about.

"No." The hoarse protest came from Jed. "Absolutely not. I hate hospitals."

The doctor chuckled softly. "As you can see, he's very much against it. The hospital's short of beds right now, and as long as his temperature stays below one-oh-two point five, I see no reason to admit him."

"Can he be moved, though?" Another hoarse protest came from the sick man, but Elizabeth ignored it. "I'd like to take him home if it's all right."

Then she remembered Amy—she'd have to take her home first, of course, and—maybe it wasn't a good idea.

"He's more than welcome to stay here," Kurt said. "He won't be that much of a burden for a few days. If he complains too much, we'll just put him in the hayloft."

"No," Jed said with a dismal croak.

"I was kidding, pal."

It was the doctor's opinion that mattered most to Elizabeth.

"Well, it probably wouldn't hurt him to be moved." The doctor looked at Jed again. "But if you Reisners are willing to take care of him, it would be best if he stayed here. No sense exposing anyone else to him on the slim chance that it is flu. Most likely it's this other bug and that's going to give his immune system a workout. We don't want him to catch anything else somewhere else. Does that make sense?"

"Of course," Elizabeth accepted his verdict with good grace.

"Okay. I'd better be getting to the hospital." The doctor pushed back the sleeve of his jacket to look at his watch. "I still have rounds to make." Glancing at Kurt, he asked. "You have that prescription I gave you?"

Kurt touched the pocket of his shirt. "Yes." He looked briefly at Elizabeth, then walked to the doctor's side. "I'll show you to the door."

Discreetly left alone in the room with Jed, Elizabeth found herself uncertain what to say or do next. His eyes were closed again. Awkwardly she moved closer to the bed, wanting to touch him, to reassure herself that he was basically okay, but she reminded herself that he was sick.

A bowl of water and a cloth were on the table beside

the bed. As quietly as possible, Elizabeth moistened the cloth, folded it into a square, and gently placed it on his forehead. It wasn't much but at least there was a little something she could do to alleviate his misery. She felt a tightness around her heart when she looked down at him. His lean features were drawn because of his illness into taut lines. When she removed the cloth to moisten it again with the cool water, she saw his eyes open.

"Ah, the young widow Carrel, soothing my fevered brow," he mocked in a weak voice.

"Be quiet," she commanded softly, watching his eyes close as she placed the damp cloth on his forehead.

"Go home, Elizabeth," Jed mumbled coldly. "I don't need you." He waved her away, but not with his usual strength. "We're alone. There's no one you have to impress."

Calmly enough, Elizabeth replaced the cloth on his forehead as if to pretend that his cutting words didn't hurt. She made no reply and Jed stopped mumbling, slipping instead into a troubled sleep.

Quiet footsteps entered the room. Their feminine lightness made it easy for Elizabeth to identify them as belonging to Freda before she turned around.

"Is he sleeping?" Freda asked.

"Sort of." The corners of her mouth turned upward in a poor excuse for a smile as Elizabeth picked up a bottle of hand sanitizer near the bed and used it liberally.

"That's a good idea," Freda said. "You never know. I just made a fresh pot of coffee. Would you like a cup?"

Casting one last look at Jed, Elizabeth nodded. "Yes, I would."

There was no sign of Amy in the kitchen. Freda read the question forming in Elizabeth's eyes. "She's outside playing with the puppies."

"Oh, my." Elizabeth ran a hand nervously through the side of her hair, the black locks curling around her fingers. "I'm sorry we've put you to so much trouble, Freda."

"It isn't any trouble," the dark blonde assured her, setting a mug of coffee on the table for each of them. "Jed's been like a brother to me and Kurt ever since I can remember. My mother swore that he spent more time at our place than he ever did at home, especially when he was a teenager, but I don't think his parents knew that."

"Yes," Elizabeth sighed heavily. "It looks like he'll be here for a few more days. The doctor didn't think it was a good idea to move him, at least for the time being. Jed didn't seem anxious to leave either."

"Well, he is ill," Freda defended him gently.

"Still, I wish—" Elizabeth glanced toward the hallway and the hidden bedroom door, but she couldn't just blurt out that she wanted to be the one to take care of him. "It's inconvenient for you," she murmured instead.

"Elizabeth . . ." Freda began, then hesitated. "If you would like to stay and lend a hand, I'm fine with that. I mean, I do have the house to take care of and meals to cook and the garden—it never ends. You could sleep in the spare room unless you'd rather not."

"Are you sure you don't mind?" Elizabeth held her breath, wanting to stay with Jed more than anything.

"It would be a tremendous help," Freda said.

"I would like to stay." Elizabeth's smile was a mixture of happiness and relief.

"The spare room has twin beds. There's no reason Amy can't stay too. I know your mother-in-law"—Freda seemed to choose her words carefully—"is quite busy with her meetings and all. It would save you having to find a sitter and constantly rushing back and forth between here and there. Amy isn't any trouble."

"Oh, Freda, are you sure you want to be invaded by us Carrels?" Elizabeth laughed.

Freda gave her a beaming smile. "I'm sure. As soon as Kurt comes back from the fields at noon, I'll have him drive you over to the house to get your things. It's a perfect arrangement."

The only one who disapproved of it was Rebecca. It was her opinion that if Jed was ill enough to require Elizabeth's attention, he was ill enough to go to the hospital. But for once Elizabeth didn't allow herself to be talked out of her plans, not even when her mother-in-law insisted that Amy should remain at home with her. The tiny wedge that been driven between them since Jed's arrival had placed a severe strain on the relationship between the two women. Elizabeth found that she didn't look up to her mother-in-law as much as she once had. In fact, there were several things about her she suddenly didn't like.

Amy was delighted at the prospect of spending several days on the Reisner farm. She was genuinely concerned about her uncle being sick, but she also knew she wasn't going to be allowed near him. The farm was a new world to her, an exciting world that she was determined to explore.

When Kurt heard his sister's suggestion, he immediately seconded the invitation, adding that he knew Freda would enjoy the company of someone her own age. And Elizabeth discovered how truly warm and friendly her neighbors were. She felt ashamed that she hadn't gotten to know them better before now. But Rebecca had never been in favor of Elizabeth becoming too closely acquainted with them.

Although she could ignore her mother-in-law's disapproval, Jed's displeasure at having her there was not so easy to overlook. Several times during the first day, Elizabeth sat with him. He had been aware that someone was there, but in his semiconscious state, the identity of the person was not as important as the cold compress on his forehead. Not until that evening when she brought him in some chicken broth that Freda had prepared did Jed recognize her.

She could have done without his comments on her presence, to be sure. Elizabeth accepted his sarcasm with forced silence, telling her bleeding heart that it was the result of his illness. She only partly believed it. He didn't want her there and she probably shouldn't stay, but she did.

There were moments in the succeeding two days when he was completely himself and others when he slept heavily, mumbling things that made no sense to Elizabeth. Sometimes she guessed they had to do with his childhood, but mostly he seemed to be going back to the time he'd spent in the Pacific and Southeast Asia.

Once he had called her name. She slipped her hand over his, feeling his fingers tighten so she couldn't pull free.

"I'm here, Jed," she said in a loving whisper.

"You shouldn't be," he muttered, barely opening his eyes. "Just go away."

"Ssh." Elizabeth bit into her lip to hold back her hurt feelings.

"Then leave me alone," Jed sighed, turning his head away from her, but letting go of her hand. Stirring restlessly, he exclaimed with unexpected forcefulness, "It's so damned hot! Doesn't anyone on this island own a fan?"

Elizabeth realized he wasn't rational.

"He's out of it again, is he?" Kurt's voice claimed Elizabeth's attention. He was standing in the doorway with Freda, who had fresh bed linens in her arms. "I thought I'd give you two a hand changing the sheets."

"We're going to need it. He's cranky," Elizabeth said with a sigh, twisting her hand free from Jed.

Kurt shook his head, taking over for a little while and

even managing to get an electronic thermometer into Jed's mouth for a fast reading, telling him, not unkindly, to shut the hell up. Peering at the tiny readout screen, he waited. "One-oh-two point five," he said to his sister.

"Should we call Dr. Miles?" she asked.

"That's the cutoff point. I'll take it again in an hour." He withdrew the thermometer, ignoring Jed's muttered rude words to him. "Roll over, Jed. And cooperate."

Jed really didn't, pushing away the hands that removed the sweat-soaked sheets from beneath him to replace them with dry ones. Finally when they had him tucked back in, he seemed to collapse with exhaustion.

"Not a model patient, is he?" Freda asked quietly.

"Maybe it's me," Elizabeth said wearily when they went out of the room. "He doesn't want me there."

"He doesn't know what he's saying," Kurt insisted. "But you can't manage him on your own. And it's not like his mother is going to pitch in."

Elizabeth silently acknowledged the truth of his statement. Alone, she wouldn't have been able to move Jed even in his weakened condition. Assistance from Rebecca would have been minimal at best. She had a very low tolerance for sick people, making her duty visits as she'd done with Jed, but never staying any longer than propriety dictated.

"How about some iced tea on the porch before we turn in?" Kurt suggested.

"Good idea," Freda said. "There's a pitcher full in the refrigerator. Would you fix a glass for Liza and me?" She'd begun using Jed's nickname for Elizabeth, but without the faintly mocking undertones. Elizabeth didn't mind.

"For my sister, anything." Kurt left the two women to make their own way to the porch.

Leaning against one of the porch's columns, Elizabeth gazed at the stars sprinkled over the night sky. "How long do you think it will last, Freda? Dr. Miles said only a few days, but it's already been three."

"I forgot to tell you—he called today. Jed's doctor e-mailed him his previous medical files and confirmed the type of tropical fever that he has. Oh, and Dr. Miles got the results back on the blood test—it isn't flu. So, as far as he knows, the fever will run its course." Freda had curled up on the porch swing, tucking her legs beneath her. Then she said something completely unexpected. "You love him very much, don't you?"

Elizabeth swung around, a denial forming on her lips. Then she sighed. "Yes," she answered simply.

Freda didn't offer any words of hope or confide anything that Jed had said to her or Kurt. If she had, Elizabeth knew she probably wouldn't have believed her. She didn't think anyone knew what Jed felt, even though he'd muttered all kinds of things in his sleep.

There was an invisible clasping of hands between Elizabeth and Freda, cementing the friendship that had been steadily growing. Elizabeth had never realized how much she missed just talking to a likeable, intelligent woman her own age, whether it was about cooking or clothes or world politics. If she got nothing else out of her stint as Nurse Nancy, at least she'd acquired a good friend.

Later, staring at the ceiling above her bed, Elizabeth waited for sleep to sneak up on her, but her mind refused to stop reliving the happenings of the past three days. Restlessly, she thumped her pillow to relieve the tension, turning on her side and gazing at the sleeping figure of her daughter in the next bed. It was no use, she thought dejectedly. She simply wasn't going to drift off if she kept thinking about Jed.

A robe lay at the foot of her bed. Slipping quietly from beneath the covers so as not to disturb Amy, Elizabeth slid her feet into the slippers at her bedside and picked up the robe. She would take a couple of minutes to check on Jed, she decided, then warm some milk in the kitchen. Wasn't that the old-fashioned cure for insomnia? She smiled to herself.

The yard light streamed in through Jed's window and she could see that he had been tossing and turning. The blankets were thrown off, exposing his bare chest. His pajama bottoms were pale, cool blue in the dim light as Elizabeth went in, but that was the only cool thing about him. She reached down to draw the top sheet up over him and found that his skin was burning to the touch. He seemed totally unaware of her presence. Taking the clean, dry washcloth left folded by the basin, she wiped the sweat from his face.

His fever was peaking—she didn't need the thermometer to tell her that. If it spiked any higher, she would rouse the others and get him to the hospital somehow.

But right now she had to do something. Cradling his head in her arms, Elizabeth pressed the water glass to his dry lips, trying to get some liquid into him. Directed by instinct, she got him to swallow a mouthful, to her relief. She wiped away the sweat again, then repeated her efforts to get him to sip water. Her heart cried out at her inability to do more to ease his discomfort as he continued to moan and toss. Her arms began to ache and her muscles throbbed with the constant repetition of her actions. She lost all perception of the minutes ticking by, still not wanting to waken Freda and Kurt.

Elizabeth didn't notice the exact moment when his fever broke. Suddenly she realized the frown had left his face and his restlessness had ceased. His lean face was still warm to the touch of her hand but without the fiery heat of before.

It was over. Jed was actually sleeping.

She practically bathed herself in hand sanitizer, then

collapsed wearily in the rocking chair beside his bed. She would sit here for a few minutes, she told herself, and let her aching body relax. Good thing she hadn't put milk on the stove, she thought with a wry smile. It would have boiled over by now and set off the smoke alarm, waking everyone. That was the last thing she remembered thinking.

Groggy with sleep, she felt shooting pains in her neck. When she tried to move, they traveled down her spine. She frowned in protest, not wanting to move again, but the stiffness in her muscles demanded it. Slowly, unwillingly, Elizabeth opened her eyes as the awareness of her surroundings gradually sank in.

The sun was well up in the sky with no traces of the golden pink of dawn. Jed was sleeping peacefully, the stubble of a three-day beard growth darkening his jaw. The sallow look was gone from his face and his forehead showed no sign of sweat.

He was all right. A faint smile of relief touched her lips.

Arching her back to flex away the remaining stiffness, Elizabeth began to gently rub away the crick in her neck, the painful result of sleeping in the rocking chair for the better part of a night. She still felt tired, but there was no point in going back to bed at this hour. As she pushed herself out of the chair, her gaze shifted to the bed. Jed was watching her. The glaze of fever was gone, his eyes cat gold and thorough in their appraisal.

"Didn't anyone ever tell you that chairs weren't meant to sleep in?" His lips quirked cynically at the corners.

Elizabeth opened her mouth to protest, her heart skipping beats, but the bedroom door was opened, effectively silencing her reply. Freda stuck her head inside, glancing in surprise at Elizabeth, then to Jed. A smile spread across her face.

"Well, looks like you're going to live," she said to him. "I don't know about Elizabeth, though."

"I'm fine," she said.

"Jed, I'll bring you a tray," Freda continued. "You must be starving."

"Don't bother." He rolled on to his back, his lazy but alert gaze moving from Elizabeth to focus on Freda. "Elizabeth can do that."

Freda raised an inquiring eyebrow, then looked briefly at Elizabeth's astonished expression. "Oh. Okay," was all she said to him. "By the way, Kurt took Amy out for an early ride on the tractor all the way to the north forty. She took a peanut butter sandwich and a milk box with her for breakfast, so that's taken care of. We'll keep her busy."

"Thanks, Freda."

"No problem." The closing of the door got Elizabeth up out of the rocker.

"I was going to shower and change," she told him tartly, resenting his expecting her to wait on him when she'd stayed up half the night with him.

The irritatingly complacent expression on his face didn't change. "I thought you were enjoying your role as angel of mercy." With disconcerting ease, he fine-tuned the sarcasm. "How long has this been going on?"

"If you mean you being pretty much out of it, the answer is three days."

"Three days?" He rubbed his hand over his chin, his stubble scraping his palm. "I hope I didn't talk in my sleep." He smiled ruefully.

"Sometimes you did," Elizabeth replied quietly. "Don't worry, you didn't make any sense."

His hooded gaze stayed on her, as if he was judging the truthfulness of her answer. She met it squarely without flinching.

"I seem to remember telling you to leave. Why didn't you?"

Her love for him made it difficult for her to answer that question honestly. "It wouldn't have been fair to stick Freda and Kurt with all the work of taking care of you. Farm chores can't wait. You know that," she added.

"So a sense of duty compelled you to stay. You get a gold star."

"I was worried about you!" Elizabeth declared angrily.

"I'm touched." Jed reached for the pitcher of water on the bedside table, nearly knocking it over when he tried to turn it around to grasp the handle.

"Let me do that," she sighed, taking the pitcher from him and filling the glass with water. Automatically she sat on the edge of the bed, cupping the back of his head with her hand and raising the glass to his mouth. She wasn't so sure he didn't still need help.

"But—"

"Hey, the next time that fever kicks in," she snapped, still smarting from his jeering at her nursing efforts, "we'll hire a big, ugly male nurse to take care of you. I'm not going to sit up half the night and listen to your ungrateful comments ever again."

The glass was jerked from his lips before he could lean back and say *ahhh*. But before she could rise to her feet, his arm circled her waist to keep her at his side.

"I'm sorry." There was a gleam in his tawny eyes. "I didn't say thank you, did I?"

"No, you didn't," she retorted, reacting with unwilling pleasure to his touch. Her hands were unable to remove his strong arm.

"Hm. Are you going to walk out?" The grooves around his mouth deepened.

"No."

"But you are angry. You know, you look just like you did the first day I came back."

"Really." It wasn't a question, and she was angry.

"Yes. All haughty and disdainful. I often wondered whether you were more afraid of my stealing the family silver or making a move on you."

"You looked like you'd slept in your clothes. Under a bridge," she added for emphasis. "So what was I supposed to think?"

"And you looked so sophisticated," Jed continued with thoughtful amusement. "Snapping out orders and warnings with all the arrogant pride of a true Carrel."

"Oh, give me a break—"

He shook his head. Evidently he was just warming up.

"The beautiful, fragile girl I remembered seemed to have disappeared," he said somewhat melodramatically.

"Yes. I grew up. Get to the point." She tried again, unsuccessfully, to break his hold, then relaxed for a second. "If you have one."

"I also remember you as being intimidated by the Carrel name and frightened that you might not be good enough for the favorite son. That's probably why I keep looking to see if that's still true. Maybe you just hide it better now. Your veneer of sophistication is very thin, Liza."

His comments hit home, but she didn't have to let him know that. "Jed . . . never mind any of that. You've been ill."

His face was only tantalizing inches from hers. "And now I'm not. Once that fever's gone, I recover fast." He smiled at the shaky breath she drew. "But I am a little weak. I'm not sure why."

His hand traced the outline of her face, his thumb lightly brushing her lips before his hand settled on the curve of her neck. At the moment, Elizabeth was positive that she was a whole lot weaker. Her resistance, what there was of it, was melting. Fast.

"I know a man isn't supposed to ask, but do you mind if I kiss you?" Jed moved his head closer to hers, hesitating a breath away from her lips.

"No." It was almost a moan.

"You objected all the other times," he murmured against her mouth. "This time I want you to want it as much as I do."

Still he teased with featherlight kisses until her lips ached to be claimed by his. She wound her arms around his neck, but he held himself a little bit away.

"I don't understand you," Elizabeth whispered achingly.

His beard scraped her cheek, then her throat, as he nuzzled the sensitive side of her neck, sending shivers of bliss down her spine. He slid his hand into her robe, caressing her waist and hips through the thin material of her nightgown.

"Please, Jed," she begged shamelessly. "Don't play games with me." Her eyes filled with longing.

"This isn't a game. But it is fun," he whispered. He nipped at her earlobe, drawing a gasp of pain mixed with pleasure.

He raised his head, his darkening hazel-gold eyes focusing on her lips, waiting deliberately. The moan that escaped her when he finally claimed them was involuntary, an almost unwilling admission of surrender. The kiss was thorough and complete, his sensual technique without fault. The wildfire raging through her blood made any other man's touch seem like a tiny match flame by comparison.

Her hunger for his full embrace was insatiable. She arched toward him, sensing that his heart was thudding as madly as hers. She could feel it beneath the palm of her hand resting against his chest.

"Were you really that worried about me?" he demanded huskily.

"You know I was," she whispered.

"Why?" With fluid strength, he pushed her back against the pillow, pinning her there with the weight of his body. "Why should you care?"

"Because." The evasive answer didn't satisfy him.

"Why?" Jed asked again, more gruffly, aware of the way his touch was dissolving her inhibitions. When she didn't answer, his grip tightened. "Answer me."

Gazing into his eyes, Elizabeth saw iron beneath the warm gold. She felt hot tears well in hers.

"Because," her voice quivered uncontrollably, "because I love you, Jed. I love you."

There was a glow of triumph in his eyes before his mouth obliterated all conscious thought with a hungry passion. She was consumed by the fiery urgency of his kiss. Not even when she had guessed how deeply Jed affected her had she ever dreamed that she would know this exploding joy.

Chapter 9

"Would it be an understatement to say that you've recovered, Jed?"

The sarcastic voice was the hiss of the serpent in the garden. It brought an abrupt end to the kiss that had been progressively leading to more than a passionate embrace. Red-faced, Elizabeth struggled to her feet, quickly knotting the sash of her robe, while Jed rolled on to his back, put off by the interruption.

"Great timing," he murmured dryly to his mother.

Smoldering outrage was evident in the disdainful set of Rebecca Carrel's features, but her self-control was as strong as her son's. She flicked a cutting glance at Elizabeth that made her disgust clear.

"Perhaps it is," his mother responded coldly. "You seem quite healthy to me. I don't see that you require Elizabeth's attention any longer. We can put an end to this charade."

"She was about to fix my breakfast," he said with a crooked smile.

"Really? Lying down?" Rebecca snapped. "I don't think so. Freda ought to do it."

Elizabeth stiffened resentfully. "She's busy. If you'll

excuse me, I'll see to it myself." Her nervous smoothing of her tumbled black curls stopped as she moved past her mother-in-law to the door.

"While you're at it, check on your child," was the waspish response. "When I came in, she was playing with those dirty puppies, letting them paw and climb all over her. She was filthy!"

"A little dirt won't harm her," Elizabeth retorted.

Rebecca wasn't finished complaining. "Did you forget that she has a piano lesson this morning? Maybe it slipped your mind that she also missed the last one." There was a deliberate pause in the condescending reminder. "For unexplained reasons."

"The reasons were personal." The tilt of Elizabeth's chin dared Rebecca to inquire further. "And I will decide if the lesson is essential."

"I don't know what possible excuse you can offer Mrs. Banks. Not now that Jed has recovered."

"Actually, that's none of your business. And have you forgotten that I pay for missed lessons—and that I'm Amy's mother, not you?" Elizabeth was shaking with uncontrollable anger as she stepped into the hall, slamming the bedroom door behind her.

She took her time in the shower and dressed with equal slowness. She couldn't recall a time that she had ever talked back to her mother-in-law or been so rude. The only twinge of remorse she felt was for losing her temper, not for the things she'd said. She didn't venture out of her room until she heard Rebecca's car start up in the drive.

Freda had left a note on the kitchen table telling Elizabeth she was out in the garden. Amy was in the porch swing, crooning to a sleeping puppy in her lap. Doubting that Jed's stomach could take a sudden jolt of heavy food, Elizabeth fixed a bowl of hot cereal, toast, and tea, and carried it into his room on a tray.

Setting the tray near him as he thanked her for going to the trouble, she walked silently to the window. It seemed incredible that a short time ago she had been in his arms, pledging her love with every breath she drew. Jed hadn't said anything besides his thanks when she'd entered the room. He had withdrawn again into that aloofness she had never been able to understand.

"You're very quiet all of a sudden," he commented.

"There's nothing left for me to say." Elizabeth let the curtain fall and turned toward him.

He seemed oblivious to her emotional state. "You should have time to pack before Amy's lesson. Freda can drive you to the house or take you on into town if you'd rather do that." Jed picked up the cup of tea and swallowed a few gulps.

"Is that what you want? For me to leave?" she asked in a choked voice that was both stiff and proud.

He held her gaze for a long moment when he set down the cup. "It isn't what I want, but it's what I'm willing to settle for," he replied evenly.

"What do you want?" Elizabeth looked down at her clenched hands, not at him.

"I thought I'd made that plain." He was studying her intently. "I want you."

Not *I love you* or *I want to marry you,* but simply *I want you,* as if she were a possession that he had coveted for a long time and intended to own.

"I'll start packing now." She turned away, her eyes downcast to conceal the welling tears.

"Liza? What's the matter?" Jed demanded as she started toward the door. "Liza!" he called to her again, angrily this time when she continued to ignore him. "Dammit! Answer me!"

She hesitated in the doorway. "I'm tired, Jed." It was true. She felt emotionally drained.

The tears slipping from her lashes released the tension that had been building since last night. She dashed them away as she began to pack her and Amy's things, but still they fell in a steady stream that made everything a blur.

Later Freda apologized for not warning Elizabeth of Rebecca's arrival, but Elizabeth dismissed it. "No harm done. She didn't interrupt anything." At least, nothing that didn't need to be interrupted, but she found she couldn't confide that to Freda.

Her fragile composure wouldn't survive another visit to Jed's room, so she left it to Freda to let him know that she had actually gone. Amy only grumbled a little, nothing more than usual for her piano lesson days. Elizabeth chose not to have Freda take her own car. Too much time in her friend's company would mean a lot of well-meaning attempts to draw her out, and until she had time to think things through on her own, that was something she didn't want.

The instant they returned from Amy's lesson and stepped into the entrance hall, Elizabeth saw Rebecca waiting for her, looking every inch the sophisticated socialite with her perfectly coiffed silver hair and dusty rose dress. Her heart sank. This morning's encounter was not going to escape without comment.

"There are cookies and milk in the kitchen for you, Amy. You may practice after your snack." Rebecca smiled amiably at her granddaughter. Elizabeth started to counter her orders out of sheer stubbornness until she met the coal-hard chips of her mother-in-law's eyes.

Elizabeth could hear the silent bell that signaled round one. It was better if the confrontation didn't begin in front of her daughter. "I put the coffee service in

Franklin's study so we won't disturb Amy," the older woman informed her when Amy left.

Rebecca's tone was pleasant enough, but Elizabeth wasn't taken in. Tight-lipped, she walked to the closed study door. Postponing this moment would be futile. Silently she endured her mother-in-law's quiet courtesy, accepting the cup of coffee that was handed to her, aware all the while that the stage had been carefully set by Rebecca. The calmness of the older woman's voice, the coffee prepared in advance, and the retreat to the privacy of the study had been calculated to inspire trust and confidence.

There were ladyfingers arranged on a plate next to the tall silver coffeepot. Leave it to Rebecca to serve a treat that made practically no crumbs and had no flavor, Elizabeth thought. She didn't take one and set the cup of coffee that was elegantly poured for her to one side.

"Please, Rebecca," she said evenly, "let's dispense with the niceties. Say whatever it is that you brought me in here to say."

Rebecca set her own cup down, folding her hands primly in her lap and hesitating for a decorous instant. She looked downward as if to study the flawless polish on her nails before she sighed discreetly and spoke.

"First of all," the silver-gray head was raised to meet the impassive greenness of Elizabeth's gaze, "I want to apologize for my behavior this morning. I was shocked. It was never my intention to interfere in your personal life or to challenge your authority with Amy. I spoke in haste and without thinking, and I'm sorry."

"Was that all?" Elizabeth knew her seeming indifference and her failure to soften in response to the apology disconcerted Rebecca, but the older woman concealed her feelings as best she could.

"No." Rebecca rose a little unsteadily, then walked

away from Elizabeth as if unsure of what to say next. "I had heard the rumors that—that you and Jed were interested in each other. For the most part, I thought it was idle gossip. People have to have something to talk about, don't they?"

Elizabeth inclined her head in a gesture that could have meant yes or no.

Rebecca continued, "I never doubted that Jed would try something with you. He's always pursued various women, with considerable success."

She glanced over her shoulder to see the effect of her comments, but Elizabeth deliberately kept her face expressionless and waited for Rebecca to continue.

"I have never understood why the wastrels of this world—it is an old-fashioned word but it fits Jed—have so much appeal for women." Her mother-in-law sighed again. Then she smiled thinly. "When men are born with good looks and charm, they don't have much need for intelligence and ambition. They get what they want with very little effort. Jed is like that."

Elizabeth said nothing, wondering what Rebecca was getting at.

"He exudes an aura of danger and excitement that makes women feel deliciously sinful. His father and I saw that by the time he was a teenager. It was a source of constant concern."

The older woman returned to her chair opposite Elizabeth and sat, leaning forward in an earnest, confiding manner, anxiety crinkling her carefully made-up eyes. Her hands were clasped in front of her in a somewhat theatrical plea for understanding.

"My concern now is for you, Elizabeth," she said a low, fervent voice. "I was foolish not to warn you about Jed. You're young, you have, shall we say, needs, which are perfectly normal, but—"

The way Rebecca was speaking made Elizabeth feel unclean. She was unable to stay silent any longer.

"Please. What I feel for Jed is love, not lust, if that's what you're getting at," she said quietly. "I didn't intend to fall in love with him. I tried to tell myself that it was only physical, but it wasn't. I love him and I'm not ashamed of it."

She was surprised not to hear a disapproving outburst, but Rebecca's softly spoken question. "Does Jed know this?"

"Yes."

"I see." Rebecca didn't appear surprised by the admission. "And what are your plans?"

"There are no plans," Elizabeth answered. The faint I-thought-so expression on Rebecca's composed face forced her to add in defense, "Jed has been ill."

"He will ask you to go away with him." It was a statement made with assurance, not a question.

"Did he say that?" The wary question was out before Elizabeth could stop it.

"No." Rebecca looked at her thoughtfully. "It's more of a guess on my part, accurate, I believe. When he does, what will you do?"

"I'll go with him. I love him, Rebecca," Elizabeth said firmly.

Her mother-in-law sighed and leaned back in her chair. "I won't pretend that I have any right to tell you what to do. You're more than old enough to make your own decisions. But I feel compelled to point out some things to you. Jed is thirty-two years old. He doesn't have a career or a job. He doesn't live anywhere, so he has no house or apartment, not even a car. Only a token sum was left to him in Franklin's will, so he has no money either. I don't mean to imply that these things are more important than love," Rebecca hastened to add in response to the obvious anger in Elizabeth's eyes. "But I am asking you to factor in everything for Amy's sake, for her future. It's true that you do receive monthly funds from her trust, but it would never support a household. However much you may believe you love Jed, you have to consider her welfare. Think about what I've said. Please, Elizabeth."

With a gentle, unruffled smile, Rebecca rose and left the room. Elizabeth sat silently. She had made no response because there was none to make. There was little consolation in recognizing that the speech and its delivery had been carefully rehearsed. Rebecca's parting shot had hit its mark. Elizabeth's vulnerable spot was Amy, and her mother-in-law knew it.

Stubbornly, Elizabeth had never looked ahead—perhaps because she wasn't convinced that Jed wanted her in more than a physical sense. If he did, what would she do then? It was impossible to cross bridges she hadn't reached.

Late that afternoon, she called the farm to see how Jed was. Secretly she was hoping that he'd be up and she would have a chance to talk to him. The shadows of uncertainty were becoming too much. Freda answered the phone.

"How's Jed?" Elizabeth asked after they'd exchanged greetings and a little small talk. She hoped she didn't sound too nervous.

"Fine. He had a big lunch and dozed off. I think he intends to sleep until morning. It's probably the best thing for him," Freda answered brightly.

"Yes, you're probably right," Elizabeth agreed reluctantly.

"Are you coming over in the evening?"

"I don't think so. I only wanted to be sure he was doing okay." There was no point in her hovering over him. As always, it seemed to be Jed's move. "I have things to catch up on here at the house."

"I'll tell him you called when he wakes up. How's that?"

"That's fine. Thanks, Freda." Slowly Elizabeth replaced the receiver.

Oddly enough, the intervening time passed swiftly. It was something of a surprise when Elizabeth realized that two full days and the morning of a third had gone by since she'd left the Reisner farm. Her inner tension had increased, though. Uncertainty and indecision gnawed at her.

Jed was recovering quickly, or so Freda told her. Elizabeth hadn't heard a word from him. He hadn't given Freda any indication when he would be returning, which didn't surprise Elizabeth. Something told her she could rely on Jed to come home when she least expected him.

Going to the raised kitchen window, she glanced out, spying Amy beside the patio table where her play cups and saucers were set out.

"It's almost time for lunch, honey. You'd better get washed up," she called. "We'll have it in the kitchen since your grandmother isn't here."

Absently Elizabeth heard the French doors open and close, and the sound of water running in the downstairs bathroom. She ladled the soup into bowls and uncovered the plate of sandwiches before setting it on the table.

A carton of milk was in one hand and two glasses between the fingers of the other when a deep voice asked, "Is there enough food for three?"

Quickly she set the carton and glasses on the counter before she dropped everything, joy surging through her. She didn't need to turn around to know that Jed had come back. Commanding her hands to stop trembling, she took down a third glass, just as if she'd been expecting him all along.

"Of course there is, Jed," she responded warmly, turning around as he approached. "You're looking better."

"I'm completely recovered." He stopped beside her, his tawny eyes intent on hers.

There was nothing about him to suggest that he'd been ill. His handsome face showed no sign of tiredness or strain. "Actually, you look wonderful." There was a breathless catch in her voice.

His eyebrow rose mockingly. "So do you," he murmured.

"Oh, boy! Tomato soup, my favorite," Amy crowed, sliding onto one of the chairs.

Jed smiled. "I think someone is hungry. I guess we should eat."

Elizabeth swallowed and nodded. "Sit down. I'll get another place setting for myself."

Food was the last thing on her mind. It did little good to tell herself to stay calm, that all the unknowns hadn't vanished simply because Jed was back. She went through the motions of eating her soup and nibbling at a sandwich.

"Amy tells me she has a birthday party to go to this afternoon," Jed commented.

"Oh?" Elizabeth looked at her daughter, who was devouring the last bites of her sandwich. "When did she tell you that?"

"Out on the patio."

"I didn't see you there," she breathed.

"I know." The grooves around his mouth deepened with amusement. "So, what are you doing this afternoon?"

"I have a meeting." She made no attempt to disguise the disappointment in her voice. What little appetite she'd had vanished as she set down her soupspoon. "It's another one of Rebecca's clubs. I'm the secretary. I have to attend."

"Okay," he answered evenly, not trying to talk her out of it as he switched the topic back to the birthday party, asking Amy about her friends.

While Elizabeth cleared the table, she sent Amy upstairs to dress for the party, reminding her to take her swimsuit and towel, since part of the fun included a visit to the town swimming pool. Jed disappeared into another part of the house. There was no sign of him when she went upstairs to change for her meeting. But he was in the front hallway with Amy when Elizabeth came back downstairs.

"Mind if I drive her there?" he asked.

"Not at all." Elizabeth shook her head. Rebecca had the other car, which left only hers to provide him with transportation. Obviously he had somewhere to go.

Conversation was minimal during the drive into town. Most of it was Amy's chatter about the party. No matter how many glances Elizabeth stole at Jed's profile, there was nothing in his expression to indicate that he sensed her disappointment.

The old familiar depression settled in. Fortunately Amy was too excited about her party to notice the sadness in her mother's smile when they left her at the birthday girl's house.

Elizabeth stared out the car window, wondering what she could say to break the silence.

"Turn left at the next corner. The Hansons' house is the third one on the right-hand side." The directions to her meeting were given reluctantly.

But Jed drove straight through the intersection without stopping.

"I meant that corner." Elizabeth pointed behind them. "You'll have to go around the block."

"I know which corner you mean." Jed glanced her way briefly and continued through the second intersection that would have taken them back to where she was supposed to be.

"I have to go to the meeting," she reminded him with a frown.

Slowing the car, he pulled over to the curb, stopping it but not turning off the engine as he twisted in the seat to look at her.

"Which would you rather do? Go to that stupid meeting or come with me?" he asked with thinning patience.

"Of course I'd rather come with you, but—" Elizabeth's frustration spilled over into her voice.

"That settles it, then." He put the car in gear and pulled away from the curb into the street.

"Jed—"

"I don't know about you, but I don't want to wait until tonight," he said firmly. "We've postponed our talk long enough. Am I right?"

"Yes." Elizabeth had to agree, ready to surrender and not caring at all about the meeting she was supposed to attend.

His slow smile seemed to reach and almost physically touch her. It was a heady sensation and a pleasurable one.

But that bridge she was worried about was coming closer. She still didn't know whether she was going to cross it or not, but she had to get there. She would never be able to come to a decision until she did.

Chapter 10

After that exchange, a silence fell between them again. Jed continued driving through town and into the outskirts. It wasn't the road that would take them back to the house. Elizabeth couldn't guess what destination he had in mind. The last place she would have thought of was the small municipal airport outside of town, but the road to it was where Jed turned. Soon enough, they were in the parking lot.

"What are we doing here?" She glanced curiously at Jed as he pulled in beside the three cars parked close to the flight office and switched off the engine.

"You might say this is my old stomping grounds." He opened his door and got out, going around to her side, smiling at her slightly bewildered expression before he helped her out. "I spent more time here than I ever did in school or at home, outside of Kurt's."

Elizabeth silently digested that piece of information, picking up on his silent contentment as he gazed at the few buildings that constituted the Carrelville Airport. A little puff of breeze was trying to fill the orange windsock.

"Do you mean"—she hesitated for a second—"that you used to fly?"

Jed glanced down, a smile curving his mouth. His arm circled her shoulders as he turned her in the direction of the flight office. She was puzzled and her expression showed it.

"Come on, I'll show you," he said. Entering the flight office, he lifted a pull-up section of the counter and led Elizabeth into the hall leading to the back offices, which were private. Her puzzled frown deepened at his easy familiarity. He opened one of the doors. "This is where Sam hangs up his shirttails."

"Huh? What do you mean?" She walked in ahead of him.

"It's a ceremony that all prospective pilots go through," Jed explained. "After a student makes his first solo flight, his instructor cuts off his shirttail and hangs it up. It's referred to as 'clipping the tail feathers.'" He led her to the wall that was patchworked with strips of cloth of every color and pattern. "That's mine." He pointed.

On a strip of pale blue material was Jed's name and a date. Elizabeth made a swift mental calculation and looked at him in surprise.

"You were only sixteen!"

Jed chuckled softly. "I had a hell of a time persuading Sam to teach me without my parents' permission. He knew Dad would come down on him like a ton of bricks."

"You mean they didn't know?"

"Eventually they found out. Somebody from town saw me landing a plane and mentioned it to Dad. I was only a few hours away from getting my pilot's license when he stopped my allowance. Fortunately Sam let me work out the rest of the money."

"Oh. You were determined. What happened?"

Jed gave her a rueful smile. "In college, I wanted to major in engineering and go into aeronautics, but Dad wouldn't hear of it. As long as he was paying my tuition, he insisted I had to take up law, like all the rest of the Carrels." His mouth twisted bitterly before he shook away the memory. "Come on, let's walk."

From the flight office, they wandered into the hangar area. In one of the cavernous sheds, a man in coveralls was working on a plane. When he spotted them, he cupped his hands to his mouth and called out, "Do you want me to roll out the twin for you, Jed?"

Jed waved at him. "Not today, Sam."

He brought Elizabeth to him with his arm, tucking her against his shoulder. She tilted her head to gaze into his face, her heart singing quietly at the warmth in his tawny eyes.

"Have you been out here often since you came back?" she asked.

He grinned. "You didn't think I spent all that time at the Reisner farm, did you?"

"I didn't know where you were or who you were with." A faint pink glowed in her cheeks as she averted her gaze self-consciously.

"I bet your imagination was working overtime," Jed teased, tightening his arm around her shoulders as they ducked beneath the wing of a tied-down plane. "If I disappear on you someday after we're married, don't check the golf course. Just go to the nearest airport and I'll probably be there."

Elizabeth stopped abruptly and her heart almost did too. A light breeze lifted the brown hair that fell over his forehead. He looked at her with a puzzled frown. "What's wrong?"

"What—what did you just say?" she murmured.

"I said—" Then Jed stopped and laughed softly at himself. "Oops. I didn't intend to propose to you like that."

"Do you want to marry me?" Elizabeth whispered, not quite believing it yet.

"What did you think I wanted?" Jed smiled gently as he turned her into his arms, locking his hands behind her back.

Closing her eyes, she leaned her head against his chest, feeling his lips moving in a tender caress against her hair. "I was afraid to think." Her voice trembled. "There was always the chance that all you wanted was an affair."

He lifted her chin with his finger. "Would you have settled for that?"

"If that was all I could have," she answered truthfully.

Possession marked the kiss that claimed her lips. It was a hard, sensual kiss that made the depth of his emotion clear. There was a determined glitter in his eyes when he lifted his head.

"Now you know I meant to have you forever," Jed said. "I knew you belonged to me when Jeremy brought you home. Remember that night?"

At this moment, Elizabeth didn't want to remember, only feel. She wanted this moment to stretch out for as long as it took to savor it completely, know that she truly was his. But forever—that was something she had to think about.

"What . . . about Amy?" She swallowed hard before lifting anxious eyes to his face.

A bemused smile spread across his mouth. "Amy is a part of you. What did you think I was going to do? Tell you to leave her with my mother?" he laughed with a trace of bewilderment.

"I—I wasn't sure," Elizabeth faltered again.

"Well, now you know," he answered patiently. "You haven't said whether you'll marry me, Liza."

"Yes, but—"

Jed stiffened. "The answer is never really 'yes' when there's a 'but' attached to it." His watchfulness returned, stealing the warmth from his gaze as he studied her guilty expression. "What's bothering you?"

There was no resistance when she pulled away from his embrace. "Jed, if I only had myself to consider, I'd—I'd marry you in a minute." Nervously she brushed the hair away from her face. "I wouldn't care if we lived in the back room of some little airport like this or a grass hut on a beach so long as I was with you. But I can't do that, because of Amy."

"What are you asking? Whether I can keep you in clover?" Jed demanded tightly.

"No," she protested.

"Then what is it? This has to be about my bank balance."

Elizabeth's stomach churned at the bitterness in his reply. "What kind of a mother would I be, Jed, if I wasn't concerned about how our marriage will affect Amy?" she asked quietly, not meeting his accusing gaze.

"You should trust me enough to know that I wouldn't ask unless I could take care of you both," he answered grimly.

"Look, I understand why you feel hurt by what I'm saying," she replied in a choked voice. "You have every right to feel that way. But please understand the way I feel. I trust you with my life, Jed. Amy trusts me with hers."

He turned away from her, raking his fingers through the thick brownness of his hair. A controlled fury darkened his eyes when he glanced at her.

"What will it take to make you decide whether you'll marry me or not?" he snapped.

"Just a little time," Elizabeth murmured. "I didn't expect you to propose—you didn't even mean to."

"You have a point there." He thrust his hands deep into his pockets, as if he wanted to keep from touching her.

"Jed, I'd . . . I'd like to think it over. I love you—you have to believe that." Her chin quivered. "I just don't want to give you an answer now that we both might regret."

"I'll never regret loving you." He stared into the cloudless blue sky for a moment before he turned to face her. "If it's time you want, you have it." He pulled a hand from his pocket and stretched it toward her, keys jingling from his fingers. "Here. I'll find my own way home."

"Jed—"

"I'd like to be alone, Elizabeth," he interrupted sharply. "I have things to think about too."

"I do love you," she murmured achingly, unable to shake the feeling that she had betrayed him as she clutched the keys in her hand.

His narrowed gaze slid to her. "If I didn't believe that, I don't think I'd let you go."

Slowly she turned away and went back to the car. The one time she looked back she saw him walking in the opposite direction, away from her. She felt miserable and sick inside.

At the car, she stopped and started to go to him. Her answer was yes. There was no other answer that she could possibly make. Without Jed, she wasn't going to be happy. She had already given him her heart and she couldn't take it back. Maybe Amy wouldn't have all the material things that Elizabeth could give her now, but her daughter would be a part of the happiness and love that she and Jed would share. And both were priceless.

But she didn't run back to Jed as she wanted to. He'd asked to be alone and she had to respect that. She would give him her answer the minute he arrived home. All she could do now was pray that he really did understand that she loved him and trusted him implicitly.

Two hours later, Elizabeth was sitting at the piano picking out the simple notes of a popular love song. A gentle breeze danced through the open French doors.

She heard the front door open and close. With her fingers resting soundlessly on the keys, she turned nervously toward the hall, a look of loving expectancy in her eyes.

It was Rebecca who appeared in the archway.

"So this is where you are," her mother-in-law said sharply. "Mrs. Hanson said you weren't at the meeting today and that you didn't even bother to call her and say you couldn't come. She said she phoned here but no one answered."

"I wasn't here." Elizabeth turned back to the piano. "I was with Jed."

There was an instant of alert silence before Rebecca murmured, "I see." She walked slowly into the room. "Where is he now?"

Hiding her dismay, Elizabeth began playing a soft melody to ease the tension that suddenly enveloped the room. "At the airport."

"He's leaving?" There was surprised disbelief in the question.

"No. No, he'll be back later," Elizabeth assured her, a faint smile touching the corners of her mouth.

"You sound very sure of that."

"He asked me to marry him. I told him I wanted to think it over."

Rebecca was silent but just for a second. "That was wise of you," she said firmly. "I knew you would make the right decision in the end. It's too bad that my son is a charming wastrel, but that is the truth. If you want to remarry, you can find a much more suitable partner," she declared complacently.

"I don't think you understand me. I didn't refuse Jed." Elizabeth felt oddly calm as she met her mother-in-law's shocked gaze. "It's the things you don't do in life that you regret. And I have decided to marry Jed. If I didn't, I would regret it for the rest of my life."

"But what about Amy?"

"Amy will be just fine. We'll both see to that," Elizabeth answered confidently.

"You can't live on love!" Rebecca declared. "How on earth will you manage when he doesn't have a job or money?"

"That's our concern, Rebecca."

"How can you be so foolish? I—"

The phone's shrill ringing interrupted her. Rebecca glared at it angrily before giving in and going to answer it. Elizabeth smiled at the barely disguised impatience in her mother-in-law's voice when she picked up the receiver.

There was nothing Rebecca could say that would make Elizabeth change her mind. Nothing.

"No, he isn't here," Rebecca said crisply to whoever was calling. "I do expect him later . . . he has been ill for a few days. Perhaps that's why you weren't able to reach him. What—oh. *Oh.*"

Elizabeth picked up on the note of sharpened interest in her mother-in-law's voice.

"I am his mother. May I take a message for him?" Quickly Rebecca began scribbling on the notepad by the phone, squinting at her writing without taking the time to get her reading glasses from her purse. "The offer was from whom? What was the amount again? Yes, yes, thank you. I'll have him call you the minute he comes in." Rebecca misplaced the receiver on the hook, staring fixedly at the notepad. The annoying buzz from the phone brought her back to reality.

"Who was that?" Elizabeth asked, on fire with curiosity.

"That was Jed's attorney in Honolulu. Jed's attorney," she repeated as if she couldn't accept what she was saying. "Some conglomerate just made an offer to buy his airline."

"I don't understand." Elizabeth frowned.

"I don't think I do either." There was a short, disbelieving laugh from Rebecca. "It seems that Jed owns cargo planes that fly between islands in the Pacific and parts of the Asian mainland. Why didn't he tell us? Did you know?"

"I had no idea."

Rebecca held out the notepad. "He's a wealthy man. Oh, Elizabeth!" A smile broke across her face as she hurried quickly to take her daughter-in-law's hands in her own. "His proposal—go ahead and say yes. I'll take care of all the arrangements for the wedding—it should be a small gathering, don't you think?"

"Can I see that message?" Jed's quiet voice slashed through the air.

The astonishment in Elizabeth's eyes changed to horror as she whirled to see him standing just inside the French doors. There was a hard look to his lean features that told her he'd overheard the whole thing. His tawny gaze held her motionless.

He ignored his mother's gushing as she proclaimed how proud she was of him and how delighted she was about his engagement to Elizabeth.

A rising sob closed Elizabeth's throat. He would never believe her now. Wary as he was, she'd never be able to convince him that she'd been willing to marry him before that out-of-the-blue phone call.

With a muffled cry of pain, she broke free of his gaze and raced from the room. She heard him call her name but she didn't want him to see her cry. She loved him too deeply to endure his caustic remarks, and he was bound to make them, to her and to his mother. Fumbling with the front doorknob, she jerked the door open, not bothering to close it behind her as she hurried down the sidewalk.

Before she could reach the car Rebecca had left in the driveway in front of the garage, a strong hand grabbed her arm, bringing her flight to an abrupt halt and spinning her around so that her other arm was captured also.

"Let me go! Please, Jed, let me go," she begged, twisting away so he couldn't see the tears streaming down her face.

But he ignored her protests, pulling her body against his and giving her a long, hard kiss. He kept right on kissing her until she stopped resisting him and the love she couldn't deny. Only then did he release her lips, allowing her to bury her face in his chest. She felt utterly miserable.

"I know you'll never believe me." Her sobs were muffled by his shirt. "But I swear I decided to marry you before that phone call. At the airport, I started to go back to tell you, but you'd said you wanted to be alone and—oh, you'll never believe me now!"

"Stop crying." He rocked her gently as he scolded her with mock gruffness. "I was on the patio."

"I know you were." Her voice throbbed with pain and confusion. "I can guess what you must think of me."

"You don't understand." Moving her head up, he tenderly wiped the tears from her cheek. "I heard everything. I was out there listening to you play the piano, telling myself to man up and just listen to whatever you were going to tell me. I hoped it was yes."

A huge sniffle from Elizabeth confirmed that for him.

He nodded, his smile wry. "Then my mother came home. You told her that you were going to marry me. I was on my way in to jump and shout and sweep you off your feet, and then the phone rang. I never guessed the call would be for me. I'd left Sam's number for my attorney in case he couldn't reach my cell, but Sam was inside that engine pulling it apart by then."

"Oh, Jed—"

"Anyway, I have my answer. You're in. For richer, for poorer. Right?"

"I was so afraid," Elizabeth gasped, her lashes fluttering shut for a second. "I thought—"

"I can guess." He folded her more tightly into his arms. "Now I have to ask you to forgive me. I wasn't being fair when I kept the truth from you and demanded that you make a decision."

"Why didn't you just tell me?" she asked softly, her hands caressing his face. "You should have been proud of yourself."

"I was proud—in that stupid Carrel way." He smiled crookedly. "I wanted to be welcomed for myself, not for the big deal I was about to pull off. My old friends Kurt and Sam were the only ones who made me feel like I'd come home. And then there was you, my lovely Liza." He kissed her lightly. "Looks like I have some business to take care of in Hawaii. Would you mind spending our honeymoon there?"

She smiled happily, still a little dazed. "No."

"It'll be at least a week before we can come back."

"You mean come back here?" Elizabeth frowned. "With your mother?"

"No way," Jed laughed. "I actually do care for her, but I could never live in the same house with her. Maybe not even in the same state." His expression became more serious. "But we have to think of Amy. Not too many changes at once, right? We'll find a place of our own—ours and hers. How does that sound?"

"Perfect."

He lowered his head and whispered into her ear, "I love you, Liza. Passionately."

She didn't get a chance to answer before he swept her off her feet and whirled her around and around until they were both giddy.

"Stop!" she cried. "I love you back! Forever!"

"Is that a yes?" He gave her one last whirl.

"Of course it is!"

Laughing, he set her on her feet and let her cling to him before he kissed her again. And again. She couldn't say no.